The Awakening

DEBRA WHITE SMITH

HARVEST HOUSE PUBLISHERS
Eugene, Oregon 97402

THE AWAKENING
Copyright © 2000 by Debra White Smith
Published by Harvest House Publishers
Eugene, Oregon 97402

Smith, Debra White.
  The awakening / Debra White Smith
      p. cm.—(Seven sisters series)
  ISBN 0-7369-0277-5
      1. Americans—Travel—Vietnam—Fiction. 2. Stalking victims—Fiction. 3. Models (Persons)—
Fiction. 4. Vietnam—Fiction. I. Title.
PS3569.M5178 A93 2000
813'.54—dc21

                                                                                    00-024160

02 03 04 05 06 / BC / 10 9 8 7 6 5 4 3

To my mother-in-law,
Mildred Smith,
for being available to care for my children
during the writing of this book,
which was completed under a tight deadline.
This book would not exist if not for your
willingness to assist with your grandchildren.
Thank You!

The Seven Sisters

Jacquelyn Lightfoot: An expert in martial arts, private detective Jac is of Native-American descent and married to her career. She lives in Denver.

Kim Lan ("Lawn") Lowery: Tall, lithe, and half-Vietnamese/half-American, Kim is a much-sought-after supermodel who lives in New York City.

Marilyn Douglas Thatcher: Marilyn lives in Eureka Springs, Arkansas, with her daughter, Brooke. Marilyn works as an office manager for a veterinarian and is planning her marriage to Joshua Langham.

Melissa Moore: A serious nature lover, Dr. Melissa Moore recently established a medical practice in Oklahoma City.

Sonsee LeBlanc: A passionate veterinarian known for her wit, Sonsee lives in Baton Rouge.

Sammie Jones: The star reporter for *Romantic Living* magazine, Sammie is an expert on Victorian houses, art, and finding the perfect romantic getaway. She and her husband live in Dallas.

Victoria Roberts: A charming, soft-spoken domestic genius who loves to cook, work on crafts, and sew. Victoria is married and lives in Destin, Florida.

The Awakening Cast

Carla Jensen: The servant in charge of the LeBlanc household.

John Lowery: Kim Lan's father. A veteran injured in the Vietnam War, he is a devoted Christian, husband, and father.

Joy Delaney: Facing the trauma of cancer, Joy is buoyed by her faith in God and her hope that her son, Taylor, will open his heart to love.

Khanh Ahn ("Con On"): A special-needs orphan in Vietnam.

Mick O'Donnel: The leader of a mission trip to Vietnam, Mick is a sandy-haired martial arts expert dedicated to serving the Lord.

Odysseus: A man of mystery. Odysseus' twisted mind seeks love and destruction.

Sophie: Odysseus' first love.

Taylor Delaney: A lifelong friend of Sonsee's, Taylor's heart was scarred by his father's abandonment.

Ted Curry: Kim Lan's boyfriend, Ted is a well-known heartthrob and movie star.

Tran My Lowery ("Tron Me"): Kim Lan's Vietnamese mother. Tran My wants to see her daughter serving the Lord and married to a man of God.

Virginia Daley: Kim Lan's sophisticated and efficient secretary.

Other Mission Trip Participants

Adam Gray
Caleb Peterson, Mick O'Donnel's younger brother
Doug Cauley
Frank Cox, Mick's assistant
Laci Emerson
Pam Cox, Frank's wife
Rhonda Ackers
Ron Emerson

One

"What do you mean, I can't go?" Tense with exasperation, Kim Lan Lowery stared in disbelief at Mick O'Donnel's obstinate face. The historical country church's foyer bustled with people who were interested in the mission trip Mick was planning. He had just spent the last forty-five minutes beseeching the Boston congregation to volunteer for the humanitarian aid journey to Vietnam. According to Mick, the trip's participants were usually set a year in advance, but this trip had fallen short of volunteers, and they were making a last minute call for more workers. The congregation had been urged to pray about this opportunity a month ago, and today was the final day to sign up. The trip was only two months away, and there was barely enough time to obtain the necessary passports and visas. Now he was telling Kim Lan she couldn't go.

Deliberately he retrieved the sign-up sheet from the table covered with a white cloth and placed it out of Kim Lan's reach. A young couple, seriously talking between themselves, picked up the paper while numerous other church members examined the Vietnamese photos, books, and cultural souvenirs.

Her stomach knotting in anger, Kim Lan speechlessly evaluated the man who looked much like a sandy-blond "Indiana Jones." Even though he wore a black business suit and exhibited the air of a professional, Mick O'Donnel looked as if he would be more comfortable on a Texas ranch wearing worn jeans and cowboy boots.

He slowly appraised her. "I appreciate your offer," he said deliberately, "but I don't think your presence would be appropriate on this trip."

Kim Lan produced several unintelligible stutters as a couple of elderly well-wishers pumped the missions coordinator's hand amid a chorus of praises for Mick's moving presentation.

"Not—not appropriate?" she rasped, feeling as if she were once again in the sixth grade trying to prove her worth to the class bully who "hated all those dirty Vietnamese." Her initial exasperation faded and was replaced by uncertainty. Uncertainty and inferiority. Inferiority and worthlessness. Those tendrils of worthlessness made her want to run from the building and cower from the view of all humanity.

Kim Lan desperately wanted to visit her mother's homeland, and she had assumed that a mission trip would be both helpful and adventurous. Her palms moistened as a new rush of anger claimed her. *How dare you!* she wanted to yell.

"I think your presence would actually distract more than help," he said discreetly. "After all…either you're *the* Kim Lan Lowery…" he waved his hand as if he were introducing royalty, "or you're a dead-ringer for her."

Kim's face warmed. Her hands clenched. Her legs shook with fury. No one had ever held her celebrity status against her. She felt she needed to defend her choice of career while at the same time she wanted to wipe the challenging expression off Mick O'Donnel's face. "I *am* Kim Lan Lowery," she said through gritted teeth. Nervously she cast a glance toward the surrounding people, hoping no one was eavesdropping on their tense conversation. Instinctively, she lowered her voice all the more. "And I just put a check for 10,000 dollars in the offering you collected to fund this trip." The note of satisfied triumph in her cool, yet angry tones left Kim sure she had won their verbal sparring. The amazed glimmer in Mick's blue eyes only heightened her sense of victory.

"I don't know why I let that surprise me," he said in an emotionless voice as he stepped from behind the table and narrowed the distance between them. "It figures that you'd want to buy your way on this trip," he muttered as if he, too, were afraid of being overheard.

"It figures?" she queried, her voice rising but a fraction.

"Of course," he replied, his words almost undetectable. "You probably think you can just throw some pocket change around and expect to get what you want." He never blinked.

She gasped as new feelings of inferiority swirled with her mounting fury.

The church treasurer, who happened to be Kim Lan's petite mother, stepped to Mick's side and handed him a sealed envelope. "I wrote a check from the church to cover the cash that came in," she said in her sweet Vietnamese voice. "The personal checks that came in are made out to the Compassionate Ministries fund, as you designated."

"Thanks." Mick's face softened as he addressed the gracious woman before him, and Kim Lan wondered if she were hallucinating. The pleasant gentleman smiling at her mother was certainly not the judgmental tyrant who had told her she couldn't go on the trip.

"I think you'll be pleased. You got a great offering." Tran My Lowery cast a meaningful glance toward her daughter.

Mick peered at the envelope. His mouth hardened into a straight line, and he purposefully broke the seal.

"Oh, there you are, Tran My. I've been looking all over for you." Kim Lan's lanky, limping father stepped from the crowd to pull his wife toward the nearby sanctuary for one of their "conferences." Kim Lan couldn't count the number of times she had seen the two consulting each other as they were now. Truly, if anyone had a great marriage, it was her parents. She thanked God her career had enabled them to break free of the poverty that had plagued the disabled Vietnam veteran and his hard-working wife.

Her attention was drawn back to Mick as he extended a slip of paper toward her. Instinctively, Kim reached out to take the paper, only to stop midway when she realized he was trying to return her check. She snatched her hand back to her side.

"Take it," he softly ordered.

"I won't," she argued, barely able to believe he would return such a significant contribution. "I put that money in the offering plate to fund the trip. I'm not taking—"

He unceremoniously tucked the check into the lower pocket of her Gucci suit coat. Narrowing his eyes, he paused and scrutinized her as if he were searching for something in the hidden recesses of her soul.

Kim Lan, who matched her father's willowy height, stared back at Mick O'Donnel eye to eye, coldly returning his scrutiny. Despite herself, something twisted in the pit of her stomach. What the man lacked in personality he certainly made up for in rugged good looks. Mick was far from handsome in the traditional sense, but his features possessed a certain appeal, a nuance of strength. Furthermore, his unusually light-blue eyes reminded her of a heaving, azure sea on a cloudless day—a warm sea that could lure a woman to explore its waters. Kim felt as if she were toppling into that sea of unknown depths, uncharted valleys, and secret treasures hidden long ago.

A flash of awareness scurried across his features like a streak of lightning amid a bank of boiling clouds. His mysterious eyes slightly widened then warmed with the attraction Kim could not deny. She became all too mindful that they stood only inches apart. Kim Lan fingered the three-carat diamond on her ring finger and reminded herself she was engaged...that her fiancé had blue eyes, too...that she had only just met this man. But the thoughts did precious little to stop the mental comparison between this blond tyrant posing as a missionary and the drop-dead handsome actor Ted Curry, her fiancé. Certainly Ted was better looking, and he never acted like such an ogre.

But... That one little word represented what the last forty-five minutes had been for Kim Lan—a lesson in trying to squelch an immediate attraction for this man before her. With every word Mick O'Donnel had spoken during the presentation, his passion for the lost and for the Lord struck a chord in Kim Lan's heart. While he certainly would turn a few heads, she had admired him more for his obvious depth of character and love for the holy. During the whole church service, she had thought, *If only Ted would somehow develop such a passion for the things of God.*

Now Kim Lan's musings mocked her. Obviously, Mick O'Donnel was a person who put on a good show and didn't live what he preached. His rude, demeaning refusal to accept her on the trip, and his rejection of her substantial offering spoke of nothing more than arrogance and pig-headedness.

"We got an excellent offering," Mick said in measured tones. "We're on target for our budget. I appreciate your generosity, but—"

"You don't want me on your trip," she stated flatly.

His slight nod was barely discernible, and Kim thought she saw a brief tremor of regret nibbling at the corners of his lips. But his next words dashed aside her assumption.

"I have a kid brother I'm trying to talk into going. He needs spiritual renewal, not two weeks with his idol." His voice held conflicting tinges of steel and remorse. "He's got pictures of you taped all over his college dorm room. He's always especially impressed with the swimsuit issues."

A rush of heat assaulted Kim's cheeks. "I stopped doing those kinds of poses," she whispered, wondering why she felt the need to defend herself.

"That doesn't change what's been done." His accusatory eyes belied the smile that suggested they were sharing the most delightful of pleasantries.

Kim Lan glanced from side to side to see that no one suspected they were engaged in a heated competition of the wills. "Look, you jerk!" she whispered, trying to keep her features from reflecting her growing distaste. "You don't even know me! You've got a lot of nerve judging me—"

"I'm not judging you," he said, his impassive expression and cold, blue eyes revealing no sign that her ire affected him in the least. That made Kim even angrier. "I'm just stating facts. The facts are..." He raised his index finger and slowly began counting off his points. "One: You want to go on the trip. Two: I think the participants, my brother included, need to focus on God, not you. Three: You assume your money will buy you a spot on the—"

"I never assumed that!" she firmly insisted. But hot tears pooled in her eyes, and she discreetly dabbed at the corners, praying that no one was noticing her show of emotions. "The Lord impressed me to give that amount and I did. That's it! That's all there is to it! Why can't you just..." Kim

Lan's quiet yet passionate voice broke as the tears dampened her cheek. At last she choked out a broken whisper, "You are the—the m-most infuriating human b-being I have ev–ever met in my whole life! During your presentation, I thought— You certainly fooled me into believing you were—"

Deciding not to give him the pleasure of discovering her initial, positive thoughts, she abruptly turned and stalked toward the aging wooden foyer closet. Feeling the curious appraisal of more than one church member, she grabbed her white fox coat from its hanger and stomped outside into the frigid January air. Furiously she jammed her arms into the coat, rushed down the numerous steps, and strode toward her black Jaguar parked in the visitor section. The pristine snow blanketing the rolling Massachusetts countryside seemed a mockery to the flaming inferno blazing in her soul.

Don't think you've seen the last of me, Mick O'Donnel! Kim raged to herself as she disengaged the car's alarm, unlocked the door, and plopped into the driver's seat. *I will go on that trip to Vietnam, if I have to go over your head and call denominational headquarters!*

In the foyer, Mick watched Kim Lan through the window as she marched across the parking lot and settled into her sports car. "Must be nice to drive a Jag," he muttered sarcastically, only to have a stab of regret pierce his soul. He had behaved far from Christlike. *What possessed me?* Mick wondered as the Jag sped from the parking lot at a telltale rate that spoke of the model's fury. *She's more beautiful in real life than she's ever been in print.* He reflected upon the tilt of her dark eyes. That waist-length hair like gleaming dark silk. The flawless, olive complexion. Even her perfume was the essence of a rare oriental bloom. *She is the personification of a rare oriental bloom.*

Despite Mick's better judgment, he was drawn to her.
During his whole presentation, he had steeled himself against
gaping at her like an awestruck schoolboy. At first he had
thought she just looked like the famous model. But soon he
knew she was *the* Kim Lan Lowery. Mick's masculine instincts
that appreciated feminine beauty had almost swept him
away. By the time Kim Lan approached him about volunteering for the trip, he was ready to run in the opposite direction. His stereotypical male reaction to a famous femme fatale
bewildered him. Therefore, Mick had turned the censure due
himself upon her. Anything would be better than feeling as
if he were a casualty of his own admiration. Anything—
including driving the object of his admiration from him.

The attraction Mick felt for her made no sense…no sense
whatsoever. Such emotions went against every fiber of who
he was: a no-nonsense man who never— absolutely never—
did anything spontaneously.

As the large congregation continued their chattering
around his display tables, Mick wearily covered his face with
a trembling hand and massaged his temples. Perhaps he was
at last feeling his age. At thirty-nine, he was slowly beginning
to realize he couldn't keep up the pace he had kept for ten
years. He had been working hard, long hours to pull this trip
together. Ironically, one of the countries that needed help
the most attracted the fewest volunteers. Furthermore, the
Vietnamese government was exacting in their requirements.
And the stress of planning and leading four missions trips a
year was only heightened by the perpetual burden he carried for his younger brother. In short, Mick felt like a water
pitcher that had been drained of its last drop. Perhaps his
irrational reaction to Kim Lan had been spawned by his own
exhaustion.

He turned back to the tables, wearily regained his post, and knew one thing for certain. Regardless of his uncharacteristic response to the Oriental femme fatale, Mick couldn't afford to let Kim Lan go on the trip. His younger brother had yet to give his final agreement to go, but their recent phone call suggested he would. Everything Mick said about his younger brother, Caleb, was true. Thoughts of Caleb's obsession for Kim left him remembering the words he had spoken to her. Next, images of her fury and the resulting tears filled his mind. *Did I overreact to her giving so much money and wanting to go to Vietnam? Perhaps I misjudged her. Maybe I owe her an apology.*

These musings caused Mick to groan. His inherent obstinacy had resulted in his apologizing more than he wanted to remember. He had a way of making up his mind and refusing to change it. Mick's mother called him stubborn, but he always told her he wasn't stubborn—just solid in his opinions. His younger brother usually rolled his eyes and said Mick was stuck in a rut.

"Excuse us, Mick?" A gentle hand touched his arm.

"Yes?" He turned to face the petite Oriental church treasurer and her towering husband.

The man, leaning on a cane, extended his hand and shook Mick's. "I'm John—John Lowery. We were wondering if you'd like to have lunch with us in our home."

"I cooked a big meal because our daughter is joining us today," Mrs. Lowery said sweetly, an Asian twist to her words. "I noticed you were talking with her, and we thought perhaps she was interested in going on the trip. She's wanted to visit my homeland for years now."

"Anyway, we thought you might like to join us for lunch," Mr. Lowery broke in. "If Kim Lan is thinking of going to

Vietnam, perhaps the two of you would enjoy discussing the trip."

Mick gazed into the eager countenance of the couple who looked to be in their early sixties. They appeared to be nothing more than average Americans. Neither of them possessed the extraordinary attractiveness of their daughter. Nonetheless, Kim Lan favored them both. She had obviously inherited her father's lithe height and straight nose along with her mother's Oriental features and coloring.

His gut reaction told him to decline the Lowerys' offer and head to the nearest McDonald's as originally planned—anything to avoid another encounter with their daughter. But a further thought barged into the forefront of his mind. He undoubtedly owed her an apology. There was no way around it. And he knew from past experience that the Lord would make him miserable with conviction until he did apologize. As a man in Christ's service, Mick had said nothing to Kim Lan that reflected his daily desire for God to purify his heart. Either he could interpret this opportunity to see her as divine intervention or he would be faced with the awkward task of offering his apology over the phone.

"I'd enjoy talking about the trip," he said, wondering if their daughter would want to discuss anything with him. He didn't want them to know he had coldly turned down Kim Lan's interest. What's more, he assumed that after their heated words any interest she had in the trip must have died. "I'd be glad to take you up on your offer of lunch. It certainly sounds more tasty than the burger I was planning."

"Great!" Mrs. Lowery said, turning to her husband. "I'll go ahead and take the car home and put the finishing touches on lunch. "Why don't you stay and help Mick get everything loaded up."

"I could use the help," Mick said, hoping the effort wouldn't be too much for the disabled gentleman.

"Well, I'm afraid I won't be able to do much more than hold the door for you." John glanced toward the cane. "This was my own souvenir from Vietnam."

"So you fought in the war?"

"Sure did," he said with a nod.

"My dad did, too," Mick said, feeling an immediate bond with the older man.

"Really?"

"Yes." Mick hesitated. "But he never came home."

"I'm sorry," the couple muttered.

The reverent silence that settled between them allowed Mick to remember the day he'd heard the news of his father's death. He had been nothing more than a scrap of a teenage boy...a boy who was man enough to eventually hate any and all Vietnamese people. His vengeful passion insisted he destroy his father's killer. Only a miracle of God had turned his hate to unconditional love and left him pouring his life out to help the needy in Vietnam and abroad.

With a flicker of compassion in his brown eyes, John Lowery placed his arm around his wife. "Well, I guess the war wasn't all bad, though. I brought home a special lady. She followed me over as a refugee. I don't know what I'd have ever done without her."

Mrs. Lowery beamed at her husband with nothing short of hero-worship. In a split second Mick wondered what it would feel like to have Kim Lan look at him like that. The instantaneous thought had precious little time to take root. Repelled by his own traitorous yearnings, Mick immediately swept the notion aside. *Kim Lan Lowery is not...* is not *the kind of woman I need for a wife. Period!*

He usually gave her type precious little consideration. In his staid opinion, she was probably spiritually shallow. Mick wanted a woman who knew how to touch heaven and understood who she was in Christ. He bolted at the very idea of any potential relationship with someone like Kim Lan, despite his initial fascination with her. His attraction smacked of superficiality; Mick was solely responding to her physical beauty. That was certainly no grounds for a solid relationship.

He would go to her parents' home, state his apologies, eat his lunch, and leave. Hopefully he would never have to see Kim Lan Lowery again.

Odysseus stood but a few feet away, listening to Mick chat with Kim Lan's parents. The conversation suggested what Odysseus had hoped for when he noticed Kim's interest in the Vietnam display. *If she does go on the trip, I simply must go*, he thought. *What better place to reveal my love for her than her mother's homeland?*

He nonchalantly paced up the aisle of the massive sanctuary and carefully scratched beneath the base of the full wig. The wig and false beard irritated him to distraction, but hopefully he would soon discard the disguise. If they both went on the trip, he would stop this cover-up and appear to Kim Lan as he really was. Odysseus originally had been more comfortable in a disguise—just in case Kim Lan noticed him following her. But after four months of discreetly watching her, he saw that she suspected nothing. During church, he decided he was ready for Kim to fall in love with the "real" Odysseus—not some hairy stranger. He considered himself much better looking in real life than the beard and wiry wig made him appear. If he went on the journey to Vietnam, he would go as himself.

Odysseus wasted no time walking toward the Vietnamese display where he observed the empty sign-up page. So far no one had committed to the trip, not even Kim Lan. Odysseus glanced at Mick, still in conversation with Kim's parents. Hurriedly, he grabbed the necessary paperwork then walked toward the front exit before Mick could notice he had been interested. Odysseus didn't want Mick to associate his real name with his present disguise since he wouldn't have to hide his identity.

After leaving the foyer, Odysseus stepped into the icy arms of the Boston winter and squinted against the glare of sunshine on snow. As he walked across the parking lot, he developed his plan. Tomorrow he would go ahead and phone Mick with his confirmation for the trip and begin processing the necessary documents for his visa to Vietnam. Mick said the registration money didn't have to be paid until the orientation meeting, this Thursday night. Odysseus would attend the meeting. If Kim was there, he would pay the fees. If she wasn't, he would assume she had not committed to the trip.

His mind spun with the opportunities the journey to Asia presented. No longer would he be held at bay by Kim Lan's celebrity status. The two of them would be part of a close-knit group. He grinned and beseeched fate to bequeath him the opportunity that was so rightfully his. Certainly Kim Lan would notice him. She would eventually speak to him. Eventually love him. She would love him, as Sophie never had.

Thoughts of his traitorous girlfriend, with her long black hair and dark eyes, made Odysseus' stomach clench in fury. Sophie had affectionately dubbed him her Odysseus—the hero from Greek mythology who traveled abroad and was widely known for his heroic exploits. At the start of their relationship, she made him feel like a Greek god, and he decided she could call him anything she wanted. But then Sophie showed her true nature, and Odysseus discovered she was not loyal to her Greek hero. The results had been less than pleasant.

One day Odysseus would have Kim Lan Lowery as his own; he wouldn't need to think of Sophie ever again. But best of all, Sophie would peer at them from her place in the afterlife—and regret her choices.

Two

~

Kim Lan, still incensed from her encounter with Mick, stepped into her parents' spacious hothouse that resembled a glass chapel. It had been her Christmas gift to them five years ago. They both loved gardening, and the ornate hothouse, custom-made from antique window frames with new glass, allowed them to have fresh vegetables year round. The small structure served as a perfect complement to their spacious, two-story frame home that sat just inside the Massachusetts state line, between Boston and Nashua, New Hampshire. One of Kim's six "sisters," *Romantic Living* magazine reporter Sammie Jones, had even traveled from Dallas to feature the unique greenhouse in the magazine.

Currently Kim Lan was on an errand for vine-ripened tomatoes. Despite her attempts to hire a cook for her parents, Kim's mother, an accomplished chef, insisted upon doing all her own cooking. Presently she was putting the finishing touches to the pot roast and vegetables. The tantalizing aroma filled the whole house and even lingered on the wool pantsuit Kim Lan now wore. Basket in hand, she walked toward the collection of a dozen tomato plants in black plastic pots.

She set the basket on the ground and pulled her cell phone from the pocket of her oversized leather jacket. Earlier, Kim Lan had called her Park Avenue penthouse and

19

checked her answering machine. Sonsee LeBlanc, one of her six "sisters," had left a message. Kim Lan was glad. She certainly needed to talk to someone about the horrible encounter she had just endured with Mick O'Donnel. Sonsee was a good listener.

Including Kim Lan, there were seven friends who had graduated from the University of Texas together where they had fondly dubbed themselves the "Seven Sisters." Over the last decade, they had maintained their friendship and even came together for semiannual sister reunions. Between the seven of them—Kim Lan, Sonsee LeBlanc, Marilyn Thatcher, Victoria Roberts, Jacquelyn Lightfoot, Sammie Jones, and Melissa Moore—they represented a wide variety of career choices and personality types. Nonetheless, they shared a strong bond that competed in many cases with their biological siblings. Certainly Kim Lan felt closer to her friends than she had ever felt to her younger, prodigal brother.

From memory Kim punched Sonsee's number into her small phone. She had decided to secretively return her friend's call because she hated to use her parents' phone and increase their bill. Considering Kim Lan's financial assistance to her parents, Tran My Lowery would insist her daughter use their phone. But Kim, ever the loyal daughter, preferred not to leave a host of long distance calls in her wake. She wanted her parents to use the sizable monthly check she always sent for their own needs.

Within seconds Sonsee answered her phone.

"Hey, it's me," Kim Lan said into the receiver. "How's my favorite dog doctor?"

"Very funny," Sonsee said with a snort.

Kim snickered. "You left me a message. What's going on?"

"I called to tell you I've been sick and to see if I couldn't get some sympathy out of you."

"What's the matter?" Kim Lan asked as she bent to pull a scarlet tomato from a vine.

"I think I've had a light case of the flu. I haven't worked since Wednesday, and I must be getting better now because I'm bored out of my mind. All I can think about is going back to work tomorrow."

"So do you have a boa constrictor tonsillectomy you just can't wait to get to or what?"

"You're just really on a roll, aren't you?" Sonsee said dryly.

"Actually, I'm not. I think I'm going to have to fight to get to go to Vietnam."

A meaningful pause followed.

"Why do you do this?" Sonsee asked through a chuckle.

"What?" Kim Lan tugged on a second ripened tomato and placed it in the basket next to the first one.

"It never fails. Just about the time I think I'm having a regular conversation with you, you throw in a curveball. What gives with Vietnam?"

Straightening, Kim Lan eyed a cardinal as it hopped along the snow-dusted wooden fence that enclosed her parents' country yard. She produced an exasperated sigh as she recalled her encounter with that tyrant posing as a missionary. "This morning at Mom and Dad's church—"

"You're at your parents'?"

"Yes. I'm on my cell phone out in their hothouse."

"Is Ted with you this time?"

"No. He just got back to New York yesterday. He's been on a shoot in California." Amazingly, that was the first time Kim Lan had thought of Ted since she stomped away from Mick. She had been so incensed by that infuriating missionary that she had even forgotten to call Ted as she'd promised. "Anyway..." she began, deciding to worry about calling Ted later, "this morning at Mom and Dad's church, they had a special service with a mission trip coordinator named Mick O'Donnel." Kim Lan couldn't hide the snarl in her words.

"I take it the two of you didn't experience love at first sight?"

"Ha!" Kim said sarcastically. "I don't think I have ever met a more demeaning person in my life!"

"And he was a missionary?"

"Yes! He was trying to recruit people to go on a humanitarian aid trip to Vietnam. Sonsee, would you believe that he accused me of trying to buy my way on that trip?"

"What?"

"Can you believe that? The jerk said I put in a check to help fund the trip in order to buy my way on his trip. And he refused to let me sign up to go—even in the face of needing participants. He said I was a celebrity so I would distract the participants from their focus on God!" Kim used the most condescending, pontifical tones she could conjure.

Sonsee whistled. "He sounds like a doozy."

"Honey chil'," Kim said with a fake southern accent, "he's a doozy-and-a-half!"

"So you're going to challenge his decision not to let you go on the trip?"

A slight movement from the corner of her eye distracted Kim Lan from watching the cardinal on the fence. She turned to see the very subject of her conversation observing her with an amused smirk. Mick O'Donnel's light-blue eyes danced with mischief as he tucked his hand into a pocket in his cloth overcoat. A leather hat, sitting at a rakish angle atop his head, only added to his pleasantly villainous expression. He reminded her of a smug pirate who discovers he's nearing a fleet of ships filled with a plethora of plunder.

Kim Lan's heart pounded furiously. Her face heated. Her mind whirled. She blinked, wondering if she was seeing things. She blinked again, but Mick didn't disappear. There he stood right between the rows of potted okra and tomatoes.

"I've been called a lot of things," Mick drawled as if he were enjoying the taste of every word, "but I've never been called a doozy-and-a-half."

Her lips trembled, and Kim Lan furiously pressed them together.

"Is everything all right?" Sonsee asked.

"Uh...I've got to go," Kim said. "Mick's here. I'll call you back later." Before Sonsee had a chance to utter another word, Kim Lan disconnected the call and dropped the phone into her coat pocket.

"What are you doing here?" she demanded, refusing to reveal that she had never been so shocked by someone's presence.

"Your parents invited me over for lunch. Didn't your mom tell you?"

"I'm here, aren't I?" Kim ground out.

"Implying?"

"You figure it out," she bit back.

"Implying that..." he looked toward the glass ceiling, "...you would have avoided the lunch hour had you known I was coming." His Midwest voice had a way of weaving itself through the atmosphere of a room and caressing the ears in a most charming—and for Kim Lan, annoying—manner.

"You got it," she said tightly, wondering why her mother hadn't informed her that Mick was on his way. When Tran My had questioned her daughter about her hasty departure from church, Kim Lan had supplied the details of her infuriating encounter with *that missionary*. Now she felt betrayed by her own mother. Not only had she not told Kim that Mick was coming, Tran My apparently sent him out to see her!

With short, jerky movements, Kim finished picking the ripe tomatoes as a tense band of antipathy tightened around her heart. Kim had never met a person whom she instantly disliked as much as the man who was watching her. An annoying voice whispered to Kim that she wasn't behaving in the most mature, Christlike manner, that regardless of Mick's treatment, she had no right to respond in such a rude fashion. But as she straightened from her task, she dashed aside that voice. In her opinion, this was not a time to worry about being Christlike. She was doing really well not to spew forth a verbal volcano all over him.

Refusing to look at Mick again, she brusquely swept past him with the intent of removing herself from his presence.

"Kim Lan, please wait," he said fervently.

Kim, feeling as if she'd hit an invisible wall, halted, her back to him, her head lowered.

"I accepted your parents' invitation to lunch so I could apologize to you," he said, his voice genuinely regretful. "When I arrived I told your mother that I had been..." he cleared his throat, "...that I owed you an apology. She graciously told me she thought that would be a really good idea and that I could find you out here."

Mick's contrite words shocked Kim Lan even more than his unexpected presence. She could have easily hastened away, but she stiffened and the ability to move escaped her. Stubbornly she peered downward at the basket filled with tomatoes. The smell of plants and Kim Lan's perfume mingled together. Only the sounds of the humming heater and an occasional bird song broke the silence, taut with emotion.

This apology, whether it was genuine or not, certainly explained her mother's not telling Kim about Mick's arriving for dinner. As usual, Tran My was up to her peacemaking tendencies. "Blessed are the peacemakers, for they will be called sons of God." That beatitude epitomized Kim's mom as none other did.

Gently, Mick touched her shoulder. As if she were under the influence of his power, Kim rotated to face him. A second before they made eye contact, she steeled herself against the impact his eyes had already induced. But once she fully peered into the fathomless depths of his azure soul, Kim refused the urge to look away. Her years as a model had taught her to be tough when the situation required it. This situation certainly required every ounce of emotional bravado she had ever possessed. Once again she felt as if she were swimming into the depths of a balmy ocean, full of mysteries and magic. Keeping her face impassive, she coerced herself to focus on the issue at hand: Mick had apologized, but did he really mean it?

"Before you walked away from me at church, you left something unsaid. Care to finish?"

"What are you talking about?" Hoping her voice didn't reveal the breathlessness that had begun to afflict her, Kim Lan never blinked in their eye-to-eye scrutiny.

He tucked both hands into his overcoat, the color of bark, and squinted. The rugged lines in his fortyish face only added to his masculine appeal. "You said something to the effect that during my presentation I fooled you into believing...but you stopped. Tell me what you initially believed about me."

"That doesn't matter in the least. You have overturned every positive opinion I might have developed," she said, her voice wavering despite her desire to keep her tones free of inflection.

"I *said* I was sorry." A shadow of regret scurried across his features. "I meant it. I really *am* sorry. I'm afraid I probably..." He took a deep breath and scrubbed his fingers through the neckline of his straight, sand-colored hair. "I probably misjudged you."

Kim Lan's eyebrows rose.

"Don't look so shocked," he said with a chuckle. "I'd like to think I really am more the man you originally assumed me to be and less the man I acted after the service."

The mellow tone of his kind voice swirled tendrils of respect through Kim's troubled spirit despite her valiant attempts to stop it. *I do not like him,* she reminded herself. *I really don't!* Out of habit, she flipped a stubborn strand of her long hair over her shoulder and planned to make a quick exit. Her legs were starting to tremble in a manner that spoke clearly of her initial attraction to Mick O'Donnel. "Well...um...Mom needs her tomatoes."

"You're engaged?" Something akin to resigned disappointment clung to his features as he examined her ring finger.

"What?" she asked, too scattered from her own pounding pulse to fully comprehend his words.

"Engaged." He paused. "You're engaged. I noticed your ring when you adjusted your hair."

She glanced toward the near-perfect diamond on which Ted had spent a small fortune. Her reactions to Mick were not those of a woman soon to be married.

"Yes, engaged," she said absently.

"To?"

"Ted Curry," she stated, wondering why she felt the sudden need to hide the ring behind her back. Instead she tucked her hand into the oversized pocket of her leather coat.

"Oh." Traces of the judgmental tyrant scampered across Mick's face.

Kim Lan could only suspect what he must be thinking. Before her short courtship and engagement to Ted Curry, he had been famous for his womanizing. Numerous tabloids on grocers' shelves had pictured Ted with his latest interest. Immediately Kim felt the need to defend not only Ted, but herself. "Ted is—isn't—has—is changing. He is more interested in the Lord and—and—we—"

Mick raised his brows, a spark of humor igniting in his eyes. "You don't owe me an explanation."

"Well, when you look at me like that, what exactly am I supposed to do?" she snapped.

"I just came to apologize," he said stiffly. "I'm sorry for the way I acted after church. And I wanted to tell you that if you still can find it in your heart to give the money, then I'll be glad to add it to the fund." His voice relaxed. "The truth is, although we're right on our budget, we can always put extra money to use. The nursing home in Cantho—that's in south Vietnam—can really use the money. They call it a nursing home, but it's not like our nursing homes. The whole operation includes an orphanage, a baby home, and also the home for the elderly—all on the same grounds. Between the three of them, that money would be put to good use."

The images from Mick's slide presentation filled Kim Lan's mind. The faces of those babies waiting for adoption twisted her heart with an unexpected desire to give one of them a home. There was one little boy in particular whom Mick said was slow to develop and desperately needed parents. She wondered if Ted would consider adopting such a child after they were married. They could provide a full-time nurse and anything else the child might need.

"Isn't the nursing home where you'll be working during the trip?" she asked as a longing to embrace those orphans swept upon her anew.

"Yes." Mick looked past her as if he no longer wanted to make eye contact. Kim almost shrank with relief when he looked away.

"So, are you saying you'll let me sign up for the trip now?" Kim Lan asked, desperately trying to keep the hopeful note from her voice. Surely part of her previous anger had stemmed from her frustrated desire to somehow make a difference in the lives of those she had seen in Mick's pictures.

Looking down, Mick hesitated. "I hate to disappoint you, but..."

"But?" she echoed, fresh irritation welling within.

"My reasons for requesting your not going still stand." Narrowing his eyes, he looked at her. "Please don't misunderstand. I'm not trying to be hard to get along with. And I *really am sorry* about earlier. If I came across—"

"Like a tyrant?" she supplied heatedly.

The vexation from earlier flashed across his features, but his words remained cool and controlled. "But I really believe that at this point you would be a greater asset as a giver and not as a participant. I have to think about all the members and the effectiveness of the team as a whole."

"And I guess you would tell me I was lying if I said I felt the Lord impressed me to give *and* go?" Kim Lan snapped.

"I never said—"

"You haven't even had a chance to pray about it! But still, you've made up your mind. Just like that!" She snapped her fingers, and Ted's diamond shimmered in the brilliant sunshine.

Mick's attention once more focused on the ring, and he spoke with a deliberate cadence that attested to an unshakable decision. "Like I already said, it's a matter of what's best for the group."

His appealing appraisal almost convinced Kim that she had been foolish in thinking she should go in the first place. Mick had mentioned his younger brother's fascination for her. *Could what Mick said be true? Could my presence distract his brother to the point that he wouldn't be open to the voice of God?* Kim thought of her own younger brother, wherever he was, of her hope for him to know the Lord. Most likely, Mick's desire for his brother were as strong as her own.

"Please try to understand," he said with resolution. "I have nothing against you." He shrugged. "Honest. And I would hate to think I'd made an enemy after such a short acquaintance."

Mick was so convincing that she came within a breath of agreeing not to go, but something inside stopped Kim Lan from even the slightest nod of acquiescence. Instead, she peered at him as his request seemed to float around the hothouse in pursuit of her agreement. But the longer she remained in his presence, the warmer she became and the more potent her reaction to him grew. Once more, she felt as if she were being tugged into the balmy waters of an intriguing sea. Her initial attraction, respect, and desire to know him better increased with renewed fervor.

The stirring magnetism in Mick's eyes heightened Kim Lan's awareness of her own surprising emotions. She had just met this man, and already he had shaken her to the core. As the seconds ticked on, she pictured his arms wrapping around her and pulling her into the ardor of his embrace.

The delicious yearning that rushed upon Kim Lan flashed between them and manifested itself upon Mick's face. His gaze trailed to her lips, lingered with longing, then found her eyes once more. "I believe you're the most lovely woman I have ever met," he muttered with awe.

The rush of pleasure left Kim Lan feeling as if she had never been told she was beautiful. Sure, she knew what all the magazines, her agent, and the fan mail said. But Mick's words held a genuine ring that much of her professional praise lacked. In her career, Kim often sensed that she would be gorgeous only until another model came along who was younger and more stunning.

"There you are," Kim's father said from the doorway. "We were wondering if the two of you had gotten lost." Leaning on his worn cane with each step, John limped toward them. "Your mother's got everything ready, Kimmy, and is waiting on the tomatoes."

"The tomatoes!" Kim Lan had completely forgotten about the tomatoes. "Of course," she mumbled. "I'll take them to her." With a vague smile thrown in her father's general direction, Kim swept past him and stepped into the frigid air.

Mick, trying his best to remain casual, watched Kim close the greenhouse door. *What possessed me? I'm acting like an eighteen-year-old with an instantaneous crush on the new girl at school.* He certainly wasn't acting like an almost forty-year-old man "set in his ways," as his brother would say. Mick had never intended to tell Kim Lan she was lovely. But the thought had begun, and before he knew it he heard the words leave his mouth. She *was* lovely. He had often seen her pictures in his brother's room and in ads. On Caleb's wall, she had seemed more like an artificial Barbie doll than a real woman. However, the effect she was having on him in real life made Mick feel less like himself and more like Caleb.

Suddenly realizing John Lowery was talking and had ended with a question, Mick smiled apologetically. "Pardon me. I was distracted."

"Yes, I noticed." Mr. Lowery's brows arched over brown eyes that twinkled with hints of approval, relief, and joy as he glanced toward the doorway. "I just asked if you and Kimmy ironed out your differences. Tran My mentioned the two of you had somehow gotten on the wrong footing."

"Yes, I apologized. That's the main reason I accepted your dinner invitation. I needed to make amends." Mick wearily rubbed his face. "I've been under a lot of stress lately, and I'm afraid that made me a bit more abrupt than I should have been."

"That's what it's all about—this relationship with Christ—making things right with Him and others," John said with understanding. "I've had to apologize more than I can remember." He smiled and motioned for Mick to accompany him.

As he followed the older gentleman's slow pace toward the door, Mick sensed that the attraction between him and Kim was obvious to Mr. Lowery. He also received the uncanny feeling that Mr. Lowery was thrilled with what he saw. But regardless of the attraction, or even John Lowery's approval, Mick would be firm about not allowing her on the trip. He would also never permit himself to see her again after today. She left him devoid of all his senses, and that was not a place he enjoyed being.

For the last several years, Mick had found a supernatural contentment in being single. However, before he was thirty-five he had regularly beseeched the Lord for a wife who was beautiful inside, for a woman whose very presence suggested she had been with the Lord, for a mate who would forever point him to the cross. He had no reason to veer from his original request simply because he had come up against a pretty face. *But how do I know Kim Lan isn't that type of woman? I barely even know her.* He recalled her saying she had stopped doing the suggestive modeling poses and wondered what prompted her decision. Could it have been an issue of obeying the Lord? If so, that certainly attested to her seeking Him. *But she is engaged to Ted Curry—the* playboy *Ted Curry. Doesn't that affirm her lack of spiritual depth? What does her spiritual depth matter anyway?* Mick lambasted himself. *She's engaged! Regardless of who the man is, she's engaged!*

He followed Mr. Lowery into the spacious home decorated in Victorian antiques. Their firm footsteps met the polished hardwood floors that produced an occasional creak in their wakes. They tread through the sunroom, down a short hallway, and into the dining room. The disappointment Mick had experienced when he saw the large diamond on Kim Lan's finger settled in his midsection like a mound of cold rocks. He shed his coat, sat across from her at the Queen Anne dining table, and refused to look at her.

"Mick, tell us more about your career," Mrs. Lowery said, as they served themselves from the various aromatic dishes. "When did you know you wanted to be involved in missions, and how did it all come about?"

A cloud of tension settled between him and Kim Lan as Mick began a mechanical rendition of the details concerning his heavenly call to missions. "Well, I was about twenty-three and working my way through a degree in criminal justice when I renewed my commitment to the Lord. At that point, I had a black belt in karate and was ready to rid the world of the ills of mankind." He paused for a tight smile and purposefully avoided glancing in Kim's direction. "But believe it or not, I was able to use my experience when I changed

majors. Between that and the college credits in law enforce-
ment, I was qualified to get a flexible security guard job at the
seminary I attended in Kansas City. So I worked my way
through a double master's in biblical studies and missions."
Mick paused, and Kim extended a basket of rolls toward him.

Mick glanced toward her, only to find himself once more
riveted by her beauty. Desperately, he attempted to look
away but seemed forever ensnared in the depths of her
dark-eyed appraisal. *What if she's the one I've been waiting
for?* The thought intensified his confusion.

His mother had finally given up on Mick's marrying. His
stepfather had dubbed him "married to his mission." And for
the most part that had been true. After years of struggling
with the anger he felt from his father's death in combat, Mick
finally relinquished his need for revenge to the Lord. That
had been sixteen years ago during a church service that had
changed his life. Then, after numerous grueling years to
achieve his education, Mick had devoted his life to coordinating missions trips for his denomination. He loved the
Asian culture now, especially the Vietnamese people, with
a passion only the Lord could have bestowed. Indeed, God
had turned Mick's hatred to inexplicable love.

But that love did not stop with the culture as a whole. In
recent years he had found himself more and more drawn to
the beauty he saw in the faces of Asian women. He had
even begun to think that if he ever did get married, his wife
would most likely be of Asian descent.

"Would you care for some rolls?" Kim Lan asked, her own
expression reflecting the heartbeat of attraction that forever
throbbed between them.

Mick continued to stare across the table into the most
gorgeous face he had yet seen, and he couldn't seem to find
his tongue. *This must be some sort of a midlife crisis*, he

thought. *I've never been so addled by a woman. What must her parents think of me?*

A muffled ring sounded from the hallway, and Kim Lan placed the basket of bread near Mick's plate. "That's my cell phone," she said as if she were relieved to have an excuse to escape. "It's in my jacket pocket. I must have left it on earlier. That's probably Ted." She glanced toward her parents, pushed back her chair, and dabbed the corners of her mouth with the burgundy napkin. "I was supposed to call him and forgot."

An aura of disapproval seeped from the Lowerys as their daughter left the room to speak with her fiancé. Mick glanced toward them and couldn't deny the grim dread cloaking both their countenances. He remembered Mr. Lowery's obvious approval, relief, and joy when he had found them together in the greenhouse. Mick's sharp mind connected all these clues and realized the Lowerys didn't smile upon their daughter's choice for a husband. But then, neither did he. Mick had only met Kim Lan today, but he suspected that she deserved a better husband than the man whose diamond she wore.

Taking one of the homemade rolls, Mick placed it on the edge of his plate and looked at the scrumptious meal. He wished he could leave immediately and board the next flight to Colorado Springs, where his homey cabin and Siamese cat awaited him. Mick's appetite had vanished.

Three

Odysseus gazed at the bedroom walls covered with a collage of Kim Lan Lowery's magazine photos. In the corner of his cluttered room, a substantial stack of magazines, several towers thick, held duplicate copies of the clip-outs on the wall. He made a point to peruse the magazine racks, and every time a photo was released of Kim Lan, he bought two of the magazines: one to add to his ever-growing stack and the other to remove the pictures and place them on his walls.

Every night when he crawled into bed his last sight before turning out the light was Kim Lan Lowery. His final thought concerned Kim Lan Lowery. His every dream centered around Kim Lan Lowery. Her glossy hair. Her enchanting eyes. Her arms, waiting to embrace him. Even her name rolled off his tongue like that of an angel.

He walked toward the old television and VCR sitting on his dresser, turned them on, and pushed in the video that he had played hundreds of time—a video featuring the numerous advertisements Kim Lan had recorded. With the sound of her melodious voice filling his quarters, he walked into the bathroom. As if in worshipful ritual, he picked up the bar of soap that bore her signature and began slowly washing his hands. Odysseus wanted her to be his so badly.

He lived for the day when she would see him...make eye contact...realize he was the only man for her.

He rinsed the fragrant soap from his hands, dried them on the worn towel, covered his nose and mouth with his fingers, and inhaled deeply of the feminine fragrance. The exotic smell seemed the essence of Kim's very spirit. With a groan, he covered his whole face with his hands and fantasized about the day they would marry. Yes, they would marry. She had to marry him. Her soul belonged to him. The rumors were flying about her and Ted Curry, but that was nothing more than a passing fancy with her. Odysseus was her man. Kim's engagement with Ted would soon end. She would have to end it.

I won't allow her to marry someone else. I'll stop the marriage. I have no choice. If Kim Lan persisted in being unfaithful, Odysseus would deal with her as he had dealt with Sophie. As with his former girlfriend, knowing Kim loved another man more than she loved him would require his action. But hopefully this pursuit would not result in death, as it had with Sophie. Once Kim Lan realized just how much he loved her, she would gladly agree to be his wife.

With determination he walked back into his tiny room and gently pushed the oversized tabby cat out of the computer chair. He sat down at the computer and logged onto the internet. Today...today was the day he would begin courting her. Soon he connected with the website that allowed him to send flowers to anyone in the United States. With an assured smile, he completed his order, typed in Kim Lan's Park Avenue address, and arranged the delivery for the next day. Surely a dozen roses would be the best romantic symbol for the beginning of the courtship.

Odysseus picked up the photo sitting on his computer desk—Sophie's photo, framed in pewter. Her dark eyes, like pools of ink, silently accused him, creating a river of guilt that rushed through his soul. He glanced toward the collection of pictures covering his wall. Sophie and Kim were alike in many ways. The same hair. The same dark eyes. The same willowy height. However, the caucasian Sophie had not been blessed with Kim's exotic, Oriental features. Odysseus, still troubled by the tragedy he'd instigated, stroked the photo as if he were caressing Sophie's face.

He remembered the day he had left for the West Coast. As they shared a final embrace, Sophie had jokingly called herself Penelope—Odysseus' devout wife. That day, he had decided he would propose when he returned from his journey. In the Greek myth, Penelope had been loyal during Odysseus' twenty-year absence, even though she was pursued by more than 100 suitors. But unlike Penelope, Sophie had proven to be a woman of less devoted intent. Indeed, her referring to herself as Penelope had been a mockery of Odysseus' love.

Tensing with rage, Odysseus slammed the photo against the desk and all vestiges of guilt vanished. He should never feel shameful for his part in the end of Sophie's life. "She deserved to die," he muttered through gritted teeth. "She rejected me. She deserved what she got."

○﹏

The next day, Kim Lan slept late at her parents' home before driving the four hours back to her penthouse. She was scheduled for a modeling show Tuesday, but there were several important details she needed to deal with. Kim Lan, who relished the freedom of driving her Jaguar, also used the driving time to plan her strategy. The sleek, ebony Jag purred to a halt under the portico of the elegant Park Avenue apartment building, and Kim Lan pondered the events of the preceding day.

She had wanted to extend the telephone call with Ted until Mick left, but due to fear of being rude, she'd promised to call Ted later. Refusing to look at Mick again, she had finished the meal without appetite. The tension between her and Mick O'Donnel had been beyond suffocating. His genuine comment about her being lovely seemed to twine itself between them, forever pulling her thoughts toward him. Furthermore, her father's occasional mischievous smiles had done little to better the situation.

Assuredly, the sparks she had felt when watching Mick during his presentation had in no way been one-sided. Despite his refusal to allow her on the trip, Kim saw that she affected him as deeply as he affected her. However, she was an engaged woman. Furthermore, she and Mick had almost nothing in common. They were from two completely different worlds. Any potential relationship between them was doomed from the start.

She put the Jag in park and stared at her eel-skin purse sitting on the supple leather passenger seat. The purse and seat blurred together in a sea of burgundy and taupe as she contemplated the 10,000-dollar check still in her possession. She had been so distracted by Mick himself that she'd forgotten to return the check as he requested. But during her drive, she had concocted a plan for returning the money and hopefully assuring her place on the list of trip participants. As soon as she walked into her penthouse, she would place a call to denominational headquarters.

Mick O'Donnel had acted as if she'd silently agreed to forget going on the trip. Actually her determination had grown. Last night, she had earnestly prayed about the trip and felt the same stirring from the Holy Spirit that she should indeed go to Vietnam. After pondering Mick's reasons for her not going, she had decided to honor his request about his younger brother and the other participants. She would do everything in her power to disguise her appearance and even assume a pseudonym. Usually when she flew Kim chartered a jet or, at times, she would fly first class with a commercial airliner. If she chose to fly on a commercial flight, she wore no makeup, shaded glasses, well-worn, casual clothing, and tucked her hair under a floppy hat. As of yet, she had never been approached, although she had endured one or two curious stares. Kim Lan would dress the same for this humanitarian aid trip. No one but Mick would know her secret.

Her plan would likely result in Mick's disapproval. However, as much as she didn't want to cross swords with Mick O'Donnel again, Kim Lan feared the Lord more. She had learned from experience to listen when God was speaking to her. The times Kim had readily obeyed the voice of the Lord, her experiences had been positive. But God had also taught her through her own disobedience. After years of spiritual struggle, Kim had finally decided that her best course of action was obedience. She was determined to listen for His voice, and she firmly believed that her desire to go to Vietnam went deeper than her own human wants.

Kim removed the keys from the ignition, inhaled the smell of new leather, and recalled her recent decision to model for a swimsuit issue, despite God's leading that she do no more sensual poses. However, the money had seduced her and Kim fell into disobedience. After the shoot, the Lord had dealt with her so strongly that she had been miserable. The feelings of conviction were still fresh. A holy conviction. A conviction that led her to heartfelt repentance.

A conviction that left her resolving to never again pose in seductive layouts. The same righteous fervor that had left her miserable now pressed her forward, toward a new journey the Lord set before her. Regardless of Mick O'Donnel's resistance, she knew God was calling her to Vietnam... to her mother's homeland...to a voyage that would lead her to those orphaned babies.

I believe you're the most lovely woman I have ever met. Mick's words from yesterday barged into her thoughts. Her pulse began the telltale tattoo in her temples and wrists. If her plan worked, and she did go on the trip, she would be faced with the difficult task of squelching her sudden propensity toward melting in the presence of the trip's coordinator. Undoubtedly, Mick could prove a distraction.

She placed her hand on the door release and scrutinized Ted's diamond as it accusingly glittered up at her. A twist of guilt tore at her heart. She had accepted the ring some time ago with the understanding that she wasn't saying a final yes to his proposal. Last week, even in the midst of misgivings, she had at last promised Ted marriage. Kim Lan was a woman of her word. They were planning to announce their engagement to the media in the near future. She couldn't back out now.

I believe you're the most lovely woman I have ever met... the most lovely woman I have ever met...the most lovely... Mick O'Donnel's sincere, startling blue eyes seemed to bore into her very soul: the disappointment when he saw her ring; the resignation flitting across his features; his assuming the worst about Kim's relationship with Ted.

This is crazy! she scolded herself. *I've got to stop thinking about him!*

With a vengeance she decided to get out and give her keys to the doorman waiting under the portico. Kim tugged on the door release and tried to shove it open, only to hear a masculine protest. She glanced up to see Ted standing inches away from the car, lovingly observing her. His dark hair, tanned skin, sensual smile, and deep-blue eyes affected her like they always did—as if the wind had been knocked out of her. Ted Curry epitomized everything she had dreamed of in a husband. Beyond handsome, he was as close to physical perfection as any man she had ever met. Even in his casual corduroys, leather jacket, and loafers he looked like royalty. His only imperfection was a slight crook in his otherwise straight nose, but even the crook gave him a charming roguish appeal. In the face of Ted's blatant allure, Mick O'Donnel's rugged attractiveness seemed... Images of Mick once again stubbornly imposed themselves upon her mind. In the face of Ted, Mick seemed... She thought of Mick's obvious love for God. She pondered his passion for those orphans. She remembered the dedication to his work that he exuded. In the face of Ted's physical perfection, Mick seemed...

"Hey, Babe, what's got you so distracted?" Ted crooned as he reached for Kim's hand and assisted her from the car. "I've been standing here for ages, just soaking you up." He placed a kiss somewhere near her ear. "I didn't think you were ever going to notice me."

"Sorry," Kim said absently. She returned Ted's brief embrace, feeling as if she were in a time warp. Although she stood with Ted, Kim found it hard to pull her attention away from Mick. With a decision of her will, she shoved images of the mission coordinator from her mind, produced a flirting smile, and dangled the keys in front of Ted. "Are you the new doorman?"

"Sure. I'm anything you want me to be," he said, the everpresent warmth in his eyes.

Amid mutual laughter, Kim retrieved her purse from the passenger seat, and Ted grabbed her suitcase. She opened her billfold and bestowed a generous tip to the doorman, who took the keys to her Jag. Despite the New York traffic and her father's constant concern about Kim Lan's safety, she clung to the Jag. The sports car represented her freedom.

As Kim closed her billfold, she glimpsed the 10,000-dollar check for Mick's mission and glanced at Ted, wondering how long he intended to stay. She really needed to place the phone call to church headquarters now. Yesterday was supposed to be the final day to sign up for the trip, and Thursday night was the first orientation meeting. Plus, if she were going she needed to apply for a visa to Vietnam tomorrow. Fortunately, her passport was current. In short, Kim didn't even have an hour to waste. However, until her spot on the trip was secure, she didn't want to tell Ted about her plans. Something told her he would not smile upon her decision to spend two weeks in Asia without him. And she wondered if he would understand her desire to participate on such a journey.

With Ted's arm possessively nestled against the back of her full-length fox coat, they stepped toward the glass doors that led into the elegant building. The nearby security guard, who admitted no stranger without proper ID, pressed the button that automatically opened the doors.

The building's foyer looked more like that of a luxury hotel than a place of permanent residence. The marble floors, exquisite front desk, and strategically placed pillars reflected the elegance of Kim Lan's penthouse. Add to that the brass and glass, exclusive gourmet restaurant, indoor pool, vintage art, gym, maid service, room service, and the opulent hostess suite available for entertaining, and the rich and famous residents usually didn't worry about the exorbitant cost. For Kim Lan, the purchase of this building had proven to be yet another smart business move that added even more earning power to her growing fortune.

"Miss Lowery, there's something special awaiting you at the front desk, I believe." The gray-haired house doorman, dressed in his usual tuxedo, bowed slightly as he spoke.

"Thanks, James," she said with a smile.

His faded gray eyes twinkled in response to their private joke. Long ago, Kim Lan had dubbed Roger Stover "the butler" and nicknamed him "James." She possessed a good rapport with her "James" and the other complex's employees. She always tipped nicely and wanted to be known for her generosity.

As she and Ted crossed the green marble floors and approached the front desk, Kim noticed a huge bouquet of roses, the color of scarlet, with "Kim Lan Lowery" scribbled on an attached card.

"These are for you, Miss Lowery," the receptionist said with a knowing smile directed toward Ted.

Kim's heart warmed as she darted Ted a coy grin and wondered how she could have ever let Mick O'Donnel sway her thoughts. Ted had proven his devotion in so many endearing ways. These flowers only attested to his continued thoughtfulness.

"You shouldn't have," she said, burying her nose in the lush petals' fragrance. "But I'm so glad you did."

"I didn't," he said, his full lips tilting downward in a near grimace. "But I'd like to know who did." He deposited Kim's suitcase on the plush oriental rug and tugged on the straight pin that attached the card to the red ribbon.

Kim's mind raced in panic as Ted opened the card. She pondered the off-chance that Mick had sent the flowers. Ted had proven himself jealous on more than one occasion, and she did not want him to know about Mick.

"Who sent them?" she asked, keeping her tone coolly disinterested. Despite her raging curiosity, Kim steeled herself against ripping the card from Ted's fingers and reading the note.

"Here." With a guarded expression, Ted extended the card toward her. "Maybe you can tell me."

She nonchalantly peered at the card to read, "With warmest regards, Your Secret Admirer." Mick's compliment from yesterday began a slow chant that wove itself into her soul. Kim Lan relived the awareness that had flashed between them when he neared her in the church foyer. She recalled that moment during lunch when she had gotten lost in his admiring gaze.

"Is there something I should know about last weekend?" Ted asked.

Kim's heart lurched. "Oh, Ted," she said flippantly, lightly touching his arm. "You get stuff like this from fans all the time, and you know it."

His face relaxed. "Sorry," he said with a chuckle. "I guess where you're concerned, I'm a little possessive." His eyes darkened with the stirrings of his deepening love.

In the past, Kim Lan had debated the genuineness of Ted's affection, but in recent days she was beginning to think that he was indeed smitten and had truly turned from his playboy tendencies. "Let's go," she said, noticing the young receptionist had grown a tad too interested in their exchange. Kim grabbed the cut-glass vase in both hands and walked toward the elevator, with Ted in her wake. Part of her figured the roses were indeed from a fan, but another side of her rebelliously wished they could be from Mick O'Donnel. Somehow, the fan scenario made more sense.

Outside the apartment building, Odysseus crouched near a flowerbed and gazed through the glass walls that constituted the front entrance. That morning he had donned his disguise and meticulously dressed himself in a khaki gardener's uniform. His presence as he toiled near the evergreen bushes had not been questioned.

His palms sweating despite winter's chill, he strained to see Kim Lan wait outside the elevator with that scoundrel Ted Curry. Kim carried herself like a princess. A princess with a knave. *Why doesn't she realize she deserves better than Curry?* His gut twisted with jealousy. Jealousy and rage. Rage and betrayal. *Kim Lan belongs to me.*

Just before the elevator door opened, he caught a glimpse of Kim burying her nose in the bouquet of roses. A faraway, whimsical look softened her features, and his heart leapt with pleasure. Perhaps the roses meant so much to her that once she met the man behind the flowers she would already be in love.

Your days are numbered, Curry, he thought as he ambled away from the bushes toward the street. Just a few short weeks, just a few more love notes, a few more flowers, and Kim Lan would be melting with adoration for her secret admirer. She would forget Ted and be ready to embrace her true love. *But what if she doesn't fall in love with me?*

That thought sent Odysseus' mind spinning into the past, into the similar doubts he had experienced when first meeting Sophie. He recalled their first dinner date…his nervousness…his wondering if a woman of such exquisite beauty could ever fall in love with him. Odysseus closed his eyes and visualized their third date when they were walking through the park after their delectable Italian meal. Sophie had allowed him to take her in his arms and kiss her. Odysseus' gut clenched with the memory of her long satiny hair beneath his fingers. Never had he dreamed that night that Sophie would betray his love. Never had he imagined her betrayal would culminate in tragedy. Never had he dreamed he would find another woman who could compare to her.

Now, not only had he found another, he had found one that thrilled him more than Sophie ever did. Certainly, Kim Lan would be a more worthy recipient of his adoration. Kim would love him. This very morning, he had called Mick and asked to be added to the list of trip participants. If she went on the trip, it would be the perfect opportunity for Odysseus to prove himself a trustworthy man deserving her love. And if she did reject him...the idea of the gorgeous model meeting Sophie's fate left Odysseus nauseous.

"She has no choice but to love me," he muttered as he neared the curbside of Park Avenue. "She has no choice."

The elevator doors whisked shut and left Kim Lan alone with her fiancé. As Ted affectionately toyed with the ends of her waist-length hair, an air of constraint descended upon him. One of the conditions of their engagement had been that the actor quit pressuring Kim Lan toward physical intimacy outside of marriage. She had been firm in her decision not to consummate their relationship before their wedding. So far, he had played the gentleman and stopped the persistent innuendoes that had characterized their early relationship.

Within minutes, she and Ted ascended to the top floor. Kim Lan unlocked her apartment door, and they stepped across the threshold of her ultra-modern penthouse, decorated in black and white with touches of oriental flair. The smell of mulberry from her numerous candles enfolded them as the telephone began a muffled, persistent peal. Kim Lan glanced toward the table in the living room where one of the cordless phones usually sat. But it was gone. She hadn't been home in two days and couldn't remember exactly where she'd left the phone. Nonetheless, the muffled ringing continued.

"I'm going to get that in my room," she said, depositing the flowers on the milky marble breakfast bar. "Help yourself to a soda."

With the phone continuing its ring, Ted set her luggage by the bar and tugged her toward him. "Ah, Kim Lan," he whispered, "let the machine get it."

"Uh, no...I don't think so." She gently pushed him away, not certain she was comfortable with the vein of his thoughts. "I—I need to go ahead and answer. It might be mom and dad."

"Okay," Ted said, a disappointed wilt to his voice. "I'm certain I've never met a woman quite like you, Kim."

"Hold that thought," she said with a charming smile. In seconds, Kim Lan stepped into her bedroom decorated with oriental antiques. The cordless phone from the living room, lying on her bed, produced another peal. Kim dropped her purse on the bed, grabbed the phone, pushed the talk button, and began the awkward chore of removing her fur coat with only one hand free.

"Hello, is this Kim Lan Lowery?"

The smooth, masculine voice left her collapsing on the black poster bed, one arm still in the coat. Her pulse leapt. Her hands moistened. Her stomach lurched. Mick O'Donnel! Immediately, she felt as if she were standing in her parents' greenhouse, feeling as if she were drowning in his mes-merizing eyes.

"Hello?" he said again. "Kim Lan?"

"Y—Yes." She cleared her throat and forced herself not to stutter. "Yes. This is Kim Lan."

"Know who this is?" he asked, a smile in his voice.

"Yes," she said again, closing her eyes in an attempt to discipline her trembling voice. "How did you get my number?" she asked, for lack of anything else better to say.

"Your mother gladly gave it to me when I called and asked."

She would, Kim Lan thought. Her parents never had been enamored with the prospects of her marrying Ted, and Kim had easily detected their heightened interest in the sparks flying between her and Mick.

"I..." He paused, and Kim thought she detected a trace of hesitancy in the voice of this self-assured man. "I called because of something you said yesterday in the greenhouse."

"Oh?"

"Yes. You mentioned the fact that I hadn't prayed about your going on the trip to Vietnam."

"Oh?" she repeated, her mind racing with the implications of his words. Nervously, Kim Lan stood, switched the phone to her other ear and finished removing her coat, allowing it to fall onto the bed. She walked toward the wall, covered with floral drapes and tugged on the curtain cord. The drapes swished aside to reveal a massive window that provided an excellent view of the expansive New York City area.

"And something told me I'd better pray about my snap decision," Mick continued. "I did. And I've come to the con-clusion that I was wrong."

Kim dropped to the nearby settee, and several silent sec-onds slowly ticked by.

"Don't you have anything to say?" he asked.

No logical thought would pose itself long enough for her to verbalize it. Kim had never been so without her wits.

"So you're going to make this as hard on me as you can?" The smile in his words only added to the delicious effect his voice had upon her.

"Did you send me roses?" she blurted, but as the words left her lips she wondered why she'd spoken them.

While weighted silence spanned several more seconds, she imagined his lips tilting in the smile that enhanced the laugh lines around his mouth and eyes. "No," he finally said with a chuckle. "What would make you think—I would never do that anyway. You're an engaged woman." Another chuckle. "Besides, on my salary, I can't afford roses. I'm a missions coordinator, remember? The best I could probably do would be a few daisies."

While another bout of silence accosted their strained conversation, a wave of heat crept up Kim Lan's neck, to her cheeks, and eventually claimed every root of her hair.

"Why do you ask? Did someone send you roses?" Mick asked at last.

"Yes," Kim said, forcing her voice into a matter-of-fact tone. "And whoever did it didn't sign a name. I've been racking my brain, trying to figure out who sent them."

"Not me," he stated.

"Thanks," she supplied a bit brusquely. But inside she was once again that young embarrassed schoolgirl who wanted to hide from the class bully. "About the trip...I'll camouflage my identity," she said, like the self-assured woman she presented to the world. "I do it all the time. If it's okay with you, I can even come under an assumed name."

"You'd do all that?"

"Of course. I think it's the best way. I don't want to distract anyone," she added with meaning. "While we can't do anything about the name on my passport and visa, what would you think if I signed up under the name...say...Kimberly Lowe. It's a derivative of my own name, so I still feel honest."

"Thanks," he said as if they were involved in a cut-and-dried business agreement. "I'll add Kimberly Lowe to the list. My younger brother confirmed that he is indeed going on the trip, and I've had a couple of others sign up too, so the more undetectable you are, the better.

"So far the whole mission team is going to be made up of people from the northeast—mainly the New England states," he said as if he were a tour guide spewing forth memorized script. "We usually try to keep the participants within a reasonably close geographical location so they can all meet each other at the orientation meetings. It's a time of prayer and some training as well," he continued mechanically. "However, if you know anyone else—*anywhere*—who wants to go, we only have nine people signed up and could still use more participants. Even if they're not close enough to attend the orientation seminars, I can mail them the information. We just need to know something in the next couple of days or there won't be enough time to get visas to Vietnam."

"And you? Where do you live?" The question arose from nowhere, but Kim Lan found herself intensely curious about Mick O'Donnel's place of residence.

"Doesn't matter," he said as if he were rankled by her interest.

Kim tensed with irritation, partly with him and partly with herself. Mick was right. It really didn't matter where he lived.

Once again, a surge of mortification washed upon her, and she lambasted herself for setting herself up for humiliation.

"Our first orientation meeting is this Thursday night, and it happens to be at your parents' church at seven o'clock. Can you make it?"

"Yes, that's fine." She mimicked his professional tone.

"Meanwhile, I need to fax you the visa application form. Get it filled out. You'll also need to attach a photo like the one in your passport. You can get one made at just about any copy store. Then you'll need to overnight the application to the Vietnamese embassy today, if possible. I'm assuming you have a current passport?"

"Yes."

"Good. When I fax, I'll also send the necessary information and instructions on filling out the visa application. It's all very simple."

After supplying the appropriate fax number, Kim Lan ended the call and tried to block Mick and her embarrassing questions from her mind. However, something he said began a haunting cadence in her spirit: *On my salary, I can't afford roses. I'm a missions coordinator, remember? The best I could probably do would be a few daisies.*

Kim recalled her father always picking wildflowers in the meadow because he couldn't afford to buy flowers, let alone roses, for her mother. She recounted the school years she had worn clothing purchased at Goodwill…never quite in style…always looking a bit more shabby than the girls who "had it all." She remembered how being dubbed "the poor girl in class" had woven threads of inferiority into the very fabric of her soul. Kim couldn't recollect the exact moment when she had made the decision, but sometime during her adolescence she had doubled her fists and pledged to one day be wealthy. No more scraping to make ends meet. No more hours in the garden because they couldn't afford a lot of food. No more meager Christmases...or birthdays...or listening to her mother crying in the den after her father went to sleep because she didn't know how they would ever pay the electric bill. No more!

Thanks to a benevolent Texas uncle, Kim Lan had been given an opportunity to attend the University of Texas. And in Texas she had been discovered by a modeling scout. Her modeling career had careened skyward. Almost overnight she had been plucked from the grips of poverty and plunked into the lap of luxury. She was able to make her dream come true. No more poverty. No more watching her beloved parents struggle to make ends meet. No more being the poor girl in class. No more! Kim Lan had kept her vow from adolescence. She was a wealthy adult. And not only was she wealthy, she was also engaged to the man numerous magazines had dubbed the most eligible bachelor in the United States.

She looked at the glistening diamond on her ring finger— a diamond she had adored from the moment she saw it. She was assaulted by questions that sent a cringe of dread across the corridors of her soul. *Would you be willing to give up the diamond for the cause of Christ? Would you be willing to sell all you have and give to the poor, should He ask?*

The dread escalated into a surge of panic that left her heart reacing as she fought the desire to run from even the prospect of sacrificing everything for Christ. Kim bolted upward. Still gripping the cordless phone, she hurried toward her bedroom door.

Ted awaited her. Ted Curry—not Mick O'Donnel. Ted represented Kim's every fantasy, her lifelong dream, her pursuit of wealth.

Four

Mick replaced the beige receiver in its cradle, propped his elbows on the worn desk, and covered his face with unsteady hands. Rubbing his eyes until they ached, he emitted a troubled sigh. Just talking to Kim Lan had shaken him to his boots. He couldn't imagine what two whole weeks on a mission journey would do to him. *I'll probably be on tranquilizers before the trip is over,* he thought with a dry chuckle.

As he gazed across the humble guest room in the quaint parsonage near downtown Boston, he wondered why Kim Lan persisted in asking such hair-raising questions.

"Why would I send you flowers?" he spit out, waving his hand as if she were present. "And what does it matter where I live?" he growled under his breath. "You're engaged!" Mick doubled his fists as a new surge of disappointment plagued him. The moment he saw Kim Lan's engagement ring, he had been plummeted into the pits of disillusionment. These unexpected emotions were confusing to say the least. They were beyond confusing. They were insane!

"Lord, what are You up to?" he mumbled. "I've done what I thought You wanted me to do. I recanted my decision about her going. But in all honesty, I just don't see where You're going on this one. If you're having ideas about me and that supermodel....Lord, You're going to have to do some heavy-duty changing on me or her because I am not her type. I can guarantee You that!" Mick abruptly stood, and the desk chair toppled behind him. After a brief session of fumbling with the chair and dropping it again, he eventually righted it.

Soon a polite knock sounded on the closed door, and Pastor Nathan Hinton stepped into the room. "Is everything okay in here?" The dark, quizzical eyes of the African-American preacher danced with a touch of concern and humor. "Sounds like you're wrestling somebody."

"I'm fine. It's this chair." Mick gave it a sideways kick. "The thing started attacking me." The two joined in mutual laughter.

Church headquarters always arranged for a pastor to host Mick while he organized the trips. This time Nathan and his wife, Nancy, had graciously welcomed Mick. During the past week, Mick had met with several congregations, stated his last-minute call for volunteers to Vietnam, and recruited participants. After the orientation seminar Thursday night, Mick would go back home to his family's Colorado acres for a couple of weeks.

In the background a baby's shrill cry broke the calm aura that had settled upon the afternoon. Immediately, the mother's soft footfalls sounded from the kitchen, and the delightful odor of baking brownies attested to her culinary talents.

"Oops. Looks like somebody is up from his nap," Nathan said with an elated light in his eyes. "Let the good times roll!" He turned from the door and followed his wife's path up the short hallway.

Mick stepped into the tiny living room and listened to the sounds coming from the baby's room. The cooing mother. The smiling father saying, "Here, let me have him." The six-month-old baby's abating cry as he found comfort with his parents.

Nathan and Nancy appeared to be around thirty. Young and in love and relishing their first experience as parents.

He glanced around the sparsely decorated living room, brightly furnished with a floral sofa, a couple of leather recliners, a cheerful woven rug, a notched coffee table, and a set of gleaming brass candlesticks on the mantle. Nancy had added the candlesticks to the welcoming decor last night and proclaimed she was the "queen of garage sales." According to Nathan, Nancy had furnished the whole house from "nearly new" stores and garage sales. No one would ever guess it from the inviting home. Mick had to admit that Nancy had great taste. Before arriving here, he had learned that they had taken the small, struggling, multicultural church out of love and devotion for the Lord. The studious Nathan, equipped with his master's degree in pastoral studies, drove a school bus for extra money. Mick always specifically requested that he stay with a pastor and wife such as Nathan and Nancy. He knew the remuneration that church headquarters supplied for his care would boost their income.

But to look at the Hintons, with the glow of the Lord on their faces and the gleam of love in their eyes, no one would ever suspect they had cause for financial concern. Nancy seemed perfectly content with her garage-sale household and wardrobe. Anything...as long as she was with her man and serving her Lord. Numerous times, Mick had heard her praying in the night, calling out the names of her husband and child and other loved ones to the Lord. Mick pondered exactly how many times he had met other "Nathans and Nancys" throughout the years—too many to count.

As he watched the couple's orange-striped cat stretch in front of the flickering fireplace, a cold ache settled in the pit of his stomach. *Will I ever meet my "Nancy"? When will it be my turn to have a wife and family?* Idly, Mick wondered if he would wind up like Nathan's ancient scrawny cat who now hobbled toward his bowl of milk in the kitchen. The cat had clearly outlived most felines. His ear was nicked. His tail was crooked. And his fur lacked a certain luster.

Just about like me, Mick mused as he rubbed the base of his neck then tucked his hand into his jeans pocket. I'm quickly moving into my middle years, and I'm just as alone as I've ever been. Before I know it, I'll be so chewed up there won't be a decent woman alive who'll even give me a passing glance.

The image of an Asian beauty swam before his mind's eye. Kim Lan Lowery. She had certainly given Mick more than a passing glance. But then he had done precious little to hide his own attraction. Instead he had gaped like a schoolboy in the grips of his first crush.

Ah, yes, a crush! The thought came upon Mick with a rush of certainty in its wake. A crush. That was exactly what had happened to him. He had developed a crush on Kim Lan. Yesterday he had wondered if he were in the midst of a midlife crisis. Perhaps he was. He had read about men doing crazy things around their fortieth birthdays. What could be any crazier than a missions coordinator becoming preoccupied with the likes of a New York supermodel! The thought struck Mick as beyond preposterous, and he laughed out loud. He looked down at his comfortable boots and jeans. A button was even missing from the cuff of his denim shirt. He had been forced to roll the sleeves up to cover the problem. Another round of laughter punctuated his thoughts.

"Sure thing, ol' boy, *the* Kim Lan Lowery is going to leave her life of luxury and join you in sacrificing all for the cause of Christ." Mick rolled his eyes in self-mockery and walked across the creaking floor, into the small kitchen, toward the refrigerator. "Get a grip," he muttered under his breath as he opened the refrigerator and reached for the gallon of milk he had insisted upon buying, along with more groceries.

Whatever the reasons for the Lord's prompting Mick to change his stance on allowing Kim Lan to go on the trip, those reasons must exclusively relate to her. At this point, Mick couldn't imagine himself in the picture at all. "My job," he firmly told himself softly, "is to be polite when necessary and ignore her the rest of the time. I'm a grown man, almost forty, biologically old enough to be a grandfather!" he sternly reminded himself. "You will not make a fool of yourself over that woman!"

Kim shoved all thoughts of Mick's phone call from her mind and stepped back into her living room. Ted, glass of soda in hand, turned from his perusal of the poster-sized picture that now graced a wall near the entertainment center. "When did you have this made?" he asked, pointing to the seven smiling faces that claimed the framed photo.

"I just got it back last week." She deposited the cordless phone in its cradle on the end table and joined Ted to gaze upon the "Seven Sisters." "We had the picture taken during our last reunion here in November."

"I must say, you are the most stunning," Ted said, toasting her with his glass.

"Oh, you're just biased." She looped her arm through his. "At least, I hope."

He disengaged his arm and began gently stroking the ends of her hair as Kim studied the various faces of her best friends. Veterinarian Sonsee LeBlanc, straight auburn hair pulled away from her slightly freckled face. Marilyn Thatcher, her brown eyes no longer haunted as they had been after her husband's desertion. Marilyn now wore an engagement ring herself. The brunette Melissa Moore, the medical doctor among them, forever practical and certain of her worth in Christ; Sammie Jones, her blazing-red hair left Sonsee's auburn tresses paling in comparison. Just as blazing as her hair, Sammie's successful career as an author and magazine reporter attested to her solid reputation. Victoria Roberts, the domestic engineer among them—a virtual Martha Stewart. Victoria, forever the soft-spoken lady, seemed to always exude a gentle assurance. Jacqueline Lightfoot, the friend of Native American descent, her dark hair cropped in the no-nonsense way that reflected her choice of career as a private detective. Then, in the middle, Kim Lan herself, wearing the same classy pantsuit she wore today. The seven of them were as different as women could be, but they had clung together through the years. Kim shuddered to think of life without these friends.

"I can't stay long," Ted said as he set his glass on a nearby table then checked his gold watch. "I've got a reading for an advertisement this afternoon."

"They certainly are keeping you busy."

"Not any busier than you." He lowered his mouth to hers for a brief, yet potent kiss.

Kim leaned into his embrace and enjoyed the sensation of being in his arms. She decided that her irrational preoccupation with Mick O'Donnel was nothing more than a distraction of sorts. But try as she might, in Ted's arms she couldn't recreate the feeling of falling into a warm ocean... the feeling of azure eyes caressing her features.

"I was hoping we could share dinner tonight," he said against her lips.

The expected surge of anticipation left her less breathless than normal. "Of course," Kim said, but thoughts of her trip to Vietnam clouded her anticipation. She needed to tell Ted about the trip. The sooner the better. However, after her recent phone conversation with Mick, Kim Lan's own determination to go on the trip now wavered. She debated whether she really wanted to be in the presence of Mick O'Donnel for two weeks. She had been a nervous wreck after only a few hours with the man.

"But," she reasoned, *"my interest in the trip spans more issues than being with Mick O'Donnel."* Kim Lan recalled those moments in the church service when she felt a supernatural tug to travel to Vietnam. She could almost perceive the sting of tears that had left her blinking as she gazed upon the photos of the orphaned babies. Furthermore, something deep within Kim, some unexplainable force, had stirred with the need she saw in the faces of the elderly who resided at the home in Cantho.

Then there had been the little special needs boy who so desperately needed a home. Many of the other children had been assigned American parents. Now they were waiting on the approval of paperwork before their adoptive parents arrived to whisk them to their new lives in America. But that one little boy...

"Have you ever thought of adopting?" Kim Lan asked as she moved from Ted's embrace and walked toward the bouquet of roses sitting on the breakfast bar.

"You mean a child?" Ted asked blankly.

"Yes." Kim absently touched her nose to one of the exquisite blooms and inhaled the heady fragrance. She could afford to take every measure to make that little boy's life the best it could be. Stroking the flower's petal, Kim wondered if his skin were as soft as the rose.

"Well, no, I can't say that I've given it much thought." Ted neared and brushed her cheek with the backs of his fingers. "Is that why you're so distracted? You haven't seemed yourself since I got here. Are you already planning our family?"

She darted a sly glance out of the corners of her eyes to see the seductive tilt to Ted's lips that made him such a hit with American women. "Maybe," she said then cleared her throat. "Um...actually, there was a mission trip coordinator at mom and dad's church yesterday. He's planning a trip to Vietnam." Kim Lan, trying to act as casually as possible, stepped into the kitchen that was more a showroom than a place of culinary endeavor. Mechanically, she opened the black refrigerator, reached for a diet cola, and popped the top. In seconds, Kim was pouring the effervescent liquid over ice and anticipating the taste.

"And?" Ted, arms crossed, leaned against the entryway.

"And I'm thinking about going." Kim sipped the liquid and tensed, waiting for Ted's negative reaction.

"Oh?" His brows raised a bit. "Should I think about going too, then?"

Kim sputtered and hacked against the cola that had lodged itself in her throat.

"Sorry, didn't meant to choke you up," he said, stepping nearer.

"It's okay." Kim coughed. "I was just surprised. That's all. I expected—" She paused to clear her throat. "I expected you to...I don't know." Kim shrugged. "I just thought you'd—"

"Be angry?" He eyed her curiously.

"Well, maybe," she said, wondering exactly how well she really knew Ted Curry. Sometimes, he completely threw her off-guard. At the moment, he seemed much less like his usually possessive self. "I mean, the trip is going to be for two weeks, and—"

He noted the time once more. "Let's talk about it over dinner tonight, okay?" Ted rushed to her side and bestowed a light peck on her cheek. "I completely understand your wanting to see your mother's homeland. Perhaps we can come to some sort of compromise. There's no reason the two of us can't charter a jet to Vietnam and go on a sightseeing tour, if that's what you'd like. We could even see China and Japan. Hong Kong is a great city. Have you ever been?"

"No."

"You'd love it." He hastened toward the door. "We'll make our plans tonight," Ted called over his shoulder before swiftly making his exit.

"But I don't want to charter a jet and go sightseeing, Ted," Kim Lan whispered as she recalled the photos of that little boy who needed a home. She took another sip of soda and pondered Ted's reaction tonight when he realized just how serious she was. Regardless of her misgivings, she could not ignore the fact that the Lord had indeed beckoned her to participate on that trip. He had then completely changed Mick's mind, which confirmed her conviction that her desires were divinely inspired. She would not disobey the Lord, even in the face of vexing her fiancé.

She glanced down at Ted's glittering diamond that seemed, of late, to be forever winking at her. That haunting voice renewed the disturbing chant through the corridors of her mind. *Would you be willing to give up the diamond for the cause of Christ? Would you be willing to give all you have to the poor?*

A tight band of tension squeezed Kim's chest until she felt she was suffocating...spiritually suffocating. *Sell all I have?* In panic, she looked at all her costly possessions. The furniture:

some custom-made, some priceless oriental antiques. The vintage artwork. Her collection of rare crystal. She pondered her extensive financial portfolio: the luxury apartment complexes she owned, the growing investments in European stock, her ownership in several import and export operations. The list went on and on. Next Kim Lan stared at Ted's diamond until it blurred.

Sell all I have for Christ?

No, no, no!

It's too much to ask!

I'll go to Vietnam.

I'll adopt the child.

I'll continue to give. I'll give 20,000 dollars to the mission fund!

But sell all I have?

The telephone rang, and Kim Lan jumped so violently she sloshed some cola on the Italian tile floor. Within seconds, she picked up the cordless phone on the end table in the living room. Thankful for the diversion from her troubling thoughts, she spoke the customary greeting.

"Hey, this is Sonsee! You never returned my call yesterday. I was going to call you again last night, but I had company and forgot." Her friend's rapid words reflected her quick-thinking nature.

Kim plopped onto the ebony leather sofa. "Are you better today?"

"Yes, much better. I think I'm on the road to recovery. I'm at work today, as planned, thank the Lord. I don't think I could have taken another day at home." Sonsee's voice held a fatigued note, despite her claims. "So I'm back at saving the lives of worthy animals everywhere." She mimicked the inflections of a used-car salesman.

Kim Lan chuckled. "Great. Well, on another note, it looks like I'm going on the trip to Vietnam after all. They need more participants. Wanta come with me?"

"You're serious?"

"Yes. I'm serious."

"Okay, sure! Let me pack my bags, and I'll be right there." Sonsee paused for her typical snort. "Come on. When do I have time—"

"It's in two months. You've got time." Kim pondered having to face Mick O'Donnel for two weeks. Then she contemplated the possibilities of having one of her very best friends there to help serve as buffer. "I'm getting a fax today from Mick—"

"Mick?"

"For an application for a visa to Vietnam. But we've got to get it in now. We'll need to overnight it. You do have a current passport?"

"Yes."

"Great. I'll fax you the visa application, and—"

"I haven't agreed yet!"

"You've got to go, Sonsee!" An irrational desperation possessed Kim Lan as she propped her feet on the glass-and-brass coffee table. "I feel like the Lord is impressing me to go on this trip," she babbled nervously. "I can't get away from this feeling. It just won't go away, and...and I don't want to have to face him for two whole weeks by myself. You've got to go!"

"Face who? The Lord?"

"Oh, good grief! No!" Kim Lan burst forth in annoyance.

"But that's what you *said!*"

"I'm talking about Mick! Mick O'Donnel."

"Oh, so we're back to Mick! Isn't he the one you said accused you of trying to buy your way on the trip?"

"Yes!"

"Yesterday you said you were going to challenge his decision to not let you go. Did you?"

"No. He actually called me today and said he had prayed about my going and had changed his mind. Now will you?"

"What?"

"At least pray about going?"

"Well, when you put it that way…" Sonsee hesitated. "Excuse me a minute."

As Kim sipped her cold soda, she heard a muffled exchange between Sonsee and her secretary, Peg. At last Sonsee came back on the line.

"Peg says Marilyn's holding on another line. I need to go. It's a hectic day, but I just wanted to take a minute and try to catch you. I think it would be good for all seven of us to have a conference call. I'll ask Marilyn if tonight is a good time for her and e-mail the rest. Maybe another of the sisters will consider going to Vietnam as well. Are you going to be around tonight, say nine my time?"

"Yes. That's ten here. I should be home. Ted and I have a dinner date tonight, but we'll be through by then. So are you saying you're actually considering going?"

"Where? On the dinner date?" Sonsee asked.

"No!"

"But that's what you implied."

"You know what I meant—to Vietnam!"

"Yes, I'll pray about it," Sonsee said with a note of expectancy in her voice. "At first, you caught me off-guard, but the more I consider it, the more I think…" She hesitated. "I don't know. It might do me good. I really need to get away. Been under a lot of stress." Sonsee's usually chipper voice held a troubled note, and Kim wondered if something was disturbing her.

"Are you okay?"

Sonsee sighed. "Actually, no. I was hoping to talk with you, but it doesn't look like that's going to happen. Marilyn's holding, so I can't get into it all. But you've met my friend who's like a brother to me—Taylor Delaney?"

"Yes."

"Well, his mom has breast cancer."

"I'm so sorry," Kim Lan breathed.

"I really want to talk with you about it all, but we'll have to catch up later. Maybe tonight. I'll e-mail you about the conference call. Maybe I can fill in all the sisters at once."

"Okay," Kim Lan said, heavy with the implications of Sonsee's news. "I'll be praying for you and for Taylor. Tell Marilyn I said hi."

"Will do."

Five

Sonsee LeBlanc disconnected the call with Kim Lan and pressed the appropriate button to connect her with her other sister, Marilyn Thatcher. Marilyn worked as a veterinary assistant to Ginger Lovelady in Eureka Springs, Arkansas. Because of Marilyn's friendship with Sonsee, Dr. Lovelady and Sonsee had become friends and now consulted each other on difficult cases. Sonsee assumed Marilyn was calling to set up an appointment for another consultation.

"Hello, Marilyn," Sonsee said. Wearily leaning back in her office chair, she stared with disinterest at the potted corn plant helplessly drooping near the window. The numerous crisp brown leaves attested that the poor thing had seen its better days. Sonsee often joked that for every animal's life she saved, she had killed a dozen plants.

"Hi. Listen, I'm at work," Marilyn said quickly. "I know you're just as busy as I am, but I've had you on my mind today. Is everything okay?"

Thankful for Marilyn's sensitivity, the young veterinarian slumped forward, propped her elbow on the cluttered desk, and rested her forehead in the palm of her hand. She wondered how much she should tell Marilyn. She hadn't told any of the sisters yet because she had only accepted the truth yesterday evening—yesterday when Taylor Delaney had arrived at her Baton Rouge townhouse, tears in his eyes.

Sonsee had openly welcomed the lean Texas rancher who had been like a brother to her since childhood. He had haltingly told her his mother had been diagnosed with breast cancer. Sonsee had lost her own mother to breast cancer only five short years ago, and Taylor had supported his friend Sonsee through the illness and funeral like the solid dependable brother he was. Last night the two of them had simply sat in silence for what seemed like ages. Sonsee felt as if she were reliving her own mother's death all over again. Taylor, clearly shaken, had tried to remain strong. However, Sonsee sensed he needed support as never before. But Taylor's visit had also forced Sonsee to admit something she had been running from for weeks now...

"Are you still there?" Marilyn asked.

"Yes, sorry," Sonsee replied, eyeing the piles of mail that had stacked up during her illness. "I'm just thankful for your call, that's all. The truth is, something *is* wrong."

"Really?"

"Yes, Taylor Delaney's mom has breast cancer."

"Oh, Sonsee, I'm so sorry. I know you and Taylor are like brother and sister."

"We might as well *be* brother and sister," Sonsee said, "except—" She stopped herself. *Except I think I'm in love with him.* Even though the words tumbled through her mind, she had yet to voice them to another living soul. She had only admitted the truth to herself last night after Taylor had left to spend the night at a nearby hotel. Somehow the admission of her love, even to one of her dearest friends, seemed too painful. For hers was a love that would never be returned. Sonsee was certain of it. Taylor had long ago declared that he would never marry. The adolescent trauma from his father's desertion and his parents' subsequent divorce had left deep scars upon his soul. Now in his late thirties, Taylor was comfortably settled as a successful, single rancher. He willingly extended his love for the Lord through helping troubled boys who needed a mentor. But Sonsee could never envision Taylor's bestowing more than brotherly love upon her. The thought of her wretched situation made her want to sob.

"Except?" Marilyn questioned after a lengthy pause.

"Marilyn..." Sonsee swallowed hard against the lump in her throat and pondered how this could have happened to her. Despite her tendencies to be a tease, Sonsee had always been the practical one. The one who made personal decisions based on common sense. Kim Lan, while she was an astute businesswoman, often seemed whimsical in her personal life. And Marilyn's feelings usually ran deep. However, the Lord had helped her emotionally survive when her husband of five years had an affair, divorced her, and married the other woman. Now Marilyn was engaged to be married to Pastor Joshua Langham, a man worthy of her steadfast love.

Through the years Sonsee had watched several of her six close friends fall in love. Marilyn had Joshua. Melissa Moore had once been engaged, but had broken away from the relationship. Sammie Jones had been married three years and had a two-year-old son. Victoria Roberts was married, but lately Sonsee wondered if all were well in that paradise. Kim Lan had Ted, for whatever that was worth. He had made a pass at Sonsee during the Christmas holidays, and Kim had dismissed the whole thing with an, "Oh, Sonsee, you know Ted's such a flirt." Thoughts of the whole ordeal left Sonsee close to nauseous. Then there was Jac Lightfoot. Jac had never married and never planned to get married. Of her six friends, Sonsee and Jac probably had the most in common.

However, Sonsee had always known she might one day get married when she *chose* to fall in love. She had long ago learned to exercise an iron will over her emotions. Yet these feelings she was having for Taylor seemed to have a mind of their own. Certainly, she had never dreamed of falling in love with her childhood friend.

At last she collected her thoughts and concentrated on responding to Marilyn, who patiently awaited her. "I don't want this to go any further. I'll tell the rest of the sisters when I'm comfortable with it, but right now, I just can't tell everyone. It's too painful. Anyway, I think I'm in love with Taylor," Sonsee said slowly. "And he's not and I don't know if he's ever going to be..."

"Oh, no," Marilyn whispered. "But this is so unlike you."

"I know."

"You've never, that I know of—"

"Been in love," Sonsee finished for her. "And if you want the truth, I'm so confused at this point—" Peg tapped on the door. Sonsee looked up to see the young, dark-eyed secretary apologetically smiling at her.

"Your two o'clock appointment—the dog who's to be put to sleep—just arrived. The family with him looks like they need a professional counselor at this point, and there's a man here who says he's your brother."

"Just a minute, Marilyn." Sonsee covered the mouthpiece. "Is it Taylor Delaney?" she asked.

Peg shrugged. "He just said to tell you your brother was here to see you. I didn't know you had a brother."

"I've got a half-brother, but he doesn't claim me," Sonsee stated the truth in a matter-of-fact voice. "This must be Taylor. He's not really my brother. He's related to my dad by my dad's first marriage. It's really confusing. I'll explain later. We practically grew up in the same house. Just tell him I'll be there in a minute. No—give me about five more minutes then send him to my office, and tell the dog I'll be with him in a minute."

"You mean the dog's owner, of course."

"Yes, yes." Sonsee waved her hand. "You know what I mean." She paused, feeling as if Kim Lan's habitual conversational curveballs were rubbing off on her. "What a day, Marilyn," she said into the receiver. "There's an ancient St. Bernard that's been with one family for fifteen years, and he's at the end of his rope, poor ol' chap. We're putting him to sleep today. He's like a family member to them. Taylor's here, too. I'm going to have to go."

"Okay. I understand."

"Thanks. We can talk about the other later. I need to talk to someone, but right now I just can't talk to everyone."

"Yes, I understand. I've been there."

"Oh—and I was just on the phone with Kim Lan," Sonsee continued.

"Have you ever been able to convince her that Ted was serious when he propositioned you, Sonsee?" Marilyn asked, a worried note in her voice.

"No, Kim Lan is convinced that Ted was just teasing or flirting or whatever…" Sonsee rolled her eyes. "I never even tried to broach the subject again. She was so ready to cut me off and brush the whole thing aside that I knew if I pressed too hard it would harm our friendship or—worse—destroy it."

"I just don't know what we should do," Marilyn said at a loss. "It seems that Kim is totally blind when it comes to Ted. She was the one who told me I needed to pray about dating Josh, and I almost feel she's living a contradiction to everything she told me."

"Tell me about it," Sonsee said. "All she ever says is, 'He's my dream man.'"

"More like a nightmare, if you ask me. And I've had that kind of nightmare," Marilyn said, referring to her ex-husband. "I can spot one of those from a thousand miles away."

"I *did* call Kim's mom about it," Sonsee said, the troubled edge in her voice reflecting the anxiety of her soul.

"What does she think?"

"She thinks we all need to pray like we've never prayed before. Tran My said she and John were uncertain of the engagement from the start, and my news only confirmed their suspicions."

A worried silence settled upon the two friends until Sonsee glanced at her sporty wristwatch. "Well, I'm going to have to go, but are you available for a conference call tonight around nine? Kim Lan's going on a humanitarian aid trip to Vietnam. I might go with her. We want to chat with all the sisters to see if somebody else might want to go. And besides, we need to do some catching up. I've got prayer requests, and I'm sure you do as well. And we still haven't set the place for our reunion."

Marilyn chuckled. "There's a reason you're your own boss, Sonsee."

"Very funny."

"Hold on a minute."

As Sonsee listened to Marilyn's muffled conversation with Dr. Lovelady, Taylor stepped into the austere office, straw cowboy hat in hand. As usual, his curly dark hair was forever in need of a trim, his cautious eyes forever the orbs of a man who has been a bedfellow with pain and betrayal. Sonsee acknowledged his presence with a smile that felt artificial. He sat in one of the chairs in front of her desk and unceremoniously propped his boots on the edge of her desk.

"Well, I've got to go, but nine o'clock for the phone call works for me," Marilyn said. "Brooke will be in bed by then. And I'll be praying for you this afternoon…and for Kim Lan."

"Thanks, Marilyn. I really appreciate it."

Sonsee hung up the phone, straightened her lab coat, and rounded the desk. She nudged Taylor's boots with her fingers. "You're getting dirt on my piled up mail," she complained.

"Sorry, Red," he said with a lazy smile as he removed his boots from the desk and stood.

Sonsee rolled her eyes. "I can tell you're back to your old self. Just as ornery as ever."

"Sure, Red."

"If you call me 'Red' again..." She picked up the golfer's paperweight from her desk. Taylor had started that annoying nickname when Sonsee was in fourth grade and her hair was more red and less the auburn shade to which it had darkened. He had been an older and wiser eighth grader. She disliked the nickname then and now, and he knew it.

"Okay, okay." Taylor raised his hands in resignation and stood. "I'll stop...*Red*."

She glared at him, glad for any diversion from her pounding pulse. Taylor would probably be speechless if he knew how she felt. The awareness of her love had started over the Christmas holiday, only a month ago, when her father had invited them both on a Hawaiian vacation. Jacques LeBlanc had retired early every night and left Sonsee and Taylor together to enjoy the evenings. They had walked along the beach in companionable silence, took in a few movies, and enjoyed the Hawaiian dining experience. Somewhere in the middle of all that, Sonsee had begun to look forward to Taylor's presence with more warmth than she had ever experienced. Now, standing across the room from this familiar jeans-clad cowboy, Sonsee pondered her father's motives. She also considered how long she might have been in love with Taylor without ever allowing herself to realize it.

"How are you feeling?" she asked, desperately trying to hide her emotions. For years, Sonsee had never given a second thought to the way she behaved with Taylor. The two of them had easily fallen into a companionable banter that characterized a normal sibling relationship.

"Fine. I'm fine, I think," he said with his usual self-assurance. Certainly the man standing before her didn't reflect the one who rang Sonsee's doorbell the night before. Last night he had struggled to stop himself from breaking under the weight of distraught emotions. Only his slightly reddened eyes suggested that perhaps he had released his pent-up passions once he was alone in his hotel room. After his father disappeared twenty-five years ago, Taylor and his mother had clung together and shared an unusual bond. Anything that affected her so deeply would undoubtedly rend Taylor's heart.

"Have you heard from your mother today?"

"Yes. I called her this morning," he drawled. "I'm heading back to New Orleans to spend the day and night with her."

"And tomorrow morning is her mastectomy?"

"Yes."

A weighted silence settled between them, and Sonsee recalled her own mother's mastectomy. The surgeons had been confident that all would go well with her. Then a short year later the cancer had reappeared. Only time would tell if Taylor's mother would have a better story. Time and the Lord.

"I just stopped by to say thanks for letting me cry on your shoulder last night." Taylor stepped forward, gripped her upper arms, and placed a firm, brotherly kiss atop her head. "You're better than any sister to me, Sonsee."

Her mind spinning in a sea of tingles, Sonsee restrained herself from telling him to kindly refrain from ever kissing her like that again. Instead, she looked into his sincere eyes and searched for any sign that Taylor's feelings for her had changed. Sonsee saw nothing new, only the fond affection he had always shown her.

She looked down at her hands, painfully knotted together. "Well, thanks," she said a bit more brusquely than intended as she stepped toward the door. "I hope all goes well with your mother. I'll call tonight to find out more details." Despite herself, Sonsee couldn't get the businesslike tone from her voice. "And I'll drive down this weekend." With her hand on the doorknob, she rushed on. "I can stay with her over the weekend, if you like, and give you time to go back to your ranch and do whatever it is you do there." She paused to smile, hoping the slight teasing tone would ease the tension that seemed to be building between them. *Or is the tension just in me?*

One thing was certain, Sonsee needed to remove herself from Taylor's presence before she suffocated. "I've got a patient waiting on me now." She examined her worn loafers; she had bought a new pair last week but liked the old ones better.

"Okay."

Sonsee sensed Taylor's curious appraisal. "Okay, see ya." She stepped from her office, squared her shoulders, and walked toward the depressed family and their pet in the waiting room. As she heard Taylor quietly taking his leave, she remembered that she had failed to say anything to him about the potential trip to Asia. Right now, Vietnam, a whole world away, sounded exactly like the place she wanted to be—anywhere away from this hopeless love that tore at her heart.

That evening Kim Lan walked into the lobby of Liambrio's, the exclusive restaurant she and Ted often frequented. Ted had punctually arrived in the hired limousine to whisk her to the top floor of the exquisite hotel and into the ambiance of dining pleasure frequented by the nation's most recognized and influential. The restaurant's low lights enhanced the elegance of the mahogany and lace, brass and crystal. Waiters, dressed in the finest tuxedos, wove their way between the intimate, circular tables, some set for two, some for four. Her stomach growling, Kim Lan relished the smells of the premium aged beef, delicate sauces, and the waft of gourmet coffee.

"Mr. Curry," the host said with a thick British accent as he produced a faint bow.

"We had reservations for six o'clock," Ted said, as another gentleman stepped behind Kim Lan to assist in removing her coat.

"Yes, of course, Mr. Curry," the tall host said with a practiced smile. "Right this way."

Ted settled his arm possessively around Kim Lan's waist, and she glanced toward him. He was dressed in a dinner suit, the color of charcoal; his dark hair gleamed in the candlelight; his dreamy blue eyes caressed her as if this were their wedding night. Kim Lan returned his admiring gaze and smiled with pleasure. As they followed the host toward the massive window that gave an excellent view of a rising full moon, numerous heads turned in acknowledgment of the celebrity couple. Kim Lan even noted with satisfaction that a few feminine glances bordered on envious. The long-faced Englishman stopped beside a cozy table for two tucked into an exclusive corner beneath the window. He assisted Kim with her chair, and she gracefully lowered herself onto the padded seat while arranging the straight skirt of her ankle-length cream-colored evening gown. With a flourish, the host placed menus in their hands.

The menu's featured delicacies blurred as Kim Lan searched for the best way to tell Ted that she planned to go on the mission trip alone; that she was not contemplating a pleasure tour of Asia; that she felt the Lord was actually beckoning her to her mother's homeland for purposes other than sightseeing. Once more Kim recalled Mick O'Donnel's slide presentation at her parents' church. The faces of all those elderly people who needed assistance...the orphaned babies...the older children, homeless and hopeless.

She blindly stared at the menu. As usual, Kim Lan gave little thought to the exorbitant prices until a new thought struck her. *The price of one meal at this restaurant would probably feed a room full of orphans for a week.*

Kim looked up to see Ted studying her, the dreamy look still in his eyes.

"You've been pensive tonight. Care to tell me what's on your mind?" He reached across the table, took her hand in his, and gently caressed her palm. "You've never been more beautiful," he continued as if he had never posed the original question.

She glanced back at the menu, grappling for the right words, and debated if there were any way she could make Ted understand her sudden, deep need to go on the journey.

"What wine will you and Miss Lowery be having tonight, Mr. Curry?" the solemn waiter asked as he placed crystal goblets full of ice water within their reach.

"I prefer tonic water with a twist of lime," Kim Lan said.

"Yes, and I'll have the same," Ted said with courtesy.

"Of course," the waiter replied, and he was off to do their bidding.

Even though Kim knew Ted indulged in liquors and wines when not in her presence, she greatly appreciated his consideration in her choice to avoid alcohol.

"I was thinking perhaps we would have the salmon with asparagus," Ted said, an expectant gleam in his eyes. "That's what we ate the night I gave you the ring." He glanced toward the diamond on Kim's finger.

"That's fine," she said, thankful to be relieved of the task of choosing from the expansive menu. "You always have impeccable taste in food."

"Yes, and in women," Ted echoed sensually, a slow simmer burning in his eyes. "I love you," he said, trailing his index finger along her wrists.

Despite her distraction with the trip, Kim's pulse leapt.

"I can't wait until we get married," Ted crooned.

Kim Lan smiled in expectation. Certainly it would be the wedding of the decade. Ted had even mentioned that he would like to have a horse-drawn carriage take her to the church. With the sounds of hushed conversation, the tinkling of crystal and silverware, and the mellow notes of harp music weaving a pleasing atmosphere around them, Kim began to fantasize about the wedding...about stepping from that carriage...about entering the classic church where Ted and she attended...about stopping at the back pew, gazing toward the most eligible bachelor in America. Her heart beat with anticipation as she pictured Ted lovingly taking her hand in his and both of them turning toward the minister.

"I've been thinking and planning since we talked this afternoon," Ted continued. "And I was wondering..." He paused with grandeur and straightened his crimson silk tie. "I was wondering what you thought about planning the trip to Asia as our honeymoon."

Kim Lan's stomach knotted as he eagerly continued.

"We could charter a jet and plan a sightseeing tour of Vietnam, like you wanted to do," his deep, mellow voice oozed with hope. "Then we could even spend a few days in Hong Kong. I love Hong Kong. And, if you like, we can tour Japan as well. Whatever makes you happy. We can take off work as long as we like. I'm free from April until June. So what do you think?"

Thankfully, the waiter arrived with their tonic water, and Ted was distracted by placing the order. Kim Lan stared across the spacious restaurant's timeless decor—the towering plants, the plush, emerald carpet, the masterpiece paintings. Even though she schooled her features into a placid mask, her mind whirled with her fiancé's suggestion...with how she would explain her desires to him and whether he would understand her need to go on a mission journey instead of a pleasure trip.

At last the waiter left them, and Ted gently toyed with the diamond bracelet she wore. He had given her the bracelet for Christmas, along with the matching earrings now clipped to her ears.

"Well, what do you think?" he asked.

Kim nervously cleared her throat. "I think it sounds like a wonderful honeymoon," she said, grateful that she had at least produced a good start. "And if that's where you'd like to go, then I'll be thrilled to go as well—"

"But earlier you said that's where you wanted to go," Ted insisted, his eyes reflecting slight confusion.

"If you're talking about today at my place..."

He nodded and leaned back in his chair.

"Well, I mentioned a mission trip to Vietnam." She licked her lips and leaned forward. "It's in two months—in March. I'm planning on going, and I wanted to mention it to you.

While I would be delighted to honeymoon in Asia, I specifically wanted to go on this mission trip to Vietnam first."

Ted tensed. "First?"

"Well, yes." Kim tightly clasped her hands in her lap. "It's just in two months."

"But I thought we'd be married by then," Ted said defensively, his lips tightening around each word.

"Ted!" She chuckled nervously. "Surely you don't think we can plan the kind of wedding we've been talking about in two months, do you? I was thinking it might be a year before we got married."

"A year?" he exploded, his eyes round in shocked disbelief. "Nobody in Hollywood waits a year!"

"Ted, please." Kim glanced toward a nearby table where a couple discreetly eyed them. "Keep your voice down."

"I see no good reason to wait that long, Kim Lan," he said intensely. "Unless you're just trying to put me off—"

"No, no, of course not, Ted," she said, so addled by their growing conflict that she wasn't even sure what she was saying.

"Besides, who said anything about us planning the wedding?" he said, raising his hand in disgust. "We'll hire someone to manage the whole thing and we'll just show up!"

"But there's my mother to consider," Kim Lan reasoned. "She wants to be involved." She pictured her mother's less-than-thrilled smile when she discovered her daughter was to marry Ted Curry. There had been numerous times when Kim knew her adulthood choices had disappointed her parents, but she had sensed their disappointment the greatest when she introduced them to Ted and announced their engagement. "Then there's the dress to make, and the—"

"I've got the money to pull it together next week if we have to," he said, fresh irritation spilling from his voice. "I don't see the problem here." He leaned forward, placed his arms on the table, and rested his weight on his arms.

"Ted, I never imagined you were thinking of our being married so soon." Although dismayed, Kim managed to keep her voice low.

"Well, exactly what did you think?" he hissed in exasperation. "That I was going to wait a whole year before I could make love to you?"

"There's more to marriage than sex," Kim said stonily as a chilling uneasiness settled between them. "Is that the only reason you proposed? Because I wouldn't go to bed with you unless we were married?"

The question seemed to form a barrier between them that Kim Lan knew could not be broken unless Ted convincingly denied her insinuations. She held his gaze, peering deeply into his angry, yet yearning eyes. She pondered the Sundays they had sat side by side at church. Ted had told her early in their relationship that he had been raised in a Christian home and that he shared her faith. However, as Kim Lan began seeking God on a new level, she likewise encouraged him to move toward a lifestyle of righteousness. Ted delighted her with signs of renewing his own commitment to the Lord. Even though she couldn't deny he had had relationships with numerous women, she had been willing to forgive him, as she knew the Lord was willing to forgive.

Kim was painfully aware that she also needed God's forgiveness. In her mid-twenties, Kim herself had been dazzled by her early career, so dazzled that she had made choices she now regretted. When an older, seasoned actor she grew up watching on television had been smitten with her, Kim blindly and foolishly tossed aside her Christian principles and made one of those choices that left her mother devastated.

Kim would never forget the night Tran My Lowery had called, her voice shaking with tears. She had just returned from the grocery store where she bought the latest tabloid that plastered news of Kim's affair across the front cover. She gently wept as Kim was forced to admit the truth. At the time, Kim Lan hated disappointing her mother, but she had also entertained the idea that her parents were a bit too old-fashioned in their beliefs and a tad too radical in their commitment to biblical standards. When the relationship with the actor broke off and he moved on to the next supermodel, Kim realized who had been wrong. She had foolishly wasted her virginity. After that sinful choice, Kim Lan had vowed before the Lord that she would never become intimate with another man until she was married. There was nothing she could do to change the past, but she certainly could honor God's standards in the present and future. She pledged to live a sexually pure life until marriage.

Now her fiancé was insinuating that he might be marrying her simply so he could sleep with her. If that were the case, Kim Lan wondered if they should continue their engagement. She wanted a marriage that would last, and physical motives alone were no basis for a solid marriage.

Silently, Ted appraised her, his expression a mixture of fury, torment, and love... yes, love. Kim Lan was certain he did feel more than just physical attraction for her.

"You know I love you," he said defensively. "And my proposal was about more than just sex. But blast it, Kim Lan..." he leaned forward and gently gripped her upper arm, "I'm a human being too, and I'm getting tired of waiting."

She looked down at the silverware gleaming in the candlelight that flickered from the ornate glass globe between them. "We've only been seeing each other for four months," she said slowly, amazed at the deliberate tones of her voice.

Assuredly her voice did not match the quivering nervousness that stripped away her hunger and left her nauseous. "I've only had the ring two months, and I only agreed to make our engagement official last week. I've been waiting a long time for the right man." Kim Lan raised her gaze to meet his. "A long time. As much as I would like to express our love in a physical manner, we need to wait. I've made one mistake. You know that, and you know how I feel about rushing into anything else—even our marriage."

The waiter arrived with the spinach salads. Silently Kim Lan accepted her salad, picked up her fork, and listlessly toyed with the deep-green leaves. Even though her relationship with Ted had survived a few tiffs, this was their most vehement conflict of yet. Kim Lan, her hands trembling, wondered if perhaps their relationship would end tonight.

"So..." Ted began, as soon as the waiter had excused himself, "you're going to Vietnam in a couple of months. And you'll be gone how long?"

"Two weeks."

"On a mission trip?" He narrowed his eyes in confusion, and Kim Lan sensed that perhaps he was stretching to give her the benefit of the doubt.

Relieved, she answered, "Yes. I really felt like the Lord spoke to me about going on the trip at church Sunday. I couldn't get away from it." She rushed on, desperately hoping that Ted would somehow grasp her vision. "There was a mission-trip coordinator giving a special presentation at my parents' church. And I knew by the time it was over that the Lord was somehow calling me to go. I've wanted to visit my mother's homeland for years now, you know that, but this is even deeper than that."

As Ted thoughtfully buttered one of the soft rolls, Kim Lan leaned forward, fork in hand, and continued to explain. "The trip is going to be centered around a nursing home in Cantho—that's in South Vietnam. There's a home for the elderly as well as a housing facility for older orphans, and then there's a baby home for the little ones awaiting adoption."

As she spoke, memories of Mick O'Donnel's passion for his work bombarded her mind. Kim Lan peered deeply into Ted's eyes and wondered if he could ever reflect the intensity of Mick's fire for the Lord. *But what does that matter? He's Ted Curry.* The *Ted Curry.*

"Is that the reason why you asked me if I've ever considered adoption?" Ted asked, some of the annoyance fading from his eyes.

"Yes." Kim debated whether she should mention the special needs child that had tormented her since she saw his photo. "Um..." She looked down at the leaves of spinach coated in raspberry dressing. Her heart drummed in anticipation and dread. "There's one little boy in particular they're having trouble placing. He was premature and slow to develop. He needs a home so badly—"

"And you want him?" Ted asked, shaking his head in wonderment.

"Well, I thought maybe we might consider..."

"You never cease to amaze me," he whispered, reaching to stroke her cheek. "I'll be honest, Kim Lan. When I first met you, I was breathless with your beauty, but I think I grossly underestimated your depth of character."

Kim blinked, not certain she had heard him right.

"I thought you were half-daft the night you told me you weren't going to do any more swimsuit poses," he said in a reflective voice.

Immediately she jumped to her own defense. "But it was because I couldn't continue to tempt men to lust after me and to disobey God—"

Ted held up his hand. "I'm not through. I initially thought you were daft, but I've come to respect your choice."

Her eyes widened, and she gaped at the man who had told her only a few months ago that he thought she was crazy for turning down the kind of money those swimsuit shoots brought in. Perhaps he was growing spiritually after all. Perhaps she had underestimated him.

"I guess I'm just saying that you're different than any woman I've ever dated. And, well, my mother is going to love you."

Her cheeks warming with pleasure, Kim Lan relaxed a bit as the knot in the pit of her stomach began unraveling. If Ted would only show this side of himself to her parents, perhaps they would reevaluate their disapproval of her marrying him.

"I'm sorry." He reached for her hand. "Really. I shouldn't have pushed you."

"I'm sorry if I disappointed you," she replied, reveling in the flood of admiration pouring from his eyes.

"Look," he shoved aside the salad and leaned forward, "why don't I plan to go on the mission trip with you? Then we could both meet that little boy and see what we think."

Stunned with this turn, Kim Lan's mind filled with images of Mick, with his probable decline of Ted's interest, with his disapproval were he to see Kim Lan with Ted. *You only just met Mick O'Donnel,* a stern voice reminded her. *Don't jeopardize what you have with Ted. You and Mick are worlds apart.*

"I'll ask Mick if there's still room for one more participant," Kim said, guarding her voice against the misgivings enveloping her.

"Oh, wait a minute." Ted placed his palm against his forehead. "It's in two months. That's March. I'm going to be in

Paris most of that month working on some scenes for my next movie. How could I have forgotten that?" He smiled and shook his head. "Some days, I think I need a new brain."

Kim Lan stopped herself from slumping with relief. Mick had sounded so grateful that she was planning to disguise her appearance, but that would prove almost impossible with Ted at her side. He was less able to disguise himself than Kim. To begin with, he had no makeup to wash off. Besides, the notion of Ted being with her in the presence of Mick left her squirming.

Ted picked up his fork, looked at his salad, then observed her with interest. "Who's Mick, by the way?" he asked suddenly, that ever-present cloud of jealousy darkening his eyes.

"Mick O'Donnel. He's the trip coordinator," she stated nonchalantly, controlling her every word.

Ted studied her, and Kim Lan returned his gaze without a flinch.

With a resigned sigh, Ted shook his head. "Okay, okay, whatever you say. I give up. Go on to Vietnam. Do whatever you have to do. But come back home, and let's get married." His pleading smile held a hint of sensuality. "Okay?"

"Okay."

"You know, babe," he said with his typical charm, "I think you've got me wrapped around your little finger."

Six

Later that evening, Sonsee LeBlanc, Dr. Pepper in hand, hurried up the narrow stairway that led to her bedroom. She sat at the new rolltop desk she had purchased the month before and, after swallowing a mouthful of soda, carefully placed the can on a coaster. The time had come for the conference call with her six closest friends. Within a few minutes, she had taken the necessary measures to set up the conference call. As the operator rang the six numbers one by one, the sisters each greeted the other.

Finally, Kim Lan answered her phone, and all seven of them were chatting together. Melissa enthusiastically talked of her new office building in Oklahoma City. Victoria shared that she had been asked to participate in a Florida television show that featured decorating and cooking. Sammie had a brainstorm about asking Victoria to write an article for *Romantic Living,* the magazine where she worked. Jac, like Melissa, was also settling into a new office building. Marilyn announced that she and her fiancé wanted the seven sisters to have their next reunion in Eureka Springs, Arkansas, where they lived. The reunion was soon set for the third weekend in May.

As the companionable banter continued, Sonsee awaited Kim Lan's announcement about the trip to Vietnam and debated whether or not to tell the group of her new feelings for Taylor Delaney. After several seconds, she decided the whole wretched ordeal with Taylor was just too confusing and too painful to share with everyone at once. Certainly she was close enough individually to all six of her friends to tell them one-on-one, but Sonsee was still too busy trying to sort out her own bewilderment to deal with the questions of the whole group.

"You haven't said much, Sonsee," Kim Lan interjected during a pause in the conversation.

"Sorry," she said, toying with the various pens in one of the desk's cubbyholes. "I'm just distracted. I hate to put an end to all this cheer, but I've got a serious prayer request, guys."

The group grew silent.

"I think at one time or another, you've all met my close friend Taylor Delaney?"

"Yes," they chorused.

"He was at your mother's funeral, wasn't he?" Melissa asked.

"Yes, that's right. You all met him there, I know for sure."

"What's going on with him?" Sammie Jones asked.

"His mother has been diagnosed with breast cancer. She's scheduled for a mastectomy tomorrow morning."

A breathless silence settled upon the friends. Sonsee leaned back in the desk chair and stared at the bed's ornate brass headboard until it blurred.

Marilyn Thatcher was the first one to break the silence. "I talked with Sonsee earlier today about this—"

"Yes, so did I," Kim Lan said.

"But, Sonsee," Marilyn continued, "you never told me what the doctors are saying at this point. Do they think that with the mastectomy her chances are good?"

"They don't know," Sonsee said with a sigh. "But you know, with my mom they thought her chances were excellent, yet still..." she sighed again and blinked against her stinging eyes. "Joy Delaney has been so good to me. Taylor and I have been close since childhood, and after my mother passed away she really befriended me. I guess she felt she should do the same thing for me that my dad did for Taylor."

"I know you've told me before, Sonsee," Sammie said, a note of puzzlement in her voice. "But would you please tell me again why the two of you aren't related? I always get confused on this."

"Me, too," Victoria added as the whining of her toddler mingled with her words.

"Well, Taylor became my father's nephew by marriage while he was married to his first wife, who died. Taylor's mother and my father's first wife were sisters. Then, after Father's first wife died, he married my mother and they had me. So Taylor calls my dad Uncle Jacques, but there's no blood relation, and Taylor and I aren't really cousins."

"Okay, whatever you say," Victoria said through a chuckle.

"I know it's confusing," Sonsee said, "but we aren't related, although we did grow up together. Anyway, he's very close to his mother. His father deserted the family when he was about twelve. That's when Father really took a bigger part in Taylor's life."

"Well, we'll remember his mom and him and you in our prayers," Jac said solemnly.

"Please do," Sonsee said, fighting back the tears. "It's almost like I'm reliving my mother's death all over again. I can't believe this is happening again. It just seems so unreal." Sonsee stood and moved the short distance toward the window covered by forest-green drapes. Listlessly she pulled aside the closed drapes and stared out the window at the cold and dank streets of Baton Rouge, Louisiana. A slow drizzle fell from the starless skies, a drizzle that seemed to dampen Sonsee's very soul. Of the seven of them, Sonsee was the only one whose mother had died. At times she became frustrated when one or two of the sisters would pass along a complaint about their mothers. More than once, she had bitten back a retort like, *Well at least you have your mother!*

After a lengthy pause, Kim Lan cleared her throat. "I have some news that's kind of exciting."

"Your life is always exciting," Marilyn drawled. "You should come chase animals at the vet's office and help me scrub my toilet for a week or two. Now *that's* excitement." All seven of the friends broke into laughter.

"Seriously," Kim Lan said, her high-pitched voice occasionally reflecting her mother's Asian pronunciation. "Looks like I'm going on a humanitarian aid trip to Vietnam in a couple of months. I'm trying to draft Sonsee into going with me. Is anybody else interested? The trip's coordinator said he could use a couple more volunteers."

"I've decided I'm going for sure," Sonsee said with resolution. *Anything to get away from Taylor for awhile,* she added to herself. *And maybe I can do something to convince Kim not to marry Ted.*

"Great!" Kim Lan cheered.

"Oh, and did you ever tell me if that Mick person was single?" Sonsee teased.

"I never said, but he is," Kim Lan said, a smile evident in her voice. "Why?"

"Well, I've also decided I'm going to marry him."

The friends produced a collective chuckle.

"Anybody who could get under your skin as badly as he has must be one fine specimen of masculinity." Even though she was teasing, Sonsee wondered about Mick and his effect upon Kim. She was anxious to meet him.

"Oooo details, details!" Marilyn said. "You guys teased me mercilessly when I first met Joshua, and what goes around comes around."

"All I know is that Mick O'Donnel is supposed to be a doozy-and-a-half!" Sonsee playfully taunted. "Kim Lan, care to fill us in on the details? Maybe *you're* planning to marry him."

"Give it a break, Sonsee. I'm engaged, remember?" Kim defended.

A chorus of wolf whistles and cheers went up.

Kim Lan's voice rose about the friendly jeers. "If you ladies would please be so kind as to tell me if anyone else might like to go on the trip—"

"I might," Melissa said. "I've been really interested in going on mission trips. There's one being planned for next year to Thailand that I was thinking about signing up for. I think this might be fun. I'm my own boss; I could arrange a visiting physician to see my patients while I'm gone. Hey! Just count me in!" she said with conviction. "I will pray about it tonight, but I don't see any reason why I can't. I'm single— footloose and fancy-free. This will be fun. We'll be together again like old times."

"Great!" Sonsee and Kim Lan said together.

"Well, as much as I'd like to be involved, I can't," Marilyn said. "I don't think I should leave Brooke that long. Having to shuffle a four-year-old back and forth between me and her daddy is hard enough on her. I don't want to be gone from her for two weeks." The group gave a respectful pause. Of the seven of them, Marilyn had certainly been dealt the most bitter medicine. Her pastor husband had deserted her and her daughter to marry his secretary. Thankfully, the Lord was presenting Marilyn with a second chance at marriage. Her special calling to be a pastor's wife would be fulfilled since her future husband was a pastor.

"Yeah, I've got to think about my husband and little one, too," Victoria said.

"Me, too," Sammie chimed in.

"That leaves Jac," Sonsee said, turning from the window and stepping toward her antique dresser's mirror to note the dark circles under her eyes. The weight of Joy Delaney's illness and her stress over Taylor was weighing heavily upon her. *Yes, the trip will do me good.*

"I can't go either," Jac said with regret. "Sorry. My plate is so full right now I can hardly leave the office long enough to go home and sleep."

"That's what you get for being such a great detective," Sonsee said with conviction. Occasionally, Sonsee had wondered if Jac would ever realize there was more to life than her career. Of the seven friends, Jac seemed the one who was the closest to the edge of their relationships. Although she still readily participated in the reunions and the fellowship over telephones and through e-mails, Jac seemed so preoccupied with her latest case that sometimes she wasn't "with them."

"I understand," Kim Lan said. "I'm having to do some rearranging to make time to go myself, but it's something I really feel like the Lord is leading me to do. I'll finally get to visit my mother's homeland."

The conversation continued, and Sonsee moved back to the desk chair. In the middle of Kim Lan's telling her and Melissa she would fax them a visa application to Vietnam with appropriate instructions, another call beeped in on Sonsee. She debated whether to take the call or just let the person call back. But something told her the caller could be Taylor.

"Just a minute, gang," she said. "I'm stepping out of this call for a minute. I've got another caller beeping in. I think it's Taylor. I'll be back." She took the other call and prepared herself for the inevitable.

"Sonsee? It's Taylor," he said softly.

"Oh, hello," she said as casually as her pounding pulse would allow. A long, awkward pause stretched between them. "How's your mother tonight?" Sonsee asked, her genuine concern evident in her voice.

"Fine. The same. Listen, the reason I called, um, you know I've never been good at apologizing, especially when I don't know what I should apologize for..." His voice trailed off meaningfully.

Sonsee rubbed her brow and smothered a groan. *He thinks I'm mad at him.* "You don't have anything to apologize for," she said, desperately trying to keep the stiff tones from her voice.

"Are you sure?" he asked suspiciously. "Come on, Red, what gives?"

"Don't call me Red," she snapped.

"Okay, okay. I give up. If you say you're not angry with me, then I'll have to accept that," his voice took on the nuance of an aggravated older brother. "But I know you well enough to know when something's bothering you. Now we can either do this nicely or I can twist your arm—literally, if I have to. Now what have I done to you?" he demanded, belying his claim of giving up.

"Nothing!" Sonsee curled her fist against the desktop. What she said was the absolute truth. Taylor had done nothing to her. Nothing but be the close friend and confidant he had always been. Nothing but be the companionable brother who would never see her as more than his kid sister. With great self-control, Sonsee stopped herself from hanging up on him. But she couldn't. *You must take control of yourself,* she firmly demanded. *You are a grown woman. If you continue like this, he will eventually suspect how you feel. And that will mean the end of our relationship!*

"I guess—guess—" she hedged. "Did I tell you I had a light case of the flu last week?"

"No, I didn't know." And the conversation took a new turn. Sonsee forced herself to interact as usual and Taylor responded, seemingly oblivious to her hopeless love.

Within a couple of minutes, Sonsee bid adieu to Taylor and went back to her conference call with her friends. Once more she contemplated Jac Lightfoot's commitment to her career, and she was brutally honest with herself. In truth, she saw much of herself in Jac. For years now Sonsee had chosen to avoid a deep relationship with the opposite sex because she had professional goals to accomplish. After surviving the grueling years of study to become a veterinarian, Sonsee had focused on firmly establishing her place in the community as a respected doctor.

But somehow love had sneaked in the back door and locked itself around her. As her sisters continued to discuss the journey to Vietnam, Sonsee pondered that Hawaiian trip with Taylor and admitted to herself what she wanted to deny. She had, indeed, been in love with Taylor Delaney long before that trip to Hawaii. She wondered how she could have been so blind to her own emotions. Perhaps she had been too certain she was in control of herself. In reality she must have been suppressing her budding love for the man whom she had depended upon more than even her three half-siblings, none of whom really appreciated her. Reflecting upon her relationship with Taylor, Sonsee realized the two of them had fallen into a comfortable pattern of relying on the other. From her viewpoint, what she and Taylor shared smacked of a long-distance, platonic marriage—if there were such a thing. She recalled her father's "conveniently" retiring early every night during their Hawaiian vacation. And Sonsee knew he had seen what she had been blind to. She was in love with Taylor. Desperately in love.

"So what do you think, Sonsee?" Kim Lan asked.

Sonsee, blinking in confusion, stared at the golf ball paperweight with which she had been mindlessly toying. "About what?" she asked.

"I knew you were too quiet to be listening to us!" Kim scolded. "Melissa says she's going to see if she can arrange to fly in for the orientation meeting Thursday night. Can you?"

"No. There's no way," Sonsee said leaning forward. "I missed part of last week because I was sick. I can't miss any more this week. We had to reschedule patients, and now my schedule is packed."

"I'll take notes for you," Melissa said.

"Yeah, and tell Mick I said hello," Sonsee teased, forcing herself to jump back into the sisterly banter.

❧

Thursday night Mick O'Donnel glanced over the small group of ten participants as they each found a seat in the church's fellowship hall. This fellowship hall at the historic church was a modern addition and looked much like many others in which Mick had been: a large, square room, tiled in brown, with the usual folding chairs, tables, customary dinner bar, and nearby kitchen.

"Okay, if I can have everyone's attention, please," he said, noticing one participant in particular. She wore no makeup, a floppy denim hat, slightly shaded glasses, and a faded sweatsuit. *Her hair must be stuffed under that hat,* he mused as he noted she was not wearing the large engagement ring. Mick wondered if the absence of the ring meant a break in Kim Lan's relationship with Ted Curry or if she was simply making a wise move by not wearing flashy jewelry. She stopped chatting with the brunette at her side long enough to glance up to find him observing her. Mick's throat tightened. That same pulse of attraction, his bane during their last encounter, flashed between them like an invisible bolt of lightning.

Mick looked back at his list, careful to keep his features schooled in a no-nonsense expression despite his sudden propensity toward aching to put his arms around her. *We have very little in common,* he reminded himself.

"Okay," he said again as the group at last settled around the tables. "It's good to see you visiting among yourselves. Already I feel a sense of camaraderie and that's good. This trip is probably going to be the highlight of your year." He paused and looked across the group of expectant faces. "For some of you, it might be the highlight of your lives." He cast another glance toward Kim Lan and pondered what she was thinking. Mick forced himself to stare at his list of eleven names.

"We are a small group. Usually our trips are larger. At first I was somewhat disappointed, but I've decided that perhaps the Lord has a purpose in keeping us small. Quite frankly, I think the Vietnamese government is more comfortable with a group closer to our size." He glanced over the group.

"Well, let's move on. As I call your names, I want each of you to come forward and pick up your introduction packet. This will give us all, including me, an opportunity to hopefully begin placing names with faces."

He pointed toward the large white envelopes lying on the table before him. "These packets contain your name tags. Go ahead and put them on. But you'll also find some basic facts about Vietnam that will be helpful to you. You'll see a map that pinpoints where we'll be. Also, there's a day-to-day guide of what we'll be involved in. Ladies, please read over the dress code carefully. If you pack shorts, make certain they are knee-length. The Asian culture views shorts differently than we do here. But within that context, remember that Vietnam has two seasons, wet and dry, and one temperature, hot. Fortunately, we'll be there during the dry season.

"Also, please make sure your shots are up to date. There's a list of those we recommend you get. I can't stress how important these are—especially the malaria pills because we will be working near a river and in an area that is conducive to mosquitoes. Any health clinic or your general practitioner can take care of the shots and medicine for you.

"Furthermore, on this international flight, you are allowed one carry-on bag and two bags to check in. However, suitcases must weigh twenty-five pounds or less. Pack light and plan to launder your clothes yourself at the hotel. Also, you'll find a list of the trip's participants as well as some general information about our flight. I'm arranging your tickets from Los Angeles for you. That's part of the cost of the trip, as you know. We want to make sure we all get on the same flight. However, you need to remember that getting to L.A. is your responsibility. We'll be going over more details on all this, so we might as well get started."

Slowly Mick called each name and paused as the participants stepped forward to retrieve his or her packet: "Rhonda Ackers." Rhonda was a middle-aged, graying widow of two years who was tired of spending her productive energies bemoaning the loss of her husband. Rhonda had decided to take definite steps toward regaining control of her life.

"Doug Cauley," Mick continued. Doug was a man in his mid-forties who looked like a direct descendent of the Irish. His red hair and mustache, ruddy complexion, and green eyes suggested a man of deep passions. Certainly Mick had been impressed with his passionate interest in the trip.

"Frank Cox. Pam Cox." Mick glanced toward the married couple in their late thirties and paused in reading his list. "Frank is my assistant on this trip," he said. "This is our third trip together. After this, he'll be coordinating trips himself." Frank, his brown eyes sincere, exchanged a brief, respectful nod with Mick.

"Ron Emerson. Laci Emerson," Mick called. Ron and Laci, both tall, lithe, and dark-complected, were brother and sister, both in college. Ron was two years older than Laci.

"Adam Gray." Adam was a tall man with dark hair and eyes. His high cheekbones and crooked nose suggested a Native American heritage. Mick knew precious little about him, except that he lived alone in New York and didn't say much.

"Kimberly Lowe." Pausing, he watched as Kim Lan joined the tight group who succinctly found their envelopes and turned back to their seats. Her graceful gait and willowy height were the only indicators of her modeling experience. As she picked up her packet, she never once made eye contact, and Mick was partially glad, partially disappointed. With haste, she grabbed the packet with her name on it as well as the one labeled for Sonsee LeBlanc. "Sonsee wasn't able to come. I'll mail this to her," she mumbled. Swiftly, she turned from the table. However, her envelope snared a couple more packets and sent them toppling to the floor.

"Sorry," she mumbled, awkwardly stooping to retrieve the packets. As she fumbled with them, he noticed her fingers shaking. Mick suspected that she was as uptight as he was about the possibilities of someone recognizing her. Sensing that she cared enough about his concerns to be so affected only enhanced Mick's deepening respect for her.

"It's okay," he soothed under his breath as he squatted next to Kim. "You're doing fine. Everything's fine. Nobody suspects a thing. I think we're going to be home free." Mick only wished he was as convinced as he sounded.

She stilled and urgently glanced at him. "How did you know?" she whispered.

"I just did." Mick started to smile but stopped himself. He could warm up to this version of Kim Lan Lowery in a hurry. Somehow, without the makeup and all the finery she seemed much less "Fifth Avenue," much more approachable, much more in Mick's league. He envisioned the two weeks on the trip—the emotional intimacy that always developed between the participants, the friendships that often lasted for years. And he wanted to groan. *What have I gotten myself into?*

Without another word, Kim Lan placed the fallen envelopes on the table and hurried back to her seat to end their brief encounter. Mick forced himself not to look at her again, but once more he felt like the gaping teenager he had turned into during Sunday's presentation.

He stared at the list and began to call the names once more. "Melissa Moore," he said, and the brunette sitting beside Kim Lan stood. So this was Kim's other friend. Both Melissa and Sonsee LeBlanc had faxed Mick their names and information and mentioned that Kim Lan had referred them.

Melissa, slightly attractive, wore precious little makeup and had the gait of an athlete. Her round, wire-rimmed glasses gave her the appearance of the class genius. Seeing a friend of Kim's that seemed so approachable only added to the model's growing appeal.

This trip is going to be the longest two weeks of my life.

"Caleb Peterson," Mick called out the last name and watched as his younger half-brother came forward. Caleb and Mick shared nothing in common except their eyes and their dry sense of humor. Where Mick was tall, blond, and broad-shouldered, Caleb barely stood five-ten and had the build of a linebacker. His dark hair, complexion, and athlete's physique usually left him with plenty of feminine company, despite his claims of being "short, dark, and lonesome." Apparently, short, dark, and lonesome fascinated women. That was part of the problem. Try as he might, Mick couldn't seem to get Caleb as interested in the things of God as he was in the opposite sex. Caleb produced his familiar smile and leaned forward. "That chick looks a little like Kim Lan Lowery. Did you notice?" he asked under his breath.

"Which one?" Mick asked, cringing inside.

"If you have to ask, you didn't notice." Caleb cast a glance over his shoulder in Kim Lan's direction and walked back toward his seat.

Swiftly Mick scanned over the names once more then peered at them as the group began chatting among themselves while exploring their packets. "Okay, it's time to get started on specifics," he said at last. "Looks like you gentlemen are outnumbered. There are six ladies and five men. For some of you, that is an answer to prayer."

Mick paused as a chorus of laughter erupted from the group.

"Actually, if you aren't married, it would appear that a mission trip is the place to find a mate. The last two trips I've led have ended with a couple getting married, and one couple has just been approved as full-time missionaries to Russia."

A round of applause punctuated Mick's words.

"We need to marry you off, Mick," Caleb said above the noise. "You're going to grow old, get gray, and *die* before you get married."

The guffaws abounded, and Mick smiled sarcastically. "For those of you who don't know it, Caleb is my younger brother. And it would appear that he is still on his lifetime mission of shamelessly tormenting me."

Amid a new round of companionable laughter, Mick began sharing the necessary details of the first orientation meeting. During the whole session, he miraculously avoided eye contact with Kim Lan. However, when they joined hands for group prayer, somehow she was standing next to him. Mick resisted the urge to quickly switch places with Frank Cox, standing on his left. Instead, he extended his hand to hers and wrapped his fingers around the back of her hand. As their palms touched, her hand trembled, and what felt like a jolt of electricity flashed through Mick's midsection. All thoughts of prayer vanished, and he swallowed hard. "Uh...Frank, would you please begin the prayer. After he finishes, I would like to encourage each of you to pray aloud, if you're comfortable with that."

All heads bowed. From within the circle, Odysseus peaked from beneath his lashes and watched Kim Lan holding Mick's hand. A surge of jealousy mixed with the heady delight that had descended upon him the minute Kim Lan had walked into the meeting. Odysseus wondered if she suspected that he'd sent the roses or if she could ever guess that his every dream was of her. He scoffed at her efforts to disguise her appearance and wondered if she really thought she could ever hide her identity from him. He knew her so well. She was what Sophie had never been: his Penelope, his model of feminine virtue. He would be able to identify her from her graceful mannerisms alone.

This session had gone remarkably well. Kim Lan had even glanced his way a couple of times. He had returned her slight smile with one of his own. His legs shaking with the force of his giddy anticipation, Odysseus imagined the progress of their relationship as they neared the time of the journey. Her slight smiles would evolve into opened arms of affection. Before the trip was over, she would return his kiss. And by the time they arrived home from Vietnam, she would be ready to marry him.

Seven

With the closing of the last prayer, Kim Lan quickly removed her hand from Mick's and walked to her chair to gather her things. The fact that she and Mick were strongly attracted to each other and that both of them knew it was an understatement. Kim Lan had trembled with his very touch, and her efforts to stop the shaking only increased her reaction. More than once during prayer, his hand had tightened on hers, leaving Kim with the impression that he understood more than she wanted to admit.

Melissa, who had been chatting with Mick, arrived to begin gathering the contents of her own packet.

This trip is beyond doubt the craziest idea I have ever come up with, Kim mentally accused herself. *Ted was right. We should have just chartered a plane and planned a tour.* However, she remembered those moments in church when she had decided to participate in this trip. Once more Kim was reminded that the idea had been less hers and more divine.

"Ready to go, Mel?" Kim Lan asked, desperately trying to keep the urgent note from her voice.

"Uh…" Melissa glanced toward the kitchen area, a ravenous light in her brown eyes. "I thought we were going to have finger foods now. I haven't eaten since lunch."

"Well, we can raid Mom's refrigerator," Kim rushed, slipping on her leather coat.

Melissa eyed her suspiciously.

"Hey, you two aren't leaving, are you?" Mick asked, breaking away from a conversation to approach them. "I was hoping this would be a time for everyone to get better acquainted."

Kim Lan, keeping her head down, grabbed the faded, denim handbag that her mother had bought at Goodwill years before. "Well, I...um...we...that is...I was thinking perhaps we would—would just go ahead and—"

Mick placed his hand on her shoulder. "There's no reason for you to rush off," he said with the faintest hint of a plea.

Don't look at him. Do not look at Mick. Kim nervously toyed with the strap of her purse, feeling as if she were once more an uncertain fifteen-year-old. "Well, I guess..." Despite herself, Kim glanced into his eyes and every trace of Ted Curry vanished from her mind. Instead, she was filled with the emotions that had plagued her all evening. Emotions now reflected in Mick's own eyes. Eyes that had become a tempestuous sea, whose depths were stirred by the whirl-pool of fascination, the gale of whimsical longing, and a swelling tide of what might have been. *If only we didn't come from different worlds. If only we'd met before the onset of my career. If only I weren't engaged.*

Caleb's brotherly chiding echoed through Kim Lan's thoughts: *We need to marry you off, Mick. You're going to grow old, get gray, and die before you get married.* Yet Kim had to admit that, although there were a few streaks of gray mixed in with Mick's blond hair, he was miles from being old. The lines that reflected his age only added a certain nuance of character and wisdom to the strength of his mas-culinity. Her pulse pounding, she frantically wondered how she was going to survive two whole weeks on the same trip with the man.

"Hey, Mick! We need you in the kitchen," Caleb called across the noisy group.

"Don't leave yet," Mick said, glancing toward the kitchen. "There's something I wanted to ask you."

"Okay," Kim rasped as he walked away.

Melissa produced a low whistle and shook her head from side to side while staring round-eyed at Kim.

With a defeated sigh, Kim observed her friend. Nothing ever got past Melissa Moore. She had graduated from college magna cum laude and basically aced medical school. After which she moved into the medical community in Oklahoma City and skillfully proved her genius as a pediatrician. Melissa Moore was too sharp to miss one detail, and Kim fully understood there was no reason to even try to hide the truth.

"I now know why Sonsee was teasing you about him."

"Sonsee doesn't even know why she was teasing me about him," Kim said wearily as she deposited her purse on the table and removed her coat.

"So she was closer to the truth than she realized, is that it?" Melissa crossed her arms and tilted her head to one side in that quizzical manner that said she already knew the truth. Of all the seven friends, Melissa was the one that was the closest to being the interrogator. She never came across as more than soft-spoken and calmly intelligent, but her questions usually pinpointed the exact problem and revealed the fact, without ever needing an answer.

As the rest of the group moved toward the long bar, loaded with a wide array of finger foods, Kim Lan adjusted her shaded glasses. "It doesn't matter," she said. "I'm engaged to the man of my dreams." She shrugged. "These things happen, you know. Just because I'm engaged doesn't mean that I won't find other men attractive."

"I think what I saw was a little stronger than finding a man attractive." Melissa arched her brow. "It verged more on 'where have you been all my life.'"

Kim caught herself nibbling on the edge of her thumbnail, and she yanked her fingers away from her mouth. "Okay, so maybe it was—is. But we come from two different worlds. There's no future in any kind of a relationship." She shrugged again and lifted her palms upward. "Ted and I are in love, and this is just one of those things in life." Kim steeled herself against a wince. Her words sounded far from convincing, even to her own ears.

"Well, whatever you say, but in your own words, 'Honey, y'all got it bad,'" Melissa mimicked the Southern accent Kim Lan often feigned.

"Go ahead. Make me miserable." She smiled as the two approached the bar. "Use my own words against me." Kim got in line behind Mick's brother and Melissa followed.

"Okay, I'll back off," she said under her breath quietly. "Meanwhile, I could eat everything here."

"I don't know how you do it," Kim said, picking up a paper plate. "If I ate like you do, I'd be the size of a door."

"I'm not half as thin as you," Melissa said, looking down at her jeans-clad figure. "I'm a size ten, now. My size eight jeans are shrinking." She grabbed a paper plate and began heaping her plate with chips and sandwiches while Kim Lan chose a few pieces from the fruit plate. She couldn't afford any extra nibbles, despite her stomach's growling.

"Excuse me," Caleb said, turning to scrutinize Kim in a most disconcerting way. "Has anyone ever told you that you resemble Kim Lan Lowery a little?" The question occurred during a lull in the group's conversation and seemed to resonate across the fellowship hall and kitchen.

Kim paused and gripped her paper plate. She felt Melissa tense beside her and sensed a couple of the trip's participants on the other side of the bar eyeing her as well. From the kitchen nearby, she noticed Mick hurrying toward the bar, and she relaxed when he approached his younger brother.

"Oh, Caleb, leave the lady alone, will ya?" Mick said loudly enough for everyone in line to hear. He rolled his eyes and gripped his brother's shoulder. "Every Asian beauty you see isn't Kim Lan Lowery." Mick turned to Kim. "I think he's got every magazine the supermodel was ever in. My goal on this trip is to hopefully teach my younger brother to focus more on God and less on women."

Everyone within earshot laughed at Mick's brotherly chiding. The group appeared to immensely enjoy the banter between the two.

"Yeah, and my goal," Caleb said in response, "is to get you to focus a little more on women. Seriously, old man, the rate you're going, you're going to be old enough to be a grandpa before you ever get married."

"I'm already old enough to be a grandpa," Mick growled playfully.

New chuckles seized the group. Yet once the laughter died, Caleb cast another glance at Kim and smiled apologetically. "Sorry."

She nodded and focused on the strawberries, grapes, and pineapple on her plate.

Within minutes, Kim Lan and Melissa had moved toward their places and taken their seats. "Whew, that was a close one," Melissa said under her breath.

"Yes, but I think Mick probably stopped any and all speculations. Might be a good thing it happened."

After Melissa had devoured most of her meal, she said, "Do you remember everyone's names?"

"No, but I bet you do."

"Everyone, I think, except the couple that was standing on the other side of Mick when we prayed."

"Oh, those two?" Kim discreetly pointed toward the couple in their late thirties, both with brown hair, amiably chatting with a young man and woman who appeared to be related.

"Yes."

"I remember them. They're the Coxes. I think Mick said their names were Frank and Pam. Isn't Frank Mick's assistant?"

"Yes, yes, that's right," Melissa said. "And they're talking to…" Pausing, she narrowed her eyes and studied the young man and woman, both with dark brown hair and olive complexions, both tall, and both college-age. "Those two are brother and sister, I would hazard to guess. I think Mick said their names are Ron and Laci Emerson."

"Yes, I think you're right," Kim Lan replied. "And aren't those two, um…" She pointed to two men who stood near the glass doors and were deep in discussion. One was tall and thin with a long face, dark hair, eyes, and brows. The other was of average height and build with red hair and mustache and complexion to match. Both men wore jeans and sweaters.

"I think the tall, dark one is Adam Gray and the shorter one is Doug Cauley," Melissa said, a ring of certainty to her voice. "And the lady sitting over there alone is Rhonda Ackers." Melissa barely jerked her head toward the plump, graying lady who sat at a table across from theirs.

"I think you're right. I guess that just leaves Mick's brother, Caleb O'Donnel—"

"No, they must be half-brothers. His last name is Peterson," Melissa corrected.

"Yes, you're right. Frankly, I hope I get all the names straight before the trip. Names have never been my forte." Kim popped the final strawberry into her mouth and glimpsed Mick chatting with a few participants who had gathered around the service bar for seconds. He'd said he wanted to ask her something, but Kim Lan was ready to go. Melissa and Kim were spending the night at her mom and dad's, and Kim had to be back in New York the next day.

"If you're through inhaling your food, I'm ready to go, Mel. I'm tired," Kim said, stifling a yawn. "Mom's going to want to sit up and talk awhile, and I've got to be back in New York tomorrow afternoon."

"But Mick mentioned he wanted to ask you something," Melissa said.

"He's got my phone number," she replied, silently beseeching Melissa to understand. "If it's urgent enough, he'll call. I really need to go."

Kim had endured all the stress she could tolerate for one evening. She felt as if Mick were watching her every move, and she fought to keep from watching *his* every move. Kim glanced toward him just as he laughed heartily at something the Coxes were saying. He seemed to immensely enjoy his work. He appeared to be a man who was at ease with himself and others. A man who lacked the nagging insecurities that seemed to be Kim Lan's tormentor. A man who would bring a mature stability into his marriage, and the promise of excitement that was so latent in the mysterious depths of his eyes. Every time she encountered Mick, Kim's respect for him took deeper root; but then, so did her fascination.

But he can't even afford roses, a nagging voice reminded her. *You've got Ted Curry—the Ted Curry—eating out of your hand!*

Another thought barged in upon Kim Lan, *But Ted isn't half as committed to Christ as Mick.* There was no question in Kim's mind that Mick O'Donnel would give every penny he owned to the cause of Christ if the Lord required it of him. His devotion to God seemed to ooze from his every pore, a devotion that made Kim's commitment to the Lord wane in comparison. Her heart pounded in dread as she once more contemplated her wealth. Ironically, she was the one in New York and Hollywood who had the reputation as a radical Christian. In the light of Mick's passion for God, Kim wondered if she had only scratched the surface of understanding the holy.

Within minutes, Kim and Melissa had discarded their paper plates and cups, bid a friendly goodbye to those nearby, donned their coats, and exited the fellowship hall. The icy air immediately wrapped its fingers around Kim Lan and seemed to sink into her very soul. As they walked across the parking lot of the large country church, the full moon's soft illumination cast a glow across the blanket of January snow that covered the scenic Massachusetts landscape. Kim's breath created a cloud of mist, and she felt an aching loneliness like she had never felt before. Something in her life was missing, something that Mick O'Donnel personified. But was it the man? His experience with God? Or both?

"Excuse me...Kim?" Mick's soft call stopped her in her tracks.

"I'll go crank the car and let it warm up," Melissa said, reaching for the keys in Kim's gloved hands.

"But…" Kim Lan had no time to even protest her friend's desertion before Melissa rushed away and Mick stepped to her side.

"Hi," he said with a hesitant smile. "Did you think you were going to get away from me?"

Slowly Kim pivoted to face him. "Well, I'm just really tired and I figured if your question was urgent you'd call. I haven't had much of a chance to visit with Mom yet. She'll want to sit up and talk, and I've got to be back in New York tomorrow afternoon for a reading," she babbled on.

"Oh?"

"Yes, there's a producer that's considering using my voice for an animated skunk named Fluff."

He chuckled. "I love it."

"I think I do too, and I'll probably do it if the offer comes through."

"Oh, I'm sure it will."

"Thanks for coming to my rescue with Caleb in there," Kim said, glancing down at the tips of her worn canvas shoes.

"Sure," he said, and an awkward silence posed itself between them.

A faint wind scampering across the bare tree limbs left a chill along Kim Lan's spine. She shivered, but couldn't determine whether the reaction came from the wind or Mick's presence.

"I won't keep you," Mick said, peering into her eyes. Even in the shadowed moonlight, his gaze seemed to pierce her soul. "I just noticed you weren't wearing your engagement ring tonight, and I didn't know if it was all part of your disguise or—"

Her gloved fists balled into tight knots. "Yes, I figured a diamond of that size might look suspicious."

"Oh."

Kim had never heard so much disappointment rolled into one word.

With a defeated chuckle, Mick stuffed his hands into the pockets of his parka and rocked back on his heels. "I guess I'm pretty obvious, aren't I?"

Not any more obvious than I am, she thought.

"Well, why not admit the obvious? There's no reason to pretend it's hidden between us, is there? You're engaged, and this trip is going to be the longest two weeks of my life. I'm beginning to wonder if I should find a replacement. Otherwise I might make a complete fool of myself—a thirty-nine-year-old fool," he said with disgust.

"You never told me where you live," Kim blurted, desperate for some diversion from his current line of thought. Nevertheless, her pulse pounded in her temples, and she yearned to feel his arms around her. Something inside urged her to beg him not to find a replacement leader.

"I'm sorry about the other day on the phone. I should have answered your question about where I live. I guess I was rude." Mick paused.

"It's okay," Kim said softly, not certain she understood all the silent communication flashing between them too fast for words.

"I've actually lived in Colorado most of my life. And you? Have you always lived in the States? You sometimes sound as if you lived in Asia at one time."

"Yes, I've been told that, but I've always lived in the United States. I just picked up some of my mother's accent along the way, I guess. That's part of the reason the producer says he wants me for this skunk voice. He says Fluff is supposed to be from Asia."

"I thought skunks were only indigenous to North and South America."

"They are, as far as I know." She shrugged. "But it looks like this one migrated or something."

"So, a skunk from Asia." He smiled. "What other surprises have you got up your sleeve?" The longing scurrying across his features left Kim Lan breathless.

"You'd be surprised by some of the offers that have come my way lately," she rushed, not even sure of what she was saying—anything to alter the current trail of her fantasies. "I thought after I decided to walk away from doing suggestive poses that my career would be hurt. My agent was even convinced of it, but I knew... I came to a crossroads where God seemed to be requiring that I make a choice." Kim gulped for air as she tried to force away longings for Mick to move closer. "Anyway, once I said no to career choices that don't please God, it's like I can't keep up with the alternate offers that are coming my way. It's amazing."

She awkwardly cleared her throat as she recalled Mick's pointed remarks about his brother's enjoyment of her swimsuit poses. "I'm sorry your brother has all my swimsuit pictures." Kim looked toward the moon and couldn't stop the new shivers that were accosting her. The icy air was starting to take its toll. Nonetheless, the heat of shame burned within. "I'm really embarassed to know th–that Caleb probably has all th–those magazines with me in compromising poses," she said, her teeth chattering. "God has forgiven me, and I've repented, but the consequences of my choices still remain. Th–there's even one swimsuit issue th–that hasn't been released. I don't even want to see it," Kim said flatly. "It makes me nauseous."

"Well, right now you're freezing," Mick said, with a warmth of approval in his voice. "Go on home. We'll talk later."

"Okay." Kim turned and took a few steps toward her father's Chevrolet purring nearby.

"Oh, Kim?"

"Yes?" Hesitating, she turned back toward him.

"You're still the most lovely woman I've ever met—even with no makeup and those glasses and that floppy hat." He stood with his hands still in his coat pockets, an aura of loneliness exuding from his words and cloaking his features.

She pressed her trembling lips together until they ached. The silence of the winter's evening intensified Mick's allure. Kim Lan fully realized she had encountered a man like no other. A man she could most likely fall madly in love with given the opportunity. But the facts remained: She was a celebrity; Mick O'Donnel was a mission coordinator. *The two just don't mix.*

"Thanks," she mumbled. "I—" She cleared her throat. "I hope—hope you don't get a replacement for the trip leader, but not just because of me. I think everyone would be disappointed now if you didn't go, especially your brother." The words tumbled from Kim before she recognized the driving force behind them. Despite her misgivings, Kim Lan did not want Mick to opt out of the trip.

"And what about you? Would you be disappointed if I resigned as leader?" The words were so soft they seemed but a whisper on the faint winter breeze.

A rush of warmth started in the pit of Kim's stomach and slowly spread throughout her body, concentrating in her face. Helplessly she held his gaze and reveled in the sensation of being tugged into the undercurrent of a balmy, blue ocean. She wondered what Mick's arms would feel like around her, and she imagined the warmth of his lips on hers.

"I think you know the answer to that," she whispered.

"Kim?" He stepped toward her, only to halt as a mask of restraint settled upon him. "But you're engaged."

"Yes. Yes, engaged," she repeated, feeling like a mindless parrot. At the moment, she couldn't even remember the name of her fiancé.

Yet she did remember how to run. Turning, she hurried toward the Chevy where Melissa waited, whipped open the door, and collapsed into the warmth of the car's interior. Violently trembling, Kim backed out of the parking lot. The headlights illuminated Mick, still standing where she had left him. She sped onto the two-lane highway and stole one last glance in the rearview mirror to see him watching while she drove away.

"You know, Kim, I think you have some praying to do," Melissa said thoughtfully.

"I'm not going to break up with—with Ted, if that's what you mean," Kim snapped. "He's my dream man. And I won't just toss him aside because I've met somebody who—"

"Who knocks you off your feet every time you're near him?"

"Exactly!"

"Did you notice the chocolates?"

"What?"

"I think he put these chocolates in the car." Melissa tapped a large flat box sitting on the seat between them.

Kim's thoughts flew to the bouquet of red roses still occupying her breakfast bar. Mick had convinced her he hadn't sent them. But what about the chocolates?

"Do they have a card?"

"Yes."

"Please open it and see what it says."

Melissa removed the small card and opened it while Kim Lan switched on the dome light.

"It says, 'With love from your secret admirer,'" Melissa said. "Wow! Mick's serious."

"I don't think they're from Mick," Kim said, an uncanny dread engulfing her. "I don't think he'd do something like that."

"What? You don't think he's romantic enough? With that smile and those eyes? He should be the hero in a romance novel!"

"Very funny. That's not what I meant." Kim reached to turn off the dome light then flipped on the radio, tuned to the soft music her father enjoyed. "What I meant is that somebody sent me roses earlier this week. The card said they were from a secret admirer."

"Well, maybe Mick sent them both."

"No, I asked him about the roses."

"You asked him?"

"Yes."

"And he said he didn't send them?"

"Yes."

"Did that embarrass you at all?"

"Yes. I wanted to melt out of existence."

Melissa chuckled. "Oh, Kimmy, Kimmy, Kimmy. Have you gotten yourself into a fix or what?"

"I'm not in a fix!" Kim insisted. "When I get back from this trip, Ted and I are going to get married. Period. We are even talking about adopting one of the children from the orphanage we'll be visiting."

"So, you've got a fiancé, a new acquaintance that leaves you swooning, *and* a secret admirer. What more could a woman want?"

As the minutes ticked by and the classical music wove its relaxing aura, Kim recalled a newspaper article she had read not long before about an unknown man who had stalked a woman then killed her. He had started the whole ordeal with love notes and flowers. The car sped south on highway thirty, and the dread from moments before increased with fervency. As they drew near to Boston, she slowed the Chevrolet, put on the blinker, and prepared to turn into the driveway of her parents' estate. She couldn't help but wonder if the person who sent the flowers and candy were indeed the same and if, by some wild circumstance, he were a participant on the mission trip.

"You know, Kim," Melissa said thoughtfully, "if you're certain Mick didn't send the flowers and chocolates, you might need to be careful."

"Yes, I know. But..." She shrugged. "The roses and the chocolates probably aren't even related. Who knows, Mick might have left the chocolates. After I asked about the roses, he might have decided to buy chocolates. He said he couldn't afford roses," she said with a smile.

"So, if he could afford them—if he were wealthy and famous, would you consider him?"

She felt Melissa's scrutiny and didn't dare glance at her discerning friend. Instead Kim concentrated on parking the Chevrolet beside her Jaguar. "Looks like Mom left the porch light on for us. She's probably got hot cocoa waiting. She's a great mom."

Mick stood in the parking lot hopelessly gazing at the stars until they blurred. The forlorn sound of a lonely owl hooting from a grove of maples seemed but a metaphor for Mick's life. He was alone. All alone. And never had he ached so much with the burden of that realization.

He slowly relived every nuance of the conversation with Kim until the final words poised themselves in his mind, *And what about you? Would you be disappointed if I resigned as leader?*

"I think you know the answer to that," she had whispered, validating every hint of the longing that had played across her features all through the evening.

"Kim?" He had stepped toward her, intent on taking her in his arms if only for a brief embrace, but he had stopped himself.

You are making a fool of yourself. Mick scolded himself with a few more accusations then shook his head in disgust. When Kim Lan walked into the meeting, Mick had vowed to barely acknowledge her—then he had promptly broken his own promise. He probably would have exercised more self-restraint, but her hand trembling in his during the prayer time had intensified his reaction to her. Furthermore, her revealing expressions testified that he affected her as deeply as she affected him. So he had chased after Kim like a love-starved schoolboy, shamelessly asking about her engagement and blatantly telling her exactly how he felt.

Groaning, Mick rubbed his eyes. He had never come on so strong with a woman. In the few romantic relationships of his adult years, Mick usually took the mature, subtle approach. There was nothing subtle or mature about his interaction with Kim Lan Lowery.

I'm acting like an idiot and can't even stop myself! Mick contemplated his fortieth birthday arriving in June, just five short months away. "This is undoubtedly some sort of a mid-life crisis! If I keep up this stupidity, by June I'll probably be driving a sports car and wearing a wide gold chain around my neck!" he muttered to himself.

Clamping his teeth with renewed resolve, Mick turned and walked back toward the fellowship hall. Through the glass doors, he noticed Caleb, his usual charming self, talking to Laci Emerson. Her brother stood nearby, a protective gleam in his eyes. Caleb, seeming oblivious to Ron's mild disapproval, sipped his Coke and focused solely on Laci. The last thing Mick needed to do was set a bad example for Caleb. He had no recourse but to redouble the intensity of his prayer life and beg the Lord to impart an extra dose of self-control upon him.

Eight

~

Clutching the massive box of chocolates, Kim Lan followed Melissa over the threshold of her parents' home, a replica of the many historical farmhouses across New England. John Lowery, leaning heavily on his cane, ushered them into the entranceway that separated the dining room from the formal living room. The elegant Victorian decor was accented with oriental rugs, brass candlesticks, and black-and-gold ceiling fans. The home Kim had custom-built for her parents was a far cry from that of the poor Arkansas farmhouse where Kim had been raised. As always, she warmed with the pleasure of knowing that the fortune she earned was making a drastic difference in her parents' standard of living.

The smell of freshly baked cookies and hot cocoa wafted from the kitchen. Kim Lan inhaled deeply. "What did I tell you, Mel?" she asked, turning to her friend. "Mom probably is prepared to stuff us full of cookies and cocoa."

"Nobody ever said I turn down food," Melissa said with a mischievous smile.

"I knew I always liked you—a woman after my own heart." John, dressed in a flannel shirt and twill slacks, rubbed his flat stomach. "And I must say that the cookies are delicious." His brown eyes twinkled with delight. "They're my favorite, chocolate chip, and I've already tested about four of them."

"Dad's the official tester." Kim smiled at Melissa. "When I was growing up, he would sample everything I cooked. If he didn't die, we all knew my latest culinary disaster was okay to eat."

"Ah, Kimmy, don't be so hard on yourself." John placed his arm around Kim's shoulders, squeezed her in a sideways hug, and planted a loving kiss on her forehead. "You never were that bad of a cook."

"I guess you forgot the gravy the dog gagged on and refused to eat." Kim set the chocolates and her purse on the nearby mahogany bench and removed her coat.

Melissa, snickering under her breath, shed her parka then hung it on the hat rack where Kim hooked her leather coat as well.

John reached for the large box of chocolates. "Yum. Looks like you've had a visit from the chocolate fairy, Kim. Care to share?"

"How did you know they were for Kim?" Melissa asked. Tilting her head to one side, she narrowed her eyes.

John's face broke into a smile, and he produced an exaggerated wink. "I'll never tell."

A surge of relief coursed through Kim Lan's veins and swept her earlier worries about a stalker from her mind. She recalled the numerous occasions during her adolescent years when her father had bought a two-dollar box of chocolates and left them on her bed with "Your secret admirer" scribbled on a card. He usually left the candy if Kim had been through a hard time, but he always gave it to her when he was especially proud of her. However, several years had lapsed since her father had bought chocolates for her, and Kim had automatically assumed the person who sent the flowers also left the chocolates.

"Dad! You left the chocolates in the car?"

"Secret admirers never reveal their identity," he said through a chuckle, a glow of approval in his eyes.

"So what about the flowers? Did you send those, too?"

A quizzical look covered her father's face. "No. What flowers?"

The foreboding hunch from earlier marched right back into her mind. What if the flowers really were from a weirdo?

"Somebody sent Kim a bouquet of roses earlier in the week," Melissa responded. "They were from a secret admirer as well."

"Wasn't me," John said as his wife called a merry greeting from the dining room.

Melissa met her by the Queen Anne dining table, and the two of them embraced.

As Kim stepped toward her mom, John placed a restraining hand on his daughter's arm. "Kim," he said, his heart in his eyes. "I *am* proud of you—so proud to know you're going on this trip to Vietnam. After I was there and saw all those needy people... For years I've wanted to go back and somehow help them, but..." He glanced at his cane, "I wouldn't be much use."

"Oh, Dad," Kim said, her eyes stinging a bit. "Thanks. That means so much to me." She thought of the times when her decisions had left her parents—and the Lord— less than approving. She determined all the more to continue seeking God and making choices according to His guidance.

John knitted his heavy, graying brows and gave a troubled frown. "And what's this business about flowers from a secret admirer? You aren't two-timing me, are you?"

"You know I'd never do that," Kim said, looping her arm through her father's.

"Seriously, you ought to be careful."

She sighed. "Yes, I know. The flowers probably came from a fan. Ted and I both get those types of things off and on all the time." She shrugged, wishing her own words would somehow relieve the doubts that troubled the waters of her soul.

Saturday morning Sonsee steered her trusty Honda along the paved driveway of her family's historic mansion. While winter's cool temperatures had robbed the grounds of their emerald hue, the sprawling LeBlanc acres still provided a scenic and impressive drive. At the end of the driveway, nestled amid a group of weeping willows, stood the white-pillared mansion that Jacques LeBlanc, Sonsee's father, had inherited from her grandfather. The numerous windows, trellises, and park benches near the rose garden brought back fond childhood memories...memories tangled with Taylor.

Sonsee's feelings for Taylor were setting her up for ultimate heartache. Something deep inside suggested she couldn't hide her love forever. Taylor knew her too well. Once he discovered Sonsee's growing love, their relationship would at best, suffer, and at worst, dissolve. Her heart heavy, she drove along the circular driveway and parked near the porch steps. Her father, who was still on friendly terms with his former sister-in-law, had graciously offered Taylor's mother a place to rest while she recovered from her surgery. Joy Delaney owned a modest home just outside New Orleans, but the mansion, with full-time staff, would better serve her immediate needs.

Sonsee, ever the loyal friend, had agreed to spend the day with Taylor's mother, and she found herself hoping Taylor was not planning on being here. After his mother's surgery on Wednesday, he had gone back home to Houston on Thursday. Sonsee hadn't talked to him since Thursday evening.

Sonsee stepped from her blue sports car and retrieved the impressive basket of peach-colored roses from the backseat. She hurried up the porch steps and opened the massive front door.

"Hello, Carla? It's me," she called as she stepped into the anteroom. The foyer's rich milieu and the faint odor of raspberry potpourri enveloped Sonsee as she carefully deposited the flowers on the floor. Swiftly she removed her vinyl jacket and hung it on the solid-brass coat hanger near the door. Little had changed in the old mansion since her childhood. The scarlet Persian rug still claimed its usual spot against the dark hardwood floor. The curving stairway with its teak banister still invited Sonsee to race upstairs to her room, to her own haven. The family portraits, hanging along the wall above the stairway, still spoke of a long line of Frenchmen who never flinched in the face of adventure.

"Sonsee, great to see you!" Carla Jenkins said, approaching from the narrow hallway that led to the servant's quarters. In childhood, the maid had sneaked Sonsee more cookies than she could remember, and the two of them still shared a pleasant friendship.

"How's it going, Carla?" Sonsee asked, taking the hands of the plump, graying brunette. The smell of her heavy perfume mixed with the faint potpourri odor made Sonsee want to sneeze. Carla was a dear, but she had always overindulged in perfume. Some things never changed.

"Everything's fine," Carla said with a smile. "Your father said you would be arriving by noon. You're early."

"Yes. I couldn't sleep last night and got up at the crack of dawn." Sonsee had missed more than one night's sleep after that trip to Hawaii.

"Well, your father's golfing, of course, but he was planning to be home in time to share lunch with you. Mrs. Delaney is excited about your being here. Do you want to go see her now or—"

"Yes, that's fine." Sonsee turned for the roses. "I brought her these. I drained the water out before I came because I didn't want it to spill in my car."

"Oh, let me get them, dear," Carla said as she took the basket. "I'll see that they're properly watered then bring them up." Flowers in hand, the diligent maid walked toward the formal dining room, which would lead to the kitchen. "Mrs. Delaney is in the green room," she called over her shoulder.

"Okay, thanks."

"And have you had breakfast?"

"Yes. I grabbed something at a fast-food place on the way."

"That won't do anything but clog your arteries," Carla mumbled as she bustled away. She always dressed in the black-and-white maid uniform that did nothing for her figure. Jacques had tried through the years to get her to wear something more comfortable, but she insisted on wearing what was proper. Furthermore, she firmly instructed the rest of the female staff to follow her example.

Smiling, Sonsee ascended the stairs that were covered with a red oriental runner that matched the Persian rug. In seconds, she stood in the wide second-floor hallway and paused outside Mrs. Delaney's door. Sonsee tapped lightly and was surprised when the door swung inward. Taylor stood on the other side, smiling a welcome. He wore the usual jeans, boots, and heavy cotton shirt. His curly brown hair was a bit damp from a recent shower, yet he hadn't shaved in at least two days. The faint shadow added to his appeal.

Oh no, Sonsee groaned inwardly. She couldn't relax. She would have to guard her every move, her every expression.

"I didn't notice your Jeep," she said.

"I parked around back. I had a load of mother's things, and it was easier to get them up the back stairway."

"So how long have you been here?" she asked as he stepped aside for her to enter.

"Oh, not long. About an hour. I stayed at Mom's last night. Carla is supposed to be bringing up breakfast for us in a few minutes. Have you had breakfast?"

"That seems to be the question of the moment. Carla just asked me the same thing."

"We're all trying to fatten you up, Red."

Sonsee looked down at her size five nylon sweats. "Won't work. You know I'll run off every pound. And don't call me Red."

Mrs. Delaney tittered from the brass bed covered with a deep-green comforter, and Sonsee walked to her side.

"You two haven't changed since you were kids," Joy said.

Sonsee settled on the side of the bed and took the hand of one of her dearest friends. *"He* certainly hasn't," she said, jerking her head toward Taylor, who busied himself pulling up the decorative blinds covering the large windows. A shaft of sunlight poured into the room, spilling its cheerful essence upon the feminine decor. The peach-and-green floral wallpaper and matching border seemed to dance with life under the sun's caress.

Taylor continued to move about the room, hovering here and there. Sonsee focused on Joy, whose pale face and reddened eyes attested to a sleepless, tearful night. "Mother isn't handling this very well," Taylor had said Thursday night when he called. Sonsee remembered her own mother's battle with breast cancer, and she wasn't certain she would do any better.

"Well, I'll go see about breakfast," Taylor said from the doorway. "I'm starved."

"You're always starved," Sonsee said.

"Hey, a man needs to eat." He opened the door.

"While you're down there, help Carla carry up some flowers. I brought a large bouquet in a basket. She's putting water in them."

"Will do." Taylor stepped from the room.

"You shouldn't have." Joy's brown eyes sparkled with appreciation. "But I'll enjoy them," she added with an impish grin.

Sonsee reached to plump the pillows, her heart twisting with the sight of Joy's gown lying flat against her chest on one side. "Yes, I knew you'd be glad," Sonsee said, forcing herself not to cry. She needed to be strong, but all these images intensified Sonsee's aching loneliness for her own mother.

"Taylor is restless. I think he's worried about me." The tall, stately woman reached toward the water glass sitting on a bedside table.

"Here, let me get that for you." Sonsee hurried around the side of the bed. The silent cloud that seemed to be hanging over all of them echoed dread whispers about Sonsee's mother's death. She was so unsure of what to say that any activity was welcomed. *Dear God,* she pleaded silently as Joy sipped from her straw, *please spare her life. If for no other reason—for Taylor's sake.*

"Taylor says you got a good report," Sonsee said at last. *But so did Mother.*

"Yes, the doctor says he got all the cancer. I'm going to be taking a mild, oral chemotherapy. Then hopefully it will all be behind us." She smiled up at Sonsee, but the shadow in her eyes attested to her grief. Joy Delaney was a woman who carried herself like a queen. A woman who had exhibited a strength of character and spiritual depth despite her husband's desertion. A woman who had succeeded in steering Taylor away from his adolescent flirtation with life on the wild side. This same woman seemed stricken with her loss, and Sonsee had no words to soften the pain.

"So, Sonsee, how are you and Taylor getting along these days?" she asked out of nowhere.

Blinking, Sonsee took the drinking glass that Joy extended to her. "Fine, I guess," she said, her stomach tightening.

"You know, this cancer business has made me do a lot of thinking and praying, and there are some things I've wanted to say to several people for a long time but have held my tongue."

"Oh?" Sonsee set the water glass on the nightstand beside the oriental lamp. Nervously, she pushed up the sleeves of her pink, hand-woven sweater.

"Yes. Anyway, I've realized I might not be around forever—"

"Don't start talking like that." Sonsee sat on the bed and gripped Joy's hand. "You're going to make it. You've got to."

"Yes, I know," she said with a faint spark of determination in her eyes. "But there are still a few things I want to tell you." Sighing, she weakly placed her other hand atop Sonsee's. "You know I've wanted Taylor to get married for years now. Even though he lives just a few hours from me and he's thirty-six years old, I still worry about whether or not he's eating right, and if he's happy or lonely, and, and,

and." She smiled languidly. "I guess that's normal for a mother, but I think maybe I'd worry less about him if I knew he had a great wife, somebody like you, Sonsee—"

Sonsee gulped. "Aunt Joy—" Without thought, she reverted to the endearment she used in childhood.

"Jacques seems to think you might care more for Taylor than you let on."

"You mean the two of you have been discussing us?" Sonsee said, bewildered.

"No, not really. There's just been a hint or two here and there." Joy grinned. "And then, I guess, seeing you with him today."

"But I've only been here fifteen minutes."

"I know a woman in love when I see one," Joy said. "I've been there. I guess in some ways I still am." A sad glimmer flickered in her eyes.

"Oh?"

"Yes."

Sonsee groped for her meaning but abstained from probing.

"Anyway, I always thought that if any woman was ever perfect for Taylor, it would be you. I would delight in having you as a daughter-in-law. You've already been as good to me as a daughter."

"So, what are you saying—that I should propose?" Sonsee's attempt at humor came out more as a sad plea as she nervously pinched the edge of the polished cotton bedspread.

"Well, have you thought about knocking him down and kissing him?"

Sonsee's head snapped up, and she caught the full force of the laughter spilling from Joy's eyes. "Oh, yeah," she said sarcastically. "I can see him now. He'd probably say something like, 'What's gotten into you, Red? Been drinking too much caffeine lately?'" she said in a deep voice.

Joy laughed outright.

"Oh, Aunt Joy," Sonsee said, restlessly standing. "You know me. This is so unlike me. I've never fallen for anybody like this."

"I always told Jacques that when you fell you'd fall hard."

"I guess you were right. And you know how Taylor feels about marriage after your husband deserted the two of you. I don't think he trusts his own reflection in the mirror."

"Sonsee, I really believe the Lord is ready and willing to heal Taylor's heart if only he'll let Him."

"I know, but..."

"Sometimes, I think my son is so busy trying to make sure nobody else deserts him that he's actually isolating himself and creating the exact situation he fears the most." Joy gazed out the window. "And when I leave this earth, Sonsee, more than anything else, I want to see Taylor happily married."

"Well, you aren't going to leave this earth anytime soon," Sonsee said, wishing she was as certain of her words as she sounded. She had said almost the exact same words to her own mother. Ironically, Sonsee had believed them, only to watch her mother die a year later. Now she didn't know what to think. Certainly Joy Delaney's life was in the Lord's hands, but Sonsee hoped with every fiber of her being that He would spare her.

"Perhaps you're right, but..." Joy struggled to sit up more, and Sonsee stepped to her side to shove another pillow behind her. "I am mortal," she finished. "And I do want to see my son married. I've been praying for years that the right woman would fall in love with him. When I started all that praying, I didn't know if you might be the one, Sonsee, even though I will admit that I had my hopes." She smiled with approval. "But I sure am glad it is you. Now all I need to do is pray that my son will wake up."

"Breakfast is 'swerved,'" Taylor called, pushing the door open before him. He stepped into the room, a solemn "butler" look on his face, a towel over his arm. Taylor held a silver tray, laden with morning delicacies and gazed down his nose. In feigned snobbery, he spoke with a comic French accent. "Today, we are *swerving* blueberry pancakes; sausage petites, browned to perfection; half of a grapefruit; and, of course, the ever-present gourmet coffee." He bent his head to sniff daintily at the ornate, silver pot. "Hazelnut, if my senses do not deceive me. Enough for three."

Joy chuckled. "It's fit for a queen."

"You are a queen, Mother," Taylor said, his heart in his eyes.

Sonsee busied herself preparing the side table for the tray. Soon Carla entered carrying the basket of peach-colored roses, and Joy gasped with delight. "My favorite color!" She beamed, and Sonsee thrilled in seeing some of the shadows scurry from her eyes. "Set them on the dresser so I can see them, will you please, Carla?"

"Of course, Mrs. Delaney."

In a matter of minutes, Sonsee had assisted Taylor's mother to the restroom and back, and eased her into a chair. As the patient began eating her breakfast, Sonsee and Taylor verbally sparred. Joy's countenance took on traces of the joyful glow that usually characterized her. Even though her eyes were still red from tears, she ate a hearty breakfast and insisted on Taylor and Sonsee sharing the coffee.

"There's plenty more downstairs," Taylor said as he poured more coffee for himself and Sonsee. "I wolfed down a couple of pancakes and a sausage or two while Carla was loading mother's tray, but I could probably eat a little more.

I think I'll go downstairs and check out what's left and get some more coffee. Wanta come, Sonsee?" He gave her a meaningful look that said he needed to talk.

"Oh, uh, sure." Sonsee picked up her coffee cup from the windowsill and followed Taylor out of the room. "We'll be right back, Joy," she said, glancing over her shoulder to see the patient give her the thumbs-up sign with an exaggerated wink. Sonsee, biting her lips to stifle the smile, walked out the door and smack into Taylor.

"Whoa there, little filly," he said in his fake John Wayne voice as he steadied her with his free hand.

"Ha, ha," she said dryly.

"Better be careful or you'll spill your coffee." But his ready smile soon turned into a thoughtful frown. "So, what do you think about Mom?" he asked, turning to walk toward the stairway.

Sonsee followed close beside him. "I think she's going to have a long period of adjustment. Looked like to me she had been crying."

"Yes, I caught her in the act when I got here," he said as they began descending the stairs.

"Well, did she open up and share with you or did she do what she usually does and put on a brave face?" Sonsee asked.

"No, believe it or not, she was fairly open with me. She even talked about Father some. She has never really talked with me about his leaving." Taylor sighed. "Oh, we've acknowledged that it knocked us off our feet, but as far as dissecting any feelings or anything—"

"Really? But that's been over twenty years ago."

"I know. I think maybe we both were so hurt over his leaving that the pain was too much to bear, so we just pulled together and did the best we could."

Sonsee shook her head. "I understand. Mother has been gone five years, and Dad and I were numb for the first two years, I think. I can't imagine what it would do to you to be purposefully deserted by someone you thought loved you."

As they arrived at the base of the stairs, Taylor paused and faced her. "I think it's worse than death," he said, his dark-blue eyes churning with clouds of pain. "Even today, as a grown man, I sometimes have to fight long seasons of self-doubt. Something inside me says that if I had been of worth, my father wouldn't have left me."

"Oh, but Taylor, the problem was with him—not you."

"I know that in my head, but sometimes my heart forgets." He gave a defeated smile.

Sonsee, not used to seeing Taylor so vulnerable, gripped her coffee cup and determined not to reach out and stroke his face shadowed by the stubble. Taylor had always been the one who livened things up around this old mansion. But looking into his pain-filled eyes, Sonsee began to wonder if all the humor he bestowed upon the world was really a cover for his pain. She groped for words, wondering exactly how to respond to the plea in his eyes. She could quote all the right Scriptures. She knew all the right "churchy" words. But so did Taylor.

"Are you growing a beard?" she blurted from nowhere.

"No." Rubbing his jaw, Taylor smiled. "Sometimes a cowboy just forgets these things," he drawled, using that John Wayne voice again.

"Would you stop it?" Sonsee rolled her eyes like a bothered sister and began walking through the ornate dining room toward the kitchen.

"Ah, come on, Red, you love it," he teased.

"Don't call me Red," she snapped, her heart pounding in fear that he might indeed realize just how much she loved his badgering.

"Touchy, touchy, touchy," he said from close behind. "How much coffee did you have this morning? You know you don't do well on too much caffeine."

She entered the mansion's spacious kitchen where Carla and another maid busied themselves with kitchen duties. The stainless steel appliances seemed to mock Sonsee. For years, her heart had been as unyielding as steel, now she had foolishly fallen for the one man she knew could never return her love. Taylor was a man who had locked his heart away in a treasure chest and buried it deep in the garden of his soul—so deep that no woman alive could ever touch it. He was too afraid of being abandoned again to really trust anyone. And Sonsee began to suspect that he had yet to allow himself to feel—truly feel—the devastation from his father's desertion.

As he amiably chatted with Carla and conned her into cooking a few more pancakes, Sonsee wondered if she even knew the real Taylor. He put forth a charming, humorous front to all the world, including her. Taylor's winning personality had enhanced his success as a rancher and a businessman. But he was so busy making everyone laugh, Sonsee wondered if he had ever shown anyone his real self.

Nine

～

Odysseus settled on his aging bed and opened his packet from the first orientation meeting. Unceremoniously dumping the contents onto the quilted bedspread, he rifled through the various papers, data, and maps until he found the notepad Mick had given each of them. The pad bore the name and address of denominational headquarters. It and a matching teal pen were provided courtesy of headquarters as a small token of their thanks.

With a wicked smile, Odysseus reached for the can of cola sitting on his nightstand. He took a long swallow of the soft drink and relished the feel of the sweet liquid as it bubbled down his throat. After picking up the pen, he lazily scratched the ears of the nearby tabby cat and began the meticulous quest of drafting his first love letter to Kim Lan. He would use the same method of courtship with Kim Lan that he had with Sophie. After the roses, the love letter. Then the jewelry. Following the jewelry, perhaps roses again. And then another love letter. By the time they boarded the plane to Vietnam, she would be halfway in love with him. The thought left his heart pounding with anticipation, his palms moist, his mind reeling with images of her in his arms whispering those three magical words, "I love you."

Gleeful with anticipation, Odysseus took another long swallow of the cola and paced to the computer desk. Below

Sophie's picture, he pulled out a deep drawer full of mem-
oirs from his relationship with her. Only hours after Sophie's
death, Odysseus had taken his key to her apartment and
removed every item that reflected their relationship—
including the personal love notes she kept in her nightstand's top drawer. Now he searched through the various
souvenirs from amusement parks, the pressed flowers, the
cards, the jewelry boxes, until he came to an envelope near
the bottom of the drawer.

Odysseus' fingers trembled in reaction to the importance
of this envelope. It contained his first love letter to Sophie.
He settled onto the bed and recalled the day she had
received the note. He had mailed the letter to her after their
third date. He had waited with urgency for her reply. Then
Sophie had called, tears in her voice, her words oozing with
admiration. That night, Odysseus had requested a lock of
her hair. He pulled open the loose flap, removed the letter
from the envelope, and gingerly opened it to view a small
plastic bag lying atop the words that had spilled from his
very soul. The bag contained a generous snip of long black
hair that Odysseus had slipped into the letter the day of her
funeral. Sophie had giggled when Odysseus reached to the
bottom layer of her silky tresses and carefully cut a thick
strand. She *said* she was flattered that he wanted some of
her hair. But there was much Sophie had *said* that she did
not mean.

Odysseus' lips pressed together as the band of fury began
to tighten around his soul. He looked across the room to
the hundreds of photos that covered his wall, to the woman
who would be more faithful than Sophie had ever been.
"Kim Lan...oh, Kim Lan," he whispered in a worshipful
chant to the beauty before him. "You will prove to Sophie

that I am of worth. When she looks from eternity and sees us together, she will regret her choices more than ever."

Turning his attention back to the task at hand, Odysseus picked up his pen, eyed the note to Sophie, and began using its contents as a guide to draft the letter to Kim.

Six weeks later, Kim Lan glanced over her shoulder as she hurried from the safety of the recording studio and straight toward the crimson Lincoln Town Car awaiting her under the portico. Modeling agencies always provided a Town Car and driver for their models. Like other supermodels, Kim relied on the car and driver so she wouldn't be forced to maneuver and park her car in the hideous New York traffic. The driver, one of several who worked for the Forman Modeling Agency, rushed around the car to respectfully tip his hat and open the back door for her.

The bright four o'clock sunshine did precious little to dispel the cold wind that had whipped in with the coming of March. And Kim, gripping the small white envelope in her clammy hands, hesitated outside the car despite the wind's biting chill. Like a hunted animal, she once again glanced over her shoulder, then she scrutinized the driver, dressed in his tasteful, blue business suit. The young black man, whom all the models knew as Kenneth, looked back at her, a curious, nonplused expression in his innocent eyes.

A wave of uncertainty washed over Kim. She no longer knew whom she could trust. In the last six weeks, her "secret admirer" had sent a typed love note that had seemed harmless enough, a pair of sterling silver earrings, and another monstrous bouquet of roses—this time white for "the purity of his love," he wrote. The typed note she now clutched had arrived in her mail that morning. Kim Lan had crammed three pieces of her personal mail into her oversized leather bag and planned to read it while waiting in the recording studio's hospitality suite.

Today, Kim began the taping for the animated movie *Fluff*. While she awaited the producer's call, she had opened her personal mail. The first letter had been from her mother. The second note from Sonsee. And this card, with no return address, had been from her "secret admirer." She had only read the note twice, but the words spun a web of terror around her heart:

> Darling,
>
> By now, you know how much I love you. Please say you'll return my love. I cannot live without you, and I'm certain you will not live without me.
>
> Forever yours,
>
> S. A.

While Kenneth curiously observed Kim Lan, images of a popular singer whom a fan murdered flashed across her mind. She wondered if she was destined to that same fate.

What exactly does "you will not live without me" mean? she wondered. *Will he kill me if I don't say I love him?* Kim's stomach tightened. In the last six weeks, she had lost five pounds. Every time she received a new contact from her admirer, her appetite diminished all the more.

"Are you okay, Miss Lowery?" Kenneth asked as she continued to stare at him. "You look like you've seen a ghost." The young man was supposed to be working his way through law school. He was new and had only been driving for the agency about six weeks. Her secret admirer had begun his "courtship" shortly after Kenneth began driving her. Kim knew well the extensive background check the Forman Modeling Agency performed on all their drivers. At Kim's suggestion, they had even used private detective Jac Lightfoot a few times to extensively investigate some applicants from the west. Kim understood that Kenneth Mylo would not have been assigned as her frequent driver if the Forman Agency did not have the utmost confidence in him. But the agency could be wrong. Kenneth's lack of criminal record, his cultured voice, high intelligence, and brilliant future as a lawyer guaranteed nothing. Many times Kim had read the headlines that stated a convicted murderer seemed like the nicest guy in the neighborhood.

Kim's legs trembled. Her palms moistened all the more, despite the chill of early March. Her heart pounded out a hard, even beat in her temples.

"Miss Lowery? Are you going to be ill?" The concern in Kenneth's kind eyes spilled from his voice. "Should I call a doctor? I'll use the cell phone. We could have an ambulance here in minutes."

"No, I'm fine," Kim choked out, rubbing her aching forehead with her shaking fingers. "I—I guess I just need to get back home."

"Yes, of course." Worry lines wrinkling his brow, Kenneth assisted Kim onto the Town Car's supple leather seat and courteously arranged her fox coat out of the door's way.

When he closed the door, Kim fought not to claw her way out of the car and demand a taxi. *That's crazy!* she told herself. *I'd certainly be less safe in a taxi with a total stranger than with a hired driver I know.* As she continued her self-talk, her pulse slowed a bit. *Kenneth has never offered a word out of line*, she reminded herself in a practical manner.

He has been helpful and gallant and pleasant. I cannot start
suspecting every man I come into contact with.

While the Town Car entered the maze of New York traffic
and began the slow trek to Park Avenue, another truth
barged in upon Kim Lan. The time had come to report the
secret admirer to the police...and perhaps think about a
bodyguard. Kim cringed with the thought. She loved her
independence and hated to think she would be forced to
forever be followed by a large male waiting to pulverize
anyone who stepped too near. However, she was certain
that once Ted heard about the latest note he would insist she
immediately hire a bodyguard. He had left for Paris yesterday in order to film the European scenes of a new
movie—a love story with Angela Swift as the leading lady.
He wouldn't return until shortly after Kim left for Vietnam.
However, Ted was scheduled to call tonight. If Kim shared
the contents of the latest note with him, he would probably
arrange a bodyguard himself—and if he didn't, her father
would.

⚬⟋

Mick slumped over the large desk in the southeast Colorado
cabin—his haven when not on the road. His home consisted
of a bathroom, bedroom, kitchenette, and living room with
a rock fireplace. Mick's mother had decorated the cabin in
a homey, yet masculine decor, and he enjoyed the refuge
from his perpetual travel.

The worn oak desk he slumped upon had belonged to
Mick's father, and so had the cabin. It had been Roy
O'Donnel's personal retreat from the world. When Mick
began his work as missions coordinator, his mother had

insisted they repair the old cabin and deed it, along with the surrounding acre of woods, to Mick. The arrangement worked beautifully. Mick had a home, and when he wasn't traveling he was still close to his parents and able to help on the fifteen-acre farm.

He glanced over the list of eleven trip participants: Rhonda Ackers, Doug Cauley, Frank and Pam Cox, Ron and Laci Emerson, Adam Gray, Kimberly Lowe, Sonsee LeBlanc, Melissa Moore, and Caleb Peterson. Mick had spent all afternoon phoning ten of the participants. He succinctly confirmed their travel itinerary to Los Angeles, made sure they were in possession of passports and visas, restated the telephone numbers of the hotels where they would be staying in Vietnam, and mentioned the plans to meet at the Los Angeles International Airport in the international terminal before boarding their midnight flight. Ten of the names bore a check beside them. Only one name remained: Kimberly Lowe.

He hadn't spoken to her since the second orientation meeting, and at that meeting he had only briefly acknowledged her presence. For once, Mick had been able to hold his tongue and act like the mature adult he was. He had barely nodded at her and had been relieved when she followed suit. Now Mick had no choice but to talk with her. This call was part of the duties of his job. He checked his silver wristwatch, a gift from his stepfather, and calculated that it would be five in the afternoon in New York. Pressing his lips together, he picked up the receiver and dialed Kim's number. She answered on the third ring.

"Hello, Kim, this is Mick O'Donnel."

The pause on the other end didn't surprise Mick, and neither did his completely forgetting why he had even called her in the first place.

"Hello," she said at last.

"How are you?" he asked, his heart pounding as if he had been chasing one of his stepfather's obstinate calves that seemed forever bent on escaping the pasture. His Siamese cat, Mao, jumped onto the tidy desk and rubbed his head against Mick's phone hand. Distracted by the call, Mick gently picked up the cat and deposited him on the nearby recliner.

"Well, I'm fine, I guess." She hesitated. "Actually, I ..."

"Is something wrong?" Mick stood as if he could somehow assist her. After another long pause, he felt as if he were dangling on the precipice of a cliff. "Kim Lan? Are you okay?"

"I'm scared," the words trembled out in a fear-filled squeak. The telltale sniffle attested to her tears.

Mick's free hand balled until his fingernails cut into his palm. "What happened?" he asked, his mind conjuring the worst of possibilities.

"I..." More sniffles. "I think I'm being followed—"

"What? Has someone hurt you?" Mick paced as far as the phone's long cord would allow then turned and walked in the other direction. He recalled the news headlines from several years ago. Everyone in America had been aghast when that pop music singer was shot and killed by a deranged fan during one of her concerts. "He—he hasn't hurt me, but..."

"Is he making threats?"

"Well," her voice continued its trembling, and Mick wanted to wrap his arms around her and shield her from the world. "Do you remember the r–roses I, um, asked you about?"

"Yes." Mick persisted in the pacing, the mere smell of the brewing caffeinated coffee seeming to increase his energy.

"Since then I've received a love note, a pair of silver earrings, another bouquet of roses, and now..." She paused.

"Just a minute. I've got the latest note here. I've practically memorized it, but I want to make sure I get it right." The sound of rustling paper affirmed her opening an envelope. "I just got it this morning. It says, 'Darling, By now, you know how much I love you. Please say you'll return my love. I cannot live without you, and I'm certain you will not live without me. Forever yours, S.A.'"

"What does 'I'm certain you will not live without me' mean?" Mick's gut clenched with his own words.

"I know," she said. "That's exactly what I thought."

"And how did he get your address?"

"He always addresses it to the apartment building. The woman at the front desk has been putting them in my mailbox."

"So he knows exactly where you are."

"Yes!" A note of terror vibrated in her voice.

Mick stopped his pacing as a new thought barged in upon him. "Do you have a bodyguard?"

"N–not yet."

Would you consider me—just until the trip? The thought pressed itself upon Mick's mind and almost found its way to his lips, but he forbade himself to voice it. Only with Kim Lan had he been guilty of breaking the self-control he had gained through years of seeking the Lord. And Mick had found a new power for exercising that self-restraint by flinging himself at the feet of his heavenly Father and crying out for strength. However, he *was* free the next two weeks. Given his black belt in karate and experience as a security guard, he could definitely protect Kim Lan.

Today marked the final arrangements for the Vietnam journey, and Mick had no more recruitment duties until after the trip. The odd jobs around the farm had been completed, and he had originally planned to take some time off to relax.

Now he would certainly chew his fingernails to the nubs worrying over Kim Lan's safety.

But it isn't my place to worry about her, he firmly reminded himself. *She isn't mine. She's Ted Curry's.*

"I was hoping it wouldn't affect the trip," she said after an extensive pause.

Mick stopped his pacing and wrinkled his brow in confusion. "Excuse me? I don't think a bodyguard could go on the trip at this point. There's not enough time for getting the visa."

"Oh, sorry. That's not what I meant." She produced a tense chuckle. "My friends are always telling me I throw them conversational curveballs. Sometimes my mind moves along, and I forget to notify the person I'm talking to."

Smiling, Mick decided he liked conversational curveballs. They would certainly keep life interesting.

"What I meant was, I wondered if I should perhaps opt out of going on the trip. If there is someone following me, would that put the rest of the participants in danger?"

Mick momentarily considered her worries. "Actually, I don't think there will be a problem. You'd probably be safer on the trip than staying in the States. Obviously this loon can't follow you to Vietnam."

"I guess you're right," she said, a relieved note in her voice. "Now, if I can only survive two more weeks."

Restless, Mick sat on the edge of the oak desk. Crossing his legs at the ankles, he gripped the base of his neck and observed his blue-eyed cat, who stared up at him through eyes half closed. *Why not ask her if you can volunteer to be her bodyguard?* The second time the notion struck him, it seemed far less impulsive. Nevertheless, Mick once more squelched the idea. Being with Kim Lan for two weeks in Vietnam was going to be nerve-racking enough. He had no business complicating his life by volunteering to be in her presence every day for two weeks before the trip. Yet his human side longed for exactly that: to be near this woman as much as possible; to get to know her better; to fantasize about what might have been...what could possibly be....

"I guess," she continued, "I need to call my secretary and have her immediately arrange a bodyguard, but really, Mick, I'm so worried at this point that I don't know if I would even trust a bodyguard. I became extremely nervous today when I realized the new driver for the modeling agency started about the time all this secret admirer stuff began. I really don't think poor Kenneth is the person behind it all; I just don't trust anyone at this point."

She would trust you. Why not volunteer to help her? Blinking, Mick started to dash aside the preposterous plan once again, but something stopped him, and he wondered if the recurring idea were human or divine. *Lord?* he asked, darting a mental prayer heavenward. *This can't be Your will, can it?* Mick's immediate answer came in the form of an overwhelming impression that he should indeed offer his services to Kim Lan. However, he resisted. He resisted just as vehemently as he had when Kim tried to sign up for the trip. Unquestionably, offering to be her bodyguard would be emotional torture. Yet despite Mick's unyielding nature, the notion that he should still volunteer persisted.

"Well, I'll get on to the reason I called..." he began, desperately trying to suppress the voice of God. Mick was almost forty. Caleb said he was set in his ways, and Mick had decided that if he *was* set in his ways, it was because he liked his ways. There was a certain comfort in understanding oneself and being sure of how to react. Even though he enjoyed the adventure of travel, he was in no way interested in surprises. Spontaneously volunteering to fly to New York and be, of all things, a bodyguard for the one woman he wanted to avoid would without doubt be categorized as a surprise.

Again, he pressed forward with the reason of his call. Concisely, Mick went through the list of confirmations, ending with the telephone numbers of the Vietnamese hotels. Like a bulldog determined not to walk through a doorway, Mick set his heels and refused to extend his services as Kim's bodyguard.

The whole idea is crazy! I just can't do it! he insisted to himself before trying to end the conversation. "I guess I will see you in Los Angeles, then," Mick said, his words stiff with the power of his resistance.

"Mick?" she said dubiously. "When you were at my parents' house eating lunch, I remember your mentioning that you have a black belt in karate and that you worked your way through college as a security guard."

"Yes," Mick answered, his heart beginning to pound with the implications of her words. If this insistence that he should be Kim Lan's bodyguard really were of the Lord, He might very well have impressed her with the same concept. The idea left Mick a tad bit exasperated—almost as if God were ganging up on him.

"I could trust you," she simply said.

The sound of the coffeepot's final stages of brewing seemed to punctuate the moment froth with expectation.

"Are you, um, by—by chance free between now—now and the trip?" she stammered, the quiver back in her voice.

"Yes," he croaked, gripping the edge of the desk. *But don't ask me!*

"And after that?"

"A few days after the trip, I'm scheduled to be in California recruiting for a trip to Romania," he rushed, relieved by the fact of his busy schedule. Surely Kim would want someone who could resume his guard duties once she returned from Vietnam.

"Is there anyway you would consider being my bodyguard between now and the trip—it would just be for two weeks."

"What about Ted? Won't he be disturbed if you hire me?" Mick asked with sarcasm. His self-control slipping, Mick stood to renew the pacing.

"Ted's in Paris."

"Does he know about this secret admirer?"

"Yes."

"Yet he left you for a trip to Paris?" Mick asked incredulously.

"He's filming a movie and couldn't exactly get out of it," Kim defended. "And he doesn't know about this latest note, anyway. Until today, all the communication from the secret admirer has seemed almost harmless. I need to be in New York the rest of this week," she rushed on. "Then after that, I'm free. I was thinking of going to my parents' house the week before the trip. I think they would be more comfortable with my bodyguard if it was someone they already knew. I think they really liked you."

And what about you? Mick wanted to ask, but he stopped himself. He already knew the answer to *that* question, and the truth left him rankled. Kim Lan understood how he felt and knew Mick was aware of how she felt as well. In short, she *did* like him. She liked him far too much for a woman soon to be married. However, she still had the nerve to put him on the spot and ask him to step into the awkward position of being her bodyguard.

"If—if you would agree, Mick, I could call my secretary and have her ch–charter you a plane to New York tonight."

Ten

The cordless phone against Kim's ear shook like an extension of her hands. After leaning against the wall near the massive window as long as her quivering legs would allow, she collapsed onto the leather sofa. Although she had been guilty of many spontaneous decisions in life, this one absolutely topped them all. The request for Mick to be her bodyguard had tumbled from her lips only seconds after the thought sprang upon her mind. Even now she wished she could somehow crawl through the phone and pluck every word she had spoken from Mick's mind.

"When do you need a definite answer?" he asked, a suspicious edge to his firm voice.

Kim bit her bottom lip until it ached, half hoping he would reject the offer and half hoping he would accept. "Well, if you can't, I will try to arrange someone tonight, so..."

"Why are you asking me to do this?" he asked with staccato urgency. "This is ridiculous. I am a grown man. If this is some kind of game you're playing....Blast it, Kim, you know how we affect each other. We're both mature adults. There's no reason to hide the truth. I'm not interested in any adolescent games! Quite frankly, the last thing either of us needs is—"

"Okay, just forget it," she snapped, thoroughly vexed. "The only reason I asked—I don't even know why I asked!" But a soft voice whispered to Kim about the real reason she wanted Mick with her. She was scared—so scared that she could hardly pray. And Mick represented a solid, dependable strength that would give her the assurance she needed. Not only would he physically protect her, but he was also a man of prayer—something Ted didn't profess to be. With Mick's powerful prayer life, he would undoubtedly summon the hosts of heaven to guard her. But instead of understanding her needs, he had expressed his lack of interest in adolescent games.

"I'm not playing games," she ground out. "I'm trying to save my life!"

A brief silence preceded his resigned reply. "I'm sorry..." he began.

"Just—just forget it!" she repeated. "Just forget I ever asked." Abruptly she disconnected the call. Kim stood on unsteady legs and tried not to ponder the extent to which she had once again embarrassed herself with Mick O'Donnel. Given his curt words regarding her request, he obviously thought she was the most impertinent, insensitive woman he had ever met. *Yet he did apologize.* As if she were running from her own thoughts, Kim Lan hastened toward her home office, across from her bedroom suite, and chose to think about the urgent e-mail she needed to send to her six sisters.

The office, another suite within itself, proved far too large for Kim's personal computer and the oversized mahogany desk where she made many of her business decisions. Therefore she had used the east wall to house her expansive collection of antique books. The most valuable books in her collection, such as those autographed by Mark Twain and Nathaniel Hawthorne, resided in a Manhattan museum, where the security system assured their staying put.

The office's west wall was representative of Kim Lan's career. Hundreds of photos and magazine covers, some framed in black and some simply pinned to the wall, lined the wall from floor to ceiling in an attractive arrangement. A full-sized mahogany bed with matching nightstand claimed the corner of the room nearest the massive bathroom. Kim's parents always preferred to stay in her penthouse when they came. For other guests, Kim arranged to have a room on the floor below where numerous furnished suites remained vacant for the sole purpose of residents housing their visitors.

Nervously Kim plopped into the rolling chair and booted up her computer. Within ten minutes, she had composed an urgent, detailed e-mail addressed to her sisters regarding the threat of the secret admirer. On the last line Kim wrote, "Pray!" and quickly pressed her e-mail program's send button. As soon as Marilyn, Melissa, Sonsee, Victoria, Jac, and Sammie received this message, Kim knew one of them would either set up a conference call or she would receive six individual phone calls by the next day.

As she stood and prepared to call her secretary, the elegant black-and-gold telephone on her desk produced a shrill ring. Kim jumped. Her heart pounded as if someone had shot at her. After the last note from the secret admirer, she was so tense that every noise left her shattered. As the phone continued its ringing, Kim stared at it, debating whether or not to answer. If the caller were Mick, she did *not* want to interact with him again. The very thought of her impulsive request in the face of their mutual attraction left Kim's face warming. She was known for being spontaneous yet self-assured, but with Mick she was anything but self assured.

At last she succumbed to the ring. Standing, Kim stepped toward the desk, picked up the ornate receiver, and said, "Hello."

"Have you called the police about all this?" Mick's urgent voice held no hint of their past conflict. His tense tone revealed only impatience and concern.

"Not yet," Kim said, forcing her words to reflect a calmness she was far from feeling. "I have a friend, Jac Lightfoot—she's a private investigator in Denver. I talked to her briefly before I received this latest note. She said at this point there's nothing the police can do other than take a report."

"Well, don't you think you ought to contact the police anyway? They'll probably take this last note for evidence." he said, a rankled ring to his voice.

"Yes. I'm about to have my secretary call them and request that an officer pay me a visit tonight," Kim said in a strained voice. The man was certainly taxing her patience. "I don't want to leave the building again without a bodyguard. It makes me too nervous."

"What about security where you live?"

"I'm covered as long as I'm here. We have security guards and cameras. Only residents and their visitors are allowed inside."

"If you'll arrange to charter the jet, I can be at the airport in two hours," he said bluntly.

Kim Lan's hand tightened on the receiver. "So you've changed your mind, just like that?" She snapped her fingers.

"I think it's what the Lord wants me to do," he clipped out. "And heaven help me, I'm worried sick about you," he said, sounding as if being with Kim Lan were a bitter trial he must endure.

"I told you to forget that I asked," she snapped, her composure wearing thin.

"Well, what you don't know is that I thought I should volunteer before you ever asked," he brusquely admitted.

Sighing, Kim rubbed her forehead. "One thing I want to make clear, Mick," she said firmly. "I am *not* playing games."

"I said I was sorry."

"I just want to make sure you have no doubts about it. I know I'm engaged. Ted Curry is my dream man." She glanced at the enormous diamond claiming her ring finger. "And just because—just because there's a—a quirky attraction of sorts between you and me, that changes nothing between Ted and me. As a *mature adult*," she emphasized Mick's own words, "I've learned to expect occasionally being attracted to men. That's the way God made us—to be attracted to the opposite sex. But I would never act upon it because I am committed to Ted. Right now I see this arrangement between you and me as a business deal only. I need a bodyguard. You're somebody I can trust, and you're available. Period."

"So you think that's all that's between us, then?" Mick challenged in a deceptively soft voice. "Just a boy-girl attraction that always exists between the opposite sex?"

Kim, her palms moistening, searched for an answer—any answer—but her mind produced only images of Mick in her parents' greenhouse; his light blue eyes alight with genuine awe, gently beckoning her to explore the nuances of who he was; her stomach doing flip-flops despite her common sense; and Mick's saying she was lovely.

"Tell me, Kim," he gently taunted, as if he were luring her to take his bait, "do you always react to men the way you've reacted to me?"

She swallowed against a dry throat and her pounding pulse assaulted her temples in a confusing tattoo. As the silence stretched like an ache between them, Kim knew she couldn't lie, but neither could she admit the truth. "That's none of your business," she snapped. "Are you coming tonight or not?"

"Yes."

"Then don't you think you need to pack?" her last words came out on a tense high note.

"Yes."

"Good. I'll call my secretary now. She'll arrange the plane and call you with the details. I'll also have her pick you up at the airport here."

"Fine," he said curtly, then he concisely stated his phone number.

Trembling with a combination of expectation and dread, Kim disconnected the call without ever saying goodbye. In minutes, she had called Virginia Daley with a request for a police officer and also asked her to make the arrangements for Mick. Kim hung up the phone and slumped into the desk's padded chair. Adjusting the belt on her silk lounging pajamas, she extended her feet in front of her and vacantly stared at the wall holding the collage of photos and magazine covers. Feeling as if Mick were peering over her shoulder, Kim wondered if all the exposure and fame she had so craved would result in her demise.

Gradually she began to examine the pictures, one by one, each representing a new step of recognition in her modeling career: at first, the teen magazines; then the women's periodicals; the spokesmodel spots; the magazine advertisements. A few shots were casual, taken backstage at a television studio where she was filming a commercial. At last, Kim Lan's gaze halted on a collection of photos that left her uncomfortable—her first swimsuit issue. Kim cringed when she remember how proud she had been of the shots once they hit the stands. Furthermore, the disappointed glimmer in her father's eyes had done nothing to dampen her sense of accomplishment. *How could I have been so spiritually shallow?* she mused, wondering why she hadn't arranged for her maid to remove the compromising photos and rearrange what was left to fill in the vacancies.

Kim pondered Mick's arrival. Even though she planned for him to stay in one of the guest suites below, he would undoubtedly enter her penthouse at some point—probably tonight. The likelihood that Mick might come into her office was slim, but Kim had precious little desire to take any chance of his seeing the compromising poses hanging on her wall as if they were something she was proud of. Once she had obeyed the Lord and stopped those types of poses, her initial pride had turned to contrite humiliation. *How many men did I tempt to lust after me?* she wondered with renewed regret. A surge of mortification burning her soul, Kim impulsively stood and tore at the first unframed photo— a picture of her in a microscopic white bikini. The image ripped in half. She snatched the rest of it from the wall and wadded it with a vengeance. Gradually she continued the process, even meticulously removing any framed shots from the frames in order to add them to the pile accumulating in the marble trash can.

A year ago Kim would have never dreamed she would be removing the glossies. But a year ago she had only just begun the journey of seeking God with her whole heart— not just showing up at church and being known as "the Christian model"—but asking God to purify her heart so she might become more like Him. Little had Kim known that posing such a request before a holy God would require some radical life changes. The journey had taken her on a voyage of repentance and restitution when needed. But truly seeking God had also begun to gradually change her focus and reverse her thought process on many issues. She had been led to crossroads numerous times, but so far the biggest had been the issue of displeasing God in her choices of modeling opportunities.

"Never again," she mumbled as she padded to her kitchen and opened the narrow storage closet beside the refrigerator. The maid kept a variety of household paraphernalia in this closet, including a red stepladder. Kim grabbed the ladder and walked back to her office. With renewed resolve, she opened the ladder, stepped onto it, and began the meticulous task of removing the images higher up on the wall.

A warm sense of approval flooded over her spirit, filling her with a supernatural peace that the Lord was certainly pleased with her actions. However, upon the heels of that blessing, a disturbing thought marched across her soul. A thought that sent chills down her spine. Kim Lan realized she was experiencing a rare moment of God's voice penetrating her mind.

"Exactly how far are you willing to go for Me? I mean more to you than your career choices, but what about your wealth? Do I mean more to you than your wealth?"

Kim stilled, her hands resting on the final compromising photo. As if a cold, dense fog were settling upon her soul, Kim's spirits wilted with the truth that she could no longer avoid. God did not mean more to her than her possessions. There was too much of the poverty-stricken schoolgirl left within her; too much of the desire for more and more and more wealth in order to prove her worth; too much of the incessant longing for the newest and the latest and the best.

Once again the voice of God impressed itself upon her mind. "Let Me heal your hurts. Place your worth in Me." And upon the skirts of that thought came a snatch of the lyrics to a tune Kim had heard recently on the local Christian radio station: "When will we realize that we must give our lives, for people need the Lord."

As she had seen so clearly with the swimsuit poses, Kim pictured with vivid clarity the new crossroads to which the Lord had brought her. She was not giving her life to draw people to the Lord. She was living her life to amass all the wealth, prestige, and human honor she could acquire. The realization, so ugly, so bitter, left Kim Lan shriveling inside. In order to take the path of righteousness at this crossroads, she would have to undergo a complete reversal of her current thought process. And she wasn't certain she was capable or ready.

Pressing her lips together, she ripped the final photo from the wall, wadded it into a tight ball, and flung it toward the overflowing trash can.

Seven hours later, Kim's personal secretary, Virginia Daley, stopped her sporty white Cadillac under the portico of a high-rise apartment building on Park Avenue. Mick opened his door and stood, resisting the urge to stretch. The flight from Colorado Springs had seemed short compared to international flying, but the hours in the plane had nonetheless affected Mick. He was ready for bed.

Virginia Daley slammed her door, walked around the front of the Cadillac and stepped toward the security guard standing near the extensive sliding glass doors. She motioned for Mick to follow and he complied. The thirty-something Virginia, dressed in a nondescript, taupe pantsuit, was the bone-thin plain sort who did precious little to improve her looks. Her black-framed glasses and the tight bun in her mousy-blonde hair intensified her lack of flair. Mick had noticed that perhaps with a little softening she might be attractive, but for whatever reason, she chose the aloof, no-nonsense look that seemed to match her personality. She was either painfully shy or despised Mick on the spot. He had gotten nothing but brief monotone responses from her all the way from the airport. Virginia seemed the absolute antithesis of Kim Lan. One of the doormen assisted Mick with his luggage, and he swept aside thoughts of Virginia to focus instead upon the woman who awaited him.

Images of Kim Lan and the seemingly senselessness of the Lord's urgency that Mick be her bodyguard sent a mist of loneliness seeping into him. The recent cold rain left the streets shiny with moisture, and the routine sounds of late-night New York traffic took on a forlorn nuance that increased Mick's hollow loneliness within. With a sigh, he peered past the sliding glass doors into the ornate marble lobby and spied a tightly knit group of nationally recognized individuals as they exited what appeared to be a classy restaurant. Part of Mick wanted to crawl into the new Cadillac and kindly tell Virginia to escort him back to the airport. He felt as out of place as a frog in outer space.

"Virginia Daley here for Kim Lan Lowery," the secretary stated concisely as she handed the security guard a small plastic square that resembled a credit card. The tall red-headed guard turned to a metal box attached to the building, inserted the card into a narrow slot, and dragged it along the computerized groove. "Yes, Virginia Daley," he said slowly, reading the blue letters that appeared in the narrow window.

"You're new," Virginia said, her voice as emotionless with the security guard as it had been with Mick.

"Yes. I started only yesterday."

With a grimace, Virginia reached into her leather purse and pulled out a billfold. She unceremoniously flopped it open to reveal her driver's license.

The security guard glanced at the license, nodded, then turned back to the box.

"Miss Lowery did notify the front desk that you'd be arriving. And the gentleman is Mick O'Donnel?"

Mick automatically reached into the pocket of his pleated dress pants and pulled out his own billfold to open it and expose his driver's license.

"Thanks," the redheaded guard said with an apologetic smile as he pushed a black button near the box. In seconds, the glass doors whizzed open and a young Italian doorman rushed out to offer his assistance with Mick's luggage.

With the doorman close behind, Mick shouldered his carry-on bag that held his laptop computer and followed Virginia into the lobby. The sounds of a waterfall mingled with piano music and laughter floated from the restaurant. The faint smells of gourmet food and exotic perfume merged to attest that Mick had stepped into a different world than his own. His thoughts raced to the poverty-stricken home for the elderly in Vietnam—nothing but a row of tattered, connected rooms that opened onto a narrow path behind the baby home. The missions team was specifically assigned the task of improving conditions for those elderly people. He wondered if Kim Lan had ever considered how the rest of the world really lived and if coming face to face with reality would in any way alter her life. She had undoubtedly grown up in the lap of luxury, considering the size and opulence of her parents' estate. Mick doubted that she could even imagine the desperation of poverty.

So here I am, in the midst of abundance, volunteering to be a bodyguard for a celebrity model—the last thing I ever dreamed of doing. Mick shook his head in bewilderment. There was no denying that the Lord was in this...this scheme of sorts that seemed to be unfolding before him with one surprising turn after another. But for his life, Mick could not make sense of it.

Virginia marched toward the elevators, and Mick followed with the doorman in his wake. While waiting for the door to open, the secretary whipped a small cell phone out of her purse and dialed a number. "Miss Lowery, we're on our way up," she said, her voice softening a bit. As the doors hissed open, Virginia said her goodbyes to Kim and plopped her phone back into her opened purse. Silently they boarded the elevator, and Virginia extended the same plastic card she had presented at the door. This time she inserted it in a groove on the wall and slid it downward. The doors hissed to a close and she punched the "P."

In the time the elevator took to ascend twenty-five stories, Mick relived his recent phone conversations with Kim Lan. He scoffed at himself for trampling every resolve to remain self-controlled, for how little time he wasted in blatantly stating exactly how he felt about her—again. *So much for subtle maturity and self-control,* he thought sarcastically.

At last they stood outside Kim's door and waited while Virginia rang the doorbell. The knob rattled, and Kim swung the door inward. With a brief, pleasant greeting, Virginia marched into the apartment, and Mick remained in the short hallway, drinking in the image of the woman before him. An image of beauty, of fear, of vulnerability. Even though Kim never moved, Mick felt as if she'd flung herself into his arms and trusted her precarious plight to his protection.

"Hi," he said his arms aching to pull her close, to comfort her, to protect her from the evil force now nipping on her heels. With a smile he hoped held at least a hint of reassurance, he said, "Well, I'm here."

"Yes," she returned then bit her bottom lip. Tears pooled in the corners of her dark, exotic eyes. "I'm scared," she said through an insecure smile.

"I know," Mick said, putting as much empathy in his expression as was in his voice. "But I'm here now, and you're going to be okay."

"Thanks," she said in a way that made Mick feel as if he were God's answer to every female dilemma. And he wondered just how many days would lapse before he succumbed to the urge to comfort her at a closer range.

Eleven

Three days before the trip to Vietnam, Mick arose at five in the morning and donned his jogging gear. Running was a way of life for him, a means to expend some energy as well as to keep him fit and give him a solid hour to think and meditate upon the Lord. During his stay with Kim and her parents, Mick had extended his jogging time to two hours: forty minutes to the nearby church; forty minutes for devotions; and forty minutes back. Kim Lan never rose before seven. Her parents' spacious house was equipped with a dependable security system. And the relief of knowing Kim had received no more gifts or notes from her supposed secret admirer added to the peace of leaving New York behind. Both of them were much more relaxed. Kim had assured him she felt perfectly safe with his rising early and exiting the premises for a couple of hours.

As Mick jogged up the dark country lane just north of Boston, he steadily neared the historic church and enjoyed the fresh morning smells of the cold countryside covered in maples. An icy March breeze stung his cheeks, and the diminishing snow on the roadside was an ever-present reminder that in the East winter weather was still a threat. Despite the snow and the cold temperature, Mick's heart was warm with the presence of the Lord. Worshipful piano music filtered into his senses through the earplugs of his portable CD player attached to the waistband of his red sweatpants. A fluid rendition of a nineteenth-century hymn filled Mick's heart with assurance of God's guidance in his life: "'Tis so sweet to trust in Jesus, just to take Him at His Word; just to rest upon His promise; just to know, 'Thus saith the Lord.'"

Mick pondered these words as he jogged to a paved parking lot and approached a white-frame church that dated from the early nineteenth century. Mr. Lowery had commented over dinner last night that as the years had progressed the classic church with its white steeple had been enlarged and remodeled without the historic feel and qualities being altered. Last Sunday, Mick had asked the pastor's permission to perhaps use a room in the church for his private devotions. The young gentleman had informed Mick that the church had recently refurbished an unused room, changing it into a chapel that was always open for anyone's use.

Mick, now cloaked in the inky shadows of the predawn countryside, paused outside the chapel's door long enough to turn off the CD player, remove the earplugs, and catch his breath. In a reverent spirit, he stepped into the small chapel that smelled of new carpet. He reached for the light switch and pressed against a knob to turn on the lights, pausing to adjust the knob until the light was sufficiently dim. The room, resembling a hospital chapel, featured a short, highly polished altar gleaming at the foot of a cross that hung upon the wall. Three mini pews graced each side of the room, and an aisle ran down the middle. The silk ferns on wooden stands near the cross complemented the rich hues of the emerald carpet and provided the only decor in the whole room.

Without pausing, Mick walked toward the altar, laid his CD player on it, and shed his jogging jacket. After retrieving the worn Bible from his coat pocket and laying it next to the CD player, he pressed the appropriate buttons on the player.

The beginnings of "'Tis So Sweet to Trust in Jesus" once again wove a melody of worship through his heart. He closed his eyes and began to meditate upon the Lord—His righteousness, His holiness, His love. After several minutes of worshipful reflection, Mick began to beseech the Father for more of the self-restraint that had been imparted to him during the last week and a half.

While in New York, the time as Kim Lan's bodyguard had proven much less emotionally stressful than Mick had ever imagined. Given Kim's hectic schedule, the two of them had precious little time to interact personally. Mick had avoided eye contact as much as possible and simply stood by while Kim recorded for that animated movie about a skunk...while she met with her agent...while she interacted with her secretary, Virginia "no personality" Daley...while she met with her financial consultant. And Mick had learned during those seven days in New York that Kim Lan Lowery was much more than a pretty face; she was an astute businesswoman who had drastically increased her earned fortune through wise investments.

Yet the four days at her parents' serene country estate had proven a thousand times more stressful than his stay in New York, and Mick once more began to wonder how long he could constrain himself against taking Kim into his arms. Under the watchful eyes of her parents, Mick and Kim had relaxed in each other's company and Mick's bodyguard job now smacked of a growing friendship, except Mick had never wanted to kiss a friend the way he wanted to kiss Kim Lan.

"Oh, Lord," he groaned, rubbing his eyes, "why have You done this to me?" As the tension between him and Kim Lan had grown over the last few days, Mick had asked the Lord that question at least a dozen times. Mick could never deny the supernatural urge that had driven him to call Kim back and tell her he would indeed be her bodyguard. There was no doubt in his mind that he was in God's perfect will. But Mick's certainty stopped there, for he saw no sense whatsoever in the Lord torturing him by putting him in the presence of an unattainable woman with whom he could fall in love. A woman so far from his world it was ridiculous. A woman who would never consider marrying the likes of him.

For even though Kim Lan's relationship with the Lord seemed far deeper than Mick had originally assumed, Mick had seen that she was still too enamored with her own wealth, still too focused on the material. He could never marry a woman with such a focus. Even if Kim waltzed into the chapel and announced she had broken her engagement with Ted, who epitomized everything she valued, Mick would not pursue a serious relationship with her, despite his heart's opposing cry. He couldn't. His call was for missions. If he ever married, he needed a wife who would share his life focus of sacrificing for the poor and needy, not pursuing wealth and luxury.

Developing a relationship with Kim Lan seemed nothing short of pure insanity. Nonetheless, that is exactly what he felt they were doing—deepening their relationship. And Mick, despite himself, was growing to like what he saw on the inside of Kim Lan even more than he liked the way she looked. Despite her material focus, Kim Lan Lowery was a delightful, intelligent, warm-hearted woman.

Mick placed his elbows upon the altar, leaned forward, knitted his brows, and desperately tried to pray. Instead he remembered the times in recent years he had beseeched God for a wife. Mick had at last decided at the age of thirty-five that if God wanted him single for life, then that would be fine. He had stopped wondering about "her." He had stopped requesting that God put "her" into his life. Instead,

Mick had started pouring his energy into an intimate relationship with God. He found a new fulfillment and a power
for living he had never known before. He had not been
looking for a wife when Kim Lan Lowery had shown up at
that church service and left him gaping.

Kim is the one you will marry. The heavenly thought
barged in upon Mick's wandering mind and sent him bolting
upright from the bowed position. The CD player spilled forth
the final, fluid notes that wove a sacred challenge into his
heart: "Jesus, Jesus, how I trust Him! How I've proved Him
o'er and o'er! Jesus, Jesus, precious Jesus! O for grace to trust
Him more!"

"But, Lord!" Mick whispered, aghast with what he thought
God was telling him, "I don't see how! She's everything I'm
not! We're poles apart!" Impatiently Mick waited for some
form of communication from the Lord only to be answered
by silence in his soul and the beginnings of a worship
chorus from the CD player.

Abruptly Mick grabbed his trusty King James Version and
flopped it open to the marked place in the Old Testament
where he had stopped reading the day before. Sometimes
when the Lord impressed nothing upon his spirit, Mick
found that divine guidance and confirmation would come
from the Word of God. While Mick had never randomly
opened the Bible and taken the first verse he read as his
communication from God, he did often find that the Lord
spoke specifically to him through his daily reading. Yesterday he finished Ecclesiastes. *Today I'll be in...* Mick
scanned the page. *The Song of Solomon!*

His eyes widened in disbelief. "Oh, get a grip!" he barked.
"The last thing I need to do is read The Song of Songs!" Frustrated, he snapped the Bible closed and stood. Mick checked
his watch. He had only been in the chapel fifteen minutes,

and six o'clock was fast approaching. Instead of feeling worshipful, he now felt torn inside and more than a tad bit exasperated. He donned his jacket, inserted the CD player and
Bible into his pockets, and covered his head with the jogging
coat's hood. In a matter of seconds, Mick trotted out of the
church's parking lot and onto the side of the two-lane
highway.

Odysseus peered over the four-foot stone wall that encom-
passed the rolling pasture behind him. His gut clenching
with rage, he watched as Mick O'Donnel trotted up the road.
Mick's early, he thought. *But I'm ready*. In the weak morning
light, Mick appeared only a distant snatch of red moving
within the tunnel of maples that covered the narrow
highway. Odysseus' fingers tightened around the barrel of
the 30.06 rifle, and he gradually raised it, laying the barrel
against the gray wall of rocks.

Fresh fury coursed through his veins like a river of molten
lava, and his right eye twitched with the force of his emotions. His hopes had soared when Kim Lan had spoken to
him at the last orientation meeting. She had even smiled into
his eyes and left him more enamored than ever. He had
come away from the meeting anticipating the time they
would spend together in Vietnam, certain that by the trip's
end she would return his love. Now she was wasting her
time with Mick O'Donnel.

Kim Lan is mine, not Mick's! For some reason, Mick had
recently been with her every day. Odysseus hated the way
she looked at Mick—the same way Sophie had looked at
that lawyer jerk. As much as he could recall, Odysseus had

never seen Kim Lan look at Ted Curry that way. Ted had seemed no threat at all. Odysseus had been sure that once Kim realized just how much he cared, she would certainly leave Ted behind. But now she seemed oblivious to Odysseus' carefully planned love notes, flowers, and gifts. Instead, she was focused on *Mick*.

A new surge of rage spun through his soul like an angry tornado deviously devouring the countryside. Originally Odysseus had planned to woo Kim on the trip to Vietnam. But that had all changed. There would be no trip to Vietnam after he killed the leader.

Odysseus had never fathomed himself a killer—not until Sophie's accident. The accident that ended Sophie's life. The shock of her death had left him initially numb. Then terrified. Finally, distraught. A taste of that distress wove through Odysseus, like a single tendril of smoke from a lone stick of incense. The incense of scorned love. He remembered the hours following Sophie's death...the fear that he would be linked to the accident...the necessary trip to her apartment to rid it of every vestige of his presence...the funeral where he was comforted, yes, comforted by well-meaning friends.

The whole ordeal had taught Odysseus so much—mainly that he could kill and survive if necessary. With cold determination, he peered through the gun's scope until he placed the jogging red figure in the center of the crosshairs. As he waited, his breath created a white cloud with each exhale. Odysseus' gloved finger touched the trigger, and he trembled with expectation.

As Mick continued in his steady stride, he desperately wanted to shove the images of the last fifteen minutes from his memory. Mick scanned the rolling Massachusetts countryside, the pastures divided by rock walls in shades of gray. Mr. Lowery had told him the walls, standing from one foot to four feet, had been present for approximately 200 years. Farmers had dug the rocks out of the ground in order to plow the rich brown soil. The rocks became markers for landowners and still served as boundaries today. Despite his attempt to enjoy the scenery now caressed in the faint glow of the approaching dawn, Mick's mind began to produce a disturbing chant that kept perfect rhythm with his footfalls:

Kim is the one you will marry.
Kim is the one you will marry.
Kim is the one you will marry.

And followed by these words came the lyrics to the song that had stirred his soul: "'Tis so sweet to trust in Jesus, just to take Him at His Word; just to rest upon His promise; Just to know, 'Thus saith the Lord.' Jesus, Jesus, how I trust Him! How I've proved Him o'er and o'er! Jesus, Jesus, precious Jesus! O for grace to trust Him more!"

The jumbled thoughts that followed intensified Mick's confusion and left a haunting question: *If the Lord is trying to tell me that I will marry Kim, can I trust Him?* The song continued to weave its melody through his thoughts, *O for grace to trust Him more!*

"Father, I need Your grace," Mick said, his throat tight. "Because I'm blowing it on this one. I just don't see how..." For years, Mick had prided himself on his logic, on his ability to prove God's existence through fact alone with his extensive knowledge of Scripture. But as he jogged along the side of that country road with the dawn creeping upon the horizon and dispelling the shadows, Mick examined himself to see that he had leagues to go in blindly trusting the Lord in his personal life. He had firmly placed his trust in the Lord for his safety in foreign countries. But somehow that seemed reasonable for God, mainly because divine protection fit perfectly with Mick's call to missions. He had trusted the Lord for the astounding supply of necessary funds to enable a mission trip and even build a needed hospital in Africa. Once again, those things had seemed so in tune with what was already in the Bible that Mick could readily muster sufficient trust.

But as he trotted forward, Mick began to realize that none of those issues involved leaping out on faith in his personal relationships. Furthermore, the whole idea of God telling plain ol' Mick O'Donnel—Caleb's older "stuck in the rut" brother—that he would marry a supermodel was ludicrous. A burst of incredulous laughter spewed from him. Either Mick was losing it, he no longer knew how to discern the voice of the Lord, or God had a wild sense of humor!

"No way!" he mumbled under his breath. He would admit his need of deeper faith in God's controlling his personal life, but actually believing that he would marry *the* Kim Lan Lowery just could not be an issue of trusting God. "This is about staring the facts straight in the eye," he resolved aloud. "It won't happen."

<hr />

From behind the wall of rocks, Odysseus adjusted the rifle until the barrel was even with Mick's head, bobbing up and down with his every step. With steady resolve, he peered through the scope until Mick's tall form once again appeared in the middle of the crosshairs. A cardinal's morning serenade echoed across the countryside and belied Odysseus' murderous motive. A tiny thread of regret twined its way from deep inside him and surfaced in his thoughts. He hated having to kill Mick because he had always been so kind. But nothing—no kindness, no ties of relationship—would change his plans. He had been instrumental in one death and had lived despite the guilt. He could do it again.

Watching Kim with Mick made him sick. Sick and betrayed. Betrayed and furious. He ground his teeth as his gloved finger quivered against the trigger. "Tell Sophie I said 'hello,' missionary boy," he sneered before pressing his finger against the trigger. The gun exploded, kicking against his shoulder with the force of its power. And Mick O'Donnel hit the ground.

Sonsee LeBlanc rolled over in bed and ferociously punched her pillow for the third time in fifteen minutes. She had slept precious little the night before, and the last thing she needed was to awaken before five. She opened her eyes to peer at the glowing red numbers on her digital clock. Four-fifty-four glared at her. With a frustrated growl, she sat up and rubbed her gritty eyes.

She had left the clinic yesterday and driven straight to the LeBlanc mansion, where she had helped Taylor's mother pack all her things and prepare to go back to her home. This morning Taylor would arrive, and he and Sonsee would take Joy Delaney to her home on the outskirts of New Orleans. By noon, Sonsee planned to be on the road back to Baton Rouge, where she would begin packing for the trip to Vietnam.

Reflecting over her busy day, Sonsee groaned. "What a day to wake up so early," she moaned, swinging her feet out of bed. She stood, reached above her head, and stretched. A drowsy yawn followed. She turned on the lamp and a soft glow fell across the room where she had grown up. The brass bed sat in the middle of a spacious room filled with memorabilia from Sonsee's life. Carla had removed numerous items from storage and redecorated the room after Sonsee graduated from college and got an apartment of her own. Sonsee's dollhouse claimed the corner beside the windows that were covered with lace sheers. Her high school bulletin board, filled with class pictures, hung on the wall beside the cherry dresser. On the wall near the marble fireplace, hung her first bicycle. The highboy, which matched the cherry dresser, held an abundance of Sonsee's framed photos from infancy to college graduation.

Sonsee padded toward her dresser and carefully picked up the ornate silver hand mirror that had once been her mother's. She looked into the mirror at her own features then glanced toward the nearby photo of her lovely mom framed in silver. Sonsee took more after her father than her mother, although she did possess her mom's green eyes.

Never considering herself beautiful in the classic sense, Sonsee had been stunned when Ted Curry made his advances. After her initial no, the actor had even called her at work. When Sonsee finally point blank asked him what he wanted with her when he was dating Kim Lan, Ted told her that she fascinated him because of her independent air.

"You're a woman who knows what she wants in life," Ted had said with a sensual nuance that traveled over the phone as if he had practiced the line a hundred times.

"Well, I don't want you! And you're going out with one of my best friends!" Sonsee had rudely insisted, much to the vain actor's surprise. "I'm going to tell Kim Lan—"

Ted had laughed outright. "She won't believe you!"

Sonsee, putting down the mirror, sighed in aggravation. Ted had been right. Kim Lan didn't believe her.

"Oh, Mom, what do I do now?" Sonsee sighed, peering at the lovely blonde woman who smiled as if she didn't have a care in the world. Sonsee's stomach clenched, her eyes burned, her lips trembled. Five years. Five whole years had passed since her mother's death. Some mornings, when Sonsee awoke, the pain seemed fresh and the loss like a nightmare.

This morning proved one of those times. Sonsee, aching to talk with her mother, lovingly stroked the photo. Life's complications weighed heavily upon her—the issues with Kim and Ted...the problems with Taylor. Sonsee's insomnia had been largely caused by the prospect of having to spend the morning with Taylor. She would love to share with her mother the overwhelming feelings of dread and anticipation that had tormented her all night. Frantically, Sonsee wondered how much longer she could conceal her feelings from Taylor. They knew each other too well to hide much from the other for very long. Sonsee cringed when she thought of his arrival in a few hours.

"What would you tell me to do about Taylor?" she whispered to the photo, then answered her own question. "You'd probably tell me to pray about it." Sonsee studied the picture and contemplated the hours she had already spent beseeching God to influence Taylor to return her love. After her mother's death, Sonsee had learned to pray in a way she had never prayed before. She had leaned on God more during those painful months than ever. Her six sisters had even dubbed her the "prayer warrior" among them. Granted, she had seen some miraculous answers to prayer. However, she was beginning to wonder if God was even listening to this request about Taylor. Recently, she had even speculated that she might be praying outside the will of the Lord. Sonsee pondered the possibility that God's will for her might not include Taylor. Restlessly, she debated if she would be willing to relinquish her hopes of marrying him to the Lord and be satisfied with remaining single for life. Two years ago, she would have probably agreed and been content. But that was before she had realized her love.

With a defeated sigh, she made a trip to the restroom, pulled her straight hair into a no-nonsense ponytail, and donned her flannel robe. Carla, who lived at the mansion, usually started her day by five in order to accommodate Sonsee's father, who liked breakfast at six. Perhaps the coffeemaker would already be percolating.

As Sonsee descended the wide stairway and neared the kitchen, Carla's freshly brewing coffee teased her senses. She walked through the ornate dining room and opened the swinging kitchen door, expecting Carla to greet her with a ready smile. Instead, Taylor sat at the round wrought iron table by the window, his demeanor that of a man deeply troubled.

Twelve

An explosion pierced Mick's disturbing thoughts. A whizzing bullet, narrowly missing his head, ripped through the air like a tiny missile. Pain, like the deep cut of a razor, tore at his left ear before he had time to duck. Instinctively, Mick tucked his body into a tight ball and rolled. He slid to a halt amid a heap of snow as another bullet, slicing through the air, menacingly pelted the snow only inches from his leg. His heart pounded in panic as warm blood trickled down his cheek and plopped onto the snow, marring the pure white with sickening scarlet droplets. Mick reached for his throbbing ear, wondering if he would find the top half gone. The brief examination proved the ear still intact—most of it, anyway.

Like a hunted animal, he scouted the surroundings and searched for a place to take cover. His only option was to climb behind the wall of gray rocks several feet away. Another loud shot splintered the maple's bark, just behind him. The shots seemed to be coming from across the road, about a hundred yards south. Whoever was shooting was serious—dead serious—and Mick wondered if climbing over the rock wall would expose him as an even better target.

The sound of a racing vehicle preceded the screeching of tires by only seconds. Mick stared in shock at the black Jaguar as it turned sideways in the road and ground to a shuddering halt only feet away. Kim Lan, gesticulating wildly, rolled down her window and screamed, "Get in!"

Another bullet, tearing away an overhead limb, seemed to dare Mick to dash for the Jaguar. His throat tightening, Mick jumped to his feet, hunched over and began a zigzagged journey to the nearby vehicle. He lunged into the car, barely slamming the door before Kim hurled the vehicle into gear. The tires squealed in protest as she stomped against the accelerator and the car lurched forward. In seconds they were racing north.

Mick's mind whirled with the danger of the last few minutes, and he stared at Kim Lan who seemed in worse shape than he was in. Her arms visibly shaking, she gripped the steering wheel so tightly her knuckles were white. She wore the casual jeans and sweater from the night before. Other than that, she had on her leather coat along with a pair of mink house shoes, and her hair was still mussed from sleep.

"Are you okay?" Mick asked, his mind numb with reaction.

Kim silently nodded and produced a telltale sniffle. "Are you?" She glanced toward him, her teary gaze momentarily focusing on his injury.

Mick reached to feel the blood freely flowing from the top of his ear. "Is my ear still there?" he asked, gingerly fingering the wound.

"Looks like it's been nicked," Kim said, her voice thick with tears.

Mick pulled down the vanity mirror and examined the lesion.

"Here's a tissue," she said, pulling one from the pocket of her leather coat.

"Thanks. I wouldn't want to mess up the Jag." Mick's feeble attempt at humor didn't succeed. He took the tissue and awkwardly blotted the stinging wound.

"I c–couldn't care less about th–this car right now," Kim said, her voice wobbly.

"What in the world were you doing out at this hour?"

"I—" She gulped. "I came for you. I think—I think the Lord woke me up. I was—was asleep and I sat straight up in bed, wide awake, and I immediately knew y–you were in some kind of t–trouble. I threw on my clothes and rushed to your room just in case you were there instead of out j–jogging. When you weren't there, I grabbed my keys and jumped into the car." She cast a wide-eyed glance toward Mick as a lone tear trickled down her pale cheek. "When I heard the shot and saw you drop, I thought—I thought you were—were dead."

"Me, too," Mick rasped. He slumped into the leather seat, his extremities violently trembling with the reality of the attempted murder. A tendril of nausea twirled through the pit of his stomach as he tried to fathom the reason for the attack. "No one has ever shot at me," he mumbled in disbelief.

"But you've never been my bodyguard before, either," Kim said grimly. She picked up her cell phone from its holder on the dashboard. "Call 911. We'll turn around in a minute and head for the police station in Boston. It's not far from here. But maybe a highway patrol can spot the gunman before he gets away."

Sonsee stepped into the white kitchen and carefully schooled her features into a bland mask. She certainly didn't expect to see Taylor sitting at the table by the window. Her heart, bound by love, hammered with the forlorn image he presented.

"Hi," Taylor said, smiling faintly at Sonsee.

"Hi," Sonsee returned, walking across the spacious kitchen toward the coffeemaker. Despite the shock of seeing Taylor, she maintained a calm expression. "I wasn't expecting you for another two hours." She reached into the glass-front cabinet and retrieved her favorite mug, decorated in a blue-striped southwest theme.

"Well, I changed my plans and drove in late last night. I sneaked in the back and slept in the room next to Mom's. Uncle Jacques gave me a key when Mom first got here. That way it's more convenient for everyone."

Sonsee poured her coffee and, gripping the cup, walked toward the table. "So you couldn't sleep either?" she asked, settling across from him.

"Oh, I snatched about four hours." He looked into his coffee cup and an awkward silence settled between them.

Nervously, Sonsee shifted in her chair and cleared her throat. She sipped the strong black coffee and savored the aroma. "You always make coffee the way I like it," she said, yet her attempt at lighthearted conversation seemed flat.

Taylor nodded in agreement and looked out the window onto the grounds well lit by strategically placed decorative lights. Sonsee followed his gaze and remembered the adolescent years and early adulthood when she and Taylor had often recruited a group of young people from church for a game of volleyball or table tennis or just to hang out and watch a movie and eat popcorn.

She recalled the Christmases Taylor and his mother had spent with Sonsee's family. Sonsee's mother, forever warm-hearted, had always treated Taylor and his mother like part of the family, even though Jacques was related only by the ties of his deceased first wife. However, Jacques' three children by his first marriage—Sonsee's half-siblings—all resented

Taylor just as much as they resented Sonsee and her mother. They never learned that Jacques paid Taylor's way through college, and it was for the best. Thankfully, Sonsee had managed to avoid those three for a year now.

With a sigh, she relived the recent years when she and Taylor entered their thirties and their friendship had matured. And sitting across the table from him now, she clearly saw that the reason she had always been able to steer clear of any romantic attachment was because her heart belonged—had always belonged—to Taylor Delaney.

"A penny for your thoughts," she said, then sipped the steaming coffee again. "You seem worried. Is it your mom?"

He peered at her, his dark blue eyes lacking the merry glimmer that always guaranteed he would be the life of the party. "I think Mom's going to be okay," he said, toying with the spoon near his cup. "I've done a lot of praying, and I really have a deep peace about her."

Sonsee nodded, wishing she could say the same. After losing her mother to breast cancer, she didn't know how to feel about Joy. "I've certainly prayed for her."

"I know you have, Sonsee." He leaned back in his chair and adjusted the collar of his denim shirt. "You've been nothing but great to my mom. I could never repay you enough." He hesitated and deliberately spoke the next words. "I guess maybe I could repay you by convincing you not to waste your love on me. I'm not worth it, you know," he said, his words barely audible.

Sonsee swallowed hard.

"What?" she gasped, desperately hoping she had misunderstood him.

For his answer, Taylor solemnly stared at her, and the silent communication that flashed between them left Sonsee's eyes stinging.

"You—you know?" she asked, her voice trembling.

Once more, he didn't answer, but rather observed her with that pathetic, lonely glint in his eyes.

"But—but h–how. How did you find out? Your mother—did she—did she tell you?"

He shook his head. "No, you told me, Red." Restlessly Taylor scooted back his chair, and it produced a scraping noise against the white Italian tile. He stood and walked to the nearby floor-to-ceiling window. His back turned, Taylor crammed his hands into his pockets.

Her head spinning with the implications of Taylor's words and actions, Sonsee prayed for the strength to calmly walk out of the kitchen. Unlike Kim Lan, who had her moments of spontaneity, Sonsee was known for her cool composure. True, she usually released her self-restraint when she was in the company of friends, and she enjoyed incessantly teasing her six sisters and participating in the never-ending banter with Taylor. But overall, she exercised a strong hand of control over her emotions. Or so she thought. Sitting at the kitchen table watching Taylor as he labored for words, Sonsee wondered if she had deceived herself.

"You might be able to come across as Miss Practical with everyone else," he said at last. "But you've never been that great at hiding your feelings from me." Taylor turned to her, his face seemingly anguished by his own words.

"So—so what are you saying?" she whispered. Her lips stiff, Sonsee gripped the hot coffee cup until the heat burned into her palms.

"I'm saying…"

"Why did you even tell me you knew?" The question erupted from her very soul. "If—if you don't—don't—aren't—"

"Sonsee, you know I can't! That's the whole point! I can't!" He closed the distance between them and gripped the top of the green wrought-iron chair. "And I didn't think it was fair to you to let you think and—and hope."

"What do you mean, you can't?" Sonsee asked, her temper, the only defense left to her, flared in response to Taylor's stating exactly what she feared the most.

"I'm telling you that my heart is as hard as a rock," he said in a tortured voice. "I can't fall in love."

"You can't or you're just so stubborn you won't?" Sonsee stood, and the hot coffee spilled onto her hand.

"I've tried, Sonsee. I've tried ever since Hawaii. With God as my witness, I *have tried.*"

The sincerity of his words dampened the flames of her fury. "You've known since Hawaii?" she whispered.

"I suspected then." Once again, he turned from her. "But by the time Mom had her surgery, I was certain."

Sonsee stared at his back, at the tall, lean lines of his physique. Somehow, she had envisioned Taylor one day discovering her love, wrapping his arms around her, and declaring he had felt the same for years. All Sonsee's prayers for a commitment from Taylor mocked her.

"I even toyed around with the idea of proposing, Sonsee." He propped his arm against the windowframe and rested his forehead against his arm. "But that wouldn't be fair to you. I'm just like any other man alive, I guess. I would enjoy the physical intimacy of marriage. But—"

"That's all it would be."

Slowly, he turned to face her. "I have always cared for you—as if you were my sister. But the kind of love a marriage requires..."

"It all goes back to your father leaving you and your mom, doesn't it?"

He didn't break her gaze.

"It's not that you can't love; you're *afraid* to love." Sonsee looked at the coffee sloshed on the table and felt as if she hadn't slept in weeks. The inner turmoil that her newfound love had stirred within drained her of all energy—emotional, mental, and physical. Recalling the last few weeks, Sonsee couldn't remember one night when she had been blessed with a full night's rest. *Love...* Sonsee had always thought that when she fell in love the experience would be like those in the storybooks. Boy meets girl. He proposes. She accepts. And they live happily ever after. Instead, love had ushered in misery.

"I love my mother," he said mechanically. "And I love my work."

"What about my father?" Sonsee exploded. "He has done more for you than—"

"I care very deeply for your father, Sonsee," Taylor said evenly. "I think I do love him, but—" As he groped for the right words, his eyes filled with tears, and Sonsee blinked in disbelief. She couldn't remember ever seeing Taylor cry except briefly at her mother's funeral. Instead, Taylor had always been more than ready to make everyone laugh. He was the class clown in school and never lacked for friends. To look at him interacting with people, anyone would think Taylor Delaney didn't have a care in the world. But now Sonsee wondered if he would ever let anyone really know him.

"Well, I guess that's that, then," she said, exercising every scrap of restraint she could muster.

"I'm sorry," he said, his eyes clouding with guilt.

Carla swept into the kitchen and stopped in her tracks at the sight of Sonsee and Taylor. "You two are certainly early birds this morning," she merrily quipped.

Sonsee tried to smile but failed miserably. Taylor produced a strained, "Good morning, Carla." The maid eyed them curiously and turned to her task of creating her famous blueberry pancakes.

"I'm leaving for Vietnam on Monday," Sonsee said. "And I need to get back home early today and start getting ready, so…I won't stay long. I'll help your mom get packed and then head on back to Baton Rouge."

"But she expected you to go with us to her house and have lunch. She was going to order pizza."

"I know, but I can't," Sonsee said woodenly. Forcing herself not to run, she turned and walked toward the swinging doorway. Once she entered the haven of her room, she would allow the tears to fall. But not now…not now. Biting her lips, she rushed for the broad stairway.

That afternoon Kim glanced over her shoulder as she walked the short distance from her parents' back door to the hothouse. She had been glancing over her shoulder all day, even inside the house. After she and Mick recounted the shooting to the authorities in Boston, they had received a report from the state patrol that no sign of the assailant had been found. The sheriff's department had conducted a thorough search of the area and discovered no major leads on the case. Kim Lan, her parents, and Mick had been on edge all day. Finally, Kim had decided to step out back for some fresh air and a change in scenery. Hopefully tending to her mother's vegetables would help release some tension. She opened the greenhouse's glass door and prepared to step inside.

"Kim Lan?" Mick called from the home's spacious back porch.

She turned to face him as he swiftly strode toward her. "You shouldn't come out without me," he said, nervously glancing toward the sprawling countryside.

"You're the one who needs protecting lately," she said, recalling that blood-chilling moment when she had heard the faint gunshot and seen a distant jogger fall to the ground. In one second she had experienced enough emotions for a lifetime. Surprising emotions. Emotions that suggested Mick was more than just her bodyguard.

"Your father and I were just finalizing the plans for tonight," Mick said, ignoring her reference to his recent brush with death. "In a couple of hours he's driving into Boston and renting a car. After dark, he'll come home and drive the car into the garage. We'll wait about an hour and get in the backseat and hide. He and your mom are going to drive us to your place then."

"I feel like we're in a spy movie," Kim Lan said, stepping into the hothouse.

"We might as well be." Mick followed and closed the door behind him.

Kim glanced at him, at the faint lines around his mouth, at his thick, straight hair touched with gray. Her fingers curved in upon themselves, as she imagined herself lovingly stroking his hair. Kim, desperate to hide her traitorous thoughts, looked down.

"Do you still think I should go on the trip?" she asked. "I don't want to endanger anyone."

"You couldn't pay me enough money to leave you in the United States while I go off to Vietnam—not after what happened," he said, a protective edge to his voice. "Besides, like I already said, you'll be safer on that trip." He shrugged. "There's no way this maniac can follow you to Vietnam. They wouldn't let him in without a visa."

"I really don't think that investigator was convinced." Kim moved toward a table filled with plants and touched the wide green leaves of a squash plant that sat amid a collection of potted vegetables.

"Excuse me?" Mick said.

Kim, darting a glimpse out of the corner of her eye, noticed the confused furrow of his brows and smiled. "Sorry. I guess I threw you off again. I was just saying that I really don't think that investigator at the police station was convinced that the person shooting at you is my 'secret admirer.'" She drew imaginary quotation marks in the air with her index and middle fingers.

"I don't guess we have any proof, but I'm more convinced than ever that it's all connected. I have nothing to go on—just a solid hunch. That last note said he couldn't live without your love. If he's that serious, he might try to harm any man who's near you. If he's crazy enough to stalk you, he's crazy enough to be insanely jealous."

A quiver raced down Kim's spine and she beseechingly searched his face. "Mick, are you sure you want to continue as my bodyguard? I would never forgive myself if…" Images of Mick falling to the ground tore at Kim. At once, Kim had wanted to throw herself into his arms and beg him not to die. "I'd completely understand if you went home for the weekend. I could call Virginia, and she'd have someone waiting for me when I got home."

"No," Mick said, his mouth set in a line that commanded no opposition. "Like I already said, I couldn't live with myself if I waltzed off into the sunset and left you now." The implications of his claim made Kim feel as if she were adrift among a collection of waves that were intent upon taking her under.

Kim Lan, refusing to directly look into his light-blue eyes, examined the squash plant once more. At the base of the wide leaves, a tiny yellow vegetable had sprouted, and Kim gently touched it. This was the first time since their drive home from Boston that the two of them had been alone, and Kim was overcome with the desire to wrap her arms around Mick and tell him exactly how glad she was that he hadn't been killed. The white bandage on the top of his left ear forever reminded her that he had almost lost his life. Even now Kim was stunned by the potency of her growing feelings for Mick. They hadn't really known each other that long. However, seeing him fall to the earth and assuming the worst had awakened Kim to a new awareness. Mick O'Donnel was gradually becoming more than a passing acquaintance. Their lives were intertwining to produce a deepening relationship. But then there was Ted. *Ted is my dream man,* she firmly reminded herself. *Mick and I have very little in common.*

Mick's words from eleven days ago filled her mind and left her all the more shaken: *So you think that's all that's between us, then? Just a boy–girl attraction that always exists between the opposite sex? Tell me, Kim, do you always react to men the way you've reacted to me?*

While Mick was her bodyguard in New York, Kim's frenzied schedule enabled her to keep a safe, emotional distance between them. She had been so busy, they had barely spoken. As long as they were in New York, anyone watching would think there was nothing between them. But during their stay at her parents' estate, his kind words, his meaningful smiles, the secrets of his azure eyes forever tugged Kim toward him. She well understood that Mick O'Donnel was not a man who entered into shallow flirtations. He wasn't interested in games, as he had so pointedly told her. When he embarked upon a romantic relationship, he would be serious.

Kim's stomach knotted in guilt. Perhaps she should have never asked him to be her bodyguard. She didn't want to lead him on to believe there could ever be anything permanent between them. She and Mick were poles apart in their life choices. Those were the simple facts.

"Do you enjoy gardening?" he asked.

"Yes, when it's like this." Kim, purposefully placing more space between them, walked toward a collection of cucumber plants next to the squash. "I don't care for the kind of back-breaking gardening I had to do growing up. That got old fast. But we had to eat, so..." She lifted the leaves of a plant to discover a cucumber ready to be picked. She removed the vegetable from the vine and deposited it into one of the baskets sitting around the hothouse.

"You had to garden when you were growing up?" Mick asked in astonishment.

"Of course." Kim Lan snapped another cucumber from the plant and placed it in a nearby basket. She looked at Mick. A veil of confusion cloaked his rugged face.

"You didn't grow up here?" he questioned.

"No. I grew up in Arkansas—actually, outside a tiny town most people have never even heard of—Quitman."

Mick scratched his forehead and shook his head in disbelief. "Then you weren't wealthy?"

"We were a far cry from wealthy," she said through a dry chuckle.

"And this estate?" He motioned toward the massive home and surrounding acreage.

"You figure it out." She stepped toward the group of tender English peas climbing up their trellises.

"You bought it for them, didn't you?" he asked, genuine admiration spilling from his voice.

With the smells of earth and fresh vegetables surrounding her, Kim Lan concentrated on picking the numerous pods of mature peas.

"I assume you're an only child. Am I right?"

"One brother."

"And where does he live?"

"Right now, we don't know. The last we heard, he was in California, but that was four years ago." Kim swallowed against a lump in her throat and concentrated on the peas. "He's been into drugs. Even spent a few years in prison. We don't even know if he's dead or alive." She forced her voice to remain steady. "A couple of years ago, Mom took down all his pictures and stored them. It's just too painful for her." As Kim recalled the years she and her brother played together as kids, her heart ached for the little boy who had grown into an adolescent—an adolescent who had made too many wrong choices.

"I would have never imagined," Mick said, his voice full of regret. .

Her hands stilled, and Kim peered at the man who had already misjudged her once. "So, you thought I grew up a spoiled rich kid and had life on easy street?" she asked, a slight taunt to her words.

His face remained impassive, but at last he glanced downward. "I guess you've done quite well for yourself, considering..." He trailed off, then tilted his head and watched her as if he were trying to put the pieces of a puzzle together. "And you probably made some sort of vow that you'd never be poor again if you could help it."

Now it was Kim's turn to look down. "Poverty isn't fun."

"So you use your wealth to help others in poverty?" A respectful awe oozed from his words.

"When—when the Lord speaks to me, and when I can." Kim Lan's toes curled inside her leather ankle boots. She didn't feel she deserved Mick's mounting admiration. Despite all the thousands of dollars she had given away, Kim had at last awakened to an ugly truth that had begun to eat away at her very core. The night she had removed those compromising poses from her wall, the Lord had painfully shown her that despite her generous gifts to the work of God, she loved her money more than she loved Him. Deep inside, she was clinging to her possessions and wealth; the thought of releasing it all to God left her panicking. If she gave everything she valued to Him, she would have nothing. She had lived on "Nothing Avenue," and Kim Lan never wanted to go back there again.

"Your donation to the Vietnam trip is going to mean we can actually add indoor plumbing to every room for the elderly there in Cantho. Did you know that?"

"No, I didn't know, but I hoped it would be put to good use." *That 10,000 dollars was pocket change. Would I give every penny to God if He asked?* The tension mounting inside Kim increased as the lyrics from that agonizing song once again played through her thoughts: "When will we realize that we must give our lives, for people need the Lord?"

"I just hope Ted Curry appreciates what a considerate woman he's marrying," Mick said with genuine concern.

As the plants blurred, Kim stopped herself from verbally denying Mick's words. Right now, she considered herself far from considerate. This struggle over her possessions...this battle of wills between her and the Lord...the knowledge that she could not let go of her money all worked together to leave Kim feeling like a defeated Christian who would never influence her world for Christ. The Lord had made it painfully clear to Kim that she was presently not willing to give her wealth so others could know about Him. She further realized that until she was willing to give her very life— her possessions, her everything—for Christ her spiritual growth would be stunted.

"Kim Lan?"

Mick's gentle voice so near startled Kim. Blinking, she glanced up to see he stood only inches from her. She had been so engrossed in her own thoughts that she hadn't realized he had moved.

"You don't really love Ted Curry, do you?"

Kim's eyes widened. Her throat tightened. Her mind whirled with Mick's unexpected question. "Of course I d–do," she stammered, frantically looking anywhere but directly into Mick's eyes. But his closeness bade her gaze into his soul...into the corridors of his heart...into the expanse as wide as the blue sky that revealed his growing admiration. Kim Lan struggled with a compulsive swallow.

Mick's tender gaze gradually caressed her every feature, then settled on her lips. Kim, stiffening her legs, prayed they wouldn't buckle beneath her. The first day she met Mick, he had looked at her exactly the same way and told her she was lovely. But this time, Mick slowly reached for her face, stroked her cheek, then slipped his hand to the base of her neck. A shower of tingles spilled down her spine, leaving a numbing sensation in their wake. Gently Mick tugged her toward him, and Kim found no power to resist his intent. His lips brushed hers with an expectant innocence that left Kim feeling as if she were again sixteen and this was her first kiss. Mick paused and pulled away only an inch. His eyes churning with the struggle of self-restraint, he seemed to be searching Kim's soul for a silent message. A voice within Kim Lan reminded her that this was nothing short of betrayal to Ted. Desperately, she urged herself to pull away, but her growing fascination for Mick left her captive in the web of his embrace, left her hungry for a closer relationship, left her longing to swim the undercurrents of everything his loving expression suggested.

"Kim..." he whispered huskily. Wrapping his other arm around her waist, Mick pulled her closer. The ensuing kiss revealed the power of their attraction and left Kim clinging to the lapel of his coat.

This morning when Mick had tumbled into her car and they sped north, she had wanted to throw her arms around him and somehow express exactly how thankful she was that he was alive. Thoughts of his brush with death left Kim reeling with the force of her increasing feelings. The kiss grew in potency.

"Er...excuse me," a soft feminine voice called from the greenhouse doorway.

Kim Lan jumped away from Mick as if a bucket of cold water had been sloshed upon them. Both she and Mick glanced toward the voice to see Kim's mother beaming like a kid on Christmas morning.

"Ted's on the phone, Kim," Tran My said, her eyebrow quirking.

Mick crammed his hands into the pockets of his overcoat and discreetly stepped aside so Kim could leave. Refusing to look at her again, he turned his back toward her and stared out the hothouse's decorative glass wall. The rolling New England countryside, adorned with patches of melting snow, sprawled for indefinite acres. Yet the beauty of nature was wasted on Mick. Despite his stoic expression, his heart pounded wildly and Kim Lan filled his mind.

Wow! He had never intended to kiss Kim when he followed her into the hothouse. Never. But as they spoke, the need to feel her in his arms had increased beyond the point of denial. Mick had so wanted to embrace her after she had rescued him that morning but he had restrained himself. Now, with her exotic perfume still clinging to his jacket, Mick's conscience suggested he should at least feel a tad guilty. After all, she was unattainable and they were far from committed to each other. Furthermore, there was still the issue of their conflict in life focus and careers. Therefore, Mick had no business whatsoever kissing Kim Lan. But as hard as he tried, he could not conjure up one thread of guilt. Instead, he wanted to share a high-five with someone and yell a resounding *Yes!*

Mick heard the door open and shut.

"I think you're the answer to my prayers," Tran My said from close behind.

Mick spun to face Kim's petite mother. "I didn't know you were still here."

Tran My's jade sweater complimented her olive complexion and made her dark, dancing eyes seem all the more merry. "Yes, and I've been wanting to talk with you. I guess now is as good a time as any."

"Oh?"

'I just want you to know that you have my and John's full blessings in your relationship with Kim Lan."

"Excuse me?" Mick asked. In their brief acquaintance, Mick had been impressed with Mrs. Lowery's kindness, grace, and dignity. He never supposed her to be the type who would pry into her daughter's affairs.

Firmly she pressed her lips together. "I have never interfered in Kim's life. But both John and I are desperately disturbed about her engagement. We both feel so strongly that Ted Curry is *not* the right one for her. Kim Lan seems so blinded by what Ted represents that she can't see she's setting herself up for a very difficult marriage. If his reputation is anything to go by, I can't see Ted being true to any woman for very long. But Kim thinks he's recommitted his life to the Lord." Tran My raised her hand for emphasis. "I believe that *can* happen, but I'm pretty certain it *hasn't* happened with him." Tran My diverted her eyes as if she were deliberating whether or not to share more. "I guess I might as well tell you," she said at last. "Sonsee—Kim's close friend—"

"Yes, she's going on the trip," Mick acknowledged.

"Well, there's seven of them, all together. They call themselves the seven sisters."

"Yes, I saw their picture at Kim's apartment."

"Anyway, Sonsee called right after Christmas, deeply disturbed. It seems that Ted made a series of serious passes at her."

"What?" Mick gasped, his uneasy suspicions about Kim's fiancé at last confirmed. "Does Kim Lan know?"

"Yes." Tran My shrugged helplessly. "Or at least Sonsee tried to tell her. Kim shrugged it off and told Sonsee that Ted was just a flirt. Sonsee said Kim got a little defensive, even, and she knew that if she pushed the subject it might mean a rift in their friendship."

Mick's eyes widened in amazement.

"So, John and I began to pray that the Lord would send another man into Kim's life—the one she should marry." Tran My laughed outright. "And right now, if you weren't a whole foot taller than I am, I'd kiss you myself!"

Chuckling, Mick shook his head, wondering if the Lord could bring any kind of order out of this mess he was getting himself into. Apparently Mrs. Lowery was convinced God had plopped Mick into Kim's life. Confusion so claimed Mick that he wasn't sure what to think. Given Ted's obvious lack of devotion to Kim, added to her parents' praying for another man to enter her life, Mick's impression that he would marry Kim Lan gained credence as a message from God.

However, if by chance Mrs. Lowery was wrong and Kim was not the woman for him, Mick was certainly tangling himself in a situation that could grow ugly. And fast. Unquestionably, if Ted Curry found out Mick had been kissing his fiancé... Mick's thoughts flashed to a potential tabloid headline: Jealous Ted Curry Dukes Missions Coordinator. Ted's lack of fidelity to Kim Lan would probably not stop the actor from possessively claiming what he believed to be his.

Awkwardly Mick cleared his throat. "I really appreciate your approval, Mrs. Lowery, but I haven't exactly proposed to Kim. I'm not certain—"

"Oh, I know," she said as she walked toward the doorway then stopped and turned around, all the while smiling as if she had won a grand prize. "I just wanted you to know how my husband and I feel. I guess I didn't want you to be afraid we would be against your interest in Kim Lan. In fact, I'm beginning to think that if I were to hand-pick a son-in-law, I couldn't do better than you."

"Well, uh, thanks, but—"

Mrs. Lowery held up her hand. "I know. You haven't proposed yet," she said, her eyes glimmering with mischief. She turned to leave then glanced over her shoulder.

"But as far as I'm concerned, you can go for it!" she said balling her fist as if she were cheering for her favorite football team.

"Go for it?" Mick echoed as Kim's mother stepped outside. Shaking his head in disbelief, he chuckled. Mick pondered the situation for several more minutes. And the longer he thought, the less he wanted to smile. At last the spark of humor was snuffed out in the harsh light of reality. Even if Kim Lan broke up with Ted today, Mick would be faced with a complicated predicament. He had allowed himself to be influenced by his desires and not his common sense. He had kissed a woman who, in his human estimation, presented no potential for a relationship.

Mick's momentary glee turned to irritation. He no longer wanted to share a high-five with anyone. When he first met

Kim Lan, he had been repulsed by his own attraction to her. From the beginning of their acquaintance, he recognized that she was not the kind of woman who would enhance his call to missions. Even though his admiration for her was growing, even though Kim was indeed leagues from the shallow socialite he had originally assumed, even though she was a woman of generous heart, she still shared a world-view Mick had long since shed, a view that said, "The one with the most toys in the end wins." That view could not co-exist with dedicating a lifetime to the service of God.

"No one can serve two masters. Either he will hate the one and love the other, or he will be devoted to the one and despise the other. You cannot serve God and Money," Mick quoted Matthew 6:24 aloud, as if to somehow pound the truth into his own head. "I had no business kissing her!" he growled.

Kim is the one you will marry. The recurring thought from this morning's prayer time barged in on Mick once more. This morning, he had doubted that he would ever marry Kim. And in the light of the afternoon sunshine, the idea of trusting God for such an impossibility still left Mick grappling for sufficient faith.

"Okay, Lord," he said impatiently, "if You really are telling me I'm going to marry Kim Lan Lowery—supermodel extra-ordinaire—then You're going to have to completely reverse her life focus and, in the meantime, have her break up with Ted."

Shaking his head with doubt, Mick walked toward the glass door and recalled Tran My's exhortation. "Go for it," he mumbled, rolling his eyes. "Get real!"

Thirteen

~

Late Monday morning, Kim Lan sat in her office and waited while the operator set up the conference call she and her friends had planned. Through e-mail, they had all agreed on the time for this special "phone prayer session." The three sisters going to Vietnam needed God's traveling mercies for their trip that would begin this afternoon.

Furthermore, all the friends had been highly concerned for Kim Lan's safety and wanted an update. Fortunately, the rest of the weekend had gone smoothly. She and Mick had been able to sneak back to her penthouse. Her parents, anxious over Kim's safety, had stayed with her as well. As of yet, Kim had received no other communications from her secret admirer. She had also been thankful the tabloids had not gotten wind of the disturbing incidents and recent shooting.

As she waited on the phone, her six friends were added to the conference call one by one. At last they were all amiably chatting and had caught up on the latest news. Finally they focused on the reason for their call. They needed to pray together, and several had specific prayer requests.

Kim toyed with the gold-filled pen lying on her mahogany desk and debated exactly what all she should share with her friends. So much was going on with her besides the secret admirer problems. Mick O'Donnel had knocked her off her feet with a kiss that left her forgetting who Ted Curry was. After that, Kim had purposefully erected an emotional barrier between herself and Mick. Poor Ted had called in the middle of his fiancée kissing another man, and he didn't even know it! Kim had asked the Lord to forgive her at least six times for kissing Mick—and for shamelessly enjoying it. As of yet, she didn't feel as if Lord had heard her. Finally, when all the sisters quieted, Kim decided to begin the prayer requests by sharing from her heart.

"Well, I guess I'll start with my prayer request," Kim said, glancing over her shoulder to verify her office door was securely closed. Mick was in the living room repacking his freshly laundered clothes and making sure all was in line for the trip. Kim's parents had stayed in her penthouse that weekend, and their presence made it possible for Mick to sleep on Kim's couch without compromising appearances. After that ominous shooting, Kim had accepted Mick's offer to keep a closer watch on her, even though his nearness cost her some emotional comfort. If this secret admirer was the one who shot at Mick, he might try to seriously injure her as well. Given the apartment building's security, Kim didn't think he could break into her flat, but she didn't want to take any chances.

"I know you all have been praying about my safety lately," she began, "but there's another prayer request. I'm really ashamed of something I've done that affects my relationship with Ted." She cleared her throat. "He kissed me a few days ago, but you guys can't tell anyone," she said quietly.

"Ted kissed you and we're not supposed to tell?" Sonsee asked.

Kim blinked and wrinkled her brow.

"I think she's talking about Mick O'Donnel," Melissa said with a smile in her voice. "You know, the 'mission coordinator turned bodyguard.' Am I right, Kim?"

A chorus of wolf whistles and teasing remarks made Kim Lan grimace. "This is not a time for clowning around," she said. "I'm serious. This is serious. In the first place, I don't need to be kissing another man. I'm an engaged woman!" Her urgent voice, tight with guilt, ended all the banter. Kim looked at her engagement ring's sparkling fire and felt a searing accusation. "Furthermore, any relationship with Mick is—is hopeless. And now I'm supposed to get on the plane to Vietnam and spend two more weeks with him. This is crazy!" She glanced toward the door and lowered her voice. "I need prayer! I am in love with Ted. I have promised to marry him. Mick and I come from two different worlds—our outlooks are too different for us to have a future together. And I'm crazy to even look at another man when I've got Ted!"

"So Ted doesn't know you kissed Mick?" Marilyn asked.

"No," Kim said, aghast. "I can't tell him. It would kill him."

Something inside Kim Lan twisted into a tight knot when she thought of Ted and Mick. Ted, the personification of physical allure, suited Kim's lifestyle and thought process much better than Mick. Mick O'Donnel was the type of man who would sacrifice his life for the Lord, and Kim couldn't seem to release her wealth, let alone her *life*. With Ted, Kim Lan was the more spiritually mature one. With Mick, Kim felt like a spiritual infant. Furthermore, after the continuing internal battle of the last weeks, Kim Lan wasn't certain she could release everything she owned for Christ. She was actually beginning to wonder if perhaps she even needed such a radical commitment to the Lord. Without a doubt, she could float along as she was and look just fine to everyone.

But what about what God thinks? Am I going to allow my fear of releasing my possessions to stop my spiritual growth? The knot inside Kim produced another wave of anxiety. She decided not to share this element of conflict with her friends.

The whole thing was too complicated and too deep. She would rather pretend she wasn't having to endure such spiritual anguish.

"Well, it sounds like you're in as big of a fix as I am," Sonsee said, her voice solemn.

The friends patiently waited for Sonsee to continue.

"There's something I haven't told any of you—except Marilyn. I've been too distraught over it myself, but I've gotten to a point now that I really need your prayers and support." She sighed. "I'm in love with my friend Taylor Delaney. Taylor knows. He figured it out himself. He isn't in love with me, and tells me he can't fall in love, period." Sonsee sighed. "Anyway, that's the good news. Here's the bad news. I feel like the Lord is trying to tell me I need to be content without Taylor—that I need to get to the place where He means more to me than my dreams of marriage. And quite frankly, I'm not there—but I want to be. I just don't know how to get there. You guys *have got* to pray for me. I'm hoping that this trip to Vietnam will somehow give me the time and space I need to really seek the Lord."

The respectful hush that followed left Kim Lan feeling even more uncomfortable. Restlessly she stood, then sat on the edge of her desk. She caught herself chewing her thumbnail and yanked her hand away from her mouth to examine the injured nail, frayed at the edges. Sonsee's problems reflected Kim's too closely. But while Sonsee had openly shared the root of her spiritual battle, Kim Lan had shied from being so vulnerable with her closest friends. However, Sonsee had also said she wanted to take this next step in her spiritual journey. Kim Lan couldn't truthfully say her desires were the same as Sonsee's.

"Well, it sounds like we're all having men problems," Sammie said, her voice deflated. "Those of us who aren't

married wish we were. And those of us who *are* married..."
She left the rest unsaid.

Kim Lan blinked in surprise. She had assumed all was
well between Sammie and her husband, Devin. Ironically,
though Sammie worked at the Dallas-based magazine
Romantic Living, it didn't sound like she was presently experiencing romance. After a lengthy silence and a few sniffles,
Kim Lan realized that Sammie was weeping.

"I can't talk about it right now," Sammie squeaked out,
her Texan accent evident even through tears, "but we really
need your prayers."

The sisters produced a chorus of supporting remarks then
an awkward silence stopped more conversation. At last, Jac
Lightfoot spoke up, her dry sense of humor supplying the
relief they needed.

"Well, I guess my life looks really good to several of you
right now. No men in sight."

The seven friends laughed outright, and Kim Lan was
glad to hear Sammie's voice among the laughter.

"So, what's your prayer request, Jac?" Marilyn asked.

"That my life *stays* this way."

New laughter spilled across the phone lines.

"Hey," Marilyn said, "I'm a woman planning a wedding.
Have some respect."

"Have you and Joshua set the date yet?" Kim Lan asked,
glad to hear the joyous lilt in her friend's voice. Marilyn and
her daughter had endured more than their share of heartache. But Kim was sure that Joshua Langham was everything Marilyn's first husband had not been.

"Well, the issue of the wedding date is my prayer request.
Joshua really wants us to make this a summer wedding, and
I..." Marilyn cleared her throat. "I'm a little scared. I had

hoped we could make our engagement last a little longer—
at least a year."

"That's understandable," Kim Lan said. "After all you've
been through—"

"Why not set the date for May, when we'll all be there for
our reunion, anyway?" Melissa asked.

Victoria, the quiet one among them, spoke at last. "Great
thinking."

"But that's just two months away. There's hardly time to
plan—"

"I'll volunteer to cater it," Victoria added. "You know how
I love to make all those tiny finger foods."

"Uh...I don't know," Marilyn hedged. "I need to do some
praying on that one."

"Marilyn," Melissa said gently, "it might be that you'll be
scared no matter when you set the date."

"Yes, that's what Josh has said, and I guess that's understandable. Really, I'm sure the Lord has put us together, it's
just... I guess my humanity is showing through right now. I
don't want to make another mistake."

"I understand," Victoria said. "I'll make sure I pray specifically for you in the next few weeks." The other friends
echoed Victoria's pledge.

"Thanks!" Marilyn said.

"Well," Sonsee began, the solemn edge still in her voice.
"I guess we need to get on with our praying. Kim, Melissa,
and I have a plane to catch this afternoon."

Kim looked at her diamond-studded Rolex and noted the
minutes ticking by. She had chartered a plane to Los Angeles
for one o'clock with plans to pick up Melissa and Sonsee in
Dallas. The morning was waning. She closed her eyes and
tried to focus on the Lord as each sister, one by one, began
their heavenward petitions. Kim Lan somehow managed to

wait until last to voice her prayer. When her turn arrived, her words came out stiff and awkward. Once again, she felt as if her prayer went only as far as the ceiling. God felt farther from her than He had been in years. As Kim grappled for the words, her mind whirled with the reasons for her lack of spiritual fervor. God had made His stance clear. She could sacrifice all she owned for Him or she could drift along spiritually defeated. This crossroads in her journey of the soul seemed the most demanding of any she had yet encountered.

As Kim stated a relieved "amen," she forced herself not to ponder her predicament a moment longer. Instead, she decided to focus on the pending trip...on the excitement of finally visiting her mother's homeland...on those orphans she would be privileged to meet. Yesterday, she had asked Mick to remind her of the name of the special needs child who had snared her heart. With an odd look in his eyes, Mick had told her the boy's name was Khanh Ahn. Kim bid adieu to her friends and pondered the moment she would meet Khanh Ahn—the child who might very well be her future son.

Three hours later, Mick followed Kim Lan onto the Lear jet at JFK International Airport. The inside of the luxury plane, decorated in taupe and white, looked more like the lobby of an extravagant hotel than an aircraft. With the smells of supple leather and a gourmet meal filling his senses, Mick shoved his carry-on bag into the closet the lone flight attendant pointed out. Without a glance at Kim Lan, he settled into one of the window seats that resembled a tailored recliner. Mechanically he fastened his seatbelt and awaited the takeoff.

Kim Lan, leaving a trail of that annoying perfume in her wake, passed him to settle into a seat near the back, and Mick tried to block her from his mind. She hadn't spoken more than a dozen words to him that weren't related to the trip since they had kissed. Instead, Kim had erected an emotional wall and barely acknowledged his presence. Mick, both relieved and aggravated, had planned to distance himself from Kim Lan anyway. Apparently the two had come to a mutual impasse that suited them both... for the most part.

With memories of the kiss tormenting him, Mick gazed out the window at the other planes in the various stages of loading, unloading, waiting, or preparing to taxi down the runway. Mick was too honest to lie to himself. While he knew he needed to keep a certain distance from Kim Lan, her aloof treatment irked him. No matter how irrational his emotions, Mick felt as if Kim were amusing herself with him—as if she had melted into his arms, only to immediately turn a cold shoulder. Logically, Mick knew that could not be the case; after all, he had behaved in much the same fashion. Logically, Mick realized that Kim Lan was engaged; she shouldn't have kissed another man. Logically, Mick understood that a relationship with Kim Lan was hopeless. But his heart screamed with the unfairness of the whole situation. He felt as if he were being cast aside by a woman who found him unsuitable by her standards. And those feelings left him attracted to her and yet repulsed by her at the same time.

Repeatedly Mick had tried to pray, to beg God for self-control and wisdom, but his prayers seemed more self-defeating than productive. Instead, Mick O'Donnel, a man totally committed to the Lord, was filled with doubts and indecision. Indecision and disgust. He doubted that the Lord had really promised that he would marry Kim Lan Lowery. He was indecisive in whether or not he should doubt. He was disgusted with himself for ever doubting, for being indecisive, and even for volunteering to be Kim's bodyguard. Then he would start all over again: *Did I or did I not feel the Lord prompting me to volunteer to be her bodyguard? Do I or do I not know the voice of the Lord? Can I or can I not completely trust the Lord when it seems that He's spinning my life into one huge knot!* And the whole cycle began anew. As the plane started rolling toward the runway, a storm raged within Mick's soul. The sun couldn't be shining any brighter, but his heart was dark with the torment of his spirit.

Within half an hour the plane rose into the air, and he and Kim were free to move about. Restless, Mick stood to pass through the luxury lobby and toward the long service bar in the back of the plane. However, in the brief journey he encountered Kim, returning to her seat with a diet cola in hand. Before they left her apartment, she had removed all her makeup and pulled her hair into a loose braid. It was somehow bound up in the back so it barely hung out the bottom of her denim hat. She wore the faded sweatsuit and worn canvas shoes she usually wore to the orientation meetings. Kim looked more like one of the attractive, thirty-something women Mick might notice in the grocery store and less the glamour girl she was. Only the alluring smell of her perfume attested to who she was in real life. That scent, so appealing to Mick, exasperated him all the more. Furthermore, seeing Kim dressed like an average woman left him with the odd sensation that she was actually in his league. Those feelings increased his aggravation.

Kim isn't in my league, and she never will be! he thought, desperately trying to control his mind and emotions.

"Excuse me," she mumbled stiffly as they passed in the narrow walkway.

"Of course," he clipped, angry with his sudden impulse to repeat the kiss that had shattered his stoic resolve to enjoy being single. Ever since he met Kim Lan, his thoughts, his serenity, his purpose in life had been nothing but a swirl of confusion. He wished he had never made her acquaintance. And if there were any way he could get out of going to Vietnam, he would. But there was Caleb to consider, so Mick couldn't abandon the trip now.

He reached the service bar and the middle-aged flight attendant filled a tall glass with the cola he requested. "Your lunch should be ready soon," she said.

"Might I ask what that would be?" Mick asked, his stomach growling. Never had airplane food smelled so good. But, of course, this was only the second time he'd ever been on a chartered luxury voyage.

"Miss Lowery ordered smoked salmon, chef salad, and potatoes basted in cheese sauce."

"I'll have two," Mick said through a faint grin.

The flight attendant, a brunette with ruddy cheeks, smiled and nodded.

Mick, walking back to his seat, neared Kim Lan. She purposefully turned her head, and Mick noticed she was speaking into one of the numerous telephones attached to the back of the seats. Her voice lowered, she seemed involved in an intense conversation. *Probably with Ted,* Mick thought in disgust, wondering anew why in the world a woman of her spiritual interests would tie herself to someone like Ted Curry. His mind wandered to that moment in the greenhouse when Mrs. Lowery had expressed her sincere concern over Ted's advances to Sonsee. Despite himself, Mick was beginning to care too much to remain unmoved by the potential heartache Ted posed to Kim Lan. Whether or not Mick was the answer to her parents' heavenward cry, he hoped Kim woke up before marrying that playboy.

As Mick passed her, he noticed a closed magazine lay in her lap. A magazine with her on the cover. She was wearing a red sequined party dress, looking as gorgeous as ever. Mick's gut tightened, and he scorned himself for his weakness. Once this journey to Vietnam was over, he vowed to forever part from her company and never think of her again.

"I wasn't trying to hide anything from you, Ted," she said, her voice rising. "You knew I hired a bodyguard and you knew why. Everything is fine, I—"

Mick figured he shouldn't eavesdrop, but found himself listening anyway. He paused at the oblong window near the low couch and looked out onto the carpet of fluffy white clouds beneath them.

"Mick O'Donnel is just a bodyguard—"

She paused, and Mick forced himself not to smile.

"Yes, he's also the mission trip coordinator, but—"

More silence.

"I know you have friends who keep you informed, Ted," she said, her voice rising in anger. "I'm not trying to hide anything from you! I just didn't want you to worry. There's no reason for you to—"

Mick bit his lips as a surge of ornery hilarity settled upon him.

"I don't see the point in my having to promise you anything," she snapped. "I promised you when I accepted your proposal. If you don't trust me now—"

Shamelessly, Mick strained his ears but heard no other comments from Kim. As the seconds ticked by and they passed over several more banks of clouds, he at last cast a discreet glance toward Kim. The phone now lay in her lap. Her head was averted, and she was blotting her cheek with a knotted tissue.

The hilarity that had descended upon Mick vanished to be replaced with concern. Concern and anger. Anger and love. Yes, love—the beginnings of a devotion that had been trying to sprout for weeks. This tenderness that swept upon Mick went much deeper than the fascination he had originally felt for Kim Lan. And with the realization of this deepening affection, came the overwhelming desire to protect Kim, to shield her from whatever her fiancé had said, to wrap his arms around her and tell her he would make everything all right.

Mick, driven by a force from deep within, purposefully deposited his cola in a holder carved in the sofa's wooden arm. He walked toward Kim, sat in the overstuffed chair beside her, and gently dashed away a warm tear streaming down her cheek.

"What did he say to you, Kim?" Mick whispered.

Stubbornly she continued looking out the window. Only the increased frequency of her tears and sniffling attested to Mick's question affecting her.

"He doesn't deserve you," he said, his voice heavy with the weight of his own emotions. Like a man desperately wanting to protect his wife, Mick experienced the primitive urge to hunt down Ted Curry and make him sorry for ever hurting Kim Lan.

"I don't know what he said, but whatever it was..."

As Mick continued to helplessly watch Kim, her hands curled tightly around the tortured tissue.

"Kim Lan..." Mick gently stroked her cheek with the back of his fingers. He was being tugged down the funnel of a whirlpool forever bent on swallowing him up. With his every pledge to move farther away from this woman came a new surge of desire to pull her closer.

Kim gave a broken sob, covered her face with her hands, and leaned toward Mick. He wrapped his arms around her and tugged that denim hat from her head. Mick gently stroked her hair bound in the braid, and wondered what it would feel like to wake up with her beside him every morning. The hunger to kiss her surged upon him with breathtaking potency, but he stopped himself from expressing his desires. Clamping his teeth, Mick coerced himself into a state of self-control he was far from feeling. The smell of her perfume mocked his restraint, and Mick strengthened his resolve.

He simply held her. Held her and waited while she released the tears Curry had caused. Mick gazed out the window toward those billowing clouds in shades of white, piled upon each other like mountains of cotton candy. He began to wonder about all the details of Kim Lan's life. Her favorite dessert, her first car, her childhood dreams. About her pets, her shoe size, her favorite movie. Whether she enjoyed roller coasters. Her most beloved vacation. If she would like his cat, Mao.

Kim is the one you will marry.

The thought that had originally left Mick reeling in confusion didn't even surprise him. For the first time, the idea didn't seem so far-fetched. Sighing, he gazed at the top of Kim's head. Her dark hair, like spun silk, glistened in the cabin's light, and the gnawing hunger in his gut swept upon him again. Mick had been single for too long. He was ready, so ready to find fulfillment with a wife. Not only would marriage mean he could express himself physically, but it would mean something even more important: He would have a lifemate to share his love for the Lord and his call to missions.

Mick debated how in the world Kim Lan could ever be that person. If this recurring thought about marriage to her really were of God, how would He arrange it? Kim was in love with Ted Curry—enough to wear his diamond.

I can't give you diamonds, Kim Lan, Mick thought. *All I can give you is me. Would that ever be enough for you?*

As if in answer to his question, she pulled away from him, fumbled for her worn purse, opened it, and pulled out another tissue. "I'm sorry," she mumbled as if she were embarrassed. "I shouldn't have—" Kim broke off in mid-sentence and made a monumental task out of blotting the tears from her face.

Mick, his arms empty and aching, groped for something to say, but no words came—nothing suitable, anyway. Oh, he could have told her that he was falling in love with her. Or he could have mentioned that he dreamed of her every night. Perhaps he could have dropped to his knees beside her and begged her not to marry Ted Curry. But none of these was the least bit appropriate. Instead, Mick forced himself to stand, walk back to the window, and retrieve his cola. He stifled a sigh. With their stop in Dallas, this was going to be a long flight. A flight that would require he exercise every ounce of willpower. A flight full of undercurrents. Undercurrents and excitement. Excitement and restraint. Before treading toward his seat, Mick swiveled to face Kim, only to be surprised to find her watching him. Respect, mixed with curiosity, flowed from her eyes. Mick longed to resume his spot beside her, but nothing could be further from what he needed to do.

"Any time you need a shoulder to cry on, I'm here," he said with a resigned smile. *I just hope you aren't crying a year after you marry him,* Mick thought. *But even if you are, Kim Lan, I'll still be here.*

Fourteen

Eight o'clock that evening Odysseus exited the main building of Los Angeles International Airport and walked along the broad sidewalk toward the international terminal. He stopped outside the sliding glass door and peered into the sprawling building filled with people from varying nations. The banners hanging from the ceiling indicated the different points of destination in Asia and Europe. Not far from the main door, a tight group of familiar individuals joyfully interacted. Kim Lan Lowery, dressed in her sweatsuit, stood between a redhead and a brunette. The redhead was undoubtedly Sonsee LeBlanc, who had not been able to attend the orientation meetings. The brunette, Melissa Moore, had been at both meetings. Mick O'Donnel stood near Kim Lan, and he scanned the crowd as if he were on guard.

With a wicked grin, Odysseus stroked his chin and wondered if Mick would ever suspect the truth. *I almost killed you a few days ago,* he thought as insane jealousy flooded his mind. *And if you lay one hand on Kim Lan, I might kill you yet.* Masking his face into a genuine-looking smile, he walked through the sliding glass doors and toward the talking group. Mick, turning to him, expressed his warm greeting. The other participants followed suit. Burning to feel Kim in his arms, Odysseus cast a charming smile toward her and her friends. The three of them acknowledged his greeting as if they were the best of friends. If all went as planned, within a matter of days Kim would pledge her undying love, and the two of them would arrive back in the United States to plan their wedding.

Kim, standing near Mick, greeted each trip participant as he or she joined the group. The final participants arrived at last, and the group walked toward the banner that read "China." From Los Angeles, they would fly to Hong Kong, and from Hong Kong to Saigon, known as Ho Chi Minh City after the Vietnam War. Mentally Kim stated the names of her fellow travelers to make sure she knew them all. The middle-aged graying woman in front of her and Sonsee was Rhonda Ackers. She had been recently widowed and was ready to do something to change her life focus from mourning. Adam Gray, the quiet man with high cheekbones and hair as black as midnight, walked beside Doug Cauley, the man with a ruddy complexion and red hair. Kim knew little about either man, but they seemed friendly enough. Frank and Pam Cox, the couple in their late thirties, strolled behind Mick. Frank, his brown hair rumpled, was serving as Mick's assistant and already looked as if he had flown to China and back. Pam, her face pale, appeared to be exhausted. Then, Ron and Laci Emerson, the dark complected brother and sister whose faces appeared to have been chiseled from fine marble, walked close to Caleb Peterson, Mick's younger brother. Caleb and Laci, who talked a lot during the first orientation meeting, had sat by each other during the second meeting. Now the two of them acted as if they had spent hours on the phone together. Thankfully Caleb seemed more interested in the fresh-faced college girl than in whether or not Kimberly Lowe was Kim Lan Lowery. Mick, who never moved far from

Kim's side, occasionally scowled because of his brother's flirting. Kim remembered his deep concern for Caleb's spiritual fervor, and she suspected Mick was not happy about his brother's pairing off with a young lady.

Their nearly sixteen hour flight from L.A. to Hong Kong wasn't scheduled to leave until midnight, but Mick explained they could go ahead and make the necessary arrangements for boarding the flight. As they neared the appropriate area, Sonsee and Melissa walked on either side of Kim Lan. Neither one of them acted as if they suspected the undercurrent of silent communication flashing between Kim and Mick—now or during the flight—but Kim was certain they must feel it. She was so distracted by Mick's presence and the confusion over their growing relationship that she could hardly concentrate on her friends' light conversation.

Kim quietly acknowledged that after collapsing into Mick's arms on the flight to L.A. she had spent several shameless minutes enjoying his warmth, his nearness. Long after her tears had abated, she clung to him, using the moment of her own weakness as a brazen excuse to revel in the feel of his arms around her. Every emotional barrier she erected since that kiss had vanished, and Kim once again found that the romantic vision of her fiancé eluded her.

Amid the raucous noise of hundreds of bustling passengers and the glare of overhead lights, Kim Lan cringed with the memory of Ted's call. He had been irate on the phone. Someone who knew a friend had informed said friend of all the delectable details about Kim's bodyguard. The friend had promptly called Ted in Paris to notify him that his fiancée's bodyguard just happened to be the leader of the trip to Vietnam and that he just happened to be mildly attractive. But even mildly attractive was too much for Ted's tolerance. He had berated Kim Lan in a horribly demeaning voice and suggested that she might be considering breaking off the engagement. Kim, hurt and confused by Ted's accusations, had eventually disconnected the call. She couldn't imagine who had been Ted's confidant, but she knew Mick had chatted here and there with a few people in New York.

In the past, Ted had thrown jealous fits but never had he been so vicious. It was almost as if he knew that Mick had kissed Kim and that she had thoroughly enjoyed the moment. Kim's stomach churned and sent a shiver of dread racing down her spine. She should have never kissed Mick in the first place; she should have never allowed him to hold her on the plane. They had no future together. They were from two completely different worlds. Their outlooks and careers were poles apart. Nevertheless, she admitted a truth that had steadily knocked at the door of her heart since she first met him. Mick struck a chord in her that Ted had never come near, a chord of respect, a chord of honor, a chord of integrity. As they approached the appropriate line, Kim dared to cast a brief glance toward Mick, only to find him observing her.

"You okay?" he asked, a veil of concern covering his rugged face.

"Yes, okay." But beneath the warmth of his light-blue eyes, Kim wondered if she would ever be okay again.

"I think once we get on that plane to Hong Kong, we'll be home free," he said under his breath. "I'm still a little paranoid, if you haven't noticed."

"I've noticed." She focused on the collar of his shirt—anything to avoid the sensation of toppling head over heels into his soul.

"Being shot at isn't exactly my idea of a good day."

She looked into his face to see his alluring eyes stirring with humor. *So, you have a sense of humor under all that steadfastness,* she thought, remembering the few times during their orientation meetings when that humor had surfaced from beneath his air of stability and maturity. Kim Lan, for a lack of anything else to do, glanced at her carry-on bag near her feet and needlessly adjusted it. When she was with Mick, her mind was determined to meander down avenues she never intended. So it was today. Kim Lan began to wonder what else she might learn about Mick O'Donnel during the trip. Soon that wondering escalated to raging curiosity.

The next twenty-four hours were a blur for Kim Lan. The flight to Hong Kong extended sixteen hours and represented a twelve-hour time gain over New York City. By the time Hong Kong's sea of skyscrapers came into view against a scenic spread of green mountainous peaks, Kim Lan had lost sufficient sleep to leave her groggy. A brief glimpse behind revealed Mick staring stonily in front of him. She wondered if he had slept at all. The plane's cramped economy section left much to be desired for Kim, who was used to first-class or a private jet. Before she left on the trip, her father had teasingly told her she was spoiled and that a little bit of roughing it would do her good.

With a sigh, she glanced toward Melissa and Sonsee, snoozing on either side of her. The flight attendant awakened them thirty minutes before touchdown, then they had drifted back to sleep. Kim shook both and pointed to the scene below.

"Look how the runway seems to be floating on top of the ocean!" Kim exclaimed as she admired the unique island airport. They moaned in chorus and turned away from Kim.

Within an hour, all the mission participants had followed their leader onto a shuttle bus that drove them to the Hong Kong airport terminal. After walking through the extensive security surveillance check manned by frowning Chinese officials, they followed Mick down a long, windowed walkway that led to the gate for their flight to Vietnam. They waited only half-an-hour before the boarding call announced the next flight to Saigon. That flight spanned two-and-a-half hours and meant the loss of another hour. By the time Saigon came into view, Kim had been on and off airplanes for approximately thirty hours.

From her window seat, she peered out as her mother's homeland came into view. The plane tilted, bringing into view a mass of run-down houses amid a sea of scrubby trees, and Kim's heart palpitated with sympathy. As they neared the airport, Kim was surprised by the evidence of age. The main building and the runways appeared to date from the late fifties to early sixties. Paradoxically, the plane that touched down on the runway with only a slight jolt represented the latest in modern technology.

As soon as the plane taxied to a halt and they were allowed to stand, Mick rose from the seat in front of Kim Lan. "Let the fun begin," he said softly, glancing toward the group. The eleven participants chuckled among themselves. Kim Lan, despite the sleep deprivation, sensed she was in for the most moving two weeks of her life.

Odysseus followed Kim Lan off the plane, down the steep ladder, and onto the shuttle bus that drove them the brief distance to the airport's main building. The whole time he was so close he could have touched her. He ached to reach out and take her hand in his, to stroke her cheek, to gently press his lips against hers, but he didn't. Instead, Odysseus sat in his seat and stared toward the airport while projecting a calm aura he was far from feeling. His heart pounded with excitement. These were the days he had been anticipating for two months.

In a matter of minutes, they stepped inside the aging building and stood in yet another line. The tired group awaited the moment they would present their passports and visas to the frowning officials who would, in turn, begrudgingly approve their entry into Vietnam. The six officials sat behind three tall desks, suited for two, separated by enough space for new arrivals to pass through once they were approved to move forward. Kim, while waiting her turn, chatted amiably with her two friends. Occasionally, Odysseus noticed her glancing toward Mick O'Donnel. Her constant awareness of Mick made him want to scream. The longer he was with them, the more he lambasted himself for botching his attempt at murder.

Nevertheless, he purposefully stood behind Kim, savoring the smell of her perfume, dreaming about the moment she would be his, planning the words he would use to woo her. She stepped toward the high, dark desk. As she presented her documents, his fists curled in upon themselves. Odysseus hoped, oh how he hoped, that she would respond to his love.

In a flash he relived that frenzied chase that had ended when Sophie's car had crashed. Odysseus had fearlessly pursued what rightfully belonged to him—and he would do it again.

More than an hour later, Kim Lan and the other participants had followed Mick through the tedious process of claiming baggage, passing it through yet another x-ray check, and exiting the airport. As the group stepped into the broad, covered walkway, a sea of people awaiting arrivals stood outside. Mick had explained that, by law, civilians weren't allowed to enter the airport unless they were passengers. Mick ushered the group through the crowd filled with soliciting taxi drivers and destitute children selling their wares. Kim Lan, absolutely exhausted, remembered Mick's repeated warnings against pickpockets and pushed forward with Sonsee and Melissa close behind. Mick's voice rose above the den of noise, and he skillfully directed the eleven participants across the street toward a cluster of taxis where a thin, aging Vietnamese man awaited them.

Mick addressed the man in fluent French, and he replied. The cab drivers picked up their luggage and stowed it into the trunks, and Kim assumed they had been waiting specifically for their group. She slid into a small red taxi with Melissa and Sonsee on either side. Mick landed in the front seat of their taxi, and soon they entered the heavy traffic, heading for the opulent Garden Plaza Hotel, a usually 450-dollar-a-night experience. However, the luxurious hotel had agreed to a reduced fee of 100 dollars per night because of the group's sacrificial mission.

"I have never seen so many motorcycles in my life," Sonsee said, gazing out the window.

"My father is always nervous about me flying—especially on international trips," Melissa said through a chuckle. "Looks like he should have been more nervous about this traffic."

Kim Lan, her head pounding, gazed out the window at the hundreds of small motorcycles zooming by them like a million purposeful bees determined to arrive first at the hive. Some motorcycles carried only one person. But more than not, they carried two or three adults. Kim Lan craned her neck as one motorcycle passed with five people on it: four adults and one child. Behind that motorcycle, another followed with one man and a box big enough to hold a personal computer with its printer. Soon she deduced that by all appearances the motorcycles coexisted without traffic laws. Occasionally another car would appear in the midst of the motorcycles, and Kim Lan noted that the main rule seemed to be that the biggest vehicle had the right of way.

"Hang on, girlfriends," she said under her breath as their taxi turned left and drove head-on into a line of racing motorcycles. Yet the motorcycles smoothly parted for the group of four taxis and arrived safely in their appropriate lane.

Mick glanced over his shoulder, a mischievous smile lighting his face. "How we doing back there?"

"Certainly an adventure," Melissa said dryly, adjusting her glasses.

As tired as Melissa looked and as pale as Sonsee appeared, Kim couldn't even begin to imagine how bad she must look. She briefly met Mick's searching gaze then averted her attention toward the window. Kim Lan would welcome a few hours in bed.

"Just wait until tomorrow when we drive from Saigon to Cantho," Mick continued with a perverse smile. "It will take us about six-and-a-half hours to drive 100 miles. Normally, it takes four hours, but from what I've gathered, most of the road is under construction. They're also in the process of widening the fifteen bridges or so between here and Cantho. Also, there's supposed to be a major bridge being built across the Cantho River, which will eliminate one of the ferry crossings. Meanwhile, we still get to ride two ferries tomorrow. And as for traffic, you ain't seen nothin' yet."

"And I guess you enjoy it?" Kim asked, a slight taunt to her words. The longer she went without sleep, the grouchier she became, and Mick's amusement with her discomfort left her less than chipper.

He shrugged. "It's an adventure. And I guess my motto is anything for the call of Christ." As soon as the words left him, Mick narrowed his eyes and looked at Kim Lan, as if he were searching for some specific reaction.

"This is just amazing," Sonsee said, her pale, freckled face alight with curiosity.

Kim Lan pretended an intense interest in her friend and grabbed the opportunity to avoid further communication—silent or spoken—with Mick.

"I was just thinking the same thing," Melissa said, shifting in her seat to better view the aging one-story buildings as they passed them. "Look at those men on the bicycles with the 'basket seats' attached behind them."

"Those are called cyclos or pedicabs," Mick said. "I've had my share of adventures with those things. Some of them are safe transportation driven by honest men and some are not. For the most part I recommend that you avoid using them and take the taxis instead."

"You know," Melissa continued reflectively, "you read about Vietnam and the war your whole life and then, boom, you're here. I never envisioned all these palm trees."

"Great minds think alike," Sonsee said.

"My mind has stopped thinking," Kim added, rubbing her temples. "All I want is a bed."

"I could use one of those too," Melissa said through a yawn.

"We're almost there." Mick glanced back at Kim. "Are you okay? You look really pale," he said with concern.

Nodding, Kim sensed Melissa and Sonsee's rising interest and could only imagine their comments later—especially since they knew about "the kiss."

"Yes, I think I have a royal case of jet lag," Kim answered, her eyes heavy with fatigue.

"It won't take long to get checked in, then you can sleep all afternoon. I planned for us to meet at seven for dinner, but you don't have to come down if you don't want to."

"No, that's fine," Kim said, aware that she and Mick were communicating more than they had in days—except for those potent moments in his arms. The telltale longing that stirred from deep within left her all the more uncomfortable. The mellow tones of his voice caressed her ears in a subliminal message that went much deeper than the pleasant comments he was making.

The protective gleam in his eyes that had surfaced with a vengeance on the chartered airplane still glowed with intensity. And Kim, so drowsy, felt as if she were being gradually tugged into the embrace of Mick's very soul. As she tried to blot out the memory of those pleasurable minutes in Mick's arms, Kim recalled Ted's horrible explosion. She wondered if he would behave so after they were married.

"They have a great buffet at this hotel," Mick continued amiably, seemingly oblivious to her friends. "I think you'll enjoy it. You'll all enjoy it," he said, encompassing Sonsee and Melissa in his charming smile, as if he had at last remembered his manners.

"I don't think two of us will even remember the buffet," Sonsee mumbled under her breath, just loud enough for Kim's ears.

The taxi came to a halt underneath the impressive portico of the Saigon Cantho Hotel. The luxury hotel that reminded Kim somewhat of her apartment building. Kim, growing more testy by the second, glared at her friend. "I'm not in the mood," she said through clamped teeth.

"Okay, okay," Sonsee responded, crawling out of the taxi. "I'm sorry."

Melissa, following them, stood and stretched then yawned. "Let's just get into our room," she said practically. "We can argue later."

The next day's trip to Cantho proved just as grueling as Mick had predicted. They had started at six, and Mick sat in the fifteen passenger van right beside Kim Lan, who claimed the middle bench seat next to the window. She held her breath while the van driver seemed to be playing an old-fashioned game of chicken with passenger buses and farm trucks loaded with crates. As in Saigon, the only traffic rule appeared to be that the biggest vehicle had the right-of-way. The van driver wove in and out of oncoming traffic, narrowly missing head-on collisions and side-swipes by only inches. Occasionally, gasps and exclamations erupted from the men and women in the van. Kim noticed Melissa gradually inching down farther and farther in her seat, and Sonsee was close behind her.

The narrow, two-lane dirt road that was under construction stretched from Saigon to Cantho and bumped past fields of rice, rows of shacks, and myriad tropical trees. The farther they traveled south the more populated the countryside, the denser the traffic, and the lower the standard of living. At last the road was lined on both sides by shacks and makeshift businesses. The van was forced to a slower pace. They inched forward while numerous people, wearing straw hats and smiles, walked up to the vehicle and tapped on the windows, wanting to sell their bottled water, yellow cakes, and soft drinks.

Everyone shot excited questions at Mick, and he answered as best he could. The inquiries he couldn't answer, he directed to the elderly man who had met them at the airport. Kim had learned the man's name was Mr. Nguyen, and he sat on the other side of Mick. Although the Vietnamese gentleman was posing as their translator, his English was limited. Therefore, Mick presented any and all questions to Mr. Nguyen in French. He answered in French, and Mick translated the answers into English. The whole process produced ample humor for all the participants.

At last the van halted at a wide river and awaited an approaching ferry. Kim Lan, her nerves on edge, noticed Sonsee turning to cast a wary glance at her. She gave Sonsee the thumbs-up sign and prayed the ferry was safe. Sonsee, her hair pulled into that no-nonsense ponytail, seemed more like her usual self today than she had the whole trip. However, the shadows in her eyes were an ever-present reminder of her own struggles over Taylor Delaney.

Neither Melissa nor Sonsee had mentioned Mick yesterday after they settled into their room. Following that long plane journey and harrowing taxi ride, all three women had fallen into bed and slept soundly the whole afternoon. The dinner last night had gone about as smoothly as Kim could have expected. She tried to avoid Mick, but as he was doing today, last night he had stuck closer to her than he had when he was her bodyguard. With the threat of Kim's stalker behind them, there was no need for Mick to hover over her. When Kim Lan asked him to be her bodyguard, he had accused her of playing games. Now she wasn't so sure that *he* wasn't playing games.

As the ferry stopped near a ramp, the group grew quiet in anticipation of the van's embarking upon the large boat. "When was the last time this ferry was inspected?" Melissa asked, and the nervous group broke into spontaneous laughter.

Kim Lan's laughter soon faded when the van rolled aboard. In the shadowed ferry, right beneath her window, lay a young Vietnamese man whose hips were so grotesquely deformed he was forced to crawl like a dog. Helplessly, he looked up at her as if to incite her with his large, dark eyes to help him. Kim's heart wrenched with the predicament of this person whose dark skin and hair resembled her own. She considered his plight if he had been born in America. In the United States, his condition might have been corrected at birth; even if it weren't, he would not have been forced to beg for a living. The cloud of hopelessness that seemed to surround him seeped into Kim's soul. The song, that was becoming her tormentor, began its slow melody in the back of her mind:

> People need the Lord.
> People need the Lord.
> At the end of broken dreams,
> He's the open door.
> People need the Lord.
> People need the Lord.
> When will we realize
> That we must give our lives,
> For people need the Lord.

Kim's eyes stung and the Lord whispered ever so gently in her spirit, *When will I become more important than what you own? I need you to give your life for Me.*

"He was here the last time I was here," Mick whispered in her ear.

"Did you give him any money?" Kim asked, turning an imploring gaze to Mick. "I know you said not to give money to beggars on the street, that many of them were just shysters. But he can't be, Mick."

His eyes glowing with approval, Mick nodded. "You're right. I gave to him the last time I was here."

Without waiting for another word, Kim dug into the money belt fastened around her waist beneath her floppy T-shirt, and pulled out a 100,000-dong note, the equivalent of about seven American dollars. But that was so little, Kim scrounged for more.

"This is enough," Mick said, relieving her of the bill. "It's more than he would normally get in a week. He'll think he's hit the jackpot."

"Are you sure?"

Nodding, Mick handed the note to Mr. Nguyen who stood, stepped around the seat in front of them and handed the money to the driver with instructions rapidly fired in Vietnamese. The driver lowered the window and nonchalantly passed the money to a young girl who stood beside the man.

Melissa turned around and faced Mick, her brown eyes pools of concern. "May Sonsee and I give something, too?" she asked.

Mick gazed across the white ferry, and Kim followed his gaze. Crowded upon the two-story ferry, between the vehicles and along the upper floor, stood numerous poverty-stricken people, some selling various odds and ends, some begging, all dressed in worn western clothing. All appeared in need.

"I think this time that we shouldn't do any more," he said as he scrutinized the passengers. "You have to be careful. I know all these people look pathetic and it rips out your heart, but some of them would relieve you of every penny without your permission. The last time I was here, my friend and I hired two cyclos to take us to the market. A cyclo is one of the many pedicabs you've probably noticed on the streets already. Melissa, you pointed some out yesterday, and I mentioned that I had had some interesting experiences with them."

Melissa nodded.

"Anyway, when I had my last adventure with one, it was close to nightfall, and the drivers asked us for a thousand dong each for the short ride. Right now, 10,000 dong is about 71 cents, so you see how little they asked. Looking back, I wonder why both of us, who are experienced travelers, didn't realize those drivers were up to no good. After awhile I suspected we had gone too far, so I leaned out to tell my friend who was supposed to be in the cyclo beside me, but he and the cyclo were gone. As my driver turned up a darker street, I told him to stop. I asked him where my friend was and where the market was, and he said he didn't know. He then demanded ten dollars. I wasn't exactly enamored by his hospitality, and I told him no. That must have been the magic word because three of his friends appeared from nowhere, and I had to fight my way out. When I eventually *did* get to the market—by taxi—I learned that my friend had suffered the same experience. Unfortunately, they got all his money. The whole ordeal toughened me up a bit, I guess. We'll be on another ferry after this one. There's an old blind man I remember who was on that one—"

"We'll give to him," Sonsee said as if she were staking a claim.

"Okay," Mick said, chuckling.

Kim, in an effort to better see the ferry passengers, discreetly removed her shaded glasses and peered past Mick's shoulder. Feeling as if someone in the van were watching her, she made the mistake of casting her gaze to the seat behind her. Caleb Peterson stared back at her, shocked admiration spilling from his light-blue eyes that were so like his elder brother's. Panicking, Kim glanced toward the other two men beside Caleb. Neither Adam Gray nor Doug Cauley had noticed her. Laci Emerson, who sat on the other side of Caleb, also seemed riveted by her surroundings. Only Caleb had seen Kim without her glasses, and she would hazard to guess by his stunned expression that he had discovered her true identity. Kim shoved the glasses back onto her nose and darted a covert glance toward the surrounding participants. Rhonda Ackers, Frank and Pam Cox, and Ron Emerson all were focused elsewhere. Kim averted her gaze out the left window, but that only forced her to stare at that poor crippled man. Her heart twisted once more. Tightly closing her eyes, she ducked her head.

"Are you okay?" Mick asked.

That question seemed forever posed upon Mick's lips. He had asked her the same thing yesterday in the cab and before that, in L.A. "I think your brother just realized who I really am," she whispered back. "I'm sorry."

"Don't worry about it," Mick replied, his lips set in a grim line. "I'll make sure he doesn't bother you."

"I'm not worried about me," Kim hissed back as if he were dense.

"Oh, that." Mick frowned. "He's so focused on Laci Emerson, I don't know whether or not he's had a spiritual thought yet. I'll talk to you about it later. Our hotel rooms in Cantho have balconies. I'll make sure our rooms are side by side. Meet me at ten on the balcony."

Taken aback by the clandestine nuance of his words, Kim stared fully into his face to see his eyes dancing, his lips twitching, and his right brow arched as if he were issuing her a challenge. *I dare you to turn me down,* he seemed to be saying.

"I'll think about it," she said, not sure how to handle Mick in his present mood. Since they'd begun their journey, he had gradually warmed up to Kim, as if their leaving the States had somehow broken all previous ties, including Ted. But the truth was, no ties had been broken at all. Kim contemplated her fiancé's near-perfect looks, his mesmerizing blue eyes, his dimpled smile that usually affected her pulse. But she also remembered the jealous frenzy he had unleashed upon her, and Mick's saying Ted didn't deserve her. She recalled that disappointed wilt in her parents' voice when she told them she and Ted were engaged. She considered the spiritual battle that seemed to rage forever below the surface of her thoughts. Kim reminded herself that Ted Curry was a perfect dream. Then she peered out the window to see the destitute cripple crawling along the ferry floor.

Fifteen

~

By one o'clock, the group had checked into their hotel in crowded Cantho, and Mick arranged for them to be driven the ten-minute journey to the nursing home where their efforts would concentrate. He sat in the van's front seat while Kim Lan occupied the first bench seat with her friends. As the van journeyed along the narrow road through the dense, tropical trees and past a few decrepit houses, Mick reflected upon his own internal journey.

From the time he held Kim Lan in his arms until the time they had landed in Saigon, he had certainly undergone a spiritual voyage—a voyage that took him through stormy waters of doubt and the dark forest of fear. But Mick had come through his pilgrimage certain of one thing: Kim Lan Lowery was indeed the woman God intended him to marry. Mick didn't know how the Lord would bring their marriage about or even how long it would take, but he could no longer doubt that the Lord was speaking to him about his future wife.

Getting to this point had brought Mick to a new level of trust in the Lord. For the first time he felt confident to step off the cliff and onto thin air in his personal life, knowing the Lord would hold him up. God, with His ever-patient wooing, had shown Mick that the time had arrived for another spurt of spiritual growth and a deeper understanding of His sovereignty.

Mick had begun to fervently pray that Kim would experience a focus change while on this trip and that she would also wake up before she married that jerk. He had decided somewhere between Hong Kong and Saigon that the best course of action would be to get to know her better, to be as friendly and caring as propriety allowed, to begin to reveal more of himself to her, and to stay in her shadow. More than once, Mick had noticed a questioning gleam in her eyes, and he knew his latest approach left her pondering his purpose.

The van drove from the trees toward a river. Slowing, the driver turned left along a narrow path that paralleled the river and led them to the nursing-home grounds. Mick turned and faced the participants. "This is the Cantho River," he said. "It's actually a tributary of the Mekong Delta, but where it runs through Cantho, it's called the Cantho River. I know this town probably doesn't seem like a hub city to you, but it's actually the political, economic, and cultural center of the region and capital of the Hau Giang Province. It's the nicest city—and the only university city—in the Delta. Cantho University is here. There's even a new riverside mall where you can sit down and have something to eat and a drink. Might be romantic for anybody who's interested." Mick glanced at Kim Lan for a split second.

"Will that ever be you?" Caleb said from the back of the van, and everyone burst into laughter.

"Yeah, yeah, yeah," Mick said, smiling at his younger brother. "Go ahead, torment me in my old age."

New snickers erupted from the group.

After the van driver maneuvered another left and drove through an iron gateway, the white, two-story, baby home came into view a few hundred yards in front of them. "That's the baby home," Mick said over his shoulder, pointing toward the structure. "To the left, just across the driveway, that barn-type structure is the schoolhouse where about a dozen school-age orphans live and have classes. They are allowed to be there four years. After that..." Mick trailed off as he considered the plight of those poor children.

"After that?" someone prompted.

"They're on their own," Mick said, glancing back again. In his line of work, seeing human suffering went with the territory, but Mick wasn't sure he would ever get used to it—or that he wanted to. "Here in Vietnam, the public orphanage system is in desperate need." Mick observed a group of six slender, smiling boys, ages eight to ten, who ran from the schoolhouse to meet the van. "These are the lucky ones," he said, waving his hand toward the boys and the baby home. "These grounds are privately owned and operated. You'll notice the cleanliness of the baby home and the sufficient number of nurses per babies. The public orphanages aren't as fortunate. In public orphanages, toddlers and babies are in the same group with children up to eleven years old. They are, for the most part, without any kind of adult supervision. All they get are meals and a place to sleep. When they're twelve, they turn them out on the street during the day, and they are allowed to come back at night only to sleep—if they can get back to the orphanage. So, what you get at that point are children, twelve and older, who are out on the streets all day long, then sleeping with the younger children at night." Mick's mouth tightened. "People call them the 'dust of society.'

"But as I've already said, the babies in this home are the lucky ones. One or two of the little guys you'll see today were actually fished out of the river by a family member.

Their mothers gave birth and promptly disposed of them."
He stopped talking momentarily in order to allow that piece
of information to make its impact. "This is a privately run
institution with an adoption agency in the States that sends
several adoptive families over every month to get their
chosen child. If any of you are interested, I'm sure it can be
arranged—especially if you'll take a boy." Mick unbuckled
his seat belt. "From what I understand, the boys are harder
to place for some reason. I can't imagine why; I'd love to
have one. Anyway, just for the record, adoption has changed
over the years. If you're in your mid-fifties or younger, single
or married, you can adopt. For the most part, these babies
are standing in line, waiting on parents. The adoption agency
is thrilled to work with just about anyone. Anything to keep
these little guys from landing on the streets. Some are
assigned to families; some are not. If one of them grabs your
heart, don't hesitate—come back and get him or her."

Mick's comments left the group in thoughtful silence as
they stepped from the van and walked toward the front of
the baby home. The baby home director greeted them in a
room unfurnished except for a long table of dark wood sur-
rounded by matching chairs. In a matter of minutes, the
middle-aged smiling gentleman led the group to the base of
a stairway and instructed them to put on hospital gowns
over their clothing.

"As I told you in orientation," Mick said, "they are highly
concerned about the health of the babies. This just assures
them that the clothing touching the babies will be clean.
They want us to remove our shoes as well." Mick slipped off
the worn boots that he wore most everywhere and set them
against the wall at the base of the stairway. "And also any
hats," he said, glancing toward Kim Lan, the only participant
wearing a hat.

When she cast a concerned glance at him, he shrugged in resignation. As she took off the floppy hat and placed it atop her canvas shoes on the floor, Mick looked at Caleb, who now wore an expression of certainty. *Oh well,* Mick thought, *it was inevitable.* Caleb and he were rooming together. Before dinner, he would have an advisory chat with his younger brother about respecting Kim Lan's privacy.

Mick, noticing that Kim had adjusted those shaded glasses for the third time in as many minutes, stepped closer to her. He laid a restraining hand on her arm as the rest of the group followed the baby home director up the flight of stairs, toward the nursery. "If you want, go ahead and take off the glasses," he said.

"But..." Her face, only inches from his, reflected her own doubt.

"I think you're right. I think Caleb already knows. I'm going to make certain he gives you some space. Anybody else who figures it out..." He shrugged. "So let it be."

Relief seemed to trickle across her every feature. "But I don't want to distract anyone," she said, removing the old-fashioned black-rimmed glasses.

"You'll have to go back and start the trip all over then," Mick said, making no effort to hide his growing feelings. "You've distracted me to the point that I can't even think straight."

Kim's eyes momentarily widened with surprise then narrowed, as if in scrutiny of his motives. "When I asked you to be my bodyguard, you said I was playing games. Now I wonder who is the one playing games."

"I don't play games. I play for keeps."

"What's that supposed to mean?"

"You figure it out."

"But I'm engaged."

"Are you?"

She blinked. "Of course."

"You don't belong to him, Kim Lan, and you know it."

"Are you suggesting that I belong—"

"Are you coming, Kim?" Sonsee called, and Kim turned to see her rushing back down the stairway, her green eyes sparkling with excitement. When she caught sight of Mick she abruptly halted. "Oops." Sonsee covered her mouth with her fingers. "Sorry."

"It's okay," Kim said, rushing up the concrete stairs. "I was coming."

Within seconds, Kim stepped into the small baby home, her mind whirling with the implications of Mick's words. Around her the group had already begun interacting with the curious toddlers who approached, some shyly, others assertively. Several babies crying, the smell of baby powder, the voices of numerous Vietnamese nurses punctuated the moment. Kim gazed across the white room furnished in wicker the color of straw. Large windows lined the entire perimeter, admitting the vivid, tropical sunlight. The whole structure, inside and out, appeared to have been plucked from the back of an ancient Spanish church and plopped near the Cantho River. Kim's gaze wandered out one of the many windows toward the tropical foliage. Her pulse pounded with Mick's words: "I don't play games. I play for keeps."

"Kim, look at this little boy! Isn't he a doll!" Melissa's air of intelligent composure was slowly vanishing as she scooped up a dark-haired toddler with large, almond-shaped black eyes. He grabbed for Melissa's round glasses, and she laughed with glee as she tickled his tummy.

Something pressed against Kim Lan's feet and she looked down to see a toddler, about twenty months old, leaning back on his haunches like a puppy, staring up at her as if she were the answer to his prayers. The face of the child was a bit flatter than that of the other children. Like most Vietnamese, his eyes lacked the oriental slant of many Asians, although their shape bore a light hint of possible Down Syndrome. Those dark, merry eyes also held a certain vacant expression, albeit he smiled up at Kim Lan as if his sole purpose in life was to charm her. A slow rush of warmth started in Kim's midsection and spread through her. She bent to pick up the toddler who immediately giggled.

Her eyes burning, Kim wrapped her arm around the baby dressed in bright red shorts and matching striped shirt. She held him close and whispered his name. "Khanh Ahn, is it you?" *Oh Lord, I want him,* she prayed as she recalled Mick's saying they were afraid nobody would adopt him. She pondered the hopelessness of his potential future, the chance that he might land on the street, the likelihood of his being "the dust of society." And a snatch of that recurring tune circled through her mind once again: "When will we realize that we must give our lives..."

"I'll give my life for you," she whispered against his cheek.

But will you give all your money and possessions for Me? The plaguing thought was like an iron fist tightening around her heart. By this point, Kim recognized the source of that thought and knew the Lord was once more knocking on the door of her heart, requesting a deeper commitment to Him. She contemplated that crippled boy on the ferry and all the poverty she had encountered since coming to Vietnam. Growing up, Kim had thought she was poor. Now she saw that she had only scratched the surface of destitution. However, she still shrank from the possibility of revisiting a lifestyle of poverty—even in America.

As a child, she had dreamed of growing up to be a princess who married a charming prince. When the opportunity came for her to embrace a princess' life she had plunged forward with abandonment and joy. And when Ted Curry had proposed, accepting him had been the fulfillment of her lifelong dream. Now she wondered how she would ever be able to release her fulfilled dreams or why God even expected that of her.

No, I can't. I can't. I can't, Kim countered as she gazed at the child. *It's too much to ask. Isn't it enough that I would extend myself to help the poor? I don't want to give all. It's too much!* These words felt as if they instigated the fall of a giant boulder, crashing across the portals of her soul, blocking out the streams of God's Spirit, of His voice, of His blessings.

"He's the one you asked me about the other day—Khanh Ahn," Mick said from close by. "Watch this." He reached to tickle the baby's tummy, and he squealed with delightful laughter. "He does that every time you tickle him."

"He's a doll," Kim said. "And I want him. I want to come back and adopt him."

"Oh?" Mick's eyes widened with wonder.

"Don't look so surprised," Kim snapped, an irrational irritation sprouting within. "I have a heart too, you know," she said defensively.

"I know that, Kim." Mick slowly shook his head as if he were amazed with their conversation. "I saw your big heart a long time ago."

"So why are you so surprised?"

"Because…" The lines around Mick's eyes crinkled with his faint smile. "I've wanted to adopt Khanh Ahn for almost a year now, but I couldn't. I travel too much."

A rush of warmth bathed Kim Lan's spirit while Mick peered into the depths of her soul. As the seconds ticked by, Kim could almost feel Mick pulling her into his arms, into the corridors of his heart, into the embrace of his growing esteem. A new bond, unexpected and unbreakable, began to form between them. A bond of respect. A bond of like-mindedness. A bond of camaraderie. And a still, small voice suggested to Kim that she and Mick weren't—and never had been—worlds apart, as she had previously presumed

Odysseus settled into a wicker chair and pretended to focus on the ten-month-old baby girl sitting on the floor. In reality, Kim Lan held his undivided attention. He watched her, discreetly speaking to Mick as if they were discussing their wedding. His gut clenched with the fury of fresh jealousy. Every day Kim and Mick grew closer—so close, he was beginning to think she and Ted Curry had broken off their engagement. If she wasn't promised to Ted, that was one less obstacle for Odysseus to overcome. He had to have Kim, even more desperately than he had ever needed Sophie.

Sophie...Sophie...Sophie. Thoughts of his former love sent Odysseus' mind reeling back in time to the night of that deadly car crash. He had arrived early from his trip to the West coast and planned to surprise his loyal "Penelope" with a late-night visit and a dozen red roses. But he reached her apartment just in time to see her get into her shiny, red economy car and speed away. On a whim, Odysseus had followed her, planning to surprise her once she arrived at her point of destination. Never had he dreamed that his beautiful Sophie was sharing her devotion with another. After Sophie stopped her car, he parked at a discreet distance and watched in horror as she exited her vehicle and approached an isolated lake-house. In the illumination of the porch light, he saw her boss greet her at the door. Then that lawyer jerk had wrapped his arms around Sophie, kissed her neck, and closed the door.

Odysseus was left in the car, left all alone, left to pull the roses apart petal by petal, left to seethe in vengeance. Two hours later, when Sophie got back into her car, he had shed every trace of honor attributed to the Odysseus of Greek legend. Indeed, he became more like a furious Zeus determined to destroy the mortal who had betrayed him.

The chase began as a game of vindictive tailgating, and it ended in an explosion that resembled the fires of Hades....

Odysseus' gut burned as if the fire were blazing within him. Blindly he stared at the child who sat nearby. He felt no emotion for the orphan—no empathy, no admiration—nothing. Only one passion claimed his psyche, an unrequited passion that urged him to action, a passion that demanded Sophie pay for her disloyalty.

Odysseus observed Sophie as she continued to interact with the baby boy, but she never got far from Mick O'Donnel. Sophie had deceived him once with that lawyer. Now she brazenly flaunted her flirtation with Mick. Odysseus' fists tightened into tight balls. Like a ravenous tiger bent on tracking its prey, he planned his desperate deed.

Kim stopped beside Rhonda Ackers as a nurse placed a three-month-old girl into the arms of the middle-aged woman.

"Isn't she precious?" Rhonda said, her blue eyes sparkling with new life.

"Yes," Kim said, leaning forward to peer into the yawning baby's face.

"They say her parents are scheduled to come get her next month." Rhonda bent to bestow a gentle kiss upon the baby's face. "I knew this trip was going to be good for me." She cast a lingering glance at Kim Lan. "When my husband died, I wondered if I would ever get over it."

Nodding in understanding, Kim reached out to stroke the baby's delicate cheek as Khanh Ahn vied for her attention. She tickled his tummy again. The child squealed with laughter, his lips curling upward like a bow. Kim moved toward Frank and Pam Cox. During their conversation last night over dinner, she understood that Frank would be leading his own mission trips after this one. The Coxes were treating this trip as a second honeymoon of sorts.

They sat on one of the wicker settees and played peek-a-boo with a curious baby girl. As if the child were determined to charm the couple, she clung to the side of the coffee table in front of them, squatted, ducked her head, then surged upward, cackling as she rose. Frank Cox glanced at Kim, a sparkle of joy in his grayish eyes. "They say this one has already been assigned a family," he said. "But I'd take her in a minute if she wasn't."

"And this is the guy who said he didn't want any more children." Smiling with anticipation, Pam Cox rolled her eyes.

Kim laughed with them, but her attention was snared by Adam Gray in the corner chair. Silently he sat alone and observed the group. Adam, the tall man of Native American descent, had interacted little with the group, although he seemed sincere enough. Vaguely Kim remembered Melissa— the source of all details—had mentioned that his only son had been killed in a car wreck about three years ago. The boy had only been four. Adam and his wife divorced a year later. Kim Lan wondered if perhaps his further withdrawal into himself at the baby home was the result of the loss of his son.

From nearby, Doug Cauley, the red-headed man Kim had gathered was a reporter, approached Adam and knelt beside him. In one arm, Doug held the little girl he had played with earlier. In the other arm, he held a baby boy. With a slight smile, Adam reached for the boy and placed him on his knee. Kim hoped this trip proved more therapeutic than traumatic for Adam.

Kim watched Caleb Peterson as he and Laci Emerson, along with her brother, Ron, sat on a floor mat and focused on twins—one a boy and one a girl—about ten months old. The two babies, sitting side by side, solemnly stared back at the three young adults, and Caleb seemed as distracted by Laci as he was the twins. Mick had impatiently implied his younger brother was so taken with Laci that he would most likely not be contemplating spiritual issues this trip despite Mick's prayers. However, if the numerous comments Laci had made over dinner last night were any indication, the young woman was a person after God's own heart. Kim mused that perhaps Caleb's interest in her was a good thing.

Caleb glanced up to find Kim appraising him. Once again, that flash of recognition flashed between them, and Kim abruptly looked at Khanh Ahn, who had developed a monumental interest in the lone hair clip holding her twisted hair at the base of her neck. Before Kim could stop him, the child managed to dislodge the hair clip, sending half her hair toppling down her back. Furtively, Kim scrambled for the falling tresses, while trying to maintain her grip on the delighted Khanh Ahn. She cast another, desperate glance at Caleb to see that any doubt that might have remained over her identity had vanished.

"Having trouble, fair maiden?" Mick asked from close behind.

"It would appear that I've had some help with my hair," she said, smiling at the baby.

"Here, let me have him," Mick said, extending his arms to Khanh Ahn.

Kim relinquished the child to him. As discreetly as possible, she twisted her hair back into its knot and firmly secured the large clip over the bun. Frowning, she mentally scolded herself for not taking the time to braid her hair this morning and fretted with the strand or two that seemed determined to escape.

"It's okay," Mick said, looking into her eyes as if he were trying to comfort her. "Just relax."

"Well, Caleb noticed. And I don't think he's got one doubt left now about who I am," she said.

"I guess your anxiety is my own fault," Mick said, his gaze caressing her every feature. "And I know I've already apologized once, but I'm really sorry about the way I acted when we first met. I shouldn't have been so...such a bore. It's just that I have been praying for Caleb for so long." As Khanh Ahn reached for Mick's chin, he lovingly intercepted the child's hand and glanced toward Caleb.

"I guess I should also apologize for calling you a jerk that day," Kim rushed, not certain she was comfortable with the increasing intimacy spawned by the shared apologies. "You're anything but a jerk." *And you'd be a great father.*

"Well, thanks." Although his face remained impassive, Mick's light-blue eyes danced like the buoyant waters of a summer sea. A burst of laughter from Caleb and his friends momentarily distracted Mick. The twins, no doubt, were gradually charming the young adults into a state of hilarity. Mick nodded toward his brother. "I hoped this trip would make a difference in Caleb's heart." Mick shrugged. "I guess I should have known all along that by the law of averages, there'd be some young woman who would distract him to the point of not being able to think straight." Mick cocked an eyebrow and held Kim's gaze in a flirting challenge as something else he said replayed in her mind. *You've distracted me to the point that I can't even think straight.* He had gone on to imply that she didn't belong to Ted, but to him.

Mick's features reflected the depth of his growing respect, along with the admiration that he had apparently decided to flaunt. If Kim didn't know any better, she would have said that Mick O'Donnel had purposed to make her fall in love with him and forget Ted ever existed. As he had already assured her, a man of his maturity would be playing for keeps. Kim's heart began to pound as if Mick had once again taken her in his arms, placed his lips upon hers, and transported her to a world where no other human beings existed, save him and her. She saw something burning in the depths of Mick's mysterious eyes, something that resembled glowing lava bursting from a hidden vein deep in an icy-blue ocean. It was something that she had never seen in Ted's eyes. For the first time, Kim Lan doubted the authenticity of her love for her fiancé.

By four o'clock Mick collapsed onto the hotel room's full-sized bed for a brief rest. He listened to the never-ending sounds of traffic in Cantho. The narrow street ran between aging buildings perched along the roadside. The ever-present motorcycles, interspersed with occasional cars, filled the street night and day. Mick, weary from the day's activities, rubbed his eyes and hoped the sounds of traffic wouldn't disrupt his night's sleep. After the group left the baby home, Mick had taken them on a brief tour of the home for the elderly that they would be improving, starting tomorrow. Then he showed them the living quarters and schoolroom that provided shelter and education for the older orphans. By now, the responsibilities of the day that started at five in the morning had taxed him, and he needed a sound night's sleep.

Caleb stepped from the bathroom dressed in a T-shirt and shorts, his hair damp. He had just showered and began rustling through his overflowing suitcase.

"So, how are you doing, old man? All worn out?" Caleb teased.

"Not quite. I could still take you on," Mick claimed.

Caleb snorted. "We won't discuss that. But I will say that you've beat me out in one area. I had no idea you were such a ladies' man."

"Meaning?" Mick asked, never taking his gaze from the straight rust-colored curtains hanging on either side of the sliding, glass door that doubled as a window.

"Meaning...the way you and Kim Lan Lowery are acting, I'd say the two of you were planning a wedding."

Mick, deciding this was as good a time as any to discuss Kim Lan, sat up and observed his younger brother.

After dumping most of the contents of his suitcase on the floor, Caleb found a pair of jeans and straightened to look at Mick. "She *is* Kim Lan Lowery, isn't she?" he asked, as if he already knew the answer.

"What do you think?"

"I think you tried to pull a fast one on me." His dark brows rose over expressive blue eyes.

"She needs her privacy, Caleb," Mick said kindly, yet firmly.

"Yeah, and it looks like she needs *you*." Caleb narrowed the space between them and punched Mick in the arm. "You old goat. I just decided you *never* would get married, and now you—"

"Cut it out, Caleb," Mick said. Standing, he lazily pushed against his brother's shoulder as he walked toward his own suitcase. "I like pretty women just as much as you do."

Caleb snorted.

"Maybe more than you," he growled. "I've been single too long."

Laughing outright, Caleb removed his shorts and donned the jeans.

Mick unceremoniously unzipped his well-traveled suitcase and examined the neatly arranged clothing. "Anyway, you need to give Miss Lowery some space. I know she's been something akin to your idol, but—"

"Hey, give me a break, will ya?" Caleb pointed to his chest with both hands. "I'm twenty-two—not ten! Besides..." Turning to the mirror on the 1970s dresser, he grabbed a nearby comb and slid it through his short, damp hair. "...I took down her pictures anyway."

"What?" Mick barked, shocked beyond any intelligent words.

"Yeah. I decided that..." Caleb shrugged. "Laci is a woman who...Laci and I have gotten to be..." he turned down his lower lip, "an item during the last couple of months. She's a woman who's serious about the Lord, and well, I guess she's made me rethink a thing or two."

Stunned, Mick stared at his younger brother, the brother over whom he had spent many hours in prayer, the brother with whom he had been disgusted for wasting this opportunity for spiritual growth on yet another superficial relationship.

"Don't look so startled," Caleb said with a grimace. "It's not like I was without hope or anything. I guess I just lost focus there for awhile."

For awhile? Mick coughed over a laugh. "Well, if it helps you any, I think Kim Lan would be glad to know you took down her pictures. She's stopped doing all those swimsuit ads."

Caleb reached to switch on the television, found a soccer game, and flopped onto the bed, his hands behind his head. "Well, there was a time when I would have said that was a cryin' shame." He smiled mischievously. "But I guess if she's really interested in following the Lord, He probably convicted her against doing those kinds of poses." He shrugged. "Makes sense to me."

Feeling as if he had landed smack in the middle of a scene from "The Twilight Zone," Mick blinked in astonishment.

"Stop lookin' at me like that, man!" Caleb grabbed a nearby pillow and hurled it at Mick.

He dodged the pillow, snatched it from the floor, and tossed it onto Caleb's face. "I'd say I'm proud of you, but you might throw the lamp at me," Mick said, beaming at his brother.

"Oh, go on and take your shower. You need one."

Shaking his head, Mick picked up a shirt and dress pants along with his shaving gear and walked toward the bathroom. He deposited his stuff on the counter and looked into the mirror to see a sandy-haired, tired man gazing back at him. Mick had never considered himself good-looking, not in the traditional sense, although he had been told that his rugged outdoorsman appearance appealed to some women.

He contemplated Caleb's admission and chuckled with relief. "Well, Lord, You never cease to amaze me," he mumbled. God had apparently been working to answer his prayers for Caleb before and during this trip, and Mick had been too blind to see it. "Now, if You will only tell me You've been working all along to bring Kim Lan to contentment with a simple life..."

Mick, preparing to shower, recalled the day's interactions with Kim. Her interest in adopting Khanh Ahn had left him initially dumbfounded. Mick had simply chalked the whole thing up to the Lord's working. With every minute in Kim Lan's presence, Mick's faith in the Lord's promises grew another mile. God was undoubtedly pulling them together, and every conversation verified His working.

Their interaction at the baby home floated through his mind, and Mick smiled at his reflection. He hoped he had given Kim Lan a thing or two to think about. The look on her face when Mick told her he didn't play games, that he played for keeps, had him smiling again. He prayed that this trip would serve as a wake-up call for Kim Lan. That she would see Ted Curry in his true light. That she would come to a point of deeper commitment to the Lord. If so, maybe by next year they would be married.

Mick envisioned them arriving home from Vietnam carrying Khanh Ahn, their newly adopted son. He fantasized about wrapping his arms around both Kim and his son, pulling them close to his heart. Mick pictured Kim looking into his face, her eyes alight with the admiration he had seen in her eyes that very day.

"But it will only happen, Kim, if you don't marry Ted," he said quietly.

Odysseus paced so swiftly across his hotel room that perspiration beaded on his forehead. He had begun writing the note to Sophie three times and scrapped every attempt. His hands shook with the intensity of the moment. This note was the most important one yet. It would prepare her for his pending visit.

A note of such importance should have taken hours to compose, but Odysseus had precious little time to draft it. He listened to his roommate, still in the shower, and checked his watch. His roommate had been in the shower about five minutes. Within another five minutes, he would undoubtedly be back in the room. Sophie needed to receive his note tonight. In the wee hours of the morning, he planned to jump onto her balcony, and tape the letter on the glass door. Now was the best opportunity to compose the letter without getting caught.

Making himself sit down, Odysseus picked up the pen and, in black ink, wrote the words that expressed his heart. The simplistic block letters did nothing to reveal his identity, which was exactly what he wanted. By now, Sophie would most likely be thinking of him as her mystery man. His plan required that he maintain the romance of that mystery. However, he signed with the initials he knew she would recognize. Hopefully those initials had become a cherished symbol to her of his steadfast loyalty. He folded the note, slipped it into one of the hotel's complimentary envelopes, sealed the envelope, and wrote "Kim Lan Lowery" on the outside. In confusion, he stared a the familiar name. Knitting his brows, Odysseus desperately tried to clear his mind of the jumbled memories that rushed upon him like a hungry hurricane. He had written the letter to Sophie...who was Kim Lan?

His roommate turned off the shower.

Odysseus' hands hands trembled. He picked up the three wads of paper he had cast aside and tucked them into one of the pockets of his jumbled suitcase. The first chance he got tomorrow, he would tear the notes into tiny bits and drop them into the Cantho River.

"And if you play your cards right, Sophie, I won't be forced to do the same to you," he muttered as images of a New York supermodel blurred with remembrances of an exploding car.

Sixteen

After dinner, Sonsee, Melissa, and Kim Lan agreed with the other trip participants that retiring to their respective rooms was the most logical choice. The day had been a long one; tomorrow the work would begin. The home for the elderly would be blessed with indoor plumbing.

While Melissa and Kim Lan chatted about their day, Sonsee plopped onto one of the full-sized beds and reached for the bedside phone. She checked her watch and calculated that it would be eight in the morning in New Orleans. Sonsee had promised her father she would call him, and even though the call would cost five dollars a minute, she wanted to hear his voice. After dialing the appropriate code numbers, she dialed her father's number from memory and waited for the phone to begin its ringing. Following the third ring, the phone was answered and a familiar voice floated over the line. The voice of Taylor Delaney.

She held her breath, thinking she must be imagining things, that all those hours she had spent weeping over him, that all those dreams she had endured about him, that all those days she had spent praying over him, were somehow making her conjure up his voice. Perhaps her father had hired a new houseman or yardman who happened to answer the phone and who happened to sound like Taylor.

"Hello, I'm calling for Jacques LeBlanc. Is he home?"

"Red?"

Sonsee wanted to groan. She was not imagining his voice. "Taylor? What are you doing there?" she asked, trying to make her voice sound as normal as possible. "Your mother, is she—"

"Mom's fine," he drawled. "But this is *my* house, and it's usually normal for me to be here."

"I thought I dialed Father's number," she said, her face getting red. Sonsee usually didn't use a phone book; most of her frequently dialed numbers were filed safely in her head. However, there were occasions when she mixed up her father's number with Taylor's or perhaps Marilyn's number with Kim Lan's. This time, she never imagined she was making such a mistake.

"Well, you must have dialed my number," Taylor said. "This is about the third time you've done this in the last year, too. I'd say you're getting senile in your old age."

Sonsee, groping for words, toyed with the idea of just hanging up, but she couldn't bring herself to do it.

"Where are you?" he asked.

"I'm in Cantho, Vietnam."

"They have phones there?" he said through a smile.

She knew him well enough to suspect he was doing what he always did—going for the laughs. Yet Sonsee wasn't in her most humorous mood. Instead, she grappled for a means to the quickest end to this stressful conversation.

"Yes," she said firmly, "they have phones. Well, this call is costing me five dollars a minute. I need to go."

"Sonsee, before you go..." he said, uncertainty spilling into his now serious voice. "I can't help but think that things will never be the same between you and me."

Biting her lips, Sonsee blinked against the tears. *You will not cry,* she insisted, but she had spent so many hours in tears that her ability to turn them off was diminishing.

"I'm sorry," he said, regret seeping from his every word. "I wish…"

"Don't," she said firmly. "There's nothing that can be done. I've acted like a fool, and…" Her voice broke and she coughed, exhorting herself not to release the emotions that left her trembling.

An aching silence settled between them.

"I would never purposefully hurt you in a million years," he said.

"I know, Taylor."

More silence. And Sonsee nervously creased and uncreased the muddled brown bedspread.

"Well, I guess I'll let you get back to your dialing, then," he said. "Do you need me to look up your father's number for you?" That ever-present humor laced his words in a teasing nuance.

"No—no thanks," Sonsee said then hung up the phone.

Abruptly she stood, walked to the sliding glass doors that opened onto a tiny balcony, opened them, and stepped out into the Vietnam night. Sonsee gripped the metal railing and gazed down into the narrow, worn street filled with motorcycles and the ever-present pedicabs. The faint acrid smell she had noticed when arriving in Cantho seemed a metaphor for the pungent disillusionment that was seeping into her soul. At last she had fallen in love, and it was the worst thing she could have ever done. Never had she felt so all alone in the world, so rejected, so distraught.

How could I have been so stupid to call him, instead of Father? She consumed several minutes chiding herself for her own absentmindedness. She completely forgot about calling her father. Melissa often laughed at Sonsee for stunts just like this one. But Sonsee wondered if tonight's mistake had been a product of her own subconscious desires to throw herself at Taylor's feet and beg him to give their relationship a chance. Last Saturday, when Sonsee thoroughly understood that Taylor would never love her, her spirits had begun a gradual downward spiral. Tonight, despite the cool tropical breeze caressing her cheeks, that downward spiral could descend no farther. She had arrived at her lowest ebb.

The sob that threatened to emerge while she and Taylor talked would be denied no longer. Sonsee covered her face with her hands and silently wept. She wasn't sure how long she stood there, releasing her emotions, but at last someone opened the door behind her.

"Are you all right?" Melissa asked, stepping beside her friend.

"No," Sonsee said. Reaching into the pocket of her khaki pants, she pulled out a tissue and mopped at her face. She hated anyone to see her crying.

Melissa placed her elbows on the railing and leaned out, gazing down onto the night traffic. Sonsee tensed, waiting on the questions she knew Melissa would calmly deliver. As the minutes ticked by, Sonsee decided to just be honest.

"I accidentally dialed Taylor's number in there."

"The two of you talked?"

"Yes."

"And?"

"There's nothing to tell. He's just terribly sorry about not being able to fall in love with me." Sonsee groaned as a new wave of embarrassment washed over her. "Of course, I am systematically making a fool of myself. It's humiliating. It's beyond humiliating! I wish I could just stay here on the other side of the world and never see him again."

"I'm sure Mick O'Donnel could arrange that," Melissa said practically.

Sighing, Sonsee dashed away the last tear and turned her back on the street below. She leaned against the rail. "Well, in reality, I don't think that's what the Lord wants."

"And what do *you* think He wants?"

"You should have become a psychiatrist," Sonsee said, rolling her eyes.

"Hey, you two, what's going on out here?" Kim said, stepping onto the balcony.

"We're talking about writing a book titled 'How to Make a Thorough Fool of Yourself in Ten Easy Steps,'" Sonsee said.

"I want in on it," Kim said. "I could give you an outline tonight."

The three sisters laughed companionably.

"You know, there's a definite odor to this place," Kim said, stepping to the other side of Sonsee. "And it's not really pleasant. Saigon didn't have a bad odor."

"You mean that faint smell of open sewage, mixed with garlic, and a boiled egg thrown in for good measure?" Melissa asked.

"Wow, I hadn't noticed," Sonsee quipped.

More laughter.

"I'm seriously thinking about adopting that little boy I was holding today," Kim Lan said.

"Really?" Sonsee looked at her. "Isn't he the special needs child?"

Kim nodded.

"What does Ted think?"

"I mentioned it to him before the trip, and he wasn't against the idea."

Melissa cleared her throat. "He looked like he might be slightly Down Syndrome," she said. "Did you realize that?"

Sonsee turned back to face the traffic and watched Kim's thoughtful face in the soft glow of the dim city lights.

"I didn't know for sure," she said at last. "But I guess if that's the case, I would still want him. He needs a home, and the thought of where he might land if someone doesn't take him makes me nauseous."

"I feel the exact same way about the little boy I was holding," Sonsee said, recalling the joy of cradling that precious two-and-a-half-year-old in her arms. "I think Mick said that the baby home is only equipped for children up to three. After that, they really are at a loss as to what to do with them. Putting them into the public orphanage system seems a crime, if you ask me." She balled the damp tissue in her hands and decided to plunge forward and reveal the whole of her anguish. "Melissa was just asking me about what I think God's will is for me. I was saying I wanted to just stay over here for life and never see Taylor Delaney again. That was him on the phone, by the way. I was trying to call Father, and I wound up dialing Taylor's number."

Kim shook her head. "I can only imagine how you must feel."

"Well, the Lord seems to be whispering to me that even if I can't have my dream man..." she raised her hand, "... that perhaps I could still make a difference in a child's life." Sonsee leaned out and gazed straight down into the sea of honking motorcycles. "I think I'll come back and adopt one of those babies for sure," she said firmly, and a pinpoint of light seemed to pierce the darkness of her soul. "I don't know when that will happen. Might be another couple of years. Anyway, I was thinking of maybe asking you guys to pray with me tonight," she continued. "I've got to get over this—this mountain of despair I feel. God seems to be trying to show me that He wants to be more important to me than anybody—any man, any relationship, anything. Quite frankly, I think somewhere along the line I fell in love with Taylor and put my dreams of marrying him ahead of my pursuit of God."

"Whew," Melissa said. "That's tough to admit."

Kim Lan remained silent.

Sonsee swallowed against a lump in her throat and wadded the tissue into an even tighter ball. "The one thing I want on this trip—if nothing else—I want to nail this problem to the cross. I don't want..." She stopped as her eyes began to sting again. "I've decided I'm tired of living my life, trying to fulfill my own dreams. I need to find out what God's plans are for me, His perfect will, and live my life to fulfill that—whether it means getting married or remaining single for life. And I need you guys to pray with me."

"Now?" Melissa asked.

Straightening, Sonsee made a firm decision. "Why not now?"

"Uh..." Kim Lan inched toward the door. "You two go ahead without me. I'm going to take a hot bath."

Swiftly, Kim stepped back into the room. When Sonsee and Melissa followed her, she rushed toward the bathroom feeling as if she were running from the hand of God. She filled the tub full of water, as hot as she could stand it, slipped out of her clothing, knotted her hair atop her head, and sank into the hot water. But the warmth did nothing to ease her tension. Confusion swirled through Kim like a tornado of never-ending conflict. A psalm her pastor had read during a Sunday service spun a recurring thread through her mind: "Where can I go from your Spirit? Where can I flee from your presence? If I go up to the heavens, you are there; if I make my bed in the depths, you are there."

"If I go to Cantho, You are there," she uttered in a distressed whisper. No matter where she turned, Kim Lan felt

the Lord was forever restating His requirements for continued spiritual growth. Indeed, Sonsee was agonizing over
the very issues that Kim Lan faced. She couldn't even get
away from her battle when talking with her friends.

Kim reflected over the last year and the choices that had
led her to this difficult crossroads in her spiritual journey.
She had always gone to church; she had always said she
was a Christian. However, one Sunday, sitting in her usual
pew, she began to wonder if there wasn't more to living for
the Lord. A voice deep within prompted her to begin seeking God on a new level. That night, Kim Lan had opened her
Bible, sat before the Lord, and essentially said, "I want to see
You moving in my life as never before. Show me what I
need to do."

From that point forth, the Lord had peeled away one layer
of unrighteousness after another within Kim Lan's heart.
Through the truths in His Word and His voice in her soul, He
had led Kim on a journey of righteousness, restitution, and
self-sacrifice. She had noticed that with each act of obedience, the Lord had increased His blessings and His presence
had grown more poignant with every passing day. But a few
months ago, when He started laying His hand on her possessions Kim Lan felt as if she had perhaps gone as far with
God as she could humanly go.

Melissa's muffled tones filtered into Kim Lan, and the
nuance of her faithful prayers seemed to caress Kim's very
soul. A tear trickled down her face to plop into the bath
water. She pressed her fingers against her trembling lips as
new tears coursed down her cheeks. She had never been as
adept at holding back her emotions as was Sonsee. When
Kim Lan needed to cry, the tears usually just flowed with no
regard to the appropriateness of the moment. Thankfully,
she had no witnesses for this crying session.

As Melissa and Sonsee's muffled prayers ceased, images of that crippled boy from the ferry filled her mind, and the tune that would not leave her soul began once more to tug at her heartstrings.

> People need the Lord.
> People need the Lord.

Shifting her position in the cramped tub, Kim Lan thought of the marble Jacuzzi in her penthouse...of those poor elders behind the baby home who didn't even have indoor bathrooms...of the excessive luxury of her whole life.

> At the end of broken dreams
> He's the open door.
> People need the Lord.
> People need the Lord.
> When will we realize
> That we must give our lives
> For people need the Lord.

A soft knock on the door interrupted her introspection. "Kim Lan?" Melissa called. "We're going down for a Coke. Want to go with us?"

"Uh, no," Kim said. "Go on without me."

"Want us to bring you anything up?"

"No...no thanks."

"Are you okay?" she softly probed.

"No, but..."

Silence.

"We'll give you some space," Sonsee said, and Kim imagined her darting a "back off" look to Melissa. Kim Lan dearly loved the brilliant doctor, but at times Melissa's penchant for details grew burdensome. The sound of the door opening and closing attested to their departure, and silence cloaked itself around Kim Lan, drawing her into deeper reflection.

As the minutes turned into an hour, Kim relived her child-hood...the years she had been the poorest girl in class...her determination to become wealthy...the hole in her heart that she tried to fill with the fulfillment of material dreams. Sonsee's words echoed through her mind, *I've decided I'm tired of living my life, trying to fulfill my own dreams. I need to find out what God's plans are for me, His perfect will, and live my life to fulfill that.*

And the Lord gently whispered in Kim's spirit, *Give Me your wealth, Kim Lan. Let Me heal the hole in your heart, so you can point others to Me. Place your worth in Me, not in what you own.*

"But I can't," Kim whispered like a child lost for knowl-edge. "I don't know how. Show me how." Kim waited as the current of her desires began to drift from the banks of mate-rialistic superficiality and gradually flow near the depths the Lord had been tugging her toward for months—the pools of spiritual maturity. The allure of the old materialistic thought process seemed to beckon her not to sail far off, and Kim momentarily resisted the Lord's gentle coaxing toward an experience with Him more powerful than any she had known before. But at long last she submitted to the wooing of the Holy Spirit completely and without reserve, and the dam of Kim's resistance broke.

She covered her face and began to openly sob. "Oh, Father," she cried between the tears. "Take it! Take every-thing I own. I will give up everything for You. I will sell every possession I have and give away every penny if that is what You want." The material things that were the most important to her swam before her mind's eye—the items she relied upon to present the right image to the world. The new Jaguar she purchased every year. The numerous fur coats. The diamonds. The rare antiques. Her extensive financial portfolio. One by one, Kim Lan released these possessions to God. By the time her bath water was chilled, she had sacrificed every material possession before the Lord. Like Abraham preparing to give up his son, Isaac, Kim's heart was at last broken, completely broken, before her God. It was spilled out and overflowing with His presence...until He presented the final request.

And what of Ted? Are you willing to break your engagement to him?

Kim's pulse began pounding with a fury that left her breathless. Her mind spun with the implications of this holy supplication. She recalled the times she had firmly claimed that Ted was her "dream man." Even in the face of his recent emotional explosion, Kim's soul cringed with thoughts of breaking the engagement with him. Every woman in America would think she was crazy.

Then Mick O'Donnel seemed to waltz into her mind and weave images of himself upon the fabric of her soul. His maturity. His monumental faith in God. His willingness to pour out his very essence for the call of Jesus Christ. Ted Curry, capricious, short-tempered, and unpredictable seemed but a child when compared to Mick. But Ted was the personification of everything Kim Lan had valued for so long.

She sat up in the cool water and furiously scrubbed herself with the washcloth and soap. In minutes she drained the tub, stepped out, and dried herself off. She donned her underwear and the oversized cotton lounging dress hanging on the door's hook. Desperate for any diversion, she whipped open the bathroom door and walked into the outer room. Wondering exactly how long she had been in the bathroom, she glanced toward the clock on the bedside table to see the ten o'clock hour swiftly approaching. The phone rang and Kim jumped, startled by the unexpected sound. Wondering who could be calling, she padded toward the phone and answered it. In seconds, Mick O'Donnel's voice floated across the line.

"Did you remember we have a date at ten on the balcony?" he asked, his mellow voice seeming to wrap itself around her.

Shivering with the effect, Kim recalled the ferry ride across the Cantho River that morning and Mick asking her to meet him on the balcony. They had been whispering about Caleb at the time, and Mick behaved as if he didn't want to say more unless they were in a private setting. However, she never promised to meet him, only told him she would think about the balcony tryst.

"Well?" he prompted. "Are you going to stand me up?"

"I..." Kim chewed her lower lip while a war raged within. Mick's comment at the baby home hit her again, as if he had just spoken the words: "I don't play games. I play for keeps." The Lord's prompting that she break up with Ted accosted her from another angle. Kim remembered Mick's observation when he first met her—*I believe you're the most lovely woman I have ever met*. However, her childhood dreams of marrying someone like Ted dragged her even further into the pit of indecision. Then she remembered those horrible accusations Ted had hurled at her before she left for Vietnam. The longer she knew Ted, the more volatile he became. Kim Lan began to wonder if marriage would improve or worsen his temper.

"I'll be out there at ten," Mick said at last. "I'll stay fifteen minutes. If you don't come out, I'll take the hint. If you do..." He paused, his voice soft, coaxing, intimate. "I'll take an even bigger hint."

The phone clicked in Kim's ear.

Seventeen

~

Mick hung up the phone and glanced toward his snoozing brother. Caleb would undoubtedly be impressed had he heard *that* phone conversation. Or else he would believe his low-key, older brother had gone off the deep end.

"Well, that's probably right," Mick mumbled with a smile. "Either God is up to something magnificent or I'm turning forty and flipping my wig."

He thought of Kim Lan's silhouette against the soft glow of Cantho traffic, and his stomach tightened with expectation. *Will she meet me? I can only hope...hope and pray... pray for a miracle.* The digital clock on the nightstand said ten o'clock was only five minutes away. Mick, afraid of being disappointed, considered not even taking the chance of standing out there like some Romeo dunce. But he knew he had precious little choice. He would never forgive himself if she came out onto her balcony and he wasn't there to meet her.

Tucking the tail of his striped shirt into his slacks, Mick stepped toward the sliding glass door, unlocked it, and walked onto the balcony. Silently he slid the glass door into place, gripped the cool, metal rail in his clammy hands, and forced himself to stare across the street at the shadowed buildings below. Mick refused to have Kim find him hanging over the rail, leaning toward her balcony, pining for the slightest glimpse of her. Yet in reality that was exactly how he felt.

But the minutes crept by as if they were each a laborious hour, and Kim never came out. Finally, Mick pressed the button on his lighted watch and confirmed his suspicions. Ten-fifteen had arrived. Mick began to accept his worst fear—Kim Lan was telling him to take the hint and back off. Unquestionably, Mick had stepped over more than one boundary with Kim from the time of their first acquaintance. However, in recent days he had been so sure of the Lord's promise that he would indeed marry Kim Lan that he had approached her with increasing confidence.

His neck throbbed with the strain of the day, and Mick massaged it. The morning had started at five, and it had been a long day for everyone. *She probably needs her rest,* he thought. *And perhaps I came on too strong.* He turned toward his room.

However, a slight movement from the corner of his eye caught his attention. Mick peered through the night as Kim stepped onto her balcony and closed the door behind her. She turned toward Mick, gripped the handrail, and silently observed him. Her hair, like a shadowed cascade, draped forward across her shoulder and hung just above the rail. The faint breeze lifted strands of the satiny tresses from around her face and blew them against her cheeks.

Mick's heart raced. He turned toward her and nonchalantly stuck his booted foot between the rods surrounding the balcony. "Nice night," he said casually.

"Yes," she answered.

The breeze wafted a faint, powdery scent across the few feet separating them, and Mick wanted to feel her in his arms. He removed his boot from between the rods and propped his forearms on the handrail, leaning toward her.

The sounds of the diminishing traffic punctuated the moment fraught with expectation.

When the silence between them became to taut to bear, Mick softly urged, "Tell me about yourself, Kim Lan Lowery."

She continued to stare at him, her dark eyes reflecting the glimmer of the lights below. "What do you want to know?"

"Whatever you want to tell me. Everything about you." *I think I'm falling in love with you, and anything you say will fascinate me.*

As if she were at a loss for words, Kim persisted in her silent appraisal.

"Well, for instance..." Mick searched for a topic of light conversation—something that wouldn't be threatening but pleasant. Anything, to keep her outside. Anything, to keep her near. "Do you like cats?"

"Pardon me?"

"Cats? Do you like them?"

"Yes, I do. I haven't had a cat in years, although we always had one around the house when I was growing up."

"I own a Siamese. My mother spoils him when I'm not at my cabin in Colorado." *I would enjoy spoiling you, Kim.*

"I love Siamese cats," she said.

"Mine's name is Mao. That's Thai for cat. Did you know?" *And "Tuht suay jahng" is Thai for "You are beautiful."*

"No, I didn't know. Exactly how many foreign languages have you conquered, anyway?" she asked.

"Who wants to know?" he teased. *I would walk across the ocean to hear you say you're dying to learn everything about me.*

Tilting her head to one side, she observed him, her lips slightly arched. "You figure it out."

"Well, I'm fluent in French."

"So I noticed."

"And it's a good thing. Poor old Mr. Nguyen. If I didn't feel sorry for him, I'd demand a different interpreter. His English is certainly not what it should be, but from what I have gathered on past trips, he needs every penny he can scrape together."

"So you've used him before?"

"Yes."

"Well, it's been somewhat humorous watching the two of you—almost like a sit-com."

"Yeah, well, the poor chap speaks almost perfect French, so at least we have some grounds for communication."

"Should I assume you're fluent in Thai as well?" she asked, curiosity scurrying across her shadowed features.

"No, just French and, I guess, English, or so I've been told." He smiled. "I know enough Thai, Vietnamese, Chinese, German, and Russian just to be dangerous and that's about it." *Do you like men who speak several foreign languages? I'll learn Greek if that's what you want.*

"The only thing I'm any good at is English," she said ruefully.

"So your mother never taught you Vietnamese?"

"I know precious little about Vietnam or the Vietnamese culture."

"Oh, really?" Mick said, surprised.

"Yes. When my mother came to the States as a refugee, she got out of Vietnam with her life, and that was about it. I don't know what all happened, but I've always had this sense that there were some really traumatic events in her past, and when she closed it off she closed off everything about Vietnam as well."

"Your mother mentioned that you had wanted to visit her homeland for years. I guess that explains it."

"Yes, I've been curious about Vietnam most of my life."

"So, what do you think so far?"

Kim Lan turned to look over the city. "I think I'm deeply saddened by all the poverty," she said slowly. "It makes me want to do more than just help out on this trip. I'd like to find out if I could donate some money to improve that home for the elderly even more than we're doing. Right now, those poor old people are living in what looks like a long row of connected huts. And then the living quarters for those school-aged orphans leave much to be desired. They're just in bunk beds in a glorified barn."

"I'll take all the money you want to donate," Mick said through a chuckle. "As a matter of fact, I could probably use up every penny you own and then some. I travel all over the world and face this kind of destitution almost everywhere I go."

She turned to face him. "I'm not sure what all is going on with me and the Lord, Mick, but I do know that...that He's requiring that I be willing to do exactly that—to give away every penny if that's what He wants."

Mick, constraining himself, stopped short of blurting out an exalted *Yes!* He schooled his features into a bland mask and slowly nodded. Inside, he wanted to jump over the balcony, land sure-footed in the middle of the street three stories below, and run up and down the road like an idiot yelling, "Thank You, God! Thank You!"

"You know, I think that's the place the Lord would like all of us to be," Mick said solemnly. "It seems everybody has a 'something' they want to hold onto." Mick drew imaginary quotation marks with shaking fingers then leaned against the balcony for support. "Or perhaps another way to put it is we all have something we hang our identity on. For some people, it's material wealth, whether they own it or just focus on it. For other people it's what happened in their past. They identify themselves as the abused one or the divorced one, and the list could go on and on." He tucked his hands into his pockets. "Then, for others it becomes a matter of releasing human relationships to the Lord. I think it's just different issues with different people, but it all boils down to a matter of the Lord asking us to place our all in His hands and take our identity from Him, not from human relationships or money or from what has happened in the past. It's a matter of giving Him absolute control of our lives. Anything less is bondage to self."

Kim Lan had bequeathed him her undivided attention, and Mick found her pensive scrutiny unnerving to the point that he couldn't concentrate on his own words. He forced himself to look toward the dark horizon. "For me," he continued, "it involved releasing some issues of bitterness, hatred, and anger to the Lord."

"Oh?"

"Yes." He allowed himself only a brief glimpse of her. "My father was killed in the Vietnam War. I was only thirteen. It devastated me. By the time I hit fifteen, I had decided that my life's mission was to find the person who killed my father and return evil for evil."

"So...you wanted to murder him?"

Mick looked at her. "Yes," he said simply. "But even worse than that, I grew to hate everyone from Vietnam."

Her eyes widened.

"By the time I was twenty, I was eaten alive by my own vengeance. My mother—my mother is a godly woman if there ever was one—spent many long nights in prayer for me." He crossed his arms and gazed absently at the tips of his worn boots as the story rolled off his tongue. Even now, sixteen years later, recalling the events of his recommitment to the Lord left Mick falling in love with Him all over again. "Then, when I was twenty-three, cocky and ready to take on the world, somehow some woman convinced me to attend a revival service with her. Looking back, I wonder if my mother wasn't behind the invitation. I had been raised in church and had even made a commitment to the Lord as a kid, but..." Mick shook his head and laughed. "I guess I was kinda like poor old Caleb with Laci Emerson. It took a woman of God to point me in the right direction. By the way," he said parenthetically, "I think God was at work all along on Caleb, through Laci. Seems he's made a new commitment to the Lord."

Kim smiled cleverly. "That's just what most men need," she teased. "A good woman to steer them in the right direction."

"Yeah, yeah, yeah," Mick said. *I think I need you, Kim. Would you be my good woman?* The thought came so strong that Mick wondered if he had actually voiced it, and he forgot everything he had been saying. He silently stared at her as his longing to hold her in his arms superseded all other intelligent thought.

"So are you going to finish?" she asked.

"I would if I could remember what I was saying. You got me off track," he said, thankful his voice didn't reveal where his mind had roamed.

"You were talking about the revival service when you were twenty-three."

"Oh, yeah. And the woman invited me and then I mentioned Caleb and Laci, and then you came forth with your words of wisdom," he recounted, to get his mind back into gear.

She laughed softly, and Mick reveled in the sound of her joy. "Well, anyway," he began, back to the subject at hand.

"That night, God got a hold of me. I knew I couldn't leave until I came face to face with my own hate and allow the Lord to clean out my heart and clean up my life. After that, before I knew it, I was enrolled in a seminary in Kansas City studying missions, and my mother was praising the Lord from Colorado to the moon and back. The rest is history." He uncrossed his arms and tucked his hands into his slacks' pockets.

"Wow," Kim said, blatant admiration spilling from her countenance.

Mick compelled himself to again observe the horizon. *So much for light conversation,* he thought.

"And now I take it you don't hate the Vietnamese?" she asked.

He coughed over a laugh. "Uh...no. Somewhere along the line, I fell head over heels in love with them. And..." Mick measured his words, desperately wanting to reveal his heart while maintaining dignity—at least this once. "I've come to the conclusion that Oriental women are the most beautiful in the world. I guess you've probably already figured out by now that where you're concerned, I..." he searched for the right words. Saying he liked her sounded too juvenile. But the words that he left unsaid seemed the most powerful choice. Those words wove a canopy of affection between them, drawing them ever closer to one another.

"Yes, I—I know," she said hesitantly. "And..."

"And?"

"I think you probably—um—suspect how I feel."

"Let me hear you say it." *One day, I hope you'll tell me you love me.*

"I—you—um—we seem to have—to have this—this thing between us. I've never—"

"Neither have I."

"And it's scary," she said.

"Yes. And thrilling."

The breeze began its slow dance around her hair, and Mick ached to feel the satiny fineness beneath his fingers. Yet his rational side thanked God the balconies separated them. Mick didn't need to be kissing her anymore. They were far from committed to one another, and the gentleman within insisted he maintain a respectful distance. Furthermore, there was that one other disturbing detail about Kim Lan Lowery: She was engaged.

"Kim?"

"Yes."

Mick, feeling propelled to discuss Ted, still wavered with introducing him into their conversation. Nevertheless, there were some things he wanted to say. "You don't deserve the way Ted Curry treats you."

She stiffened, and an uneasy silence settled between them.

Straightening, Mick clutched the rail and, in an attempt to feign relaxation, slowly placed his boot back between the rods. Mrs. Lowery was so concerned about her daughter's pending marriage that she had desperately prayed for another man to enter Kim's life. Mick recalled Kim's telephone conversation with Curry on the airplane, and he understood Mrs. Lowery's desperation. The protective instinct that had bid him hold Kim on their flight to L.A. manifested itself again.

"I've seen Curry's type before, and I'm afraid that he's using marriage as a means to just get what he wants from you. When he gets bored, he'll move along regardless of your wedding vows."

"You don't even know him," she softly defended.

"I know his reputation." Mick waved his hand for emphasis. "And I know he made a pass at Sonsee." The words sprang from Mick before he realized what he was saying. Breathlessly, he stared at Kim as she observed him in stunned silence.

"How did you find out?"

"Your mother told me," Mick said, cold dread settling in his midsection.

"But how did she—*Sonsee!*" Kim said with certainty.

Mick stifled a groan and wondered how he had managed to unequivocally place *both* his feet in his mouth.

"I told Sonsee Ted was j-just flirting," Kim sputtered, the rising ire evident in her shrill voice.

"Well, she doesn't think he was, Kim Lan. Neither does your mom."

"I don't appreciate their or *your* interfering," she said, resentment lacing her words.

"I didn't mean to come across that way. I'm just worried you can't see the forest for the trees or something, that maybe—that maybe you're so enthralled with what Ted is, you're blinded to—"

"Excuse me," she snapped. Opening the sliding glass door, Kim stepped into her room and slid the door shut.

"Well, great," he said under his breath. "Chalk up another zero for Mick O'Donnel."

Kim, breathless with the intensity of the conversation, paused inside her room and allowed her eyes to adjust to the lamplight. She turned the worn lock on the balcony door as a determined knock sounded on the front door. Sonsee's tired voice called into the room, "Kim Lan, this is our last call. Are you in there?"

Rigid with anger, Kim rushed to the door, unlocked it, and swung it inward. "What happened? Did you lose your key?" she asked, her voice tight with irritation. At the sight of Sonsee entering the room, Kim could barely curb expressing the onslaught of pain and betrayal. Kim wanted to yell, *How could you! How could you talk about me to my own mother!*

"I thought my key was in my money pouch," Sonsee said, removing the pouch from her waist and dropping it on the dresser where the missing key lay. "But looks like I left it here." She picked up the key and dangled it. "I'm so exhausted I could sleep a week!" she said with a yawn.

"Me, too," Melissa echoed. "By the way, Kim, where were you?" Melissa asked. "We've been standing out there about three or four minutes knocking our brains out."

"I was on the balcony talking—" Kim Lan cut herself off.

"Talking to Mick?" Melissa tilted her head in that curious way of hers and examined Kim Lan as if she were already convinced of the answer.

"Figures," Sonsee said, flopping onto the bed. Her pale, freckled face revealed her exhaustion.

"What's that supposed to mean?" Kim Lan challenged, an edge to her voice. With each passing second her ability to hide her aggravation diminished tenfold.

"We might as well just get it all out in the open," Sonsee said practically. "Lord help us all, I certainly spilled my guts tonight." She tugged on the black elastic band holding her ponytail and her hair fell to her shoulders as she plopped back on the pillow. "Anyway, Melissa and I have put our heads together and come to the conclusion that Mick O'Donnel is falling in love with you."

Melissa adjusted her round wire-rimmed glasses. "Are you aware of just how serious he is, Kim?" she asked as if she were Mick's protective older sister.

Kim looked at both her friends. "Whose side are you two on, anyway?"

They exchanged a meaningful glance, and the stress of the evening coupled with their sisterly treason sent a whirlwind of fury through Kim Lan. Her palms moistened. Her pulse pounded. Her legs shook.

"We were just worried that…" Sonsee started to sit upright, as if a change in position would better enable her to express herself. "You said he had kissed you, and considering Ted, we were concerned that, well, the way things look, we just don't want to see Mick get hurt."

"Neither of us has known him that long, but he seems like a really special man, Kim," Melissa added.

Kim's annoyance mounted to mammoth proportions.

"You have a lot of nerve, Sonsee LeBlanc," Kim Lan blurted out, ignoring their concerns about Mick.

"What?" Her eyes as wide as if she had been slapped, Sonsee stiffened.

"I know you told Mom that Ted made a pass at you," Kim ground out.

"Oh, no," Melissa muttered.

"How?" Sonsee gasped.

"Mick told me. Just now—on the balcony."

"But how did *he* know?" Sonsee asked, her face growing paler by the second.

"Mom told him. It looks like the few people I trusted the most have been the most disloyal." Kim's shaking voice broke with the fresh rush of tears.

"The person who betrayed you is *Ted,* Kim," Sonsee insisted. "The only reason I told your mother was because I was beside myself with worry—"

"*I told you Ted was just a flirt, Sonsee!* Why can't you believe me?" Kim waved a hand for added emphasis.

"And I tried to tell *you* that he was *dead serious!*" Sonsee's voice rose in a frustrated crescendo, and she held Kim Lan's gaze as if she were determined to stare the truth into her friend. "He even called me at work, Kim," she added, shaking her head.

Melissa nervously cleared her throat. A taut silence descended upon the friends. Grinding her teeth, Kim turned her back on her silent friends, grabbed her silk pajamas from her open suitcase, and stormed toward the bathroom. Before entering the restroom, she pivoted toward Melissa and Sonsee and stonily glared at them. "You're both so concerned about Mick! Do either of you even give a flip about me? Do either of you *care* whether or not *I* get hurt in all this—this mess?"

"Kim Lan," Melissa soothed. "We didn't mean it to come across that way at all. We were just afraid that maybe you didn't see how serious Mick was and...about Ted..."

"And what a lecher Ted is. Is that it?"

"If the shoe fits," Sonsee said, her cold voice and tight lips proclaiming her anger.

Kim whirled around, went into the bathroom, and slammed the door with an ominous finality that seemed to sever all bonds of friendship. She flung the red pajamas onto the floor and clenched her fists as tears of wrath erupted, creating hot rivulets down her cheeks. Her spine stiff, Kim covered her face and bit her lips, refusing to emit even the faintest sniffle that would attest to her crying. After fifteen minutes of silence laden with potent emotions, Kim sat on the side of the bathtub. Her body, weak from the adrenalin rush, acted as if it were a jellyfish, molding its form to the contour of the tub.

The sounds of her friends preparing for bed floated into the room, and Kim's heart cringed with the magnitude of their actions. Never had she felt so alienated from them. *True friends aren't supposed to gang up on each other,* Kim fumed. *If they really loved me, they would be loyal and not discuss me behind my back. And Sonsee stooped so low! I can't believe she discussed me and Ted with my mother! And Mom!* Kim Lan stood and paced the small room. *How could Mom have turned around and told Mick, almost a complete stranger, what Sonsee told her? None of it is Mick O'Donnel's business!* She snatched a tissue from the box on the counter and scrubbed her cheeks. Furiously Kim blew her nose, and a new thought barged into her turbulent mind.

But what if Sonsee is right? What if Ted really was serious in propositioning her? Despite her penchant for defending Ted, Kim Lan's recent dinner date with him at Liambrio's broke across the canvas of her mind. She recalled his furor over their waiting a year to get married. *"Well, exactly what did you think? That I was going to wait a whole year before I could make love to you?"*

Kim pondered all the marriages among fellow celebrities that had ended as quickly as they started, of the actors and actresses who had walked out on their families for their latest fling, of the possibility that Ted was no different, despite his claim of a deeper commitment to Christ. Her musings traveled back to her one romantic indiscretion. Kim Lan had been starstruck by a famous actor who had promised her heaven, only to cast her aside when he grew tired of the relationship. She had been so devastated that she cried herself to sleep every night for a month, then spent the next year in a state of emotional numbness. Finally, Kim Lan had vowed that with God as her helper she would never— *absolutely never*—fall prey to another such relationship.

Have I done it again? Kim asked herself. *Is Sonsee right?* Icy dread draped across her shoulders and a chill of apprehension shot down her spine. Kim Lan couldn't stay the compulsive shiver that left her teeth on edge. *Perhaps Sonsee told Mom about Ted's comment because of her loyalty and* *love for me....*Kim's stomach churned with nausea, and she stifled a groan as she covered her face with quivering hands. As if the pieces of a jumbled, complicated puzzles were clicking into place, she recalled a comment made by a fellow model a few weeks before. *Aren't you concerned about Ted going to Paris with Angela Swift as his leading lady?"* Kim had not given the passing remark a moment's concern. Just as she had with Sonsee's claims, Kim had dismissed the whole exchange from her mind. She so desperately wanted Ted to be her prince, to fulfill her childhood dreams, that she had refused to even consider he might be less than devoted.

Immediately Kim Lan sensed the Lord tugging her back to the place where she had been when she stepped from the bathtub. It was time to make a choice. The crossroads once again presented themselves. One road was marked with the blood-stained, sacrificial steps of a holy Savior. The other path was marred with the determined footprints of selfish goals and self-centered gratification. Ted Curry represented everything Kim had valued her entire life. But even if he were faithful, he still was not a man who hungered after the things of God...a man like Mick O'Donnel.

At last Kim accepted the truth. Ted was not and never could be faithful. *He values me because I make him look good and I'm a challenge. That's no basis for a healthy marriage.* Exhausted with the intensity of her battle but strangely at peace, Kim Lan donned her silk pajamas and brushed her hair. She pictured the three-carat diamond engagement ring she had left in her apartment building's safety deposit box.

Kim looked at the bathtub. An hour ago, she had cried in that very spot and began the process of releasing all she owned to the Lord. Yet when He pointed to Ted, she bolted.

The psalm from earlier once more scampered across her soul: "Where can I go from your Spirit?" Kim Lan understood that the Lord would not allow her to skirt the issue of releasing Ted any more than He would allow her to avoid making a choice about releasing her possessions. Ted was the personification of her materialistic thought process. If Kim Lan was going to release her wealth to the use of the Lord, she would also have to release Ted. Anything less was hypocrisy.

A deeper peace settled upon Kim as she realized she no longer desired Ted. The reason went much deeper than the evidence of his philandering. It was an issue of a pure heart, of being purified by a holy Creator. Kim closed her stinging eyes and imagined herself opening the safety deposit box that held the engagement ring. She picked up the near-perfect diamond. In her mind, Kim Lan examined the ring as its glistening depths produced copious sparkles like a thousand shooting stars ready to light up her spirit. Kim imagined slipping the ring upon her finger.

Do you love Me, Kim? a gentle voice whispered from the recesses of her soul.

"I do," she breathed.

Will you release this ring? Will you release Ted? Will you give your life, your wealth, and all you own so others will know My love?

"I will," Kim whispered, tears streaming down her cheeks. *"I will,"* she said again. The materialistic chains dropped from her captive soul, link by rusty link, and Kim Lan Lowery was free. A joyous sob spilled from her inner being like the fragrance of a rosebud that has awakened from a suffocating night to erupt into full bloom with the splendid dawn of liberty.

Eighteen

Odysseus sat up in bed and peered at the digital clock on the hotel's nightstand. Four-thirty. He rubbed his face and lambasted himself for sleeping so late. He had planned to awaken by two in order to deliver his letter to Sophie. Due to Vietnam's proximity to the equator, the sun was up by five-thirty. The darkness would begin to fade by five. Odysseus had wanted to give himself plenty of time to deliver his note and get back without being seen. He did have thirty minutes, maybe an hour. The task shouldn't take more than fifteen minutes. However, pressing so close to dawn disturbed him. If something went wrong...but he couldn't think like that.

The finalized plan involved jumping from his balcony to Sophie's—an approximate four-foot leap. Then he would tape the note to the balcony door and pray that she saw it soon after she arose. Odysseus had thought of slipping the note under the door or taping it to the room's hallway door, but he was afraid some passerby might take it—or even worse someone might see. He had even considered leaving the note at the hotel's front desk, but that would mean the receptionist would be able to link him to the note. Finally Odysseus had decided that taping the note to the balcony door made the most sense.

Silently he slipped from the bed and walked to his jumbled suitcase. He pulled on a pair of black slacks and matching T-shirt, then inserted his feet into thick-soled canvas shoes. Odysseus turned to his bed to place the extra pillows under the covers and arrange them to appear as if he were still in bed. He glanced at his roommate whose back was turned to him. That idiot slept so soundly he didn't envision his waking up for a thing. But if the imbecile were to stumble to the bathroom, he would at least see the outline of what appeared to be a person in the next bed.

Odysseus retrieved the note from the inside pouch of his suitcase, then inserted his hand even deeper into the pocket to find the roll of duct tape. He had specifically chosen duct tape because it tore easily and served numerous purposes. He slipped the note into the front pocket of his pants, gripped the tape in the other hand, and took one step toward the balcony door. Odysseus stopped. As an afterthought, he moved back to the suitcase and fished out a black ski mask and a thick butcher knife he had stolen from the hotel kitchen. He shoved the ski mask into his other pocket and held the butcher knife with the tape. The sinister blade glistened in the limited street light, seeping in from the window. He contemplated what he would do if he were able to use the blade to break the lock on Sophie's balcony door and decided to take his room key as well. Odysseus retrieved the key from the dresser and dropped it into his other pocket. Having the key would broaden his options.

In seconds, he opened the sliding glass door, stepped outside, closed the door, and paused to peer into the room. No movement from his roommate. An occasional honk sounded from the sparse yet steady traffic below, and the distinctive smell of Cantho penetrated his nostrils. He walked to the side of the wide balcony and gauged the distance between his rail and Sophie's. Once again, he estimated the leap to be a mere four feet, four-and-a-half at the most. He glanced down to the dimly lighted street, three stories below. The jump appeared a simple one. In spite of that, he recognized he had no room for error. One miscalculation, and he would be gravely injured or killed.

Stealthily he climbed onto the rail, gripping the hotel's bricks for balance. Refusing to look down, he held his breath and leaped. His feet thudded against Sophie's balcony. Odysseus fell forward on hands and knees. His pulse pounding, his knees burning, he stilled and waited, expecting any minute to hear someone stir within the room. Only the sounds of traffic. Odysseus smiled his pleasure.

Noiselessly, he stood, removed the note from his pocket, and tore off a section of the duct tape. He frowned as a deluded mist settled upon his mind. The name on the envelope said, "Kim Lan Lowery." Through the mist, the forms of two women emerged. Both with waist-length hair, the color of black satin. Both tall, lithe, and lovely. Both with eyes like dark pools of fathomless mysteries. As one specter stepped in front of the other, the images blurred together, increasing the chaos in Odysseus' mind. He secured the note to the glass, with the front facing inward so the name could be seen from inside the room. Odysseus' explosive emotions twisted together like a gyrating tornado, heightening his need to feel Sophie in his arms once more. The intensity of his desires demanded that he at least try to open the balcony door. His first attempt failed.

He thought of Sophie, of her soft lips against his. A frenzied force urged him on. Odysseus placed the butcher knife's strong blade between the sliding door and its facing and tried to pry it open. The locks on these doors lacked much to be desired. He increased the pressure and the lock broke. The door jolted open six inches. His heart raced. His palms perspired. His mind whirled with glee. His fantasy was realized. The opportunity that lay before him left him heady with delight.

Odysseus waited to be sure no one stirred within. When the seconds ticked by and no sound came from the room, he removed the ski mask from his pocket, slipped it over his head, and tore a six-inch piece of duct tape from the roll—just long enough to securely cover Sophie's mouth. He stuck the end of the piece of tape to the front of his shirt and tore off two more pieces. One long enough for her wrists. The other, for her ankles. These he attached to the front of his shirt as well.

He tarried while regretting the necessity of binding his love. *Once she understands it's me,* he thought, *she won't struggle.* But until then, he was forced to use the tape. If Sophie were startled and screamed, she would awaken her roommates and perhaps Mick O'Donnel. Odysseus needed her total silence when he took her into his own room and slid her under his bed. He would leave her there until his roommate went to breakfast. Feigning illness, he would stay in the room. While the rest of the group ate breakfast, he and Sophie would fulfill their thwarted dreams and run away together. The thought of the other trip participants missing them blew winds of discomfort upon his soul. He decided that by the time the other group members realized they were really gone, he and Sophie would be far away.

Mick sat in the congregation of a historic New York church and cringed while the wedding march erupted from the organ. At the altar stood Ted Curry, his face marred by lust. The elderly minister, dressed in black, stood near Ted and gazed up the aisle. Behind them, a wide array of greenery accented the sanctuary, announcing the significance of the day. The crescendo of the organ music announced the pending arrival of a special lady—the bride.

"All rise," the minister said, lifting his hands.

Joining the congregation, Mick stood, turned, and strained to catch a glimpse of Kim Lan while she descended the aisle. As she neared his pew, about the middle of the sanctuary, Mick wildly waved to her, trying to halt her progress, but her focus rested steadfastly upon Ted. Mick screamed, "Kim Lan, don't! This is a mistake! A terrible mistake!" But she never heard him.

Perspiration trickled down his back. Desperation overwhelmed him. He violently trembled.

"Kim!" Mick bellowed as she passed him, heedless of his presence. "Listen to me! I love you! Don't...don't...don't... you're throwing yourself away!" Mick, frantic to stop her, tried to move into the aisle, but he couldn't. He continued to push against the unseen restraints that bound him. More sweat. More desperation. More trembling.

"Kim Lan!...Kim Lan!...Kim Lan!" he screamed.

She stepped toward Ted, took his hand, and the congregation was seated. Yet Mick continued to stand, continued to yell, continued to hopelessly try to lunge for Kim. His head spun. His heart ached. And his soul felt as if he were dying.

The minister persisted in his duties. The "I dos" were stated. The "I wills" were agreed upon. The kiss was exchanged. At last, Kim and Ted turned toward the congregation, and Ted's lascivious face appeared to be that of a ravenous wolf. The minister said, "I present to you Mr. and Mrs. Ted Curry."

As if the minister's words released the ties that bound him, Mick lurched forward, stumbled toward Kim, and fell at her feet. "NOOOOOOOOOOOOOOOOOO!" His agonized cry echoed off the sanctuary walls like the wail of a desolate soul, torn asunder.

∽

The faint pressure against her mouth disturbed Kim Lan. Knitting her brows, she stirred from sleep and groggily reached for her mouth. But her hand was snatched away from her face. Her eyes popped open as a band bound her wrists together. A shadowed figure hovered over her. In panic, she mutely screamed and kicked at the covers. He dashed aside the covers and tightly secured her ankles together with what felt like tape.

Her forehead beaded in sweat. Her stomach churned with nausea. Her mind raced with hysteria. The masked stranger placed his mouth near her ear. "It's just me, Sophie," he said in a gravelly whisper, his hot breath enveloping her ear. "Come with me. It's time to celebrate our love." Effortlessly, he scooped her up and slung her over his shoulder as if she were a bag of potatoes. Her head hung downward, her arms extended below her head.

Oh, Lord, no! she wailed inwardly as tears gushed from her eyes. Every note, every gift from the secret admirer flew through her consciousness. Mick had thought she would be safe in Vietnam.

No! No! No! God save me!

She squirmed against the intruder's tight hold, only to have him increase his grip. His steel-like fingers crushed into her thigh. His labored breathing reverberated throughout the room like the deranged pants of a rabid panther dragging his prey to its cavernous den.

As he neared the room's door, it beckoned Kim like the portals of a burning abyss, yearning to suck her flesh into its pulsating jaws. She shrieked in terror, only to produce a weak scream. She screeched again and again and again, desperately hoping that her faint cries would somehow wake up Sonsee or Melissa. Yet the sickening memory of her friends saying they were so exhausted they could sleep a week took away her hope. Kim pounded the man's lower back and produced another round of mouselike squeaks.

"Kim?" Sonsee's dazed call incited Kim Lan to kick her captor with all the furor she could muster. Her captor's fingers seemed to tear to her very bone, and a shriek of pain erupted from Kim in the form of another faint squeak.

Sonsee snapped on the light. "Kim!" she yelled.

The invader unceremoniously dropped Kim. She collapsed against the floor like a rag doll, thudded first to her feet, then to her bottom, and onto her back, the hard floor brutally impacting her tender flesh with each jolt. The intruder raced around her and out the door as if he were a blurred, black spirit afraid of the light.

~

Quivering like a spent race horse, Odysseus stepped the few feet to his room, unlocked the door, and entered the darkened quarters. His roommate, still asleep, appeared to have never stirred. Silently, he removed the ski mask and rushed to his bed. He knelt beside the bed. Reaching under it, he lodged the tape, knife, and ski mask between two slats and the mattress. He stood and removed the black pants and shirt, then stuffed them between the slats and mattress as well. In seconds, he slipped off his shoes and crammed them into the bottom of his suitcase. He shoved aside the pillows on his bed and crawled under the covers.

Gazing across the dark room, Odysseus relived the previous minutes. The feel of Sophie in his arms. The smell of her perfume. The realization that she had fought him.... He closed his eyes. Fury burned beneath his lids like the fires of Hades, like the flame of a car exploding against a mountain. If this interlude with Sophie had taught him nothing else, it had taught him that she hadn't changed, that she didn't want to hear of his tender love, share his heart, or spend her life with him. Therefore, he would take what was rightfully his, what that lawyer had stolen from him. He had no choice.

⁂

Mick, sprawling at Kim Lan's feet, looked up into her face. At last, she had acknowledged his presence at her wedding. She smiled curiously and said, "Do I know you?"

"It's me, Mick!" he yelled. "Remember?"

Sadly, she shook her head as church bells clanged in celebration of her marriage to Ted. The bells soon took on an odd resonance, a regular meter of a long ring, followed by a pause, and another long ring.

Mick shook his head from side to side. "No...no, Kim, no. Don't marry Ted. Don't...don't. Please God, stop her...stop her..." he begged as she stepped over Mick and walked up the aisle. The bizarre church bells' ringing continued, their rhythmic peels steadily growing more annoying than joyous.

"No...no, Kim, no," Mick muttered moving his head from side to side. Now, he was lying on his back in the church aisle, gazing directly at the baroque ceiling. Somehow, a pillow had found its way under his head, and his whole body rocked with the intensity of his heart, breaking under the burden of his emotions. Those shrill wedding bells beckoned him to reach out and clasp them, and Mick flailed his arm until he gripped one of them. He placed it against his ear to hear a frightened female voice calling his name.

Mick sat straight up in bed, his body drenched, his mind filled with the sorrow of his failure to stop Kim's marriage. Against his ear, he held a phone. From that phone poured panic-filled cries.

"This is Sonsee! Mick, are you awake?"

"Yes, yes, awake," he mumbled. Attempting to regain his equilibrium, he rubbed his eyes, and his heart thumped with heavy beats of relief. *It was a dream. Only a dream,* he told himself.

"You've got to come to our room now!" Sonsee urged. "Someone tried to kidnap Kim Lan."

His body went rigid. "What!" he barked.

"A man came through our balcony door, taped Kim's mouth and hands and feet and was carrying her out the door when I woke up!" Sonsee's words tumbled out like the rapid fire of a machine gun.

"Kim Lan, is she—"

"She's fine. Bruised but fine."

"I'll be there in two minutes." Mick dashed aside the covers, slammed the phone onto its receiver, clicked on the lamp, and reached for the slacks and shirt lying on the foot of the bed.

"What's going on?" Caleb muttered, his voice thick with sleep.

"Someone tried to kidnap Kim Lan," Mick ground out. His protective instincts burning within, he crammed one foot, then the other into his pants, pulled them up, and fastened them.

Caleb, rubbing his eyes, sat up and observed his brother as if he were trying to comprehend what Mick had said.

Mick threw on his cotton shirt. He grabbed Caleb's shorts and T-shirt from the dresser and tossed them at him. "Get up. Get dressed. And see if you can find any traces of anybody who looks suspicious," he demanded.

Nineteen

~

Kim, shaking uncontrollably, waited while Melissa tore the duct tape off her wrists and ankles. The adhesive that had stung the skin around her lips exacted similar pain on her arms and legs. One sob after another ravaged Kim's soul and seemed to keep perfect rhythm with the firm knock that sounded against the door.

Sonsee rushed to the door. "Mick?" she called.

"Yes, it's me."

Melissa tore away the final inches of tape from Kim's ankles, and she swiveled to face Mick as he stepped into the room, his rugged face the pale countenance of a man in mental torture.

Looking up at him, Kim's face crumpled as she wailed in agony, "Mick, he's here. The secret admirer is here."

Mick, dropping to her side, wrapped his arms around her and pulled her against his warmth. Kim Lan clung to him, wishing she could somehow absorb the calm strength he exuded.

"Did he—did he physically hurt you?" Mick asked, wanting to hear confirmation of what Sonsee had already told him.

"N–no." Kim buried her head more snugly against Mick's chest as he stroked her hair. His heart's rapid beats seemed the nuance of a haven of safety.

"He just taped her up and was hauling her out when I woke up," Sonsee said grimly.

"Look at this," Melissa said from across the room.

Kim Lan pulled away from Mick to turn toward Melissa's voice. She stood at the sliding glass door holding an envelope. "It was taped outside and has 'Kim Lan Lowery' written on it."

"Open it and read it," Mick said grimly.

Like a child in denial, Kim's palms itched to cover her ears. She didn't want to hear or see anything else that would further stress the dangerous canyon into which she seemed destined to plunge.

Melissa slid her finger beneath the seal, opened it, and removed the piece of paper. She reached to turn on the corner lamp and picked up her glasses from the dresser. "Sophie," she read. While pushing the glasses onto her face, she reread the name in puzzled deliberation. "Sophie, I am here. I felt you wanting me to come. So I followed you. At last, the moment we have awaited is upon us." Melissa's voice shook. "I love you, and I have taken special pains to make sure you love me. We mustn't be kept apart a moment longer. I am coming to you, and you'll be mine. Please do not reject me. I beg of you not to reject me. I do not want to harm you." She looked toward Kim and Mick, her face solemn. "It's signed 'S.A.'"

Nausea knotted Kim's stomach. Sonsee stared at her, eyes round with dismay. Covering her face with quivering hands, Kim shook her head in disbelief. "He's—he's h–here. Dear God help me! That—that crazy man has followed me to Vietnam."

"Why does he think you're somebody named Sophie?" Melissa asked.

"Who's Sophie? Do you know, Kim?" Sonsee asked.

"He's nuts!" Kim choked out.

Mick gently gripped her upper arms and urged her to face him. "You've got to go back to the States," he commanded. "If we hire a car back to Saigon, we might even get you on a flight out today."

"But..." Kim, her mind spinning with the urgency of the moment, wasn't even sure what she had said.

"No buts. That maniac has somehow followed you. And if he decides to harm you then gets out of Vietnam before he's caught, according to international law there's no punishment awaiting him in the U.S."

"Shouldn't we call the police?" Sonsee asked.

"Yes," Mick said, his eyes tormented. "But they're so busy keeping up with the masses here, we have no guarantees. Their first loyalty is for their own people."

"And what about the American embassy?" Sonsee countered.

"There's not one in Vietnam," Mick said grimly, "for obvious reasons."

Kim's heart wrenched with the wretched reality. "I s–so wanted to help those—those old people. And today—today was the first work day." Her eyes stung with new tears.

Mick's gaze gently caressed her features and stirred with respect. "I know you did, Kim, I know," he said. "But I can't watch you like I did in New York, and I'd never forgive myself if—"

"I'm not arguing with you," she said in defeat. "I want to get out of here as much as you want me to." She recalled the heat of the man's breath against her ear. "And the sooner the better, but..." She swallowed. "I just hate that it all had to happen this way."

Dismay filling his eyes, Mick pressed his lips together into a grim line as if a new thought had just struck him. "Oh, no." He released Kim and pressed his thumb and forefinger against his eyes. "It couldn't be."

"Maybe this secret admirer is someone on the mission trip," Melissa said, her uncanny sense of observation firmly in place.

Dumbfounded, Kim swallowed against her tightening throat.

"We've got to get you out of here," Mick said, gazing past Kim to the cluttered room. "How long will it take you to get packed? Can we leave in an hour?"

"But—but what about the work day?" Kim asked. "Don't you need to be there to get it all started?"

"The nursing home director knows everything we're planning to do," Mick said. "Plus, Frank Cox is my assistant. Remember? This is his third trip with me, so I think he'll do fine. Also, Caleb knows his way around construction projects. I'll call the nursing home director now and tell him what's going on. If I can get you safely on the plane, I can be back at my duties by tomorrow."

"But what's going to stop this guy from following Kim Lan to L.A.?" Sonsee asked.

"Nothing," Mick snapped. "But if we act quickly, maybe she can be a day—or at least a flight—ahead of him. Her chances of survival are better in the States than here, even if he is on the flight behind her." Mick looked at Kim Lan. "We know he's here. We know he means business. And we know the police protection is close to nonexistent. As soon as we find out what flight you'll be leaving on, I want you to call your secretary and have her meet you in L.A. with the two biggest brutes she can hire so they can escort you home. Tell her to charter a flight from L.A. to New York—that's probably the safest thing. Also have her alert the police in L.A. and in New York as well."

"Okay," Kim said as she nodded, tears of regret, sorrow, and panic streaming her cheeks.

Mick's intense expression softened to one of compassion. "Oh, Kim," he said, his gaze roving her face.

She pressed her fingers against her lips and slowly shook her head from side to side. Kim Lan had never been so frightened in her whole life. Mick wrapped his arms around her, and she readily leaned into his embrace.

Resting his head on Kim's, Mick censured himself for believing this stalker wouldn't follow her to Vietnam. Foolishly he had relaxed once they entered Saigon, never imagining that the man could have trailed Kim. Mick contemplated her journey to Los Angeles. Every instinct within urged him to go with her, but that would be a breach of his employment contract and could very well mean the loss of his position. He pondered the importance of his job compared to Kim's life. There was no comparison. But Mick wasn't convinced that she would be under any threat on the journey home. In the first place, he didn't think the stalker would be able to catch the same flight. In the second place, all the way from Saigon to L.A. she would be in a well-populated, well-lighted, high-security situation—much safer than a hotel room in Cantho, which the intruder had already penetrated.

He contemplated the identity of this unknown man and again wondered if he might be one of the trip's participants. Mick scrutinized the male volunteers, pondering the potential culpability of each. Doug Cauley, the red-headed news journalist. He seemed nice enough. Harmless, even. He had told Mick several times that he had dreamed of participating on a trip like this one for years. Seeing Doug as a stalker would be a stretch to anyone's imagination.

Frank Cox, married to Pam. He was an excellent assistant. Mick had known him for a decade. Frank's solid reputation and effectiveness in ministry preceded him. Immediately he dismissed Frank.

Ron Emerson, Laci's tall brother. Ron had seemed so distracted over Laci's interest in Caleb, Mick couldn't imagine him having time to stalk anyone.

Adam Gray. Mick mulled over the possibilities of the reticent Adam being a stalker. Adam had said precious little to anyone the whole trip, except to mention that his son had been killed a few years back, and he and his wife were divorced. Other than that, his only open communication had been with Doug Cauley. Perhaps the loss of his son had somehow affected Adam's mental health. A pall of distrust settled upon Mick.

The only other male participant was his brother, Caleb. Mick immediately dismissed any possibility of Caleb's being the stalker. Then he thought of all those pictures of Kim Lan on Caleb's wall. Furthermore, Caleb had discovered who Kim Lan was. Whoever had written her the note likewise knew her true identity. But Mick could never believe that his kid brother would hunt down a woman. He was too busy successfully charming them the traditional way to waste time as a stalker. Mick, loyal to the end, rejected the whole idea. Furthermore, he reminded himself that he had no proof that any of the volunteers was the stalker. But whether the stalker was a trip volunteer or not didn't change the fact that the lunatic was close. Mick looked toward the balcony. "He came in from the balcony, then?" he asked.

"Looks that way. The lock is broken," Sonsee said as she grabbed various items around the room and tossed them into one of Kim's opened burgundy suitcases.

"So he would have had to either climb up the building with a rope or jump from one balcony to the next," Mick mused, stroking Kim's silky hair in an attempt to still her trembling.

"Exactly," Melissa said. She bent down and zipped one of Kim's suitcases. "And I'd cast my vote for hopping from one balcony to the next."

"Makes sense to me." Sonsee, clad in oversized pajamas, tossed a hair drier into Kim's suitcase and stopped to place both hands on her hips. "I don't see him climbing up the front of a building on a rope, even in the dark. There's traffic out there all the time. A passerby might see him."

"Right," Mick said. "So if he did jump from one balcony to the next, he'd have to be on this floor."

"Or..." Melissa extended the handle on the suitcase and rolled it toward the door, "if he was on the floor above us, he could have tied a rope on a balcony and swung down to this floor. It would only have taken him a couple of seconds to swing down and no one on the street would probably even notice." She stepped into the bathroom and came out, inserting her arms into a terry cloth bathrobe.

"Is there a fire escape?" Kim Lan asked, her voice muffled against Mick's shirt.

"Yes. But I think it's on the other side of the building. I'm not sure." Mick sighed. As Melissa and Sonsee finished Kim's packing, Mick coerced himself into once more contemplating the possibility that a trip participant was the stalker. All the participants were on the same floor and their rooms were all side by side. The likelihood of someone jumping across one, two, or even three balconies seemed feasible. But he doubted a stalker would have hopped the balconies from six or eight rooms away. That was a lot of leaping. The possibility that the intruder climbed down a rope from one or two floors above seemed logical as well. However, Mick's thoughts centered upon the occupants of the rooms closest to Kim's—the trip volunteers.

Rhonda Ackers and Laci Emerson shared a room two doors down from Mick's room. Frank and Pam Cox were next to Mick. Then Mick and Caleb. Kim, Sonsee, and Melissa were on the other side of Mick and Caleb. Doug Cauley and Adam Gray's room was next to Kim's. On the other side of them, Ron Emerson had a room to himself.

A knock sounded at the door, and Kim Lan jumped. "That's probably Caleb," Mick said, pulling away from Kim. He stood, gripped the knob, and uttered a suspicious, "Who is it?"

"It's me, Caleb."

Mick opened the door, and Caleb stepped into the room. "Didn't see anything or anybody out of the ordinary," Caleb said, discreetly glancing at Kim Lan.

"Did you check out all the floors or—"

"Yes," Caleb said. "Every floor from this one down. I looked over this floor first then took the stairs down. I figured he'd more likely be on the stairs than the elevator. I didn't go to any floors above this one because I couldn't see him going that direction."

"Might not hurt to check them out anyway," Mick said.

Kim Lan, rubbing her wrists, gradually stood. "Should we report this to the hotel management before we go?" she asked.

"Yes. I'll take care of that," Mick said. "I hope they take the whole thing seriously. And I guess the local authorities also need to be notified, in case there's any other instances like this one. I'll tell the hotel security to do that," Mick said, his gut tight with anxiety. "But we need to concentrate on getting you out of here. The hotel management has always proven itself conscientious, but that's no guarantee, and who knows if the police would be able to catch this guy. And big-otry against Americans is still an issue here. Not with everyone, but there's an underlying current—so much so that there are many Vietnamese who hate the idea of Amer-icans coming over and adopting their orphans."

"But that makes no sense," Melissa countered, settling on the end of the bed. "It doesn't look like anybody in Vietnam will take them, and they'd eventually be on the streets."

"I know," Mick said. "but that's the way it is." He watched Kim Lan as she sat beside Melissa and stared at the floor. She appeared to be as stunned as he felt. There she sat in that red silk lounging suit or pajamas or whatever they were, her dark hair falling around her shoulders and down her back. That magazine she had been holding on the plane featured her on the cover wearing a red-sequined party dress. Without doubt, red was her color. She was his lady in red— the woman he had been waiting for. And she was promised to Ted Curry. The recent nightmare assaulted his mind, and the panic that had accompanied the dream seemed to tiptoe up behind him and sink its bony fingers into his neck. *I won't let you marry Ted, Kim Lan,* he thought. *If I have to throw myself at your feet during your wedding, I will.*

Mick stepped toward her, leaned forward, and placed his hands on her shoulders. She looked up into his face, her dark eyes the churning black orbs of a hunted animal. Mick's heart clenched when he thought of what that maniac might have planned for her. "Are you going to be okay?" he asked.

"Yes." She swallowed and nodded. "I'll feel better once I get on the plane, but I'm—I'm okay...as long...as long as you're here."

Holding her gaze, Mick sensed their audience's height-ened interest. He leaned forward and placed a gentle kiss on

Kim's forehead. "Well," he said, "I'm here. And everything's going to be fine. Just fine."

"Thanks," she said, reaching for his hand.

Mick squeezed her fingers. "I'll be ready in about thirty minutes," he said softly. "I need to make a couple of phone calls to take care of today's responsibilities." He looked toward the clock to see that it was five-thirty. "By the time we get ready, we should be able to hire a car or van "

"Okay," she said, releasing his hand.

Mick turned to Caleb and nodded toward the door. "Let's go."

As soon as Mick closed the door, Kim stood and rummaged through her suitcase, searching for a pair of jeans and shirt. Melissa and Sonsee hovered here and there as if they didn't quite know what to do with themselves, and Kim Lan recalled their argument the night before. She owed them an apology. She would be leaving soon and didn't have time to put it off. Kim glanced at two of her dearest friends. "I need to apologize," she said.

They both stared back at her as if they had no idea what she was talking about.

"I'm afraid I've been blind to Ted and his—his faults. Sonsee, I—I should have listened to you in the first place. I..."

The two exchanged silent, startled glances.

"And..." Kim sighed, "if it makes you feel any better, I'm going to break my engagement with Ted."

"That's the best news I've heard in months." Sighing, Sonsee shook her head.

"Whew!" Melissa dropped into a chair. "We—all the sisters have been praying you'd do exactly that."

"I'm sorry I got so defensive," Sonsee said, moving to lay a comforting hand on Kim Lan's shoulder.

"It's okay." Kim spontaneously embraced her friend, thankful that their relationship was strong enough to withstand such a difficult conflict.

At last they pulled away from each other and Kim massaged her wrists, still red from the tape. "There's a lot I need to talk with you both about but we don't have the time. The long and short of it is, I've been going through a spiritual battle similar to Sonsee's. Right now, I've still got some things to decide. I know Mick is falling in love with me, and—and I think I could probably fall in love with him, but I've got some soul searching to do." Kim pulled a pair of jeans and a T-shirt out of the suitcase into which Sonsee had been heaping her things.

"I just hope I live long enough to do some soul searching."

Sonsee and Melissa walked to Kim Lan's side and placed their arms around her. Kim shuddered and clamped her teeth in an attempt to hold the threatening tears in abeyance. She didn't have time for another cry. She would rather spend the time falling in a heap at Mick's feet and begging him to escort her back home. Kim was frightened to her bones.

"We're going to be praying for you," Sonsee said.

"Would you like us to go home with you?" Melissa offered.

"No," Kim said, but seriously considered the idea anyway. In the face of the facts, she quickly dismissed the whole notion. "What kind of protection would either of you be?" Kim looked from Melissa to Sonsee and back to Melissa. "If either one of you were Jac Lightfoot, detective extraordinaire, I'd take you up on it. She's got a black belt in...in... whatever that is."

"Tae Kwon Do," Melissa supplied.

"Right," Kim agreed. "Besides, I know how much you both looked forward to coming on this trip."

"But we'd never forgive ourselves if—" Melissa started.

"I'm going to be fine," Kim Lan said, amazed at how sure she sounded. "Once I get on that plane, I'll be okay. Together, the two of you have spent several thousand dollars to be exactly where you are. And they need the workers." The faces of those elderly people tore at Kim's heart. "I can't let you leave," she said firmly. "They need all the help they can get."

Squeezing her shoulder, Sonsee shook her head. "You're as stubborn as we are," she said.

"Speak for yourself," Melissa shot back.

"Oh, get real," Sonsee quipped. "You're worse than all of us put together."

The three friends joined in mutual laughter—a laughter that was hollow, anxious, and full of fear.

Twenty

By six-fifteen Kim settled onto the hired van's backseat and waited while Mick and the driver loaded their luggage behind her. Mick had decided to arrive in Saigon prepared to spend the night just in case they couldn't book Kim a flight for today. According to him, the flight from Saigon to Hong Kong wasn't the problem; but the Hong Kong to L.A. flight was often full—especially in the economy section. However, business class and first class were likely to have last minute openings. Kim prayed they would or that she could arrange to charter a flight back to L.A.

She slumped further down in the van, pulling the denim hat closer to her brows. She felt as if a pair of eyes followed her everywhere she went and watched every move she made. In a matter of minutes, Mick settled next to her, and the driver claimed his position behind the wheel. When Mick placed a protective arm around her Kim Lan didn't resist. Instead, she leaned next to his torso and constrained herself against clinging to him.

"So, what did I do to earn this?" he asked, a hint of humor lacing his words. "Whatever it was, remind me to repeat it."

The van eased into the river of honking motorcycles that increased in density with every passing hour. Kim glanced up at Mick. A mixture of sweet agony, anxiety, loneliness, and love cloaked his features. He stroked her cheek with the backs of his fingers, and Kim drank in the pleasure of his touch.

An uncertain smile nibbled at the corners of his mouth. "You gave me quite a scare back there."

"I'm still scared," she said, clutching his heavy cotton shirt.

Leaning forward, he placed a light kiss on her forehead. "It's okay. You're going to be okay."

"I hope you're right," Kim said.

"We've got to trust the Lord on this one."

"Sometimes that's tough, especially when you've been taped up and toted around by a maniac."

"I know, but Sonsee could have not awakened. I really see the hand of the Lord in all this. He certainly woke you up to come to my rescue when I was being shot at."

"How's your ear?" Kim peered toward the top of his left ear, to see the brown scab still intact.

Fingering it, Mick produced a slight wince. "Still a little sore, but okay."

"This man is playing for keeps," she said, thinking of Mick's near brush with death.

An awkward silence settled upon them. Kim purposed to observe the back of the seat in front of them until she could conjure a logical statement, yet nothing coherent entered her mind.

At last Mick cleared his throat. "Uh…if my memory isn't failing me, when we left off last night, we weren't, um, on the best of terms. I'm sorry I—"

"I should be the one apologizing," Kim interrupted, returning her undivided attention to him.

He blinked, his face impassive.

"I think you were right about everything you said."

Only the faint dancing of his eyes attested to any emotion.

"I've done a lot of praying and reflecting in the last months, and last night I decided I'm going to have to break off the engagement with Ted."

He raised one eyebrow. "Would you mind if I asked the driver to stop and give me time to run up and down the road and shout for about an hour?"

Kim broke into a smile, while Mick continued.

"And while I'm in a candid mode, I guess now is as good a time as any to tell you again that I think I'm falling in love with you." His hungry gaze settled on her mouth, and Kim recalled the heat of that kiss in her parents' greenhouse.

"I gathered that," she said as the van bumped along the narrow road full of potholes.

"And?" He searched her eyes. "Do I dare to hope that you could ever feel the same about me?"

"I...I..." Kim Lan closed her eyes, took a quivering breath, and pondered the vast changes the Lord had wrought in her heart and soul within the last year. She had gone from being a woman who possessed a Christian belief system to one whose most passionate desire was to pour her life out for Jesus Christ... and all because she had begun to seek the Lord with all her heart. Yet, because of her change in heart, she had made and still needed to make important decisions.

Thoughtfully, Kim gazed out the window at the Vietnam roadside lined with humble hovels and people who so desperately needed the Lord. Last night, after prayerfully deciding to break the engagement with Ted, Kim had gone to bed feeling as if she were beginning life anew. She recalled snuggling under the covers, stretching languidly, and noticing a difference in her muscle tone. She hadn't been able to enjoy a strenuous workout for almost a week. With a sigh, Kim Lan had pledged to work out with extra vigor before the fall fashion shows scheduled for April.

But the same question that hit Kim last night, posed itself today. *What if the Lord wants me to quit modeling?* Her answer from this morning was the same from last night: *Then I'll quit.* Prayerfully, Kim wondered if the Lord would eventually direct her into a new career. At one time, she would have balked at walking away from modeling. Now she only wanted God's perfect will for her life—no matter what that might be. Clearly she still had many decisions to consider. In fairness to Mick, she didn't want to make any rash promises. Kim already had one engagement she dreaded breaking. She didn't want to have to break two because she hadn't taken the time to ponder God's will. Add to that the pressure of some crazy man breathing down her neck, and she didn't possess the presence of mind to even think about a commitment.

"I'm sorry. I'm rushing you," Mick said, regret clinging to his every word. "I'm not about to pop the question, if that makes you feel any better."

Kim shifted away from him and sat up in the seat. Nervously she looked out the back window, only to see numerous motorcycles in their wake. Mick followed her glance and peered behind them for several silent seconds. She watched him, remembering the first time she had seen him, when he was putting his soul into that presentation about Vietnam. Kim had been impressed with Mick O'Donnel even then and, like Sonsee and Melissa, considered him a special man.

"But..." he continued, at last taking her hand in his, "I want you to know that I'll be here, if and when you decide you would like to pursue a relationship. I just didn't want you to get on that plane to Los Angeles without knowing exactly how I feel." He gave her hand a light squeeze. "I know we come from different worlds. Compared to your income, my retirement nest egg looks like pennies," he said with a faint grin. "I own one cat, one cabin, and one Ford pickup."

"But I like cats, cabins, and pickups," Kim said, her heart melting with the sincerity of his tones.

His smile increased. "And the way I travel, you'd think I was part gypsy. For some women, that's a problem."

"I love to travel."

He chuckled under his breath. "I spent the first part of our acquaintance thinking I was crazy to think a woman like you would even glance at a man like me, but…" Narrowing his eyes, he looked back at her. "From the first time I met you, your eyes seemed to reflect the same things I was feeling."

"Even when you were telling me I couldn't go on the trip?" A flutter of awareness flitted through her midsection as she recalled their first meeting and the temptation to topple into the balmy essence of his sea-blue eyes.

Those blue eyes glistened with mischief. "I could hardly give my presentation that Sunday for looking at you in the audience," he said, glancing down. "At the time, I didn't think there was any question about whether there could be a relationship between us, and the last thing I needed was you on this trip and me so distracted I couldn't even lead it."

"So it was you—not Caleb—you were worried about?" she asked, shaking her head in disbelief.

"Well…" He softly bit his lower lip and shrugged.

Spontaneously, Kim reached forward to stroke his face, shadowed with need of a shave. Never had Ted been so open with her, and her reluctance to break their engagement now seemed ridiculous. "Well," she whispered, "I do care for you, Mick O'Donnel. I do. I think you're the most fascinating man I've ever met, but—"

"But?"

"I need to do some praying about a lot of things. I've gotten so far out of the will of the Lord that I don't even know what He wants of me. I don't even know whether I'll continue to model. Last night I laid everything on the line. I told God I'd even sell everything I own and give away every penny I've made if that is what He wants."

He covered her hand with his. "It might very well be that the Lord just wants your willingness," he said, "like with Abraham and Isaac. The Lord didn't want Abraham to really sacrifice Isaac, He just wanted Abraham's willingness."

"Well, I'm willing," Kim said. "For the first time in my life, I can say that I'm really willing to do anything the Lord has for me. If that means leaving a life of fame and digging ditches in...in..." she waved her hand, "Hungary, then so let it be."

"But," Mick said, "you would be a powerful witness for the Lord to continue in your career. I'm certain many young women look up to you. And there are few people with your earning power. If you chose a lower standard of living and gave sacrificially, think of how many missions trips you could fund."

"I like the sound of that," Kim said pensively.

"Well, like I told you last night, I've got the scoop on every mission field from here to South America to Siberia and back. If you've got the money, I can find the projects that need funding. We'd make a great tag team for God. There are kids starving all over this planet—street children that just need a place to sleep at night, three meals a day, and somebody to give them a chance in life. And that's just the tip of the iceberg."

The song that had haunted her for weeks began to weave its melodious tune through her soul: "People need the Lord. People need the Lord. At the end of broken dreams, He's the open door." She hummed a few bars and Mick joined her until they were softly singing together.

"I want to give my life for Him," she whispered when the tune was over. "And it might very well mean that I keep my career and give away a lot of what I make. But I'm going to pray like crazy first. More than anything else, I just want to be where God wants me."

"And while you're at it," Mick said, "pray like crazy about us too, will you?"

"I will," Kim said, solemnly gazing into blue eyes that stirred with respect mixed with love and masculine frustration.

At six-twenty, Odysseus walked into the hotel restaurant rich in the hues of dark wood. He settled at the long section of tables that the mission group occupied. Disappointment dripped into his spirit when he realized Sophie had yet to come down for breakfast. The windows that spanned from wall to wall provided an excellent view of the shabby buildings and abundance of motorcycles buzzing up and down the street. He gazed out the windows, counting the seconds until Sophie arrived. With the smells of breakfast tantalizing his senses, he picked up his menu and joined the others in making choices. The group chatted among themselves and reveled in the anticipation of the occasion. Today's activities began the reason they had come to Vietnam—the work on the home for the elderly.

After everyone had placed breakfast orders, Caleb Peterson stood from his spot at the head of the table and lightly tapped his water glass with his knife. The bell-like sound focused all attention on Caleb. That was when Odysseus noticed Mick O'Donnel was missing, too. Something wasn't right. He felt it in his gut. Sophie was gone. Mick was gone. And he wondered if they had run away together. The flame of raging jealousy burning in his soul increased to a roaring inferno.

"If I may have your attention, please," Caleb said, inserting his hands into his jeans pockets as if he were uncertain of himself. "Uh...Mick asked me and Frank Cox to take over some of his duties today. There's been an...emergency," he said as if he were hedging. "Kimberly Lowe had to return to the States, and Mick is escorting her back to Saigon today."

Odysseus' face went cold. His heart sank. All appetite vanished. This was worse than he had ever imagined. Kim Lan...*no, Sophie* had committed the ultimate betrayal and run from him. This was even more devastating than her fighting him last night. She had turned her back on him and run away with another man—*again!* Odysseus' fingers curled into his palms until his fingernails painfully dug into his skin.

"She looked exactly like Kim Lan Lowery," Rhonda Ackers said, shaking her head. "Did anyone else notice that?" Several in the group nodded.

Nervously, Caleb glanced toward Melissa and Sonsee. Melissa, adjusting her glasses, cleared her throat. "She is Kim Lan Lowery," she said simply. "We've been her friends since college—before she was famous."

No! She's Sophie! Odysseus wanted to roar. Instead, he stifled the urge. His face twitched with the effort.

A stunned silence settled onto the group. Odysseus' roommate leaned over, a concerned expression in his eyes. "You don't look very well," he said. "Are you okay?"

"I think I have food poisoning. I was up most of the night," he lied, grabbing the first logical excuse he could conjure. And what a great excuse it was. Mick O'Donnel had warned them from the start of their trip to only drink bottled water and sodas, avoid fresh fruit from roadside venders, and only eat hotel food. Otherwise a traveler opened himself up for food poisoning or severe intestinal difficulties. The food poisoning scenario would suit him perfectly. He would feign illness, go back to the room, and pack while the rest of the group finished breakfast and went to work at the baby home. As soon as they were gone, he would hire a car to Saigon. He had a plane to catch.

❧

Mick stood beside Kim in the small Cathay Pacific ticket office while she booked her flights to L.A. The office resembled many Mick had been in around the world, including a few in the States. The usual counters. The usual tiled floor. The usual smiling clerks. Fortunately, Cathay Pacific did have a few openings in first class and business class on today's flights to Hong Kong then L.A. Kim's hands shook as she presented the credit card to the clerk, and the woman began the necessary paperwork.

A war raged inside Mick. A war that had begun from the first time he saw Kim crumpled in a heap in her hotel room. He knew beyond doubt that she needed to get out of

Vietnam. Due to his pressing duties with the nursing home, Mick couldn't watch her twenty-four hours a day. All it would take would be one slip and that creep could snatch her up, do what he wanted, and toss her away. She would be lost, never to be heard from again. She needed to leave. Period. However, the closer they came to her actually doing that, the more Mick bemoaned allowing her to leave alone. If he went with her, his visa would be stamped at the point of exit and he would not be granted reentry to Vietnam. The trip would have to continue under the supervision of his assistant, Frank Cox. This was Frank's third trip to share Mick's responsibilities, so Mick didn't doubt for one instant that he was capable. Nonetheless, denominational head-quarters would probably frown on his decision at best. At worst, they would fire him.

But so what! a voice within him urged. *She's worth more than your job. Besides, you have a spotless record with them. Why not call the director now and tell him the situation? Perhaps he'll understand....*

Her head bent as if in defeat, Kim fumbled with the credit card that the clerk extended back to her.

"Wait!" Mick gripped Kim's arm. "I'm going with you."

"What?"

"I—I'm going with you."

A relieved cry escaped her. "Oh, Mick, I wanted to ask you so badly, but I—I was afraid it would—it would in some way jeopardize your job, or—"

"It will. It *will* jeopardize my job," he said. "But I've got to take the chance. I can't let you get on that flight without protection. I just can't."

"So is that two first-class tickets then?" the clerk asked, her English laced with a Vietnamese accent.

"Yes," Kim Lan said as if she had been relieved of a great burden. She gave her credit card back to the clerk.

Mick had arranged to get special rates, economy tickets for the whole group. Unfortunately, the cheap rate meant the tickets couldn't be changed to first class, and there were no more vacancies in economy. Mick debated allowing Kim Lan to foot the bill for his ticket. Regardless of her ability to afford it, he did have some pride. Mick spotted the public phone on the far wall and decided to argue the point later. He had some phone calls to make. He dug through his money belt for his international calling card and decided to report his decision now. In Kansas City, where his boss lived, it was almost one o'clock in the morning. "Rise and shine," he said under his breath.

Odysseus walked to the window of the Cathay Pacific office on the corner of a busy street in downtown Saigon. Around him a collection of what looked like street bums squatted and talked while pedestrians walked here and there in pursuit of their goals. The taxi driver he had hired in Cantho waited in the car at the curb of the street filled with motorcycles zooming along at an insane rate.

He strained to see into the ticket office and at last spotted Sophie at the counter. Odysseus smiled in appreciation of his own genius. He knew when he left Cantho that in order to catch them he would have to make up for lost time. He had told the driver that if they made it to the Cathay Pacific office in time, there was a fifty buck tip involved. In Vietnam that represented the salary of a college professor for one month. The cliché "money talks" couldn't have been truer. Indeed, money not only talked. It drove...and drove very fast.

On the other side of the ticket office, Odysseus noticed Mick O'Donnel talking on the telephone, his back turned to the door. He scanned the rest of the office to see a group of maybe six Caucasians clustered in the corner as if they were waiting to meet someone. Near them stood an approximately six-foot-tall plant. Beside the plant sat a life-sized cardboard replica of a Vietnamese airline flight attendant. The image of the woman plus the advertisement written beside her provided an excellent spot for him to crouch behind should the situation require it.

Odysseus glanced at Mick on the phone. He crossed his legs at the ankles as if he were in deep conversation. Sophie's back was also turned. This was as good a time as any to slip into the office. He opened the door and scurried behind the group of what sounded like Canadians. He tuned out the occasional comments from the Canadians and peered toward Sophie as she arranged to buy two tickets— the two o'clock 767 to Hong Kong and the eight-thirty 882 flight from Hong Kong to L.A. The clerk verified that they had asked for the two o'clock Airbus flight from Saigon to Hong Kong and not the four o'clock flight.

He smiled as he planned his strategy. Odysseus would wait and catch the four o'clock flight to Hong Kong. That would stop them from being on the same flight and reduce his potential of being detected before he made his move. However, once in Hong Kong, he would enact his strategy. Odysseus hated Mick O'Donnel for stealing Sophie's heart. And he hated her for giving it to him. He would kill them both in Hong Kong, then board the flight home a free man.

He reeled with an onslaught of maniacal hysteria. "I'll kill you, Mick O'Donnel. I'll kill you in Hong Kong. Oh, Sophie, I'll have to kill you, too," he whispered, his voice cracking. "You betrayed me...again."

"I understand that this violates the terms of my contract," Mick said into the phone. "But I've been conducting missions trips for over eight years, and I've never done this before. I fully believe this is a matter of life and death."

"Well, I can't guarantee that the missions board will support your decision," Mr. Kleiner said.

"I understand that, sir," Mick said. "But I think you'd do the same thing if this were your wife."

"Good grief, son," Kleiner exclaimed. "I didn't know you'd gotten married. When did that happen?"

"Well, we aren't married—*yet,*" Mick said, tapping the side of the phone. "But there's a pretty good chance..." He left the rest unsaid.

"I see. It sounds as if you've made your choice."

"I've made it," Mick said firmly but respectfully. "And quite frankly it's been one of the hardest decisions I've ever made in my life. But given Frank Cox's experience I think the trip isn't in the least bit jeopardized. I'll call him when I get to Hong Kong. I'll also talk with my brother, Caleb. He knows his way around any kind of construction. They should both be in their rooms by the time I get to Hong Kong. So, the work will be done, your promises will be fulfilled. And I'll make sure someone gets home with her life intact."

"Okay, son, okay," Mr. Kleiner said, his voice still groggy. "You do what your gut tells you. But, like I said, I can't promise—"

"I know," Mick said. "I understood that when I called."

Mick hung up the phone and walked back to Kim's side. The clerk was in the process of handing her their tickets and going over all the necessary details once more. When the clerk had finished, Kim Lan looked up at him and he drank in the image of her lovely features. She still wore the hat and glasses, but they did little to mask the full force of her silent appraisal. Her eyes stirred with esteem, adoration, and perhaps a glimmer of true love. Mick, not even attempting to hide his feelings, returned her gaze.

He certainly hoped this growing bond between them continued to strengthen once she arrived in New York. Mick respected her desire to pray about their relationship, but as they turned toward the door he was overwhelmed with the old plaguing doubts. Kim Lan said she was going to break her engagement to Ted Curry. Mick calculated that a man with the looks and charisma of Curry could be highly persuasive. He hoped Kim followed through with her decision. Sometimes decisions made abroad were altered under the lights of home.

Stifling a tired yawn, Mick once again left a ticket office and prepared for yet another flight home. He had felt the Lord telling him that Kim Lan would one day be his wife. He would have to cling to that promise and trust God. Otherwise, he would despair. Mick had just put his whole ministry on the line for Kim. But he knew that even if she never committed to a relationship with him, he would not regret this decision to escort her home.

Twenty-One

By one-thirty, Mick had followed Kim into the first-class section on the Airbus headed for Hong Kong. He relieved her of her carry-on luggage and stowed it on the floor under the seat in front of theirs.

"I'd feel more comfortable if you'd sit by the window," he said.

"Me, too."

Mick stepped aside for Kim to settle into the window seat. Glancing around the plane, he claimed the seat beside her while Kim Lan likewise observed the group of people trailing onto the aircraft. The anxiety playing across her features matched Mick's feelings. She glanced backward then across the cabin. The buoyant sunshine spilling through the windows seemed a mockery of the darkness cloaking Mick's spirit.

"We're going to be fine," Mick soothed, wishing he was as convinced as he sounded.

"You don't look like you believe yourself," she said with a nervous smile.

"We've got to trust the Lord to protect you."

"If that madman could follow me to Vietnam, he could follow us home, Mick," she said. Twin pools of tears filled her dark eyes.

All morning Mick had restrained himself from pulling Kim close, but all restraint fell away in the face of her need. He placed his arms around her and tugged her into his loving embrace. As if she had been longing for his touch, Kim clung to him, and he wanted to hold her forever.

"We're probably going to be in the safest environment in the world," he said, stating the facts for himself as much as for her. "The way suitcases are x-rayed, especially on these international flights, there's no way someone could come on board with a gun. He'd have to be on the same flight to harm you anyway, and the chances of that are almost nonexistent."

A flight attendant approached. "Would the two of you like anything to drink?" she asked.

They placed their orders for sodas and Mick continued, "We're tucked away in first class, coddled by the attendants." He waved toward the exiting woman. "And Virginia said she'd have the chartered flight and the bodyguards waiting in L.A." The facts, as rational as they seemed, did precious little to ease Mick's troubled mind. He would do his level best to protect Kim, but that lunatic had shot at him.

"Would you pray?" she asked.

Mick's arm tightened around her shoulders. "I've been praying almost nonstop since that phone call woke me up this morning," he said. "But I'll—"

"I—I need to hear you."

"I know. Anything for you, Kim Lan," he said. Lowering his voice, Mick briefly beseeched the Lord for their safety. He could barely concentrate on his own words as she cleaved to him like a lost child. After his short prayer, Mick muttered a soft amen and pulled away far enough to cup her face in his hands. He rubbed her cheeks with his thumbs. Deciding to toss all caution to the wind, he gently brushed his lips against hers, expecting her to pull away. Instead she leaned toward him and drank of his passion. Mick, tempted to deepen the kiss, considered their location and kept it brief. *Brief and potent,* he thought as his heart reacted accordingly. *Even in the den of danger, she affects me.*

By the time the plane took off and rose above the clouds, many of Kim's anxieties had eased. However, once the Hong Kong skyline seemingly rose from the ocean against a backdrop of majestic green mountains, the wariness of the hunted surged upon Kim again. In a matter of thirty minutes, she and Mick disembarked the plane and boarded the shuttle, about the size of a passenger bus, that transported them to the terminal to wait for the next flight. Surreptitiously she scanned the faces of each of the male passengers, searching for a sign of awareness in any of their eyes. From her vantage near the front, she couldn't see each passenger, but the men she could see looked unfamiliar and none seemed to recognize her.

When the bus stopped, she and Mick shouldered their carry-on bags and joined the others in line. As she stepped from the shuttle, the airport, recently constructed on an island off the coast of China, seemed to beckon her to enjoy its rare location. On any other occasion, Kim would have paused to soak in the scenery of the surrounding ocean and the popcorn clouds hanging in the sky, but the urgency of her situation bade her waste no time. Instead, she grasped Mick's hand and marched forward with purpose.

Within an hour they had made their way through the security check, found their designated gate for the Los Angeles flight, and decided to eat at one of the various restaurants in the airport. Their plane didn't leave until eight-thirty. Given the one hour time gain from Saigon to Hong

Kong, Kim and Mick had a four-hour wait ahead of them. But they had chosen the earlier Airbus flight because both preferred waiting in Hong Kong over waiting in Saigon. They knew the lunatic was in Vietnam. Whether or not he would follow them to Hong Kong was still a moot matter.

By the time they finished their meal, their wait had been reduced to three hours, and they ambled toward their departure gate. Kim Lan neared the half dozen other people who sat in the chairs available for waiting passengers.

Mick squeezed her arm. "Let's wait a minute before sitting down." He looked up the windowed walkway then glanced at his wristwatch. "I need to find a phone and call Frank and Caleb. It's six-thirty in Cantho. They should be in their rooms by now."

"There's one this way," Kim said, pointing toward two phones near the restrooms.

"Okay. Why don't you come with me?" He bent to pick up her bag and shouldered it with his. "I can see you from there, but I want you close."

Agreeing, Kim Lan fell in beside him to walk the short distance to the phones. With every hour that passed, Kim's attachment to Mick grew, despite her logical needs for some prayer time about their relationship. Secretly, Kim took in his rugged features and the attitude that reflected a man of high integrity. Never before had a man put his whole career on the line for her. But she had the feeling that Mick O'Donnel did what was right because it was right and that, even if she had declined his offer for romance, he would have still escorted her home. As Mick unzipped his money belt and retrieved the international calling card, Kim decided that unless the Lord strongly showed her otherwise, she would invite Mick O'Donnel to wrap his arms around her for life. In the Hollywood scene, Kim could always find a man who was fatally handsome and had more money, evidenced by Ted Curry. However, she was slowly realizing that she might look the rest of her life and never discover another man as honorable as Mick O'Donnel.

While he began the tedious process of punching in a long line of appropriate numbers, Kim Lan pondered her friend, Marilyn Thatcher. She thought of Marilyn's former marriage to the man Sonsee often referred to as Greg "The Jerk" Thatcher. Greg had decided after five years of marriage that he liked his secretary better than his wife and daughter. He had abandoned them and his pastoral calling to marry the secretary. Devastated, Marilyn had vowed never to marry again and initially refused Joshua Langham's overtures. But now she and Joshua were engaged.

When Kim Lan met Joshua last summer, she had thought Marilyn was crazy for rejecting his interest. Furthermore, in her mind Kim had compared Joshua to Ted Curry and realized that Ted didn't fare well in that comparison. She had assumed that the possibility of her meeting a "Joshua" was nonexistent. Kim observed Mick as he waited for the phone's ring and realized she had met her own "Joshua." Mick and Josh were as different as two men could be, but they were men of equal valor.

Looking back, Kim wondered how she could have been so blinded by Ted, but she reflected that perhaps she had been less blinded by Ted and more by her erroneous life focus. That wrong focus had almost caused her to make a few other wretched mistakes. From the first of their relationship, Ted Curry had pressured Kim Lan toward physical intimacy. She had put up a solid resistance initially but had found the temptation more appealing as her relationship with Ted grew. Cringing, she remembered the one time the temptation had been almost too great to deny. But a renewed resolve had descended upon her, and she had at last drawn a firm line and told Ted to back off or forget their relationship. She thanked God that He had given her the strength to draw that line with Ted. Flinching within, Kim pictured what a mess her life would be now if she had been intimate with Ted, how remorseful she would have been, how afraid that Mick might find out. As things stood, Kim dreaded having to tell Mick about the one affair she had allowed Satan to drag her into years before. However, she took comfort in knowing that Mick seemed to be a man who was more interested in what she was becoming and less in what she had been. Kim Lan reveled in the memory of their time on the balcony last night. The memory of the respect and appreciation in his voice warmed her with gratitude. Certainly, as a woman of God, she would forever fix her eyes on Jesus and allow Him to continue releasing her from the wrong choices of her past.

That continued focus left her free to live a life completely committed to Jesus Christ. Free to base her worth not on material gain but on who she was in Christ. Free of the nagging sense of inferiority that told her the more she owned the more worthy she would be. As soon as Kim got home, she planned to consult with her financial advisor and make some radical changes in her portfolio. Right now, she didn't know if that would mean selling everything and abandoning her modeling career or if that would mean continuing in her career and giving more of her salary to missions. Whatever the Lord directed, she was at last ready to obey.

Kim observed Mick as he asked to be connected to Frank Cox's room. After a brief wait, Mick spoke into the receiver and began the necessary explanations. From what Kim heard of the conversation, Frank wasn't the least bit ruffled by his sudden inheritance of the trip's leadership role. Relaxing with every word, Mick explained that he had informed the missions director in Kansas City. As he was wrapping up the conversation, a startled "What!" erased all evidence of relaxation from him. He gripped the metal phone cord and peered up and down the walkway, his body tense and alert. Kim Lan followed his gaze as a sense of danger crept upon her like an invisible monster hovering above, its jagged teeth dripping with blood.

"When did you miss him?" Mick asked, his gaze roving toward the row of windows to a landing plane.

"Uh huh. Uh huh," he said, his voice sounding like the rapid fire of a machine gun. He looked at Kim, and the troubled clouds churning in the depths of his eyes left her nauseated.

"Oh, no," Mick said, covering his eyes with his free hand. "Yes, I understand. Okay...okay, I will. Yes...right....Did you alert the police?...Good...Yes, I understand. He was already long gone." After a few more minutes of tense conversation Mick ended the call.

By the time he replaced the receiver, Kim's curiosity and fear were raging out of control. "What did he say?"

"Doug Cauley is missing," Mick said, grimly observing her. "Frank said he told them he had food poisoning at breakfast, and he needed to spend the day in bed. When they got back from the nursing home at four, Doug and his luggage were gone. The hotel clerk verified he had checked out and that she had made arrangements for him to hire a car to Saigon."

Kim's throat tightened. "Do you think he's the one?" she whispered, feeling as if every drop of blood drained to her feet.

"It makes perfect sense,' Mick said. "His room was next to yours. Whoever hopped onto your balcony wasn't far away."

Recalling the feel of the invader's hot breath against her ear, Kim shuddered against a chill that zipped down her spine. "I would have never suspected him," she said, shaking her head in dismay. "He seemed so polite."

"I think many evil people know how to mask themselves," Mick said looking up and down the walkway again as a lone cleaning lady wearily pushed by her cart. "That's part of what makes them so wicked."

"Did they notify the police?"

"Yes, and the police are reporting everything to the authorities in Saigon, but Doug had all day to leave Vietnam." Mick peered past Kim Lan as if he were determined to maintain a constant surveillance of the area.

"But...but if Doug Cauley's the one, how did he know we left for Saigon?"

Mick rubbed his eyes again and shook his head in disbelief. "This morning at breakfast, Caleb told the whole group there had been an emergency and that I was escorting you to Saigon so you could fly back home."

"Oh, Mick," Kim said, laying a hand on his arm. "Caleb must feel terrible."

"Yes. That's what Frank said." Mick rubbed his whole face as if his emotional exhaustion matched the physical exhaustion marring his expression. "One side of me wants to feel sorry for Caleb, and another side wants to throttle him. What was he thinking?"

"He probably was so disturbed by the whole thing he wasn't thinking. And the others were probably asking where we were."

"Yes, and in all fairness to him, I don't guess I ever told him that we suspected someone on the mission trip." Mick continued to stare down the windowed corridor. "I never told him not to tell where we were going, either. I guess I just assumed he'd use that woman-focused brain of his to piece it all together," he said in exasperation.

"Mick, don't be too hard on him." Kim gripped his arm.

"Don't be too hard on him? If Cauley catches up with us..." He left the rest unsaid and examined his calling card. "Frank says Caleb really wants to talk to me. I was going to call him anyway and tell him I won't be back." Wearily, he sighed. "I need about all the self-control I can muster right now."

"Did you ever do anything stupid when you were his age?" Kim asked, reflecting on her own stupidity in agreeing to marry Ted—and she had left her early her twenties behind several years ago.

Mick raised one brow and examined her as if he were mildly surprised. "I guess I stand corrected," he said.

By seven-thirty, Doug had made his way through the security check and stealthily walked toward the boarding gate. The flight to L.A. would depart in one hour. The boarding call would begin within the next half hour. He had no time to waste. He fingered the rope in his pocket. He had bought it in one of the many shops not far from the ticket office in Saigon. Soon, he would have to use it.

"I love you, Sophie," he muttered under his breath. "I love you, but you don't love me. After all I did for you, after all these years, you still don't love me." His mind, demented from his growing hate and obsession, continued its contorted journey.

Like a tiger sneaking up on an unsuspecting lamb, he crept forward, alert for the one thing he needed to complete his strategy—a closet or stairway door, a secluded space to which he could lure Mick O'Donnel and eventually Sophie. Doug would do what he had to, then calmly board the plane for L.A.

A tired-looking cleaning lady approached, pushing her cart in front of her. Doug slowed to a stop. Casually he leaned against the wall and watched her pointing her cart toward a door about thirty feet in front of her. The door had a sign on it. The first line was written in Chinese, the second line said "Employees Only," typical of all the signs in the airport that catered to an international clientele. The short, shabby woman stopped her cart outside the door and pulled a set of keys from the square pocket of her blue cleaning smock.

As she unlocked the door and turned on the light, Doug nonchalantly walked toward her. She opened the door, stepped through, and turned to pull the cart behind her. Cauley produced his most polite smile and said, "Here, let me help you." He pushed against the door. She nodded in understanding and grinned her thanks as she pulled the cart into the room. Doug followed the cart and closed the door behind him. The smells of soap and antiseptic greeted him. As his victim spewed forth a protest, he dropped his carry-on bag, doubled his fist, and hit her between the eyes with the full force of his masculine power. The petite woman, about half Doug's size, crumpled and fell to the floor in an unconscious heap. Not giving her another thought, Doug shook his stinging fingers and looked around the small room lined with shelves of cleaning paraphernalia.

The door whisked open behind him. Surprised, Doug swiveled to see a glowering Chinese police officer holding a shining black nightstick. Incited by his murderous mission, Cauley grabbed the policeman by the arm, flung him against the opposite wall of the closet, and kicked him in the face. The guard scrambled to right himself and Doug relieved him of his nightstick. He slammed the stick against the policeman's temple and watched without emotion as he dropped beside the unconscious maid. Doug stooped to remove the handgun from the policeman's holster and deposited it atop the cleaning cart. Next he retrieved the maid's keys from near her legs and stuffed them into his pocket.

Shoving aside the cart, Cauley opened the door, calmly slipped out, then clicked the door shut behind him. He looked up and down the windowed walkway to confirm that no one had noticed anything out of the ordinary. With long, purposeful strides he approached the boarding gate for the flight to L.A. At last the appropriate sign came into view, and he looked below it to see a line forming in front of the doorway that would lead to the passenger waiting room. Mick O'Donnel and Sophie stood toward the end of the line.

Doug slowed his pace and stopped about fifteen feet from them. He stared at Sophie, absorbing her beauty, wishing she had never rejected him, had never run from him. They could have had so much if only she hadn't betrayed him. His plot, so carefully planned, began to unfold when Sophie turned from talking to Mick and noticed him.

While standing in line, Kim had kept her gaze downward, her mind alert, and her heart in a constant state of prayer. If she and Mick could just get on this flight without incident they would be safe. Impatiently, she had awaited their turn to have their tickets validated. After expressing her impatience to Mick, Kim looked up to see Doug Cauley observing her. A knot of dread settled in the pit of her stomach, and the hair on the back of her neck prickled. Kim, momentarily paralyzed with terror, mutely returned his appraisal. His keen green eyes bore twin points of panic into her soul. As she held his gaze for those brief seconds, Kim felt as if a shaft of ice entered her heart. The lust, fury, and distaste marring his features spoke of demonic intent.

"I loved you," he mouthed, his lips twisted in aversion.

Kim's heart raced as she focused on his moving lips.

"But now I have to kill you. Kill you...kill you" he continued to mouth as if he were crazed with his purpose.

Her eyes widened. She debated if he had really said he was going to kill her or if she were imagining the whole thing. Her skin crawled. Her stomach threatened to reject her last meal. Violently trembling, Kim grabbed Mick's arm and gave it a hard yank. She stifled a terrified cry and pointed toward Doug Cauley.

Mick pivoted toward Cauley and stilled. A muffled exclamation spilled from him. He dropped his small bag as Doug turned and ran up the hallway. Mick started to race after him, then whirled back and grabbed Kim Lan by the arms. "Find a security guard!" he roared. "I'm going after him."

Kim seized Mick's bag and ran to the front of the line where the departure gate agent was preparing to validate their tickets. Her legs quaking, Kim plopped the two pieces of luggage at the woman's feet.

"There's a man who's been trying to kill me," Kim blurted. Her eyes burning, she looked toward Mick's retreating form. He recklessly dodged a group of chatting Asians then disappeared around a slight curve in the hallway. "My friend is chasing him now." Kim pointed to where Mick had been. "The killer followed us from Vietnam. We need a security guard! Quick!" The dismay in Kim's voice held a the ring of truth.

The numerous passengers in line joined the startled agent in looking down the hallway. Each passing second seemed to predict the gonging of Mick's death toll, reverberating against Kim's soul. The official turned to her assistant and spoke in rapid Chinese. The assistant dropped her clipboard and dashed up the hallway.

"Sir! Stop!"

Mick blocked out the startled call of the airline pilot he had almost run into. He plunged forward, searching for Cauley. He had lost him about three minutes before. Mick dodged a cleaning cart and a cluster of airline employees who watched him pass. As he reached the glass doorway that led to the runway, he shoved it open then stopped. There was no sign of Doug. The man had disappeared.

Winded, Mick turned back to retrace his steps. He jogged in the direction he had come, scanning the hallway for any signs of a doorway or stairway that might have given Cauley a place to hide. Right before rounding the corner to the boarding gate, Mick noticed a door open and a man with red hair briefly peering out. He scanned the passersby until he encountered Mick's gaze.

Mick dashed forward, slammed open the door, and pushed his way inside to face Doug who was poised and ready to destroy his prey. Over his head he clutched a menacing nightstick. Without a blink Cauley sucked in a lungful of air, pressed his lips together, and smashed the nightstick toward Mick's temple. Taken by surprise, Mick grunted and extended his arms in self defense. But it was too late. A black pall of unconsciousness descended upon him. As he sank to the floor, his last coherent thought centered upon Kim Lan.

Twenty-Two

~

Kim, her exhausted mind spinning with dread, strained to see any sign of the returning assistant. Only three minutes had passed since she left to get a security guard, but Kim Lan felt as if each minute were an hour. At last a scowling security guard appeared, with the assistant agent beside him. Kim sped toward him as the clerk rushed to resume her duties. Not attempting to temper her emotions, she grabbed his upper arms and, panting like a winded horse, screamed, "There's a killer after us! My friend is chasing him down. You've got to help us!"

The guard's stony eyes glared back at Kim. Chinese airport officials had a reputation for being tough and unbendable. This one, in particular, acted as if he didn't appreciate being touched. As Kim released her hold, she could only pray he would take action.

"The killer's name is Doug Cauley. He's got red hair. He ran that way." She pointed down the hallway.

"Do you know for certain this is what you are saying?" the official demanded with a heavy Asian accent.

"Yes!" Kim roared. "When I was in Vietnam, he broke into my room and tried to kidnap me. He's been sending me threatening notes. And he just told me he was going to kill me. That's when my friend started chasing after him."

"Come with me," he said. The guard's brisk pace didn't seem quite fast enough for Kim. Praying like mad, she restrained herself from bolting forward and leaving the guard behind. But the longer they walked, the more she suspected that something dreadful had happened. Neither Mick nor Doug were anywhere to be seen.

"You are sure this is what you say?" the guard demanded again.

"Yes! Yes!" Kim insisted as a movement from the corner of her eye snared her attention. A door marked "Employees Only" slowly opened and a man with red hair cautiously peered out. When he saw Kim and the security guard, he snapped the door shut.

"That was him!" Kim said, pointing toward the closed door. "I just saw him in that room."

"The room should be locked," the guard said, as if he still doubted Kim's claims. He crossed the hallway, turned the knob, and opened the door.

Kim peered past him to catch a glimpse of Mick, lying on his back on the floor, eyes closed, head tilted at a limp angle. She choked on a sob as the door opened farther and beside Mick stood Doug Cauley holding a gun.

"Both of you come in here—and don't make a sound," he growled.

The guard, at last convinced of the emergency, stepped into the room, and glanced over his shoulder at Kim who hesitated. Once she stepped into that room, she might very well be sealing her own doom and ending any possibility of the authorities capturing Doug.

"If you don't come in here now, I'll put a bullet in Mick's head," Doug growled.

Dismayed, she noticed a trickle of blood flowing from above Mick's brow. Frantic, Kim stepped into the room to notice two other unconscious individuals—a cleaning woman and a policeman. In panic, she scrutinized Mick's chest to see if he was still breathing. A rush of relief warmed her midsection as she noted the steady rise and fall of his chest.

"You should be ashamed of yourself, Sophie," Doug Cauley sneered. The door sighed to a close and Doug locked it. "You betrayed me! After all I did for you!" The demonic glaze in Cauley's eyes, the trembling of his gun hand, the fury spilling from his face struck so much terror in Kim's soul she didn't even attempt to argue that she wasn't Sophie. "I followed you for six months before seeing you sign up for that mission trip. I spent thousands of dollars to go to Asia with you, and then you run off with another man! I'm going to have to punish you," he said. "You leave me no choice." He dug into his pocket and pulled out a thin rope that resembled twine and extended it to Kim. "Tie his hands and feet with this," he demanded, waving the barrel of the gun at the guard.

The guard cast an uneasy glance toward Kim who hesitated.

"If you will give yourself up, you will not be as—as held as responsible," the guard said, glancing toward the unconscious police officer. "But if you continue, the Chinese laws, they are not favorable for such behavior."

"Take it, Sophie," Cauley barked, shaking the rope.

She jumped and reached for the rope. Doug's hand brushed hers, and he reached to stroke the top of Kim's fingers. The feel of his perspiring fingers on hers made her skin crawl, and she relived those repulsive moments early this morning when he had whispered in her ear. She jerked away, and he spewed forth his hatred in a long stream of irrational accusations.

Seeming to lose all sense of logic, he reached for her throat and left himself open for the security guard to firmly plant his foot in Cauley's gut and shove him across the room. Doug slammed against the far wall, knocking over a row of aerosol cans with his flailing arms. Instinctively, Kim grabbed one of the cans, pointed it at Cauley's face, and filled his eyes with antiseptic. Roaring like a furious bear, Doug pawed at the air then covered his ruddy face with his hands.

The security guard, grinding out exclamations in rapid Chinese, retrieved the gun and held it against Cauley's temple. "Get help!" he yelled at Kim.

Within minutes Kim found another security guard. The two guards handcuffed a muttering Doug Cauley, then turned to the victims on the floor. "He will not be home to America for many long years," one of the guards said, looking at Kim Lan as if he were trying to assure her that Doug would receive the punishment he was due.

Relieved, Kim flung herself at Mick, laid both hands on his face, and began calling his name. She gently slapped his cheeks, desperate for some sign that he was going to be okay. And she knew...she knew beyond doubt that her heart would never be the same because it now belonged to Mick O'Donnel.

"Mick! Mick!" she said fervently.

He turned his head from side to side and moaned.

"Oh, Mick! Mick! Tell me you're going to be okay." With abandon, Kim Lan repeatedly kissed his face.

Groaning, he opened his eyes briefly then struggled to open them again. At last he focused on Kim, and she showered him with another array of kisses.

"What a way to wake up," he muttered groggily while trying to smile.

Kim Lan stood in the church fellowship hall observing Marilyn, who was dressed in a tea-length, off-white wedding gown. Her blonde hair, brown eyes, and fair complexion glowed with the beauty of her wedding day. Joshua Langham, dressed in a black tuxedo, stood beside her as the two of them greeted the numerous guests who had attended their June wedding. In Kim Lan's estimation, Marilyn had never looked more beautiful.

"She's stunning today, isn't she?" Melissa asked from close by.

"That's just what I was thinking," Kim said. She and Melissa were dressed as all their sisters were—in knee-length, navy-blue dinner dresses that complemented the Victorian style of Marilyn's dress.

They had all stood beside Marilyn as her bridesmaids and witnessed her and Joshua exchanging their wedding vows. Kim Lan had been thrilled to serve as the maid of honor. Now the sisters flitted here and there. In May, during their semiannual sister reunion, they had helped Marilyn plan the wedding and assigned themselves to specific reception duties. Before the reunion, Marilyn announced during a conference call that she and Josh had set their wedding date for June. They wanted to keep it small and simple and desperately needed the help of all the sisters.

Last night, Marilyn had asked her friends to pray for her. Even though she had known Joshua a year, she had still been a bit apprehensive, but nobody would guess that today. Marilyn told the sisters before the two o'clock wedding that she awoke that morning certain she was doing the right thing.

Kim Lan and Melissa, who were in charge of the guest book and gift table, companionably stood at their post and sipped their tangy punch. They observed Victoria as she took the lead as chief chef and overseer of the reception. Victoria, her curly brown hair piled atop her head, appeared to be the consummate, delicate lady. Usually she remained in the background at public functions unless she was involved in a reception such as this one. During these endeavors, she was in her element and able to exercise her best gifts.

Mick O'Donnel, who had gotten acquainted with all the sisters, approached Kim Lan after chatting at length with the groom. Joshua Langham, a man of average looks and extraordinary charm, acted as if marrying Marilyn was equivalent with going to heaven. Mick, indulgently smiling, stopped at Kim's side and said, "It's always good to see a happy groom."

"Well, if ever a man was happy, it's him," Kim replied. She smiled into Mick's face and reveled in the feel of his possessive arm on her waist. He looked dashing in his dark, blue-gray suit. The color contrasted with his fascinating eyes and complemented his light tan hair. "I must say, you have never looked more handsome either."

"Maybe it's because *I'm* a happy man," Mick returned, smiling into her eyes. "And..." He hesitated as a hopeful dubiety scampered across his features. "Maybe it's because I'm praying that I'll soon be as happy as Joshua."

A flutter scurried through Kim's midsection as she clearly understood the hint Mick had so skillfully trotted out between them. After breaking the engagement with Ted Curry, whose rage confirmed her choice, Kim had asked Mick to give her two weeks to sort through her feelings and pray about their relationship. Those two weeks turned into the longest days of her life. They also confirmed that the Lord really had put her and Mick together and that His perfect will rested in her having a lasting relationship with Mick. Since then, they had continued to fall deeper in love. Kim Lan now felt as if he were indeed becoming a part of her.

He had even been with her during the recent meeting with her financial advisor. Mick, proving some financial savvy of his own, had helped her redirect some of her interest bearing investments from herself to numerous missions projects. As Mick had mused during that van ride from Cantho to Saigon, the Lord had shown Kim Lan that she was to continue her modeling career and earn the money that would fund God's work and His kingdom. Fortunately, the missions board had supported Mick's decision to leave his post and escort Kim home, and she looked forward to further interacting with the people who trusted Mick to represent them abroad. Assuredly, she and Mick O'Donnel made a great tag team for God.

Now she sensed that it was time to move one step closer to consummating what God was joining together. If Mick proposed, she would gladly accept.

After consulting with Marilyn and Josh, Victoria stepped in front of the bride's table and raised her voice. "Okay, everyone! The bride is ready to toss her bouquet. All you single maidens need to line up."

Marilyn, smiling as if she was the winner of the grand prize, joined Melissa in front of the bride's table and stood holding the ivory-colored bouquet she would toss to "the next woman who would get married."

"Go on out there," Mick urged, pressing against Kim's back.

"Are you coming, Mel?" Kim asked, turning to her friend who adjusted her glasses and set her punch on the nearby gift table.

"Might as well," she said dryly. "You never know! There may be hope for even an old-maid doctor."

"Oh, right," Kim said, rolling her eyes.

Sammie Jones, the other sister who was married, corralled Sonsee LeBlanc, and a protesting Jac Lightfoot. They stood in the group of young women clustering near the bride. Holding the camera, Sammie adjusted her red hair and brushed her bangs out of her face before snapping a quick shot. Then she posed, ready to catch the important moment on camera.

Before Marilyn turned her back on the group of waiting women, she winked at Kim Lan. Then, Marilyn swiveled and tossed the bouquet over her shoulder, high in the air, directly to Kim. Whistles and cheers erupted from the group as Kim gracefully reached up and snared the bouquet. A round of applause ensued and the group diffused. Mick approached from his spot near the guest book.

"I told her to make sure you got the bouquet," he said. A faint smile tugged at the corners of his mouth and accented the laugh lines around his eyes. Yet the smile gradually faded as he searched her face for confirmation.

Kim Lan, breathless with the implications of the moment, silently returned his gaze.

"From what I understand…" He looked away, narrowed his eyes, then held her gaze once more. "There's a path behind this building that leads to a small waterfall. Would you like to join me on a stroll?"

"Of course," Kim said, never hesitating. The way she felt today, if Mick didn't pop the question she might.

Only his expectant eyes revealed Mick's emotions. His stoic expression never changed. "After you," he said, extending his hand in chivalrous fashion.

Before leaving the smell of gourmet coffee and bride's cake behind, Kim glanced over her shoulder to see her five sisters huddled around Marilyn. All of them smiled as if they were conspiring among themselves. Sonsee even wiggled her fingers in sisterly salute.

"Break a leg, Mick," Josh softly called from near the groom's table.

Mick chuckled under his breath. Kim Lan, stepping out of the fellowship hall, wondered if the whole lot of them were in conspiracy behind her back. Taking her hand in his, Mick led Kim down the narrow worn path and through a tunnel of rich, Arkansas foliage. The trees formed a canopy overhead and blocked out the hot June sunshine. Kim inhaled deeply of the smells of the forest. The soft sound of falling water soon mingled with the birds' cheerful chirping. Mick slowed his pace, directing Kim to a moss-touched stone bench that sat beside a dainty waterfall. The lacelike water cascaded from the rocky ridge so common among the Arkansas Ozarks. The water splashed to the pool twenty feet below and merrily flowed along as part of the narrow stream.

Mick nudged Kim to sit on the bench, and he knelt beside her in a traditional stance. Kim's eyes filled with tears as he looked deeply into her eyes. She did nothing to conceal the answer to the question she knew he would pose. He pulled a red-velvet ring box from his coat pocket and opened it with fingers that were far from steady. Inside the box a lovely jade stone, set in gold, glistened in the patches of light dappling the forest floor.

"My dad sent this ring home to my mother before he was killed," Mick said. "Vietnam is known for its excellent jade. And...for producing excellent women." He turned love-filled yes upon Kim

Her lips trembling, she dashed aside a tear that splashed onto her face.

"When Mom married again, she gave the ring to me, and I decided to save it for the woman I would marry. This ring means the world to me. It represents my father's love for my mother, but even more, the jade symbolizes my love for you." He reached for her hand and kissed the backs of her fingers. "And I do love you, Kim Lan. I love you more than my own life. Would you wear my ring and be my wife?"

Kim, no longer able to contain her emotions, blurted, "Yes!" and threw her arms around his neck.

Caught off-guard, he lost his balance, gave a muffled cry, and toppled onto his backside. Kim landed on the ground next to him, and a light's instantaneous flash punctuated the moment.

Kim turned to see all her sisters clustered behind the bench, laughing as if they were kids on Christmas morning.

"You were spying on us!" Kim accused.

"We had license," Sonsee said.

"The photographer invited us for the journey," Marilyn finished.

Sammie Jones, her journalist's camera in hand, said, "That would be me. I decided you two would like a memory of this moment. But I wanted a picture of *the kiss,*" she finished through a chuckle.

"Well, you didn't exactly get a picture of that," Mick said dryly.

"So kiss her!" Melissa urged. Sammie focused her camera and the sisters cheered as Mick leaned toward Kim and securely placed his lips on hers.

Author's Note

Dear Reader:

In 1998, my husband and I traveled to Vietnam to adopt our little girl, Brooke Debra Smith. Her Vietnamese name is Kim Lan Tang, and she will be four years old September 29, 2000. Excluding the stories of the pedicab thief and stalker, most of the Vietnam travel events come from our personal experience, including the crippled boy on the ferry. He really exists. I have also held and tickled Khanh Ahn, the special-needs child. If you are interested in adopting a child from Vietnam (or any other country), please visit my website.

In a sense, Kim Lan's trip to Vietnam symbolizes her spiritual journey and her awakening to a deeper experience in the Lord. As the trip to Vietnam is based on my personal experience, so Kim Lan's awakening is really mine. When I started panting after God "as the deer pants for streams of water" (Psalm 42:1), He began to purge me on a deeper level than I ever imagined. While I have never owned Kim Lan's wealth, I have been affected by the materialistic mindset that so permeates our society, a mindset that says, "The one with the most toys in the end wins." However, just as God did with Kim Lan, He required that I be willing to sell all I have for His cause and, if He asks, be willing to die for love of Him.

This kind of relationship with the Lord does not come cheap and only happens after we commit to an intense, daily pursuit of Him. But when we "turn [our] eyes upon Jesus and look full in his wonderful face, the things [and wealth] of earth become strangely dim in the light of His glory and grace" (Helen Howarth Lemmel).

Are you turning your eyes to Jesus? Are you seeking Him with your whole heart? Are you willing to give your life because people need the Lord?

Whatever issues you are facing, whatever difficulties you must endure, this one thing is the key to peace: a deep, deep intimacy with Jesus Christ. In order to have such a purity of relationship with Him, He will indeed require that you release everything that clouds your soul. Release... release...and find a power for living you have never known before.

In His Service,

Debra White Smith

In four years nearly 500,000 copies of **Debra White Smith**'s nonfiction and fiction books have been sold! Her award-winning writing, entertaining humor, and solid biblical knowledge have made her a reader favorite and a much-sought-after conference speaker. Debra holds an M.A. and B.A. in English with a minor in communications. She lives with her family in East Texas.

You may contact Debra at:

P.O. Box 1482
Jacksonville, TX 75766

or visit her website:
www.debrawhitesmith.com

BOOK 1

❧ ❧

SECOND CHANCES

Marilyn Thatcher and her daughter needed a new start, a second chance...

❧ ❧

"You couldn't pay me to get involved with another man," Marilyn Thatcher insisted. Shattered by her husband's abandonment, she vowed to protect her heart—and the heart of her four-year-old daughter, Brooke. After returning to her hometown, Marilyn and Brooke nave settled into a life of quiet routine—a life without a husband or father, a life without God.

Then Marilyn meets ner charming neighbor, Joshua Langham. Irresistably attracted to his infectious smile and compassionate spirit, she reluctantly accepts his friendship. As their relationship deepens, Marilyn's fear of betrayal intensifies when she accidentally sees Joshua's mysterious tattoo. When Joshua's past erupts into the present, a whirlwind of danger engulfs them both. With renewed faith and courage, they risk everything to protect Brooke...and their love.